SUCH
A
LOVELY
FAMILY

ALSO BY AGGIE BLUM THOMPSON

I Don't Forgive You
All the Dirty Secrets

SUCH A LOVELY FAMILY

AGGIE BLUM THOMPSON

TOR PUBLISHING GROUP
NEW YORK

SUCH A LOVELY FAMILY

Copyright © 2024 by Agnes Blum Thompson

A Forge Book
Published by Tom Doherty Associates / Tor Publishing Group
120 Broadway
New York, NY 10271

www.tor-forge.com

Forge® is a registered trademark of Macmillan Publishing Group, LLC.

The Library of Congress Cataloging-in-Publication Data is available upon request.

ISBN 978-1-250-89199-0 (trade paperback)
ISBN 978-1-250-89197-6 (hardcover)
ISBN 978-1-250-89198-3 (ebook)

Our books may be purchased in bulk for promotional, educational, or business use. Please contact your local bookseller or the Macmillan Corporate and Premium Sales Department at 1-800-221-7945, extension 5442, or by email at MacmillanSpecialMarkets@macmillan.com.

First Edition: 2024

Printed in the United States of America

0 9 8 7 6 5 4 3 2 1

For my mother-in-law, Kathleen Calhoun Thompson

(whose only resemblance to these characters,
I am grateful to say, is a shared name)

SUCH
A
LOVELY
FAMILY

Everybody loves the Calhouns.

They are such a lovely family. Thom and Ginny Calhoun have lived in the same house on Sycamore Lane for thirty-five years, and raised all three children in their classic white colonial with crisp black trim.

So what in the world are the police doing here?

The neighbors gather in small groups to gawk at the squad cars parked askew on the wide, tree-lined street. The sirens are off, but the cars' flashing blue lights announce their presence.

What happened? The neighbors whisper to each other as an ambulance arrives. *Was it Thom? His heart?* The consensus is no—Thom, with his mane of thick silver hair, is in such good shape for a man in his midsixties. Maybe it's Ginny, one woman says, but no one takes her seriously. Ginny of the wide smile, always in her tennis whites—she can run women half her age around the courts.

Must be one of the children. *They were all here for the party this afternoon*, sniffs one neighbor, who has never appreciated the noise and hubbub that the Calhouns' annual cherry blossom party brings to their quiet street. It's bad enough that the tourists descend on the Somerwood neighborhood every spring to photograph the explosion of white and pale pink blossoms. But the Calhoun party seems like such an ostentatious display of wealth.

Can't be Nate, another neighbor says about the Calhouns' middle child. *Such a wonderful young man. A marine biologist, I believe. I hear he's in from California for the party. Have you seen his little boy? Adorable.*

I hear he's engaged, and thank goodness. That little boy needs a mother!

I certainly hope Ellie Grace is not involved. She's the whole reason I joined Instagram. I love seeing what she's up to.

That leaves Trey.

It's what they're all thinking. The eldest Calhoun child was kicked out of two D.C.-area prep schools and military school. His father pulled some strings to get him into college. Everyone knows Thom made a DUI go away for Trey, as well. After two years of college, Trey dropped out and left for LA to work in the movie business. Things went south, and now he is back, living in the house next to his parents, a bungalow they had bought for guests.

Everyone's pulling for Trey, though.

Despite his youthful mistakes, he has so much potential. And it's been wonderful for Ginny to have her oldest son back; she really dotes on him. If anything happened with Trey, she would be devastated.

Ask Renée, someone says. *She'll know.*

Despite their superficial differences, Renée Price and Ginny Calhoun have been close friends for years. The two are often seen walking their dogs—French bulldogs for Ginny and a bichon frise for Renée—early in the morning.

Renée is seated at a cocktail table in the Calhouns' front yard. Hours ago, it might have been a party guest she was chatting with. Now, it's a police detective questioning her.

The Calhouns' whole front yard was recently filled with guests in their spring finery—friends, family, select neighbors—sipping cocktails and chatting. Nature had obliged, providing cherry blossoms in peak bloom as a backdrop to the party. Now the evening breeze sends the little petals fluttering onto the grass like freshly fallen snow. And the guests have been joined by dour-faced uniformed officers and several plainclothes detectives. The white bunting swapped for yellow caution tape.

Renée hugs her little dog to her chest. From the way she keeps glancing at her house across the street, it's obvious that she wishes she were back home and not in the middle of a crime scene.

She already told the police what happened.

How she was in the powder room when she heard the loud *pop, pop*. How, when she'd opened the bathroom door, her dog had bounded away from her. She had followed, calling Mumbo's name, worried he might be headed for the kitchen to inhale more of the bacon-covered scallops. But no. He was heading deeper into the house. She had followed and caught a glimpse of her Mumbo tugging at a blue-and-white-checked tablecloth from the party that lay crumpled on the floor.

Only when she got closer, Renée told the police, she saw it wasn't a tablecloth at all.

It was a blue-and-white gingham dress with a pair of legs sticking out akimbo.

Drenched in blood.

No, she won't be going home for a while.

1

Trying to be this perfect hurts.

The silk dress compresses Danit's ribs, the three-inch espa-drilles squeeze her toes, and the incessant smiling for the photographer makes her face sore. But pain is a small price to pay to belong. To finally be, at twenty-six years old, part of a family.

And not just any family—the Calhouns.

Ellie Grace slips her arm around Danit's waist as the photographer calls out, "Fromage!" The pressure of her future sister-in-law's arm against Danit's ribs unleashes a warm feeling, the same sensation she used to get as a child when her mother would play with her curls. An almost primordial sense of belonging. *I will finally have a sister*, Danit thinks.

Danit fell hard and fast for Nate last year. That first month or two, it was hard to imagine wanting or needing anything more than him. But then she met his little boy, Malcolm, and saw pictures of his parents and brother and sister and realized that he came with this incredible family. And that by marrying him, she would instantly belong to his family as well. It was more than she had ever dreamed of.

Although this morning did get off to a rocky start with El-lie Grace, Danit attributes that to the stress of organizing the annual Calhoun cherry blossom party. When she and Nate and Malcolm arrived late last night to Nate's childhood home, Ginny and Thom were already in bed. So her first introduction to the Calhoun family was this morning, when she came down for breakfast and found Ellie Grace fuming about missing flowers. When she turned on Danit, she was abrupt, bordering on rude.

"You're not wearing blue-and-white gingham." It wasn't a question but a statement. Ellie Grace was wearing a sleeveless shirtdress in the checkered pattern.

"I . . . didn't know I was supposed to," Danit stammered, ashamed to have stepped in it so soon with Nate's sister. When Danit was back in California packing for the trip, she had asked Nate if there was something special she should bring for the party. It was the first time she would be meeting her future in-laws, and she wanted to make a good impression. She knew they were wealthy, and she was nervous that what she had would not be good enough. But Nate had said nothing about blue-and-white gingham.

Thank goodness Ellie Grace had shown up with a collection of shirts, dresses, skirts, and wraps—all in gingham. Ellie Grace hustled Danit into the wood-paneled study off the living room to change. "I knew someone would forget. I'm sure I've got something in here that will fit you. Coastal Cues, that's one of the brands we collaborate with, sent me a whole bunch of these. Here we go, this is cute!" She held up a sheath dress—navy blue on top and gingham from the waist down. You're what, a size eight?"

"Ten, actually."

Really, Danit is a twelve. Sometimes a fourteen. But it was nothing that a little Spanx and holding her breath wouldn't take care of. And she wanted to please Ellie Grace.

"Give me that Calhoun smile!" the photographer orders with the verve of a cheerleading captain.

The Calhouns shift ever so slightly for the photographer, their stately white house in the background. From the corner of her eye, Danit glances at Nate's parents—Thom, with his athletic build and perpetual tan, and Ginny, whose smooth, unlined face belies her sixty-two years. She hasn't had a chance to really talk to them yet, not with the chaos of the party, and she has no idea what she will say to them when the opportunity arises.

Danit worries she might pass out from the warmth of everyone's bodies and the constriction of the dress. The late-spring sun isn't helping. It was much cooler in Mendocino when they left yesterday. Next to her, Malcolm fusses in Nate's arms, and she takes the baby happily. He plays with the diamond on her ring finger.

"Since you're not yet technically a Calhoun . . ." Ginny winks at Danit, letting her finish the thought for herself.

"Oh, of course!" She steps away from the group and out of the photo.

"That's ridiculous," Nate says, but Danit shakes her head at him and smiles to let him know she understands. Which she doesn't, of course. She's never been in a family portrait—there was just her and her mom growing up. But she can kind of see where Ginny is coming from.

After all, Nate has already been divorced once.

This photo will go out this Christmas and feature the whole clan, all of them wearing some iteration of blue-and-white gingham. The men in button-downs, their sleeves rolled up, a little bow tie for baby Malcolm, a headband for Ginny, and so on. Even matching collars for the two French bulldogs, Asti and Spumante.

Ginny might be worried that the marriage will not go through and they will be stuck with photographic evidence of a failed relationship.

But it will. Danit is sure of it.

Out of the corner of her eye, Danit can see the first guests arriving. And just like that, the photographs are over and the party has begun. Light jazz begins to play from hidden speakers, and it seems to Danit that the pink and white tulips planted along the front border stand up and salute as if on cue. The Calhouns scatter and, almost like magic, waiters appear, circulating the lawn with shrimp puffs and mini quiches and trays of fizzy pink drinks.

Suddenly finding herself alone, Danit grabs a drink off a tray and takes a big sip. She doesn't want to get drunk, of course. She wants just enough to take the edge off. Meeting all your future in-laws at once is tough to tackle sober.

2

This party will do the trick, Ginny Calhoun thinks. *It has to.*

Ginny smiles widely, knowing that is the only thing, short of a facelift, that will make those awful little marionette lines around her mouth disappear. The Botox takes care of the grooves on her forehead, and the filler plumps up the hollows under her eyes, but nothing short of surgery is going to get rid of those god-awful lines.

Thom will see the young Ginny in her, won't he? That's what they say about long marriages. The men sometimes need reminding of the youthful beauties they fell in love with so long ago. She will help him remember at this party. All this other nonsense will fade into the background, and things will return to the way they were supposed to be.

After all, they are the Calhouns.

"Excuse me!"

A young woman in a catering outfit rushes by her and through the front door of the house. Ginny jumps back to avoid being hit.

"The staff should be using the back door; the front is for guests," Ellie Grace says. "Want me to speak to Sunniva?"

"Sunniva has been catering the party for seven years, darling. She knows the drill."

"Sometimes these newer hires need to be reminded."

"I'll handle Sunniva." Ginny adores her daughter, but she sometimes senses in her a desire to assume the mantle of power without putting in any of the hard work.

Ginny surveys the scene before her like a queen surveying her castle grounds. The huge cherry tree in the front yard is in full bloom, casting a pink sunlit glow over the cocktail tables covered in checkered cloths. A corner lot really is the best for entertaining. The guest list is a mix of Thom's business connections, friends from the Somerwood Country Club, and neighbors, some of whom the Calhouns are genuinely fond of and others who needed to be invited lest they complain about the noise.

And of course, her children.

Ginny smiles for real this time. It's so rare to have all her children—Trey, Nate, and Ellie Grace—together like this. A horrible thought intrudes—*This will be the last time.* She gasps. Where did that come from? She shakes the thought away.

"Those photos will make a wonderful Christmas card, Mommy," Ellie Grace says. "All of us in gingham. I thought the ones last year were a little gloomy. Tartan plaid doesn't photograph well."

So many Christmas cards over the years. The white linen at the house on Nantucket, the pinks and greens in St. Barts for spring break. It was so right for so long. Where did things go wrong? Had she taken her hand off the rudder?

When the hydrangeas didn't arrive this morning, her heart sank like a stone.

She knew that this time was different.

Ginny looks at her watch—it's almost three fifteen—and goes in search of Thom, taking two champagne flutes with her. She finds him and hands him a glass. "Darling, shall we get things started with a toast as always?"

He takes the glass from her, a glimmer of resentment in the slight flare of his nostrils. He used to like how she managed all the little details in their lives. But a month ago, he snapped at her when she asked him to grab *The Washington Post* on the front path, telling her he wasn't her trained dog.

They walk to the front stoop of the house. She knows what he's thinking—he needs to put in about another hour of face time before he can retreat to the silence of his beloved study.

It wasn't always this way. He once relished these get-togethers—years upon years of them. Not just the cherry blossom parties but so many other celebrations. It is hard for her to reconcile this taciturn man with the Thom who enjoyed hosting friends, holding court with a bourbon in his hand, bragging about his golf exploits, telling shaggy-dog stories about deep-sea fishing in the Keys.

"Ding, ding, ding," Thom calls out like so many times before. Ginny watches his face scan the crowd and then alight on a woman with long red hair in a short pink dress that makes her slender legs look miles long. Ginny recognizes her as a recently hired employee of Calhoun Development. Over the years, there have been many pretty girls with long legs and easy smiles. But they never last. Ginny's never been able to figure out if Thom was involved with any of them, or if he simply likes having pretty girls around the office. That's not quite true. She's never *wanted* to figure it out. Thirty-five years is a long time to be married, and you have to allow your partner a little leeway, a little privacy. It's their policy. He's never looked too closely at how she spends money, and she's never asked too many questions about the pretty girls.

But those damn hydrangeas. Could it have been an honest mistake?

Ginny lays her hand on Thom's forearm and gives it a gentle squeeze to shake him out of his reverie. "Something wrong, dear?" Ginny asks.

"Not at all." Thom shifts his gaze away from the redhead to the faces peering up at him. "I'd like to make a toast." His booming voice quiets the crowd. Someone turns down the music.

"We are gathered here once again to celebrate the cherry blossoms. The Japanese may have gifted Washington these beautiful trees back in 1912 as a token of friendship, but you have gifted us with your presence—this year and over the many years. Here's to friendship!"

He holds out his glass, and everyone raises theirs. "Hear, hear!" someone calls out.

"Oh, darling." Ginny leans in for a kiss. "That was wonderful."

Thom keeps the smile on his face and his champagne glass in the air as he leans in to her as if to kiss her cheek.

But it is not a kiss he delivers.

It's a message.

Only the most astute onlookers would notice the subtle change in Ginny's face, the smile morphing from one of joy into one of horror.

3

Ellie Grace scans the party, looking for her husband, but sees no sign of him. Zak isn't one to blend in with a crowd. It's not only his golden hair, olive skin, and striking green eyes that cause heads to turn, it's the way he carries himself. And he photographs so well. But while charm comes easily to him, punctuality does not.

She's going to give him an earful when he comes. He missed the family picture that will go out on the Christmas cards. People might get the wrong idea, think their marriage is in trouble.

To alleviate her anxiety, she opens Instagram on her phone. Her account, Gingham Life, got a nice little bump this week when it was mentioned in a South Carolina lifestyle magazine. A flurry of new followers has brought her total up to 190,000, a number that would have seemed astronomical to her when she started, but now that she is deeper in the influencer game, she realizes how small it is. One day, she'd like to be in the same ballpark as DCGirlsWearPearls or Beltway Prep, or even TrulyTrudy, the influencer who has perfected the preppy, classy lifestyle vibe and has 1.5 million followers.

But she'll need something to go really viral to get that kind of following. And so far, her upscale Washington, D.C., lifestyle brand isn't cutting it.

Just because life is messy, doesn't mean you have to be!

That is her tagline, and everything she posts illustrates how to make order out of chaos. Sorting by color, finding the perfect planner, coordinating your clothes into capsules so that you always look pulled together, no matter what you grab from your closet. She has a loyal following, all right, but nothing *explosive*. But how do you make organizing your matching office accessories explosive?

Ellie Grace scrolls through some pictures that she asked a catering waiter to take while the family was being shot by the photographer. Zak should have been there to take these. But they aren't terrible—after all, a professional photographer had already seen to the lighting and the staging.

A few are actually pretty good, like the ones in which she's holding Malcolm. Pictures with babies get a ton of engagement. Quickly, she writes a caption and presses Post.

"Are you trying to pretend Malcolm is your child?"

Ellie Grace turns to see her brother Trey smirking beside her.

"No. I say he's my nephew in one of the hashtags." Like the rest of her family, Trey has no idea how much work goes into Gingham Life. He thinks it's just a vanity hobby.

"I don't see the point of these family photos. Aren't you supposed to stop sending Christmas cards once the kids have grown up?" Trey asks. "I mean, no one cares."

"It is important to some people," Ellie Grace responds. She will not let her brother get under her skin.

"Shallow people."

"No. Conscientious people."

"Remember what Mom said, Smelly." He wags a finger at her. "Be on your best behavior for the party."

Ellie Grace feels annoyance burn within her. Trey has always been able to push her buttons. She stiffens. "I am. You be on your best behavior."

Despite her mother's insistence otherwise, Ellie Grace knows that her mother favors Trey. Lots of mothers dote on their firstborn, but in this case, it didn't stop when Trey's childhood ended. Maybe Ginny felt sorry for Trey because as soon as Nate was old enough for school, he outshone his big brother in every department, from athletics to academics. But Ellie Grace is sure her parents' many excuses for Trey's behavior—the expulsions and scrapes with the law—made things worse. Perhaps if they had been tougher on him when he was younger, California would not have happened.

Not that she knows the details.

"You look adorable!" John Cooke from down the block, known by all as "Cookie," bends down to kiss Ellie Grace on both cheeks. His husband, Bob, stands in his shadow, about a foot shorter and fifty pounds lighter, offering a shy wave. "Your mother has outdone herself. And such perfect timing! Right, Bob?"

Bob leans forward. "There's supposed to be a big windstorm tonight. It's going to blow all the cherry blossoms down."

"Well, that is lucky timing," Trey says with a cheer that sounds obviously false to Ellie Grace's ears but does not seem to register with either Bob or Cookie.

"And I love the gingham theme." Cookie taps the gingham pocket square that is sticking out of his linen jacket. "Message received."

Ellie Grace beams. "Thank you, Cookie. I knew you'd appreciate it."

"I hope I'll make it onto your Insta one day." He pivots to Trey. "And, Trey, love the bow tie."

Trey grins. "Why, thank you, kind sir. Ellie Grace has impeccable taste."

Ellie Grace refrains from snorting.

"That she does." Cookie wiggles his bushy eyebrows. "So what's the scoop on Nate's fiancée? She's adorable. And I love those curls."

"She's super sweet," Trey says and nods toward Ellie Grace. "Don't you think, Ellie Grace?"

"Of course. I mean, I don't know her that well yet. We all just met her today, but it's so much fun to have a new member of the family!" Ellie Grace smiles wildly. What was she supposed to say? That everyone is disappointed Nate proposed to his kid's nanny, a woman who was flummoxed this morning when Ellie Grace used the word *canapé*?

"Now we have a fourth for tennis," Trey says. "I'll have to remember to reserve a court at the club while she's here. Right, sis?"

"You two kids are just the most adorable," Cookie says.

Trey throws his arm around Ellie Grace's shoulder. "Family is everything."

No, Ellie Grace doesn't know what happened in California. It involved a car crash, that much she knows, but it must have been much more than that. Whatever it was, it was bad enough that Trey came back, tail between his legs, and is now doing a stunning impersonation of an upstanding, churchgoing young man.

So it must have been pretty bad.

4

"My idea."

Danit turns to see an older woman holding a goblet of pink liquid. "The Cherry Smash. It's the signature cocktail. Try it."

Danit takes a sip. "Mmm, delish."

"Careful. It's stronger than it looks." A small white dog yips at their feet, and the woman bends down and scoops it up. "This here is Mumbo."

Danit takes the dog's paw in her hand. "Nice to meet you, Mumbo. What a unique name."

"I named him after the sauce," the woman says. "That's a D.C. thing. You ever had it?"

Danit shakes her head.

"Well, my Mumbo is just like the sauce," she says. "Mostly sweet with a little bit of a kick. This little guy loves parties." The sunlight catches the woman's close-cropped silver curls, which seem to glow against her dark skin. "And I'm Renée. I live over there." With a manicured hand, she gestures to a large stone house across the road, beyond the Calhouns' neatly clipped box-wood hedge. "I've lived there going on fifteen years, so I know everything. That means I know you're Danit."

"Yes, that's right." Danit holds out her hand. "Danit Shapiro. Nice to meet you. I love your outfit."

"What, this old thing?" Renée gestures toward her pink silk jumpsuit adorned with a red cherry blossom print. "Not too on point?"

"Not at all. And I love pink and red together. Very bold."

"I was worried Ellie Grace might not approve. She's very particular about her dress code."

"The cocktail is genius, Renée." Ginny materializes beside them, along with Nate, who is holding a squirming Malcolm. "Nathaniel, put the child down. Let him explore."

"Sorry I disappeared," Nate says to Danit. "We couldn't find Mr. Panders."

Danit nods, understanding. Mr. Panders is a well-loved stuffed panda bear missing one ear. When they first started dating, Danit once spent a cold evening in a local park with a flashlight trying to locate Mr. Panders after a picnic with Malcolm and Nate, eager to prove herself.

"Perfect weather," Renée says to Ginny. "I hear there's a little wind coming in tonight, so your timing couldn't be better."

Ginny shivers with fear. "I detest March weather. So unpredictable."

"Right. *March when the sun shines hot and the wind blows cold,*" Danit says. "*When it's summer in the light, and winter in the shade.*" The ensuing silence makes Danit want to disappear into the soft earth. "Sorry. That's Charles Dickens. *Great Expectations?*"

"Of course!" Renée snaps her fingers. "What a terrific memory."

"Impressive," Ginny says dryly. "You must have been the most literary nanny in all of Mendocino. How lucky Nate was to have hired you."

Danit understands the words Ginny has said but is not sure of their meaning. Was she just complimented or insulted? She knows being a nanny is probably not high on the list of occupations Ginny had in mind for her daughter-in-law. On the other hand, she did call her *literary.*

"I sure think so," Nate says, grinning. "Danit studied English literature at UC Berkeley."

Danit nods silently. Technically, that is true.

"Danit, darling, don't you dare go back to California without spending a day with me at the Red Door." Ginny places one cool hand on Danit's arm. On her ring finger is a giant diamond-and-emerald panther that looks as heavy as a paperweight. Danit starts counting the little diamonds—one, two, three—but loses count at eleven. "Olena's facials are unparalleled. You feel like you're being sandblasted, but I swear she takes five years off your age. Not that you have anything to worry about, dear. Danit, I am saying that correctly, aren't I? It's dann-it? Such an unusual name . . ."

"It's Hebrew. My father was Israeli."

"Oh." Ginny's fingers flutter to the strand of pearls around her neck. "How utterly fascinating."

"But I never knew him. My parents met in San Francisco. My mom was a nurse, and he was doing his residency, but by the time I was born, my dad had moved back to Israel. So it was just us two. But she died when I was twenty." She is talking too much. She *is* too much. Too big for her dress, her wild hair exploding in the D.C. humidity. She feels Nate give her shoulders a squeeze and tries to relax.

"I'd love to go to Israel," Renée says. "It's on my bucket list."

"Me, too," Nate says.

"Oh, I'm too boring for all that." Ginny waves the idea away. "I'll stick to Lake Como and the British Virgins, thank you very much."

"Well, you'll have to visit us in Saipan, of course," Danit says.

Ginny doesn't flinch, but she blinks twice. "Saipan? Where in the world is Saipan?"

"It's a US territory in the Mariana Islands. In the South Pacific." Confused, Danit turns to Nate, but his face gives nothing away. Surely, he's told his mother. They've been planning for months. He has an opportunity to lead up a whale survey off the Mariana Islands. She was excited to go with him as his girlfriend, of course, but as his wife, the trip has taken on a whole new meaning. Not a trip. A move. They were going to start their lives afresh there.

"I've been meaning to talk to you, Mom—"

"Nathaniel, darling, we simply must say hello to Caroline Smith. I've had to listen to her drone on about her grandchildren for years, and now it's my turn." Ginny scoops up Malcolm. "Let's go, my beautiful baby boy, and say hello to some old friends."

Danit watches them walk away, Nate turning back to offer a shrug. He must have a good reason for not telling his parents about the move. Danit is sure it will all make sense once he explains it to her. When she turns around, she finds that Renée has melted into the crowd. Danit is alone.

She swallows the rest of her drink in one gulp. The alcohol hits her empty stomach. Not good. She needs something to eat. She shouldn't have said all that about her family—about not knowing her dad, or her mother dying. Mentioning death at a party like this? And she should have said *passed away*, not *died*. Her face warms at the embarrassment.

Allergic to shellfish, Danit bypasses a waiter offering shrimp puffs and heads toward the large, white house, past a steady stream of waiters marching in and out of a side entrance. She wonders how many people are working at this party. When Danit was growing up, her mother's idea of hosting was inviting Charmaine Wu, a sculptor who lived in the downstairs apartment of their duplex, up to drink rum and Cokes on the small balcony that overlooked the traffic on their busy street. She hadn't realized quite how overwhelming it would be—meeting Nate's family, being photographed, the party—until just now.

Danit exhales deeply and enters the large living room. She wanders between the two sitting areas, one near the fireplace and the other in front of a large bay window looking out on the backyard. When she gets nearer to the window, she can see two caterers outside standing close to each other. A young Black man with starter dreads and a white girl, her long sleeve pushed up to reveal an elaborate tattoo covering her arm. The girl passes something—a vape pen, Danit guesses—to the man. This must all seem ridiculous to them. It seems a little that way to her. Back in Mendocino, she and the boys—that's how she thinks of Nate and Malcolm—live simply in a rented wooden house a few blocks from the ocean. She can't imagine what it was like for Nate to grow up in a house as grand as the one she is standing in now.

Danit looks around the beautifully appointed room for clues. How did her down-to-earth fiancé, whose preferred Saturday date is a slice of pizza from Frankie's and a long walk on the beach, come from this kind of wealth? She may not know much about antiques or furnishings, but it's obvious how much care went into decorating—the pale yellow walls and cream-colored sofas, accented by blue-and-white ceramics.

But she isn't simply looking. She is searching.

Nate never talks about his ex-wife, Helena. Only that she didn't want children and left as soon as Malcolm was born. The few times Danit pushed him for details, he simply had nothing to say. It was a surefire way to end a conversation. But Danit has so many questions. How could a mother just walk away from her baby? It was impossible for Danit to imagine. In the past few months, she fell as hard for Malcolm as she had for his father.

"You can't move to Saipan with a man without knowing what happened with his first wife," Charmaine scolded her. After her mother died, Charmaine had stepped in as best she could and now occupied the role of an eccentric aunt. "What if it's like *Cast a Dark Shadow*?" The two shared a love of film noir, and in that film, Dirk Bogarde played a handsome psychopath who keeps marrying, and killing, rich older wives. "Maybe this Helena was a wealthy spinster he murdered, and now he's looking for victim number two."

"Then he's barking up the wrong tree, because I'm broke." They both laughed. Charmaine had been kidding, of course. But still. She was right. If the situation were reversed, Danit would not be happy to see her adoptive aunt move halfway around the world under these circumstances.

Last week, Danit asked Nate directly, *Tell me about Helena. Like, what was her maiden name? Where did you meet?*

She caught a glimpse of irritation cross over his face before he said, "Helena is my past. And you are my future. You are my everything."

And then he proposed.

Danit stops short at the grand piano, her eyes riveted to a simple silver frame nestled among others. She picks it up. In it, Nate is holding a tiny newborn Malcolm, who sports a shock of black hair. She glances at the collection of photos before her, family through the ages. But no signs of Nate's ex. She's been erased from the Calhoun narrative.

But then again, why would there be photos of her? Families don't keep pictures of ex-wives, do they? Her own mother had only one photograph of Danit's father, an out-of-focus snapshot that she kept buried in the back of her bedside table.

Danit knows what she has to do. Find the right time, ask Nate these questions, and get some answers.

It's perfectly reasonable. So why does the thought make her stomach clench?

Because she knows if she demands answers, she is going to have to provide some of her own.

5

Shawna takes a small rip off the vape pen and passes it back to Jamal.

She doesn't want to be high, but one hit won't do that. She planned to do this whole thing completely sober, but being here stresses her out even more than she'd anticipated. And she'd anticipated that being in the Calhoun house would be very stressful.

"I like your tattoos." Jamal nods at her left arm.

"What?" Shawna looks down in a panic. She must have pushed up the white shirt sleeves of her catering uniform without realizing it.

"Oh, shit, thanks." She quickly rolls down her sleeve and buttons it at the wrist. The tiniest tendril of a honeysuckle vine that climbs up her left forearm before wrapping itself around her bicep peeks out.

"Yeah, you don't want Sunniva to see it." Jamal tucks the vape pen into his chest pocket. Sunniva is their boss. An efficient, petite woman who wears her black hair in a bun so tight it looks painful.

Before they started setting up for the party that morning, Sunniva gathered the catering staff and asked, "How many of you are vegetarians? Have tattoos? Piercings?" Almost everyone raised their hands. "Terrific," she said. "Now keep it to yourselves. I don't want to see it or hear about it at work, and neither do the guests."

"I heard she fired a guy for trying to talk a guest out of eating prosciutto at a party," Jamal says with a laugh before opening the door for Shawna to reenter the kitchen. They step inside the large room. It's three times bigger than any kitchen she's ever stepped foot in. Catering staff are everywhere—laying food on plates, pulling trays from the oven, washing glasses and goblets. "Sunniva does not mess around."

Shawna nods, grateful for the cover that a strict boss provides. The truth is that she doesn't want her sleeve tattoo to show, because it's the most instantly recognizable thing about her. And she doesn't want the Calhouns to know she is here.

Not yet, at least.

Someone hands her a plate of small slices of toast topped with a small lump of what looks to Shawna to be tuna fish.

"If people ask, this is hickory-smoked Chesapeake Bay bluefish," Jamal explains, carrying two platters of the same. "Sustainable, locally owned business, of course."

"Of course." Shawna marches behind him, hopeful that with her tattoo hidden, no one will recognize her. She has one thing going for her—people never pay attention to the staff. Shawna has worked service jobs her whole life—from summers at the frozen custard stand when she was in high school to serving tourists at Bubba Gump's in Universal City. And as a webcam girl.

She shakes off the memory of Los Angeles—it seems a million miles away.

Outside, she holds the tray before her and pauses at the little groupings so guests can help themselves. She reminds herself, as she circulates among all these rich people who barely acknowledge her existence, that she has every right to be here.

It's just one big poker game, she tells herself, and she holds the winning hand.

Or at least some decent cards.

Shawna pauses in front of a couple to allow them to sample the bruschetta. Both are dressed entirely in shades of beige, their hair faded to a grungy yellow, not quite gray. They offer wan smiles, then turn their backs to her and continue speaking in a low murmur.

To a younger Shawna, these people would have looked des-
titute in their drab clothes, but now she knows better. The details tell a different story. The linked gold Cs on the woman's
quilted, patent-leather flats—Chanel. The diamond tennis
bracelet hanging off her bony wrist—worth thousands. This is
a different kind of money, she thinks as she steps away, than
what she imagined when she was a kid. Growing up in a small
town in Oregon, she thought all rich women had plastic surgery, wore tons of makeup, and teetered around on four-inch
heels, with miniature chihuahuas peering out of thousand-
dollar purses dangling from their wrists. That they wore de-
signer clothes with obvious logos and dressed in shimmery
fabrics as if they were headed for a night out.

That was before she moved to LA—the land of the five-
hundred-dollar white T-shirt. There she learned about under-
stated wealth. Why go to Old Navy and buy a white T-shirt and
jeans like a normal person when you could spend ten times as
much? Because they knew they had spent more money, and that
gave them confidence.

Shawna rounds the corner of the house and heads into the
expansive side yard. She has managed to avoid the woman so
far. Shawna tells herself that she's working up the nerve. It's why
she's here, after all—to see Ginny and Thom—but there's no
need to rush into anything. Just the thought of the two of them
sends Shawna's pulse racing. They will not be pleased to see her,
she knows.

She might need one more hit of Jamal's vape pen, after all.

*   *   *

Ginny drags Nate to an empty cocktail table on the periphery
of the lawn. She needs his full attention. But when he turns to
her, there is no other word to describe the look in his eyes except
dreamy.

"I wanted to talk to you about the wedding," Nate says. "We plan to have it on the beach, in Saipan, but we'd like to have an engagement dinner in Washington before we leave. Since most guests won't be able to make it over. Nothing fancy, but something like this."

Ginny blinks hard. "An engagement dinner?" When the party is over, she'll have a proper talking-to with him, get him to see that marrying that creature is out of the question. He didn't always have such lowbrow taste in women. Helena was exquisite: a champion tennis player, a graduate of Stanford Law. Too bad she didn't have a maternal bone in her body. But still, the nanny? It's such a cliché.

"We could do it right here. I have a lot of good memories here," Nate says. "I'd almost forgotten all the good stuff, but being here brings it back. Trey and I biking around, shooting baskets in the park. Remember Snowmageddon? We built these huge snow tunnels that ran down the street. All the kids were practically living in them. We had this crazy idea to camp out one night. Ellie Grace had read about snow camping." He lets out a laugh. "God, that was a disaster!"

Ginny puts her fingertips together and cracks her knuckles, a terrible habit that she has never been able to break. "If you're done reminiscing, I'd like to discuss something with you."

"I just thought it might be nice, since Danit has no family, to have something with my family here. Before we move."

"Let's table this marriage talk for a moment, shall we?"

"*Table this marriage talk?*" Nate narrows his eyes. "Mom, I'm getting married. It's happening. I'd love your support."

"Don't get mad. Danit seems like a very nice, sturdy young woman. And you've always had a soft spot for misfits."

"*Misfit?*" Nate recoils at the word. "That's my future wife you're talking about. Danit is the furthest thing from a misfit, Mother."

Ginny forces a smile. This is not going as she'd planned.

"Don't be annoyed with me, darling. I hate when we quarrel. My nerves are frayed already. Now tell me, what is this business about Saipan? You're going on a trip? For how long?"

"I know I should have told you earlier, but I'm telling you now. I've been awarded a grant to study humpback whales in the South Pacific."

"For how long?"

"Do you mean *congratulations*? It was very competitive. It took a lot of work to get it. But to answer your question, it's a two-year grant."

"Two years! For God's sake." She puts her hand to her mouth as if doing so might stuff her hysterical reaction back inside her body. "What on earth do you plan on doing in Saipan for two years?"

"Well, considering that I am a marine mammal acoustician, my plan is to fulfill the terms of my grant by planting underwater listening devices and then collecting data to establish the patterns—"

"Enough." She holds up a hand. She hates when Nate gets like this. Imperious. Holier-than-thou. As if science and knowledge and rational thought are the highest virtues. "That's quite enough."

"Of course, you know that I'll need the paperwork."

"To leave the country?"

"And to marry Danit."

Now her smile is genuine, and she feels her shoulders relax a little. "Oh, is that right? I suppose that's the real reason you're here."

He glances away and smiles. Ginny follows his gaze. Danit. Ginny snaps her fingers in front of her son's face. "Hello?"

"Mom, it's the opportunity of a lifetime." His tone is infuriatingly calm.

"And have you discussed this *opportunity of a lifetime* with your father?" She can barely keep the tremble out of her own voice.

Nate sighs. For a moment, she can see the little boy in him. The one who preferred digging in Penobscot Bay for sea creatures over sailing lessons. The one who would sneak out of services at St. Giles's to go wading in the creek behind the church. He was always a bit odd. She tried her best to balance him. Make him more *normal*. But a mother can only do so much.

"You know I haven't," he says. "But you should also know that it's not a discussion. You two don't have a choice."

"We can talk after the party."

"There's nothing to talk about. Get the papers ready. I want them signed this weekend. Danit and I are leaving next week."

"Oh, is that a fact?" A woman across the lawn catches Ginny's eye and waves. One of her neighbors, a real busybody. Ginny returns the wave. She'll have to get back to the party soon. A hostess must mingle. "And if I don't get the papers ready?"

"I'm not sure yet," Nate says.

"You'd destroy this family?" She keeps her voice low. The neighbor, not satisfied with a wave, is walking over.

"If the family gets destroyed, it's Dad and you that killed it. Not me."

"Well, if you think your father and I are going to allow you to take our only grandchild across the world, you are kidding yourself."

"You really can't stop me."

"Oh, Nathaniel, dearest. After what happened in California, you of all people should know what we are capable of."

And with that, she turns on her heel and intercepts the neighbor with a hug. "Darling, I was just coming to find you. Love the dress!"

6

Trey makes an exaggerated choking sound as his sister straightens his bow tie. He longs to rip off the stupid thing and drop it in the garbage. He feels like one of those trained monkeys, all dressed up and forced to dance to a tune for his supper.

"Very funny," Ellie Grace says. "I've always thought a man looked dashing in a bow tie."

"Am I imagining it, or are you making it tighter?" The teeny, tiny bump he snorted a few hours ago is wearing off, and he is jittery.

Ellie Grace jerks her head back. "Are you high, Trey? What the hell is wrong with you? Daddy will *kill* you."

Drug testing at the house is a Friday-afternoon ritual, so he has until Monday to indulge just a little. The tests only pick up substances from the previous five days. He has to strike a balance with his drug activity—not so much as to draw attention but enough to make parties like this bearable.

"We all have to go one way or another, Smelly. We're just big sacks of slowly decaying meat that will eventually stop functioning."

"Stop. You're not funny."

His little sister scrunches up her nose in irritation, a quirk that has always evoked in Trey a desire to lovingly torture her, ever since they were kids. "Everybody that you know and meet and love will eventually die."

Ellie Grace plasters on a plastic smile, but her eye twitches. He's gotten to her. Penetrating her super! cheery! upbeat! façade has been a lifelong hobby of his. "You'd better watch it. Here he comes."

Trey turns and sees his father striding toward him, followed by a couple he does not recognize. His stomach does a flip. He'd love to split and head next door to the guesthouse, where he could blast a Kings of Leon album on his stereo and drink himself into a daydream in which he is back in California. The California before the accident, that is.

Yesterday, he found *Youth & Young Manhood* on vinyl at Joe's Record Paradise in Silver Spring. Walking into that store was like stepping back in time. Being a tween in the early aughts, pre-iPhone. All that freedom. No obligation to carry his very own tracking device. The customers in the record store, those were his people, not the chinos-wearing automatons at Calhoun Development. There, at Joe's, he caught a glimpse of his younger self, the Trey who had his whole life ahead of him like an open highway that was just waiting to be driven on.

But what happened in Cali changed all that.

Now it's Sundays in the pews at St. Giles's.

Thursday dinners at the Somerwood Country Club.

Gingham bow ties.

No drugs. No alcohol. No overnight guests in the guesthouse.

Those are the rules of his life now. If he follows them, he gets to live in this gilded cage. Break them and—and what? What would they do?

Would they really turn him in?

Would parents really do that to their own son?

"There you two are. Come say hello." Thom joins Trey and Ellie Grace. "This is my daughter, Ellie Grace, and my eldest son, Trey. This is Craig Piercy, whose time you wasted last week. And his lovely wife, Yasmeen."

"Sorry about that," Trey says, extending his hand. "Something came up at the last minute." He's not sorry he missed the dinner at the club—sitting on display with his parents for everyone to gawk at, ingratiating himself with his father's business cronies. Not sorry to have missed pushing rubbery chicken or overcooked salmon around his plate, rehashing the same boring conversations.

Piercy lets out a hearty laugh. "No worries, Trey. I'm sure a young buck like you has a lot on his plate. Call my office and we'll set another meeting. We'll get your dad's tile order sorted."

"That sounds great."

A member of the catering staff approaches, and Trey grabs a glass of something pink. Immediately, his father takes it from him and passes it to Piercy's wife. "For the lady."

"Lovely color." She holds the drink up to the sunlight before taking a sip.

Thom takes a different glass from the tray and passes it to Trey. "And lemonade for the boy. Find me a scotch, will you, sweetie?" he asks the waitress.

Trey holds the unwanted glass. Message received. Alcohol is for the grown-ups, and his father does not consider Trey, at thirty-three, a grown-up.

"Scotch isn't on the menu, Daddy." Ellie Grace's voice is sweet but sings with tension, like a guitar string tuned too tightly. "Try a Cherry Smash. It's Renée's secret recipe."

But Thom is smiling at the young waitress, ignoring his daughter. "You can rustle up a scotch, can't you, darling?"

Looking from Ellie Grace to Thom, she says, "Yes, sir. Of course."

"Good girl."

Trey watches his sister flinch. Poor Smelly Ellie. She should know that their father always gets what he wants, whether it's on the menu or not.

"Your father was just telling us you live next door, Trey," Piercy says. "You know, you could tear that down and have a five-million-dollar house on that lot by the end of the year."

"Oh no!" his wife says. "I love how cute and storybook it is."

Trey makes a noncommittal noise into his drink. The fucking

house. Real estate. Properties. The same damn conversations over and over again. How he wishes someone would say something unexpected, something offensive, just to shake things up.

Ellie Grace turns to the woman. "The house is so nice to have for when guests come in to town. Hotels can be so unpredictable. Staff shortages and whatnot. And this way, they're near the club if they want to use the pool or play some golf." Ellie Grace gestures toward the country club just beyond a bank of cherry trees. Trey smirks. She's doing a bang-up Ginny impersonation.

"And of course it's perfect for Trey, now that he's back," Thom says. "We love having him so close. My golf buddy. Isn't that right, Trey?"

All eyes turn to Trey as he struggles to fake an enthusiastic response. Inside, he seethes. His parents have him on one of those giant retractable dog leashes. He screwed up once and *snap!* they yanked him back to Washington, D.C. If the beautiful guesthouse he lives in is like a prison, then his father is a warden in gabardine slacks. Trey catches himself. He should be grateful, after what he did, that he didn't end up in a real prison. For murder. Or would it be manslaughter? He shudders despite the afternoon sun.

"You all right, son?" Thom's eyes are narrowed.

"Of course, Dad. Couldn't be better." Trey can feel beads of sweat breaking out on his forehead. Can his father sense his anger? Behind closed doors, Trey could rage for hours about his dad. He's broken every plate in that adorable *storybook* house and punched more than a few holes in the walls. But in his father's presence, he shrinks into a meek little boy.

"Must be nice to have the whole family together," Piercy says, nodding his chin at Malcolm, who, a few yards away, is running at full speed at the neighbor's small white dog, collapsing, and then dusting himself off to try again.

Trey watches Malcolm stumble on the grass and roll onto his

bottom. He sits stunned for a moment, then slowly pulls himself to his feet again. Trey's heart sinks for the little guy. When Trey met his nephew for the first time this morning, he wanted to grab his tiny shoulders and yell, *Run! Run as far and as fast as you can!* But Malcolm couldn't run for more than a few yards without falling. He had no chance.

"So tell me, Trey. Your father says you were in LA doing some entertainment work?"

"I was. I went in on a direct-to-consumer entertainment model. But Hollywood's a tough market to break into." He is pretty sure neither Craig Piercy nor his wife, Yasmeen, would be interested in hearing about his efforts to get a high-end camgirl subscription service off the ground.

"Sure is," Piercy says. "Very tough. What is a *direct-to-consumer entertainment model?*"

Trey narrows his eyes. He can't very well say, *It's where dudes pay a monthly fee to see young women do household chores in weird kinky outfits.* "Well, it's a monthly service, tailored to the interests—"

"The important thing is Trey is back home," Thom interrupts. "He had some time to sow his wild oats, but we need him at Calhoun Development. What with the new fifty-five-plus community going up in Centreville, I can't imagine what we'd do without him. Right, Trey?"

The group looks expectantly at Trey for confirmation, but Trey can't make his mouth move. Ellie Grace breaks the hush by launching into the difference between Yoshino and Kwanzan cherry trees, for which Trey is grateful. Piercy and his wife join in as if nothing has happened, but Trey burns with humiliation. As the chatting crowd ignores him, a white-hot fury fills every pore of his being. He doesn't like to think about why he had to leave LA. He is more than the single worst thing he ever did. That is why he needs to get out into the world and do something, be somebody. He longs for the kind of success that could blunt his own self-hatred.

Will they ever let him go? They said, *Come home, follow our rules, straighten out your life.*

One year, they said.

But that year has come and gone, and nothing has changed. And nothing will change unless he forces it to.

7

When Zak shows up at the party, thirty minutes late, Ellie Grace does her best to squelch her annoyance.

"Sweetie, over here!" She'd told him how important it was that he be here for her.

"Sorry I'm late, babe." He kisses her on the cheek. "Did you have a chance to talk to your dad?"

"Umm, hello to you, too."

"Sorry. It's just on my mind."

"Zak, come on. It's a party." She loops her arm through his, pleased to see he is wearing the gingham shirt she picked out for him. It hugs his body, the thin fabric stretched nicely across his broad shoulders.

"You said you would ask him."

He's right. She did promise. But she doesn't like how much he's been talking about money recently. It just wasn't the way she was raised. If he would just be a little more patient with Gingham Life, she might not need to ask her dad for a cash infusion at all. So far, her business has received more offers of free stuff than actual cash. Her basement is chock-full of merch—boxes of checked flannel pajamas, floral-patterned gardening tools, vegan handbags. But she is working on a few sponsorships.

"I will, but maybe we should wait and see if one of the sponsorship deals comes through? I guess I think we should give Gingham Life a little longer," Ellie Grace says. "I think it's going to turn a corner soon." She feels funny still asking her parents for money at twenty-seven. They let her and Zak live in one of Calhoun Development's model houses for free. True, the Chalfonte isn't the top of the line, but the location in East Bethesda is great. And her mother is always slipping her a little cash. Last Thursday at the club, her mother sneaked an envelope of ten one-hundred-dollar bills into her bag after dinner. *Just for funsies.*

"Babe, Gingham Life is going to be huge. No doubt. But we're tight on cash flow. We could use a little help. I mean, running Gingham costs money."

"Well, yes, there are monthly costs." There are the photography sessions, the Photoshop software, video editing, graphic design, email marketing, web development, search engine optimization, clothes, props, travel—it all adds up to a few thousand a month. "But you have to spend money to make money. And once we have a baby, that will mean more sponsorship opportunities."

Zak ignores her mention of a possible child. "They'll help you if you ask. You just need to get over your pride, Ellie Grace. You're their only daughter."

His words are like little pinpricks at her heart. When she first met him a year ago, just being with her was enough for him to be happy. But these days, he seems so focused on money. Then she chides herself. He grew up with so little that of course he has anxiety about finances. "I will talk to him, sweetie. I promise."

"I need a drink, babe. Be back in a flash."

A few moments later, he returns balancing two glasses of pink prosecco in one hand and little Malcolm in the other. "I swiped him from your mother. Which do you want—baby or booze?"

"What a cutie!" Her voice is shrill. She takes a glass of prosecco. She desperately wants a baby, or two, or three, but it hasn't happened yet. Not that she hasn't done everything she can do on her part—fertility yoga, smoothies, tracking her ovulation on an app. The past few years have been filled with one friend's baby shower after another, while each month she cries when she gets her period. Zak says she's too stressed and that's why she hasn't gotten pregnant, but she thinks something might be wrong. The thought that she might not be able to have a child is enough to induce a panic attack. She *needs* a baby. Otherwise, what is the point of, well, anything? And why would Zak stay with her? A baby would cement Zak to her for life in a way that even a marriage cannot. Not to mention, having an adorable baby like Malcolm can more than double a social media influencer's followers. She would definitely become a brand ambassador.

"Aww, look at him trying to grab my drink!" Zak says loudly as he jostles Malcolm. Loudly enough for some of the nearby partygoers to look. It's quite a sight, Zak so handsome and the baby so cute.

"What a wonderful father you are!" a woman says. Her companion nods approvingly.

"Oh, I'm not the dad, just the doting uncle. But I can't wait 'til I have one of my own." He flashes that stunning smile. The women practically swoon.

"I'm glad to hear you guys want to make me another grandchild." Her father has appeared and stares down at them from his full height of six foot four. He played basketball at the University of Pennsylvania and never lets anyone forget that he was a starting player for the Quakers the year they went to the Final Four. "So what's the holdup?"

"No holdup, Daddy." She has an idea, a way to kill two birds with one stone. She can frame her request for money as a need for fertility treatment. If she slightly exaggerates how much a fertility workup would cost, she can pay for the best specialist and pocket the rest.

"We're working on it, sir." Zak grins at Thom, but Thom does not return the smile.

"Are you, now?"

Ellie Grace watches as her father and husband lock eyes for an uncomfortable moment.

"Better get this little guy back to his dad," Zak says.

As she watches him walk away, she gets the sinking feeling that she's just witnessed some subtle communication between him and her father, something terrible.

* * *

Nate peers up at the large, white house, fronted by four two-story columns. It is, objectively, a beautiful house, he can see that now as an adult. But to him, it is one of those glue traps that you put in the basement to catch crickets. They hop on and, unable to escape, they die trying. Like Ellie Grace and Trey.

"Nate, it's wonderful to see you back in D.C." Renée Price is by his side again.

"Yes, it's wonderful to be here." It's an uncanny habit of hers, showing up seemingly out of nowhere. He was already in high school when Renée moved in with her family. Her friendship with his mother has always confounded him. A Black middle-school teacher, she was married to some kind of finance guy but is now a divorcée in her late fifties whose laugh lines telegraph her relaxed approach to life. Renée seems an unlikely buddy for his mother—a Lilly Pulitzer–wearing boomer whose battle against aging, both on the tennis court and at the dermatologist's, seems to be inspired by Sherman's siege of Atlanta.

"I feel like our conversation got cut short. How are you?"

"Great. How are Eva and Seth?" Ellie Grace used to babysit the Price twins, who are about ten years younger than Nate. He searches his brain for any details he might have heard from his mother over the years, but comes up with nothing.

Renée launches into a summary of Eva's and Seth's accomplishments. Eva is at Duke. Runs marathons. Seth is about to graduate from Columbia and is applying to medical school.

"Wow. Good for him." He has never been very good at playing this game. Remembering names and occupations and degrees and lobbing the conversational tennis ball back with just the right inquiries. The constant comparing of status was an invisible but inescapable web that had been spun around him since he was a child. When he was in elementary school, the stakes were low—like which child was playing Chopin at the piano recital while the others banged out "Twinkle, Twinkle, Little Star." They ramped up a bit through middle school (who made the travel soccer team, who was cut) and peaked in high school (Ivy League versus, well, everything else). But it didn't end at college. Even now, his mother pours gossip into his ears whenever she calls. And for what? To elicit guilt, or jealousy, or perhaps competitive striving? After all, he can't possibly be happy living on a marine biologist's salary in California.

"Oh, and that little prince!" Renée nods at Malcolm, who sits at Nate's feet, busy pulling up fistfuls of grass. "Isn't he a handsome devil. Has that telltale Calhoun black hair."

Nate winces before offering a tight smile. It's a throwaway statement. And anyway, it's true—he, Trey, and Ellie Grace all have the same thick, glossy black hair. A Calhoun trait. His mother is the only blonde in the bunch.

A man his father's age in a crisp, pink button-down matching his ruddy face joins them. Nate dips in and out of the conversation, but he is anxious. Renée's comment about Malcolm has unnerved him. Where is Danit? She's the only person at this party he really wants to talk to.

He tries to survey the crowd for his fiancée without being too obvious about it. Danit stands out, which he likes about her. Her glorious, wild curls that range naturally from dark brown to sun-kissed blonde. Her wide hips and wide smile, both of which she is self-conscious about, seem to signify a kind of warmth that is so rare. As soon as he saw her standing in the driveway of the Steins' house, he knew he needed her in his life. She was like vitamin D in human form.

"Is that right?" The man with the red face peers at Nate. Frank? Fred? Nate can't recall his name, only that he is an old golfing buddy of his dad's.

"Sorry. I didn't catch that," Nate says and leans down to pick up Malcolm.

"Saipan. Renée here says you and yours are off to Saipan."

He opens his mouth to answer, but before he can, the man launches into the history of golfing on the islands. "There are ten courses that are worth their salt. Number one, of course, is Tara Iti, just north of Auckland . . ."

Nate's stomach roils as he recalls the scene earlier. He had wanted to break it to his mother that they were moving in a more delicate way. Not that he faulted Danit for blurting it out. He had never asked her to keep it a secret. But he knew how Ginny hated to be the last to know. The secret to getting her approval is to convince her that moving is somehow her idea. He was going to say it was safer for Malcolm, that he would be thousands of miles from his past. That no one and nothing, not even the truth, could find them in Saipan.

"Cape Kidnappers!" Renée says. "Sounds terrifying!"

"Oh, it is!" The man grins. "But Adam Scott calls the par-five fifteenth his favorite golf hole in the world. And he would know, wouldn't he?"

Nate smiles and chokes out a laugh. By now, his mother has no doubt told his father about the move. They'll present a united front. It will get very ugly. But he is not going to shy away from a confrontation.

Not this time.

His parents made a promise that night two years ago, and now he is asking them to make good on that promise.

And if they don't say yes? If they refuse? He doesn't know what he will do.

But he knows he won't end up like Trey and Ellie Grace, cowering in their parents' shadows.

Nate swoops up Malcolm and looks deep into the boy's dark eyes.

"Dadadada." Malcolm pats Nate's cheeks and shoves two tiny fingers into Nate's mouth. "Dibby do dadda."

"*Dibby do dadda*?" Nate responds. "That's just what I was going to say."

Nate leans in close and smells the boy's breath. It is reminiscent of maidenhair ferns in the woods, uncurling after a long winter, ready for spring. It's hard to remember what life was like before him, but everything he has sacrificed—sleep, career opportunities, his marriage to Helena—all of it was worth it to have this little person who has given his life meaning that he didn't even know was missing.

8

After finishing off her second Cherry Smash, Renée deposits the empty goblet on a table, bids Nate and the others goodbye, and goes in search of a third.

She's a little wobbly on her feet. Maybe kitten heels on a damp grass lawn aren't the best combo. She should have worn espadrilles. She keeps a wide grin on her face and her chin up as she navigates the crowd in search of a waiter. Every year, for the past fifteen years, she has helped Ginny plan this party. That means sipping Bellinis or mimosas while Ginny frets over finger food and the guest list. The Cherry Smash was Renée's contribution this year, and as far as she can tell, it's a hit.

The alcohol is doing a terrific job of quieting that little voice inside her head, the one that's been keeping her up at night. When she got the house in the divorce, she thought she was set. She could barely afford the mortgage payments and insurance. But her ties to the community were deep. Plus, she wanted a home for Eva and Seth to come back to—for holidays, and yes, if they ever hit a rough patch. Lord knows their father's high-rise apartment in Dubai, Hong Kong, or wherever his job took him next wasn't going to cut it.

Then the roof began leaking. And the basement flooded.

And Seth would be starting medical school, which cost upward of sixty thousand a year.

But Ginny is helping her make it right. Renée can depend on her friend.

The Calhouns have so much money, will Thom really miss it?

Renée's eyes alight on a young man with dreadlocks holding a tray of drinks. "Excuse me, honey," she says. "I'll take one of those."

He pauses long enough for her to remove a Cherry Smash from the tray.

"Yes, ma'am." His tone is respectful but his smile wry. For a moment, they lock eyes, something passing between them. They are two of only a handful of people of color at the party. Then the moment is gone, and she turns away quickly, almost bumping into Thom.

"Easy there, Renée." He holds his hands up as if in defense, even though he towers over her.

"Sorry, Thom. I didn't see you there." If she had, she would have gone the other way. She'd spotted him earlier, across the lawn talking to his three children. But she tries to stay away from Thom in general. She's never liked him, an opinion she learned to keep to herself over the years for the sake of her friendship with Ginny, but that dislike has hardened into something else recently.

"Enjoying those drinks, I see."

"Absolutely, I am." She takes a big gulp of her Cherry Smash to prove it. And why shouldn't she? She's a fifty-seven-year-old woman. He doesn't have any claim on her. A little thought scratches at the back of her mind, like a cat wanting to be let out. Does he know? "It's a terrific party, Thom."

"Isn't it? Seems when the liquor is flowing and the food is served on silver platters, you've got no shortage of friends."

Renée tries to think of something clever to say but finds herself speechless. Over the years, she's watched Thom routinely build up his family members only to cut them down again. The comments about Nate's determination to be the exception to the rule that Stanford graduates were big earners. The way he would tell Ellie Grace not to "worry her pretty little head" about things. How often he threw out the phrase "You'll have to forgive Ginny" right before insulting her, and then chortling, as in *You'll have to forgive Ginny, she only reads the Style section.* He likes having people dependent on him, she thinks. And no one has paid a bigger price than Ginny. But her friend is one of those women who cannot conceive of life without her man. Whereas Renée had no choice when Drew left her.

"Friendship is everything," Renée says. "And everyone appreciates the hospitality. Ginny is a wonderful hostess."

"I'm glad you're enjoying our hospitality," Thom says. "Once again."

"Hmm?" Renée leans in, pretending not to hear him, but there is no mistaking the hostility in his voice. But he can't know about the money. Ginny said he never checks that particular account. She swore up and down it would be their secret.

* * *

Because this side of the yard is packed with people, it is more difficult for Shawna to navigate with the large tray. Back when she cocktailed, she learned how to balance a tray high above her head and hold it steady even if someone pinched her ass. But here, the whole point of carrying the tray around is that guests can reach what is on it. Sometimes that means she simply has to stand and wait for people to notice her. She is like the opposite of Moses parting the sea—people seem to converge in front of her as she approaches.

Taking a sharp left around a group of laughing women in kelly-green and pink shifts, Shawna sees her and stops short.

Ginny is wearing a crisp, white button-down shirt tied at the waist and a long gingham skirt with a slit up the side. Her blond bob is expertly tousled, her deep tan set off by the white of her shirt. When she opens her mouth wide to laugh at something her companion says, revealing gleaming white teeth, Shawna recoils farther back into the boxwood hedge. It's like looking into the jaws of a lioness.

At once, the bad feelings rush in—the doubt, the self-hate.

"You have nothing to be ashamed of," she whispers to herself. "You have every right to be here."

She's been working on this plan for a while. First, she had to save enough money to come to Washington, D.C. It wasn't cheap. She found a room in an apartment to rent in Gaithersburg and a job at an upscale chain restaurant off Rockville Pike. The money has been all right. There were moments when she thought about putting the past behind her. Maybe returning to the West—not to LA, not home to Oregon, but somewhere new, maybe Arizona or Texas. But something kept her here.

A sense that she is owed more. The kind of money she is after could be life-changing.

On one of her drives by the house, she saw a van pull up and a small woman—whom she now knows was Sunniva—get out. The side of the van said *Capitol Catering*.

She watched Sunniva disappear into the house and then reappear a few minutes later, Ginny towering over her as they walked and talked, pointing to parts of the garden.

Shawna visited the website address on the van right then and there and filled out a contact form for employment. It was a long shot, she figured. But even before she returned to her small room, her phone rang. And a short interview later, she had a job.

Shawna passes a napkin to a woman in front of her who is evaluating all the bruschetta on the tray as if one might have a secret pearl tucked among the smoked bluefish.

"Locally sourced from the Chesapeake Bay," Shawna says. "Sustainable." Her arm is growing weary, and she'd like to keep moving, put a little more distance between herself and Ginny.

At that moment, Ginny turns, looking directly at her. Their eyes lock. Shawna swallows a small shriek. The tray she is holding slides out of her grip and onto the grass. She falls to her knees, her head swimming. She came here to confront the Calhouns, but coming face-to-face with that woman has transported her back to that vulnerable state she was in two years ago. Who did she think she was fooling? Tears fill Shawna's eyes, making it hard to pick up the bits of food scattered in the grass.

When she has finished cleaning up the mess, Shawna stands and looks around, but Ginny is nowhere to be seen. Maybe she imagined the look. Maybe Ginny didn't recognize her. She has to pull herself together if she is going to go through with this plan. She can't let them intimidate her again.

Shawna takes the tray of ruined bruschetta and marches back to the kitchen. She is sure her face is red and sweaty. Her throat feels constricted.

Once inside, she deposits the tray and tells the kitchen staff she'll be right back, she needs a bathroom break—cold water on her face to revive her and five minutes alone to gather her thoughts. Rethink her plan.

Jamal stops her on her way to the powder room.

"You okay? You need this?" He taps his chest pocket.

"No. I'm fine."

"I have some Vyvanse if you're tired."

"Thanks, but no."

"You sure?"

She offers a weak smile and continues walking. She isn't sure. She used to love the adrenaline rush and focus of speed. But a hit off a vape pen is one thing, popping pills is another, right?

In the powder room she collects herself. She looks in the mirror and tells herself to get it together.

"Stick to the plan," she says to the girl staring back at her.

Shawna leaves the bathroom, shutting the door behind her. Her nerves feel less jangly now. She can handle Ginny and Thom. *She holds the cards.* As she rounds the corner back to the living room, a hand grabs her arm from behind. Shawna spins around to face Ginny, who has an icy smile on her face. Shawna gasps.

"You clever little bitch." Ginny tightens her grip around Shawna's arm. "Well, now that you've found us—what do you plan to do?"

9

"You have one week, Renée," Thom says. "I want the money back in full."

Renée takes a step back, checking that no one around them has heard him.

"How did you . . . I thought—"

Thom laughs. "You really think Ginny is capable of pulling off something like this? Without my knowledge? Oh, Renée."

Renée feels her chest seize up. His open cruelty sickens her. But the person she really feels for is her friend who is married to this man. Poor Ginny. Who spends so much time perfecting a body that long ago ceased to comply with fad diets and Pilates. Manicuring hands riddled with age spots and veins like rural routes on a road map. Ginny really thought that this garden party might win back a man who's having the best sex of his life with a thirty-year-old.

"I saw you," Renée says. "At Filomena in Georgetown."

Thom's mouth opens in shock. "What?"

"I said I saw you. With that woman." Renée takes a sip of her drink, savoring his discomfort. He looks a fool. Loafers without socks, a new Tesla, a fake tan. Chasing a girl the same age as his own children.

"You're spying on me?"

"Spying? Hardly." The Italian restaurant is a D.C. institution, with over-the-top décor and killer risotto. It isn't a spot you go when you want to hide; it's where you go when you want to announce to the world you are in love. It's a baby boomer's equivalent of posting a "couple picture" on Instagram.

Thom takes Renée by the elbow and marches her toward the privacy of an immense rhododendron. "And so what?" he hisses. "You think that means I'm going to let you rob me blind?"

"No one's trying to rob you," Renée says, trying to strike a conciliatory tone. Maybe if he knew about the HELOC. The roof. Seth's tuition. Maybe, just maybe, he would be sympathetic. "It's a loan."

"Well, I'm not the bank of Chevy fucking Chase," he snarls. "And I didn't okay the sale of those stocks. She didn't mention that part, did she? Because that's a federal crime."

Renée shakes free of his grip, her whole body trembling. She doesn't know if he's telling the truth—would Ginny really sell stocks out from under Thom without his knowledge? She knows Thom has a temper. He is known as a ruthless businessman.

For the first ten years of their warm but casual friendship, she thought Ginny and Thom had the perfect marriage. It certainly seemed that way from the outside. Renée can remember the exact day when that perception was shattered. She had spent a lovely September afternoon at Ginny's drinking gin and tonics in the garden and sorting through spring bulbs. When she got returned to her house, she realized she had forgotten her phone on the back patio. She was just through the garden gate to retrieve it when she walked in on Thom dressing Ginny down. It was impossible not to hear. It wasn't the words he used so much as the tone, dripping with contempt. Although she can easily recall one line he delivered, *You can't breathe without spending a thousand dollars.* At first, Ginny tried to brush the whole thing off, but slowly, over the course of the following months, she began to confide in Renée. And then there was the occasional blue bruise on Ginny's arms, her shoulders, her neck once.

Renée tries to take a step back, but the sharp twigs of the shrub dig into her back.

"Ginny never said—"

"Ginny!" He laughs. "I don't give a damn what Ginny said.

Ginny is not going to be my problem much longer. And where I eat and with whom is none of your goddamned business. You're going to keep your mouth shut if you know what's good for you." Thom leans in so close to her that she has the absurd thought he might kiss her. "And as for the money, let me be clear: you have one week to return it or I'm going to the police. Understand?"

She nods.

"I can't hear you."

"I understand," she whimpers. At her feet, Mumbo lets out a little whimper, as well.

Thom turns on his heel and walks away, leaving Renée shaking in the bushes. Thom is a monster. She can't get him that money in a week. It's already gone. If she is forced to pay him back, she will lose her house. And Ginny, poor Ginny—how can she tell her friend what is coming down the road? *Not my problem any longer.* She knows what that means. The loss of Ginny's life as she knows it. Utter and total humiliation in front of her friends and family. Shame at the club, at the grocery store, pitying questions and looks, avoidance. As if being cheated on and left for a younger woman were a contagious disease. And knowing Thom, he will hide his money. Tuck away their assets before the divorce, drag out legal proceedings for years while Ginny gets nothing.

Ginny's never held a job a day in her life. How will she survive?

Renée knows all about it. She lived it herself. What she doesn't know is what she should do.

With a trembling hand, she brings the glass to her lips and downs the last of the Cherry Smash. As she watches Thom work his way through the crowd, laughing and slapping backs, a rage she hasn't felt in a long time begins to bubble up. These men, who use women up and then toss them aside. Ginny fretting over the cocktail napkins and the choice of music—she was rearranging the deck chairs on the *Titanic*. The iceberg is almost here, and she has no clue.

* * *

Ginny is surprised at the fury in her own voice, her use of foul language. So unlike her. But it's fueled by the terror gripping her insides. That little slut cannot be here. Not today of all days. Not with everyone here. But what to do?

The girl pulls free. She rubs her arm, but her chin juts out, defiant. "We need to talk."

Ginny looks her up and down. Shawna is *almost* unrecognizable. The last time she saw her, Shawna's hard living was etched on her sunburned face, visible in her lanky hair and protruding collarbones. She had the worn-out look of a woman twice her age.

"We don't have anything to talk about." Ginny tries to keep her voice low so as not to attract attention, while still sounding authoritative. The girl has her cornered, but she can't let her see that. "Do I need to remind you of what you signed? And what can happen if you break your word?"

A man looking for the bathroom comes in. Ginny smiles and directs him toward the right door. She can feel the sweat break out on her hairline. What was that old deodorant commercial? *Never let them see you sweat.* Shawna holds power over Ginny, over their whole family, but Ginny can't let her know just how much.

"I'm not afraid of you anymore," Shawna says. "And I want to renegotiate."

"Renegotiate?" It comes out as a half laugh, half bark.

Shawna flinches but does not recoil. "I think I have some pretty good cards in my hand."

Ginny straightens up. "You need to go now. Or I'll call the police."

It's an empty threat. The last thing Ginny wants is a marked police car pulling up to her front lawn, guests gawking.

"I'm not going anywhere. And if you won't talk to me, I'll go find your husband." She puts one hand on her hip. "Or your son."

Ginny turns, sensing someone nearby. It's Cookie from down the block, standing there with a woman she recognizes from the club, a harried mother of two teens.

"Cookie, darling!" Ginny kisses the air on both sides of Cookie's face before turning to the other woman as Shawna stands by. Ginny tries to position her body so the girl cannot leave. She's not done with her. "Simmons, you look lovely as always. That dress."

"Oh, Ginny, you have outdone yourself," Cookie coos.

"How on earth did you manage to get those tulips to bloom the same time as the cherry blossoms?" Simmons asks. "You must have God on speed dial."

"I stagger my plantings. Early bloomers for March, then April bloomers, and I even have tulips blooming well into May. I can send you my bulb source. Direct from Holland."

Simmons clasps her hands together. "I had no idea tulips could have such a long bloom time! I have a brown thumb. I'm lucky to get a few daffodils to grow. Maybe I have too much shade." As Simmons expounds on her gardening woes, Ginny's pulse speeds up. She senses Shawna's impatience beside her. Ginny needs to get her off the property before anyone else recognizes her.

But Simmons won't stop talking.

"Excuse me, ladies, sir," Shawna says. Before Ginny can do anything, the girl has slipped away.

10

Ellie Grace pauses outside her father's study and peers through the crack in the thick door. This is his sanctuary, and she hates to disturb him. She can see him sitting in a leather club chair, a drink in one hand, looking at his phone. The dark wood-paneled room reeks of masculinity—it's the adult equivalent of her brothers' clubhouse out on the roof when they were little, with the *No Girls Allowed* sign tacked on the window that led to it. When Ellie Grace was growing up, her father would indulge his love of classic rock by blasting his old records in here: the Who, the Stones, and—his favorite—the Doors. Mercifully, the heavy wood paneling made it almost soundproof; Ginny made sure of that.

Ellie Grace knocks on the door while nudging it open. "Daddy, you in there?"

Her father waves her in, and Ellie Grace shuts the door behind her, taking in the 2019 Developer of the Year award, her dad's UPenn jersey, family photographs, and other testaments to the success of Thomas Banks Calhoun, Jr.—in business, sports, and family affairs.

He rises from his chair, walks over to a large mahogany desk, and sits down behind it. "Taking a break from the festivities?" He twirls a tumbler of scotch in his left hand, while the fingers on his right hand tap a manila envelope that lies on his desk. It is the only thing on the massive desk besides a Waterford crystal figurine of a golfer that her mom bought him for Christmas a few years ago. The sounds of the party are quite muted in the study, as if they are coming from a faraway place.

Ellie Grace sits on the arm of the chair he has just vacated. "Well, Daddy, I wanted to talk to you about something."

Her father has always flummoxed her. Other girls she grew up with seemed to have their dads wrapped around their fingers, but her dad seemed immune to her charm and annoyed by her tears. Ellie Grace always felt like she was a nuisance to him, or maybe a household chore that her mother was responsible for.

Sometimes she wondered if she had been a mistake. She was four years younger than Nate. Maybe her parents had never wanted her. Her father turns to the window, before scowling. She follows his gaze. Zak out on the lawn, talking to a cute blonde. Her dad won't understand. That's just Zak's way. He's super friendly. After the family dinner at which Ellie Grace and Zak announced they were engaged, she overheard Thom talking to Ginny in the kitchen. *Anyone could see this pretty boy con man coming from a mile away. Anyone but our daughter, that is.*

It was a brutal and unfair assessment, and all because Zak had declined a job on her father's construction crew. It's true that six months was a short time to know someone before marriage, but the heart wants what the heart wants. She was sure that once they really got to know Zak, they would love him, but so far, it hadn't happened.

"Daddy, don't tell Zak I told you. But I think we need to look into fertility treatments. And those are, like, really expensive."

"Is that so?"

"Daddy, we really want this. We want to be a family."

"If it's so important to your husband, why doesn't he get a job and pay for it? The average salary in this country is sixty K. Our construction workers can take home more than that."

"Daddy, Zak is not a construction worker."

"You don't get to have it both ways. Either he takes care of you, or I do."

Ellie Grace recoils in shock. "What does that mean?"

"You're a married woman, sweetie. He's an adult fully capable of caring for his wife. This enabling has got to stop."

"What *enabling*?"

"I've been patient." He takes a deep breath. "We're going to need you to vacate the Chalfonte model. Construction is complete, and we'll be putting it on the market in April."

Ellie Grace grips the side of the chair, her nails digging into the leather. "April? That's next week! Why are you doing this to me? What have I done?"

"It was only supposed to be for a year. I told you that when you moved in. That once the elevator was installed, and the home theater in the basement, once everything was done, we'd be putting it on the market."

"Where are we supposed to go? To live?" Tears spring to her eyes. This is the last thing she was expecting. Maybe a no on the money, but to be kicked out on the street?

"You'll figure it out."

"You own so many houses! Why can't we stay in one? I don't get it. My friends' parents help them out all the time." She hiccups and wipes at her eyes with the back of her hand. "I don't bring in enough money to support us both. We have bills, Daddy," Ellie Grace says, sniffling. "We have car payments."

"So does most of America. Get a real job, come work for me. We need a sales rep out in Centreville for our next fifty-five-plus community."

Ellie Grace shudders. "Sales? Centreville? Where even is that? Besides, I have a job."

He laughs. "That internet thing?"

She winces at his casual dismissal of Gingham Life, into which she has poured almost every waking moment of the past six months.

"We all make choices in life, honey. You are at a crossroads.

Make your choice, but then you will have to live with the consequences. You'll need to be out of the house by the second week of April."

He smiles, which infuriates her. He's enjoying this, she realizes, a hot lump of rage forming in her throat.

"I'd like to add that if you should ever find yourself on your own, I will always be here to help you get back on your feet. No matter what, there will always be a room for you in my home."

"Wait, what? Are you saying if Zak and I broke up for some reason, I could move home, and you'd support me?"

"I'm saying, should you find yourself in an unfortunate circumstance, my door is always open."

"Are you seriously incentivizing me to leave Zak?"

"No shame in divorce, Ellie Grace. Lots of young people make mistakes with their first marriages. Doesn't mean you have to live with the consequences forever."

The d-word feels like a cord tightening around her neck. She gasps, doubling over, struggling to breathe. She lands in the leather chair, still warm from her father's body. "How could you even suggest that?" The words come out strained and hoarse. She looks up at the man who raised her, trying to identify any compassion in his neutral face, and finds none. "I love him, Daddy. Doesn't that mean anything to you? He makes me happy."

Again, her father drums his fingers on the manila envelope. "What is that?"

"This? This is the nuclear option. Let's hope it doesn't come to that."

Ellie Grace stiffens. Her father is not a man who makes idle threats. "What do you mean *nuclear*? What are you going to do?"

"You just turned twenty-seven. You're not getting any younger, Ellie Grace. You married this guy over my objections, and I've been patient. It's been over a year. I gave him a chance, but he cannot support you."

The tears come gushing now; she is unable to stop them.

"Money. That's all you care about. What about my happiness? I'm your only daughter!"

"You are playing at marriage. Playing at adulthood."

Ellie Grace stands up, mouth open, but no words come. His lack of emotion and total composure only make her more upset. A strange vibration runs through her. *This is what hatred feels like*, she thinks. Thom stands up, grabbing a tissue as he rounds the desk. "Chin up, sweetie." He hands her the tissue and holds her uncomfortably by the shoulders in a simulation of a hug. Ellie Grace stiffens, enduring his touch. "Trust me, this is all for the best."

Ellie Grace presses her lips together and doesn't say a word. She knows if she opens her mouth, a torrent of terrible things will come out.

"Now go fix your makeup and go back to the party," her dad says. "And when you see that husband of yours, please tell him I'd like a word."

He steps away from her and opens the study door. It takes her a millisecond to get the message—she's been dismissed.

11

Trey is sitting on the roof of the sunroom, smoking a cigarette. To get here, he had to climb through the window of the upstairs bathroom that he and his brother once shared, a feat that is a lot harder in his thirties than when he was a kid. From up here, he has a view of the Calhoun backyard, which is relatively small compared to the size of the house and the lot. Most of the land consists of a large, L-shaped lawn in front of and on the side of the house, where his parents always host their parties, including this one.

When he was younger, his mom would keep him, Ellie Grace, and Nate in the back under the watchful eyes of that year's nanny while the adults partied out front. Trey smiles remembering those days. All he and his siblings had to do was keep clean until their presence was required, make the rounds of the party, and then they were free. Free to run around the backyard, which didn't seem so small back then, climb trees, get dirty—be young.

Now his mother has taken over the backyard with her gardening. A huge shed, which she refers to as the *she-shed*, sits at one end, while a large flower bed occupies most of the other half, serving as a cutting garden for her annuals in the summer. As of this moment, the long, rectangular beds of earth lie dormant, but even Trey is impressed in midsummer when they overflow with pink, yellow, and orange flowers, turning the backyard into a butterfly magnet. His mother is nothing if not industrious. *She's always loved a good project*, he thinks. Unfortunately, that includes her three children.

Trey stretches his legs out, remembering all the hours he whiled away up here. The roof is relatively flat, with a slight incline, and most of it is taken up by a large skylight. But on the far end, where he is sitting now, this little spot nestled under the shade of a giant oak was his unofficial clubhouse. His and Nate's. They never let Ellie Grace up here. And then later, as a teen, he came here when he wanted to smoke or drink without his parents noticing.

Trey rubs out his cigarette, stands, and brushes off the oak catkins that have collected on the roof and stuck to his pants. A few feet away is the house's second chimney, rendered obsolete years ago when the addition was put on, but which his mother insisted on keeping due to *symmetry*. He walks to it, curious to see if the hidey-hole of his childhood is still intact. *Hidey-hole* is a misnomer of sorts. The summer he turned eleven, he pried a few loose bricks free from the back of the chimney and wedged a metal box in their place. He and Nate would use the box to leave secret messages for each other, purloined candy, and later, at least in Trey's case, joints.

He reaches around the back of the chimney, a surge of excitement hitting him when he touches the familiar metal box. He pulls on it gently, slowly wrestling it free. Trey stares at the grime-covered box in amazement. After all these years, it has survived the weather, nocturnal creatures, and his mother's endless home-improvement projects. But that elation disappears when he opens it and finds it empty. His heart sinks. But what had he been expecting? A letter from his teenaged self? Some kind of time capsule? He closes the box and works it back into the side of the chimney. Maybe when Malcolm grows up, he'll teach him about this place. Be the cool uncle.

He sits back down, scooching close enough to the edge to make him a little woozy. At once, he is flooded with a powerful nostalgia that hits right below his stomach, causing him to tear up. When he was ten, Nate and Ellie Grace would follow him everywhere, and he was the best diver on the country club's summer swim team. But somewhere between then and now, he has screwed up royally. And not just what happened in California, although that will haunt him forever.

Up until then, he had never really believed that he was a bad person.

Trey wipes the tears away with the sleeve of his shirt. He tries never to think about that night because what's the point? He can't change it. He can't go back and not get behind the wheel. That whole time period is a blur. One minute, he's a free man in LA, trying to launch his adult subscription service, and the next he's in his parents' guest cottage, working for his dad, trying to live with the fact that his careless actions cost someone their life.

Maybe it didn't happen quite that quickly, but that's how it felt to him.

He has a few memories of being in the hospital in LA, frozen in excruciating pain, each breath an exercise in masochism because of his three broken ribs. His father had been in town at the time of the accident, and Trey awoke to find him by his side. He was too zonked on painkillers to ask questions. He barely remembers being transported back to D.C. What he does remember is those groggy first days in the guesthouse, alternately tended to by a night nurse and his mother. When he was finally well enough to have a real conversation, he mentioned looking forward to returning to LA.

"That's not happening," his father said. "The girl riding in the car with you did not survive the crash. I had to call in a few favors to get you out of the state, but it was made very clear to me that if you return to California, you will be held criminally responsible for her death."

And that was that. No further explanation or discussion. He had crossed over and was no longer a charming scamp. He was reprehensible.

Hearing the back door of the house slam below him, Trey freezes, praying it is not a family member searching for him.

"You okay?" a man's voice asks, a voice he doesn't recognize. "You kind of ran out of there."

Trey gets down on his stomach and inches closer to the edge to get a look at who is out there. Seeing two figures in white shirts and black pants, he relaxes.

Only waitstaff.

"I'm okay, just stressed out," a woman's voice responds. "I'll be fine."

A zap of electricity shoots through his brain. That's a voice he *does* recognize.

But it can't be. His mind is playing tricks on him. He was just thinking about her, about the crash, so his crazy brain is doing a number on him. It's not the first time he has imagined he's seen her or heard her voice. It happens sometimes, most recently in the line at Starbucks, and also twice while walking down the street in Bethesda. But he is always wrong.

It's never her.

But when the girl below laughs in response to something unintelligible the guy has said, the sound hits him at the center of his being and cracks him open. It's the laugh of a ghost. Only he doesn't believe in ghosts. He must be going insane. The roof spins, and for a moment, he thinks he might roll off.

It can't be.

She's dead.

Dead in a car crash on the side of Tuna Canyon Road.

Dead because he was high out of his mind.

The back door creaks again. "Shawna? Jamal? What are you two doing?" a woman's voice, clipped and irritated, asks. "Let's get back to work."

Shawna. The reality smacks him with the force of a large wave, sending him reeling. He grips the edge of the roof tightly.

That was real. He didn't summon her name out of his imagination. Shawna is here. Alive and well and *at his parents' annual cherry blossom party.*

Trey scoots back until he is at the bathroom window. He has to go find her, talk to her. He won't really believe it until he sees her face-to-face, but already there's a thrilling flutter in his heart, like a bird about to take flight. *She's not dead. I didn't kill anyone.* Distracted, he knocks his head on the windowsill as he reenters the bathroom, but keeps going, his heart pounding in his chest. Once inside, he takes a moment to catch his breath and fix his hair in the mirror.

A sweaty, red-faced version of himself stares back at him. Frantic-looking, but with a glimmer of hope in those wide eyes.

If Shawna is alive, then his parents have no leverage over him. The thought is intoxicating.

He yanks the bathroom door open. He has to find her, fast.

12

Ellie Grace approaches her husband, who is standing by the croquet game, chatting up a blonde in a floral maxi dress. After clearing her throat several times unsuccessfully, she gently shoves her husband to get his attention. She spent the last ten minutes in the bathroom trying to fix her face so it does not look like she has been crying, but he notices right away.

"What happened?" She cannot tell from his tone if he is concerned for her, or angry because it is obvious the conversation with her father did not go well. The blonde excuses herself in search of a cold drink.

Ellie Grace pulls him a little farther away, out of earshot of the croquet players. "He said no."

"No? Just 'no'? What were his exact words?"

Ellie Grace can't meet her husband's eye. How can she tell him the cruel things her father just said to her? If she had to repeat them, she would burst into tears again, or do something worse. She swallows hard. "They can't help us." She quickly adds, "Right now."

"But they can help out Trey?" Zak spits out her brother's name. "Your parents gave him a Range Rover. A goddamn Range Rover, Ellie Grace, while we drive an Audi A3. But they can't help us out? That's bullshit. And you know it!"

Ellie Grace squirms. "That's not fair. How was Mommy to know how much she would hate driving such a big car? She's basically only driven convertibles. It seems silly for no one to drive it."

"Not the point, Ellie Grace." There's a part of Zak that makes her deeply uncomfortable, but she tries not to think about it.

Like last week when they saw a man buying an ice cream for his daughter. The man unknowingly dropped a twenty, and Zak pocketed it. She was horrified. Had he always been like this and she just didn't see it? No. He was just more conscious about money, that was all.

She met Zak at Equinox a year and a half ago when she was at the lowest point in her life. She was fifty pounds overweight, depressed, and with her self-esteem in the basement. Her three-year relationship with Camden had ended when he went on a business trip to Miami and came back engaged to a twenty-one-year-old Pilates instructor.

It didn't help that at the same time, her mother was going gaga over her first grandchild, Malcolm, who had just been born, while motherhood seemed further out of reach than ever for her. Ellie Grace was furious with Camden for leading her on, but even angrier at herself for sticking around, waiting for that ring, for as long as she did. Camden was never going to marry her, and she never really loved him. On paper, they were perfect—they had met her senior year at Vanderbilt at a charity silent auction run by his fraternity and her sorority. But they were just going through the motions. She sees that now. After six months of binge eating and watching Netflix, she joined a gym. And on the first day she went to the gym, she met Zak. Having him in her life was like plugging in the lights on a Christmas tree. She felt alive again. She had never known a man as beautiful or as kind as Zak. And he seemed equally excited to get to know her. It all seemed predestined—the long engagement to Camden, getting dumped. It all led up to meeting Zak. Within six months, she shed those fifty pounds, and they were eloping to Hawaii. Her parents disapproved—of his tattoos, of the fact that he had attended Arizona State for two years before dropping out, of almost everything about him. But she knew they would come around once they realized how happy he made her. After all, that's what they'd always said: *We just want you to be happy.*

"Look at this party," Zak grumbles. "They have more than they know what to do with."

Ellie Grace cringes. But he does have a point. She was the one who'd arranged the catering, and she knows the bill was upward of ten thousand. And that didn't include the cost of the alcohol. She turns to the house. Through the dining room window, she can see the cabinet displaying her mother's Royal Copenhagen Blue china. Worth a small fortune. Each salad plate cost more than a hundred dollars. In the middle of the cherry dining table sits a William Yeoward punch bowl that cost at least thirty-five hundred, and the vintage Baccarat candlesticks were another few thousand. But it isn't her mother's fault that she likes nice things.

"So how did you leave it?" Zak asks.

She doesn't want to tell him about having to move out, or about her father's not-so-subtle suggestion that she leave Zak.

"Daddy said he wants to talk to you. He's in his study."

Zak sighs. He's always been intimidated by her father, which her dad takes as a sign of weakness. He walks to the front steps of the house, and as soon as he is inside, panic grips her. Sending him was a mistake.

She is seized by a horrible thought—her father might offer Zak money to leave her. The idea sends adrenaline coursing through her veins. She can't let her father take away the one good thing in her life.

"Excuse me." Ellie Grace pushes past Danit, who is about to take a swing with her croquet mallet.

She has to get to the study before Zak does.

* * *

Danit brings her mallet back and takes a whack at the blue wooden ball, sending it flying across the lawn.

"Nice hit!" Cookie says.

Malcolm starts to run after the ball, but Danit reaches down and grabs him by the shirt. "Not so fast, buddy. This is your ball." She kicks a small rubber ball a few inches in front of him, after which he rushes.

"I understand that one of the hallmarks of a successful party is that everyone is so busy having fun, they don't realize that the hosts have disappeared. Right, Bob?"

Bob nods. "Absolutely."

"But where are Thom and Ginny?" Cookie looks around. "I haven't seen them for a while."

"I know. I haven't seen Nate either," Danit says, following his gaze. Although she is enjoying herself, it would be more fun if he were here. "He said he would be back in a flash, but it feels more like an hour."

"I think you're next." Danit hands Bob a white-striped croquet mallet. The party is a huge hit. Guests are drinking and chatting, and the croquet game is in full swing. Malcolm kicks the rubber ball, but it doesn't roll very far in the thick grass.

Bob steps up and takes a swing, connecting mallet to ball with a quiet thud. The white ball bounces along, knocking Danit's green ball through the hoop. "Yeah!" She gives a little jump. "Thank you!"

Bob beams at her. "Happy to help."

"All these lookie-loos clogging up the streets," Cookie says, leaning in close. "The cherry blossoms in Somerwood used to be a hidden gem, a local secret. Thanks to the internet, we get as many visitors as the Tidal Basin now."

Danit turns and takes in the sight. Cookie's right, the streets are clogged with people, couples strolling with their dogs and families posing for pictures on the banks of the creek that runs down the median of the wide, tree-lined street. Across the road, two well-groomed kids are selling organic lemonade from an expertly constructed stand.

She watches as a couple wanders onto the Calhouns' lawn,

mistaking the private party for some kind of public event. The woman in charge of the catering rushes over, gently shooing them back onto the street.

"The weather's perfect, though," Danit says. "Nate said I should prepare for temps between forty and eighty degrees."

Cookie laughs. "True, the weather is not something we can count on in late March in the Washington area. More than a few of these parties were forced indoors by rain. And there was 2012. We had a heat wave. Oh, look, there's Ellie Grace." Cookie waves her over.

Ellie Grace picks her way across the lawn. When she gets closer, Danit can tell she's upset. Her eyes are a little puffy, and she's wearing more makeup than usual. Danit wonders if she was crying.

"Everything all right?" Danit touches her on the arm, and Ellie Grace jumps back.

"What? Yeah. Totally fine." Her eyes dart around and land on Danit's face. "Hey! Let's get a picture! Excuse me, sir!" Ellie Grace taps a waiter walking by and gives him her phone. "You, too, Bob, Cookie." Her voice is shrill, bordering on manic.

Bob takes a step closer to Cookie, and Danit positions herself on the other side of Ellie Grace. Right before the photographer takes the photo, Cookie yells, "Hold, please!" He pulls a small, brown, leaflike thing out of Ellie Grace's hair.

"Eww, what is that?" Ellie Grace recoils.

"Just an oak catkin." He shows them the oblong-shaped object. "This is actually the flower of the oak tree."

"We ready?" the waiter asks, his impatience evident.

They freeze while he takes a few shots. Ellie Grace takes the phone back, taps furiously at it for a minute, and then says, "Voilà!" She holds the phone so Danit can see. "It's a photo dump of the party. Like just a ton of shots capturing the vibe."

Danit nods along with Ellie Grace, but can't help but recoil internally. Why is it so important to her that every moment of her life be shared online with strangers? A movement at the corner of her eye catches her attention. Renée has appeared in the front doorway, but it takes Danit a moment to realize there is something off about Renée's appearance. Her eyes are wide, her mouth open.

"Cookie, look." Danit motions toward the front door, and they turn in unison. They're not the only ones, as Renée's still form on the stoop is beginning to draw attention. Soon most of the guests around Danit are watching Renée, anticipatory smiles frozen on their faces.

"Maybe she's about to give another toast," Bob says.

That's when Danit sees the blood.

And then Renée begins to scream.

And scream and scream and scream.

13

Nate paces outside the study door, on the other side of which several EMTs are working. Behind him, Ellie Grace is leaning against the wall, chewing on her nails like she used to when she was a teen.

"Don't chew your nails," Nate says as kindly as he can. "Mom wouldn't like it." He can recall screaming matches between his mom and his sister, including the time his mother painted Ellie Grace's nails with something foul-tasting in an attempt to force her to quit.

Ellie Grace looks down at her splayed fingers. "I just had them done, too." She walks over to Nate and grips his arm. "I want to go inside."

"You can't." Nate unpeels his sister's fingers, and in a gentler voice adds, "Not yet. Let the medics do their work."

"Is she going to make it?" She looks up at him wide-eyed, and for a split second, he can see the little girl Ellie Grace used to be, the one who would follow him around, hoping to be part of whatever adventures he and Trey were heading off on.

"I don't know. She's alive, at least, so there's hope." He gives her what he thinks is an encouraging smile, although he is anything but confident. There was a lot of blood in the study when he'd gone in earlier.

Ellie Grace whimpers and turns away, busying herself by rearranging a vase of calla lilies on a side table. Nate wishes Zak were here to comfort her—isn't that a husband's job? A flash of irritation hits him. *And where the hell is Trey?* Nate experiences a fleeting panic about where Malcolm is and then exhales, remembering he is still outside with Danit. Malcolm is safe.

Nate was the first person to run inside after Renée began screaming on the front stoop. He tore through his childhood home and into his father's study, where he stopped abruptly in front of the bodies of his parents on the floor. At first, he thought they were both dead. His father's large frame lay splayed out on the silk rug, while his mother was draped atop him, blood drenching her checked skirt. A strange thought occurred to Nate, that they looked as if they had been struck down while in the middle of dancing, the way his mother's arm was flung over his father's shoulder. It was only after he bent down that he realized his mother was still breathing.

Nate turns just as a tall woman strides through the front door and right past him into the study. He pokes his head in and watches her bark orders at a technician—she is obviously in charge, an assumption confirmed when someone refers to her as "Detective." Nate paces by the entrance to the study, feeling useless, and is forced to jump back as two EMTs rush past him, wheeling his mother in a stretcher.

"I'm going with her," Ellie Grace tells Nate and rushes out after them. Left alone, Nate moves closer to the entrance of the study, trying to get a sense of what is going on inside. When he peers in, he can see the detective standing above his father's body. Bile rising in his throat, he swallows hard. The room evokes so many memories from childhood. It was his father's refuge and the only place the two of them really interacted one-on-one.

As a child, he was summoned into this room countless times, to stand exactly where his father lies now, to account for his actions. He can still recall the shame that accompanied these conversations—standing at attention while his father sat in his leather club chair and dressed him down. The last one happened during his senior year in college, when Nate informed his father he wouldn't be coming back to D.C. to work for Calhoun Development but was staying in California instead to pursue a master's in marine biology. The conversation did not go well.

Nate watches the detective poke around the trash can next to the desk with a pencil. She says something he cannot quite make out, so he takes a step closer. A technician in a white polo shirt with the word *FORENSIC* across the back in black letters joins her, and the two of them peer into the trash can.

"What do these look like to you?" the detective asks.

"Used tissues?"

"Look more closely."

Nate watches the technician lean in and peer at the empty trash can more closely. "Looks like a pile of trash can liners."

"Exactly," the detective says triumphantly. "But what's missing?"

"Garbage?"

"Bingo." The woman's face breaks into a grin. "These are the refills. So where's the bag that was in use?"

The detective turns, meeting Nate's eye. Startled, Nate jumps back, bumping into the side table, knocking over the vase with the calla lilies. He grabs it before it spills any water, setting it upright just as the detective enters the hallway.

"Hi, sorry, I was just—" He doesn't finish his sentence because he has no idea what to say.

"Detective Jacqui Washington." She hands him a card. "Montgomery County Police. Are you related to the Calhouns?"

"I'm Nate Calhoun. I'm their son. One of their sons. My older brother, Trey, is around here somewhere. So is my younger sister, Ellie Grace." His hands are sweating, and he rubs them on the side of his pants.

Detective Washington nods. Nate estimates she is almost as tall as he is at six feet, because even in the flat boots she is wearing, she can look directly into his eyes when she speaks. "Do you live here? With your parents?"

"Oh, no. I'm visiting." Nate lets out a little nervous chuckle.

"But this is the house I grew up in. I'm in from California with my son and fiancée, and we're staying here this week."

"Got it." She takes out a small spiral notebook and scribbles something down. "First of all, I'm very sorry for your loss, and I know this must be a terrible shock."

Nate bristles. "Thank you. My mother is still alive, though."

"Of course. And I'll be heading to the hospital shortly to try to speak with her. But I'd like to ask you a few questions before I do."

Nate nods. "How can I help?"

"I take it there was a party going on at the time?"

"Yes, my parents throw a cherry blossom–themed party every year around this time. They've been doing it for as long as I can remember."

"I see. I'm going to need a copy of the guest list, as well as the name of the caterer and their information, so we can get a staff list as well."

"Sure. Ellie Grace is the one who'd have all that. She helped my mom with the party."

"We noticed your father had a safe under his desk."

Nate nods. "That's right."

"It was open and empty. Who, besides your father, had access to that safe?"

Nate blinks hard, trying to picture the safe beneath his father's massive desk open and empty. It's difficult to imagine since he's never seen the thing open. "No one. Only recognizes my father's fingerprints. No one else's."

"Not even your mother's?"

Nate shakes his head, wondering if there is some hidden implication in her question. He's never really given it much thought, but maybe it was strange that his father didn't allow his mother access to the safe. What was so secret that he didn't want her to see?

"Any idea what your father kept in that safe?"

"I have no idea. I would guess documents, maybe business stuff, but I really don't know. My father didn't really talk about that kind of stuff."

This last sentence seems to grab Washington's attention. If she had antennae, they would have perked up. "Would you say you were close to your father?"

Nate measures his words before he speaks. "Well, I've lived in California for several years now."

"I meant emotionally, not geographically."

"Yes, I know. I was getting to that." His father never visited him in Mendocino, even when Malcolm was a newborn. When business brought him to California, it was Nate who was expected to drive down and meet him. And he showed little to no interest in Malcolm, never bothering to join the weekly Zoom calls that Nate had with his mother on Sunday afternoons so she could visit with her grandson. Nate did get an occasional email from his father, usually forwarding an article in *The Wall Street Journal* or some alumni news. "We were not particularly close. He was a very private man."

"I see."

"And he didn't approve of my being a marine biologist. He wanted me to come back here and work for him." Nate presses his lips together. *Why the hell did I just say that?* The stress of the situation is getting to him.

Detective Washington shuts the notebook and pops it into her jacket pocket. "We'll need to talk again, soon, but now we'd better get the fingerprinting started."

"Fingerprinting?"

"Yes, we're going to need prints of everyone who was inside the house today. You, your family, and any of the catering staff. We'll set something up outside for the staff and guests, but let's get your family in here"—she gestures toward the living room—"and a technician will take care of you soon."

In a dreamlike state, Nate walks into the living room and sits down on one of the sofas to wait. He stares at the back of the house, where tall windows look out on the backyard. A memory of one Christmas morning comes to him. He had gotten a baseball mitt as a gift, and his dad took him outside in the back to play catch. It's one of the few happy memories he has of his father. Nate thinks about what the detective asked him, about what was in the safe.

He has no idea what his father kept in that safe because he didn't really know his father at all.

And it hits him—now he never will.

14

Mumbo trembles in Renée's lap. He's not a fan of the bright lights of the police cars and the ambulance. Renée coos to him as she strokes his head, waiting for the officer who said he would be right with her. She sits at one of the cocktail tables, piled high with empty glasses and crumpled-up napkins, a sense of doom settling on her shoulders.

A uniformed officer with a thick neck and a shiny bald head pulls up a folding chair and sits across from her. "Officer Amatangelo. Mind if I ask you a few questions?"

"Not at all," she says. "I want to help in any way that I can. I just don't want to go back inside there." She shudders.

"Understood. So, who's this guy?" He reaches for Mumbo, who emits a low, guttural snarl.

"Oh, Mumbo-wumbo," Renée coos into the dog's ear. "Don't bite the officer." She eyes Amatangelo warily. Mumbo is a very good judge of character. "This is Mumbo."

"Mumbo." He smiles. "Like the sauce. Well, do you mind if we clean Mumbo up? It looks like he may have some trace evidence on him."

"Evidence?" Renée recoils, squinting at the small dog. Now that she's looking closely, she can see a dark smear on his fur. She gasps. "What is that? Is that . . . blood?"

"We can't be sure until we process him." Amatangelo reaches his hand out, and Mumbo snaps. The officer yanks it back in time. "More of a cat guy myself," he says.

"Process him?" Renée hugs Mumbo closer, horrified. "I do not like the sound of that."

"Oh, it's no big deal. Just a swipe of a cloth. We'll give him right back." Officer Amatangelo motions for someone beyond Renée's field of vision. A moment later, a small man appears.

"This is one of our technicians. He can take your pup to be proc—checked out."

The technician reaches out and pets Mumbo without incident. "Hello, Mumbo," he says in a sweet voice.

"Looks as if he likes you," Renée says, allowing her dog to be lifted from her arms. She doesn't really see what choice she has. "Take good care of him," she says. "Hold his bottom. He doesn't like to dangle."

Once they are gone, Amatangelo opens his notebook. "So, you were a guest at the party. Where do you live?"

"Across the street," Renée says, pointing to her house.

The officer glances across the street at Renée's large, stone house. "Oh yeah? You live there?"

She winces at the note of surprise in his voice. "Yes, I do. And I have for fifteen years." Renée realizes she sounds a bit snippy, but she's been answering this question for too long. She knows an African American woman with a teeny white dog is not the typical Chevy Chase resident, but she hates how people react. It's exhausting.

"Let's start with how you discovered the bodies," Amatangelo says.

Renée blanches at his phrasing. "Ginny Calhoun is not a body. Ginny Calhoun is one of my dearest friends. And Thom deserves more respect in death."

"Yes, ma'am. I didn't mean any disrespect."

"It started when I was in the bathroom with Mumbo—"

Amatangelo raises his eyebrows. "The dog came in with you?"

"Mumbo comes with me everywhere. He's very attached to me, and he doesn't like to be alone. That's why I took him with me to Ginny's party. Plus, everyone loves Mumbo." She sniffs a little. "Especially Ginny. Asti and Spumante—those are her

Frenchies—and Mumbo are pals. I'm sorry." She grabs a cocktail napkin off the table and dabs at her eyes.

"No, please take a moment."

After she's done wiping her eyes, Renée continues. "Well,
I was finishing my business when I heard a loud pop. Like a
firecracker. And then when I was washing my hands, I heard
another."

"How far apart are we talking? Ten seconds? Five minutes?"
Amatangelo jots something down.

"Oh, I don't know. However long it takes to flush and wash
your hands. Ninety seconds? Not longer than two minutes,
that's for sure."

"What did you think the sounds were?"

She shrugs. "I'm not sure. A firecracker? An accident in the
kitchen? My mind most certainly did not go to gunfire."

"Uh-huh." He scribbles some more. "And then what happened?"

"And then I opened the door, and Mumbo shot out." Renée
recoils at the memory. If only she had stayed in the bathroom a
little longer—maybe fussed with her hair, reapplied her lipstick.
If she could do it again, she would lock the bathroom door and
not come out. But there are no do-overs in life.

"Is that unusual? For him to run off like that?"

"Not really. He's a killer with a terrific sense of smell. You
know all these little terriers were bred to kill rats. It's in their
blood."

"That's very interesting."

"Well, I called him. I didn't want him getting into anything—
like chocolate, for instance. Chocolate is toxic to dogs. But he
didn't come back. And Mumbo always comes back." Renée's
shoulders slump as she relives the moment, calling after Mumbo,
wandering deeper into the Calhoun house. Little did she know
what she was about to stumble across. "But this time, he didn't
come back."

"So what did you do?"

"He started barking. I could hear him in Thom's study. So I went after him and . . ." Her voice trails off.

"And?"

Renée can tell the officer is impatient by his fits and starts. *He has some work to do on his people skills*, she thinks.

"I followed Mumbo into the study. And that's when I saw . . ." She pauses to sniff. "Well, first I saw the blue-and-white checks and I thought it was a tablecloth, but then I realized." Her voice catches. "It was a skirt. And I saw the legs." She brings her hand to her mouth at the memory. She doesn't want to fall apart here, not in front of all these people.

"So you saw Mrs. Calhoun first?"

Her hand flutters at her chest. Through tears, she describes finding her friend lying on top of Thom. "And then I saw Thom."

"And what did you do then in the study, after you found the bodies?"

Renée shifts. "Well, I checked to see if they were alive. And Ginny was."

"Did she say anything?"

"Nothing. She was in so much pain, in and out of consciousness. I called 9-1-1. And then I guess that's when I ran out of the house screaming."

"Ms. Price—do you know of anyone who might have a grudge against the Calhouns?"

"Against Thom and Ginny? Don't be ridiculous; they are widely admired."

"Maybe a disgruntled worker or employee? Ever hear of anything like that?"

"Absolutely not."

"And what about the children? Did they get along with their parents?"

"The children?" Her eyes widen. She peers past him to the front yard of the Calhoun house. Trey is outside, but she can locate neither Ellie Grace nor Nate. Fifteen years ago, when she first moved in, she had a front-row seat to watch the Calhoun children grow out of childhood, through adolescence, and into adulthood. She watched them for clues as to what her own children, several years younger, would be experiencing and saw, on the whole, growth and success. Yes, the Calhoun kids had their share of struggles, but what kids didn't? Ginny, as far as she was concerned, had been an exemplary mother, fiercely devoted to her children. She was offended, on her friend's behalf, by the officer's implication. "Thom and Ginny have given those children everything they could need and want. They've been wonderful parents. And if you need evidence of how much they loved each other, you need not look any further than this party. It's a family tradition."

"I wasn't implying they didn't love each other, but sometimes there are tensions in a family."

"Tension is one thing. Murder is another."

Properly chagrined, Officer Amatangelo's cheeks turn a rosy hue. Renée sits back, satisfied. Decades teaching middle school has taught her a few things about dealing with impudence. "Is that all?"

The officer nods. "For now."

"Good. I'll just go find Mumbo, then."

Renée walks toward where the technician took her dog. She looks back to see Officer Amatangelo heading up the lit path that leads to the front of the house. Expertly placed lights at the base of the cherry trees illuminate the pale pink blossoms against the darkening sky, lending them an air of artificiality like a theater set. She remembers when Ginny had the lights installed. Thom thought it was a waste of money, but Ginny prevailed. And she was right, Renée thinks.

Ginny always had good instincts on how things would look.

15

Danit straps a fussy Malcolm into a stroller. By focusing on the task in front of her, she hopes to keep the reality of what has just happened from sinking in.

Nate's father is dead. Not just dead but murdered.

Danit longs to be with Nate, comforting him, but she knows the best way to be of help right now is to settle Malcolm down. She can't imagine what Nate is feeling. She knows he wasn't close with his father—but she also knows he would never wish for this.

Nate always said that whenever he didn't know what to do with Malcolm, he just did the opposite of what his dad did. It was why Malcolm often spent the night cuddled between the two of them in their king-size bed. And Danit loved him all the more for it. He was determined to give Malcolm the kind of unconditional love he said he never felt.

Danit wipes at her eyes with the back of her hand and bends down to focus on the stroller straps. That is how she will get through this night, focusing on Malcolm and on the tiny things that need to be done for this child.

It's not easy. Malcolm wriggles, in no mood to be constrained, and as soon as she gets one of his pudgy arms through the harness, he slips the other one out. It's like Whac-A-Mole. Sensing someone breathing behind her, she turns to see Cookie, the Calhouns' neighbor. He crouches beside her, loosening the top button of his lilac shirt. "Let me help."

Together, they wrangle the baby into the harness. Cookie proves surprisingly adept at clicking the infernal little buckles. Malcolm rubs his eyes with two balled-up fists.

"Aww, he looks so tired," Cookie says.

"He's been crying." Danit gets up, too. "I'm hoping taking him for a walk will help." She pushes the stroller back and forth in a rhythmic motion, but Malcolm keeps fussing. "He doesn't like the bright lights."

"I'm with him. It's awful." Cookie touches her arm. "I'm so sorry about your father-in-law—well, future father-in-law. Poor Nate. Is there anything I can do to help?"

"I'm just so shocked. It feels so unreal." She swivels her head. "And all these people, just hanging around."

Cookie nods. "Gawkers, that's what they are." He clucks a few times. "I wonder which hospital they're taking Ginny to? Probably Suburban. How can Bob and I help?" He gestures to Bob, who has just caught up to them and is sheepishly stuffing a mini-quiche in his mouth. "Anything. Anything at all. Would you like us to watch the baby? We've turned one of our spare rooms into a nursery for when our granddaughter, Willow, visits. And we are happy to watch Malcolm. We have everything he could possibly need. Certainly more than what I had when I raised Olivia." He lets out a laugh. "Although that wipes warmer is a godsend, I have to admit."

"I think we're okay for now, but thank you for your offer," Danit says. "I'll let Nate know."

"Of course. What a good mama you are. Those boys are lucky to have you."

Danit smiles, touched by the compliment.

"And you two are free to stay over as well. There's plenty of room. I mean, you can't possibly stay *there* tonight." He gestures toward the big house.

"You're right," Danit says. "We can't stay there. It's a crime scene."

"Nate might want to stay with his brother or sister," Bob offers.

Cookie makes a face. "Not at Trey's, I hope. Don't take this the wrong way, but Trey and little babies don't seem like a good mix."

Danit looks around, taking it all in—the party guests, the police, the onlookers. "This is all so crazy."

"I feel a little guilty," Cookie whispers. "But this is kind of exciting, isn't it?"

Bob scowls. "Cookie."

"Too soon?" Cookie asks, straightening up. "Oh, Lord. Here comes Marty. Something about that man just brings out the worst in me."

Marty from down the block strides up to them, his anemic-looking wife trailing behind. Cookie introduces Danit and Malcolm, but Marty barely looks in her direction. "It's a robbery, that's what it is." He looks from Cookie to Bob and then to Danit, as if challenging anyone to disagree with him. "I would take a hard look at that catering staff. We had our Thanksgiving catered a few years ago, and half the silver walked away."

His wife nods in agreement, her straw-colored hair frozen in place with what Danit guesses to be half a can of hairspray.

"Marty, we don't know that," Cookie says. "People always blame the help. They get scapegoated."

"It was one of the catering staff, I'm telling you," Marty insists. "It's why we bother keeping a list of approved companies and businesses." Marty stabs the air with his finger. "Any SNOB member has access—"

"Did you say *snob*?" Danit asks, startled.

Marty's thin lips stretch into a small smile. "I know how it sounds, but it stands for the *Somerwood Neighborhood Oversight Board*. We are a very inclusive group—anyone in Somerwood can join, even the renters. We meet once a month to discuss issues related to our community, and I have always said, hire someone not vetted by SNOB at your own risk."

"Well, it looks like that's exactly what happened," his wife says in a meek voice.

Bob lets out a series of small dry coughs, and Cookie puts his hand on his husband's arm.

"I'd love to stay and listen to all these theories," Cookie says. "But Bob and I have to go."

"I'll walk with you," Danit says.

"Well, lock the doors," Marty says. "There's a killer on the loose."

Danit pushes the stroller alongside Cookie and Bob. They are halfway across the lawn when a uniformed police officer steps into their path. "Officer Cruz," she says, adjusting her thick black eyeglasses.

"Hello, Officer Cruz," Cookie says. "We were just heading home."

"Mind if I ask you a few questions before you go?"

"Not at all. We don't mind, do we, Bob?"

Bob looks at his watch. "I like to be home by eight."

Danit wonders if she's supposed to stick around, but it feels weird to leave now.

"Won't take but a minute," Cruz says, taking out a notepad. After she jots down everyone's names, she asks, "Did any of you notice or hear anything unusual at the party?"

Danit shakes her head. "Nothing. It was a really nice party."

"Everything was fine until Renée appeared on the front stoop," Cookie says.

"Do you happen to know what time that was?"

"I do—it was 5:50 exactly. My Apple Watch goes off at ten to the hour to remind me to move," Cookie says. "And it had just gone off when Renée came outside. Of course we didn't think anything of it at first. Renée is one of Ginny's closest friends. We're all in the garden club together. We're responsible for all the daffodils along the median and the upkeep of the creek. It may look entirely natural, but it does take work. But when we saw her there, we all sort of paused, didn't we?"

"I thought she might be about to give a toast, the way she just stood there." Bob rubs his chin, lost in thought. "Which is odd, now that I think about—"

Cookie blanches. "That's more than odd, Bob. That's silly. Why would Renée give a toast?" He shakes his head as if Bob is the most ridiculous creature on earth and turns back to the officer. "Well, that's when I saw the blood. And I just knew. I just knew."

"And of course, there was the screaming," Bob says.

Cookie nods. "Yes, there was also the screaming. A lot of screaming."

As if on cue, Malcolm lets out a loud scream of his own, and Danit turns the stroller away from everyone. "We'd better start moving."

"Well, the offer stands. Come by anytime," Cookie says. "Right, Bob?"

"Right," Bob says.

Danit nods goodbye at the officer before pushing the stroller through a scrum of onlookers, not slowing down until she is far from the crowd. The quiet is a balm to her pounding head.

After a few moments of brisk walking, Malcolm settles down. But Danit feels raw, on edge. This was most definitely *not* how she'd imagined her first meeting with the Calhouns would go. She had hoped this trip would be a chance to get to know each of the Calhouns, to win them over, to make them see what a great addition to the family she would be.

That she was just as good as Helena.

Feeling her phone buzz in her pocket, Danit stops beneath a streetlamp to check it.

It's from Nate.

Hi sweetie, can you come back to the house
The cops want our fingerprints

16

Ellie Grace watches the ambulance pull away with her mother, a sinking feeling in her stomach. She wasn't allowed to get into the ambulance, which outraged her, and the EMT, the one with the ginger beard, wasn't particularly nice about saying no. Although he informed her she could meet her mother at the hospital, he used a very dismissive tone.

Ellie Grace squeezes her eyes, forcing the tears back. She's aware that everyone is watching her. The neighbors and party guests have staked out spots on the lawn, close enough to observe but at a respectful distance.

Ellie Grace marches over to the nearest uniformed officer, a squat woman with large glasses. She crosses her arms and stands there until the officer finishes interviewing one of the party guests, feeling a strange mix of entitlement and vulnerability. *Do what I say. Take care of me.*

"Can I help you, ma'am?" the officer asks.

To Ellie Grace, her tone sounds anything but helpful. "Hi, I'm Ellie Grace. Thom and Ginny's daughter?"

Ellie Grace waits for the softening of the woman's face, an offer of condolences—something to indicate she knows who Ellie Grace is and that she is suffering. But the police officer stares at her impassively. "And I am Officer Cruz. How can I help you?"

"How can you help? How can you help?" The words tumble out before Ellie Grace can stop them. "My father is dead. My mother is on her way to the hospital, fighting for her life."

Officer Cruz offers the tiniest of smiles but says nothing. This just makes Ellie Grace more frustrated. All she wants is a little sympathy, a little warmth. She is aware people are watching, maybe even filming, so she forces herself to calm down and, in the sweetest voice she can muster, continues.

"I am heading to the hospital, but when my mother was being wheeled into the ambulance, I noticed that her jewelry was missing. And I just thought you'd want to know. Like, that seems really important."

"All right. I'll make a note of that, ma'am."

"A platinum-and-diamond anniversary band from her right hand. And her Cartier panther ring. It's diamond pavé with emerald eyes and sapphire spots. Do you want to write this down?" She can feel her left eye twitch. She should be driving to the hospital right now. But if she doesn't do this, who will? Her brothers?

Cookie and Renée appear, flanking her. "Is everything all right, Ellie Grace?" Renée asks, stroking Mumbo, who is curled in her arms.

"Oh, thank God you're here. My mother's jewelry is missing." Her voice breaks, and she hiccups loudly. "Her rings, her bracelet. Do you think the person that . . . the man who . . ." Ellie Grace inhales sharply, unable to finish her thought. Shifting Mumbo to one side, Renée takes a packet of tissues from her purse and hands it to her. Ellie Grace nods appreciatively, taking one from the packet. At the periphery of her mind, the truth lurks like a monster waiting for the bedroom lights to go out before it attacks.

Her father is dead.

Her mother has been shot.

And where the hell is Zak?

She pushes the monster back under the bed. "And she always wore a tennis bracelet on her right wrist."

Cruz taps her chin with her pen. "A tennis bracelet? Like little tennis rackets?"

Ellie Grace uses all her strength not to shriek at this policewoman, whose stoic demeanor inflames her like lighter fluid on a barbecue grill. "A tennis bracelet is simply a string of diamonds," she says through clenched teeth. "Only this one is Cartier. All of it was Cartier." She sniffs and turns to Renée. "That was Mommy's favorite jeweler."

"*Is* her favorite, sweetie. Your mother is going to pull through," Cookie says.

"Cookie's right," Renée agrees. "She is one tough lady."

"I know." Ellie Grace nods. She texts her mother at least three times a day. Life without her would be unimaginable. But they are right. Ginny might look like a typical country club housewife, but beneath her Lilly Pulitzer, she is made of steel.

"Can you spell that? Carty—?" the officer asks.

"Cartier," Cookie says. "*C-A-R-T-I-E-R*."

"And what is the estimated value of the missing jewelry?"

"Oh, I don't know. You'd have to ask my fa—" Ellie Grace chokes up and bites her hand. *Don't lose it in front of all these people.* But how is one supposed to behave under these circumstances? What is the proper etiquette when your parents have been shot?

"Oh, darling. You poor thing." Cookie pats Ellie Grace's back. "Listen, Officer, I'm sure you can get that kind of information from the insurance company. I'll just take it from here."

Officer Cruz snaps her notebook shut. "Yes, sir."

Cookie waits until Officer Cruz has returned to the crowd and is out of earshot. "You poor dear. I am so sorry for your loss. Your father was a wonderful man."

"Wonderful," Renée repeats.

The two of them stare at her with expectant looks on their faces.

"Yes, he was," she says, because she knows that's what they want to hear. Ellie Grace looks past them at the people on the lawn, the officers hanging yellow police tape around the front door, the catering staff huddled in one corner. She can see onlookers standing in the street, some of whom have their phones out and are filming the chaos. It's only a matter of hours until the murder goes viral on social media, sensational news sites, and true crime sites—and is linked to Gingham Life. The thought mortifies her.

"I should go," Ellie Grace says, taking a few steps toward her Audi and unlocking the car with her fob.

"Aren't you going inside?" Cookie asks. "I think your brothers are there. In fact, I believe the police want to talk to all the family members. Purely for informational purposes, of course. No one could possibly think any of you kids were involved."

Ellie Grace peers past Cookie at Officer Cruz, who is chatting with another police officer. They both turn and look directly at Ellie Grace, and her stomach sinks.

"I have to go to the hospital to see my mother." Ellie Grace grasps Cookie's arm. "Can you find Zak and tell him? That I've gone to the hospital?"

"I'm sure that . . ." Cookie follows Ellie Grace's gaze to see Officer Cruz striding toward them, waving her hand. "I believe the officer is trying to get our attention."

"Great. Thanks." Ellie Grace slides into the car and slams the door in her neighbor's face. A moment later, the black Audi peels out into the night. Looking in the rearview mirror, she sees a stunned Cookie and Renée staring after her.

Ellie Grace presses hard on the gas. She knows she can drive away from this terrible scene, but she won't be able to drive away from what happened here tonight.

And tomorrow is going to be even worse than today.

17

The scene outside the house reminds Shawna of the county fair her dad would take her to each summer. There were so many things to see and focus on that she always felt like she was missing out—if they went to the duck races, she felt she ought to be riding a Ferris wheel, and on the top of the Ferris wheel, she longed to visit the baby lambs.

What is she supposed to focus on right now? The TV truck that has arrived, or maybe the gawking onlookers who fill the streets? Or perhaps the party guests who are still milling around, baffled looks on their faces.

Whatever it is, it has to be external because she is not prepared to explore how she feels about what she just witnessed. It never occurred to her, in her months of planning, that Trey would be here. And when she saw the pure fury written across his face, she knew things were about to take a bad turn. And they did.

She shudders and sinks a little farther into the crowd of catering staff that is off to one side. In their white shirts and black pants, they remind her of her high school soccer team, waiting to take the field.

She finds Jamal in the small crowd and bumps him with her shoulder. "Hey."

He turns, smiling. "Hey, there you are. I was wondering where you went."

"What do you mean? I didn't go anywhere. I was working just like you."

"Whoa, Nelly." He pulls back. "I didn't mean anything."

"Sorry, I'm just on edge. Are those cops coming to talk to us?"

Jamal turns toward where she is gazing. A tall woman in a blazer and jeans approaches, with a short uniformed officer behind her.

"Yeah," Jamal says. "And if they split up, I hope I get the woman. That dude looks like a bulldog."

"Funny, I hope I get the guy." Shawna thinks the uniformed cop doesn't look too bright, and maybe if she acts really friendly, he'll go easy on her.

"Sir? Can we have a word?" The officer approaches Jamal.

"Of course." Jamal follows the cop, grimacing over his shoulder at Shawna.

Shawna steps back, close to a large tree, hoping that if she lingers in the shadows she can avoid being interrogated. But no luck—the woman detective finds her.

"Hi. I'm Detective Jacqui Washington from the Montgomery County Police. Mind if I ask you a few questions?"

Shawna smiles. "Sure," she says in a peppy voice. She does mind, but has anyone ever said *no, thanks* when a homicide detective approaches them?

After getting Shawna's name and age, the detective asks, "And where do you live?"

"I'm staying in Gaithersburg," Shawna says.

"Staying?" The woman cocks her head to one side.

"I mean, I live there. I haven't been in the D.C. area too long."

"How long would that be?"

"A month or so," Shawna says.

"Well, welcome to the DMV. How long have you been with Capitol Catering?"

"Not long. This is my first job, actually."

The detective follows up with a battery of questions: Did you see anything? Hear anything? Notice anything? But Shawna insists there was nothing unusual or out of the ordinary about this party. If the detective can sense that she is lying through her teeth, Shawna can't tell.

"Did you have an opportunity to go inside Mr. Calhoun's study?"

"No." The word pops out before she can stop it. Immediately, she regrets it. What if there are cameras inside?

"Let me ask you something—you're not worried about ruining such a nice silk shirt?" Washington asks, pointing with her pen. Shawna glances down at her clothing as if she is surprised to see that she is, indeed, wearing a silk shirt. *Damn it*, she thinks, *there's no way that the uniformed cop would have noticed.*

"I don't know," Shawna says, flustered. "I've never really done anything like this before." *Lie.* She started waitressing at sixteen, and it has been pretty much the only job she's ever had. Before Trey, that is.

"Hmm, seems pretty risky to me. And it's okay with your boss? Everyone else is wearing oxfords. You're wearing a blouse."

Shawna starts to cross her arms, then drops them by her side. She doesn't want to appear defensive. "I hadn't really thought about it, but I guess you're right." She breathes deeply. "I think catering isn't my thing, after all." She forces out a light laugh, the kind she is sure would have worked on the bald cop. She's gotten out of more than one speeding ticket with that laugh. But Washington is unmoved.

"I worked as a waitress one summer," the detective says. "Management made us wear khaki pants and mustard-yellow sweaters. I mean, look at my complexion. Mustard yellow? I looked sick every dang day of work."

Shawna offers a noncommittal "Uh-huh." She doesn't like where this little story is going, but she can't let the detective see how nervous she is.

"I hated that stupid cotton sweater," Detective Washington says. "But I still took such good care of it." She narrows her eyes as she speaks. "Every night, I checked for even the tiniest stain. I bought a toothbrush just for the job. If you don't get the stains right away, they set. Don't you think?"

"I guess. I'm not a stain expert. Like I said, this is my first catering gig." She wishes the detective would drop the topic, but she knows if she acts weird, the woman will probably dig deeper. Shawna pushes out a light laugh. "Lesson learned!"

"All right, we're done here." The detective turns her body three-quarters and points to a man at a table wearing a baseball cap. "See that guy? He's a technician who's running prints. Go get your prints taken. Purely routine."

Bile rises in Shawna's throat. Did she touch anything in the study? She can't remember.

"You all right?" Washington asks.

Shawna nods. "Sure. Just a crazy night."

"Well, if you remember anything, no matter how small"— Washington scribbles something on a card and hands it to Shawna—"call me. My cell's on the back."

"Absolutely, thank you." Shawna pockets the card before walking away toward the tech to get printed. Beneath the silk shirt, her body is soaked in sweat. An early-evening breeze sweeps across the yard, and Shawna shivers.

The shirt was a dumb mistake.

But how could she have predicted she'd be interviewed by the one cop who knew the difference between silk and cotton?

* * *

Danit holds a wiggly Malcolm on her hip as she paces the Calhouns' living room. Nate is upstairs, packing up some things so they can go stay with Ellie Grace and Zak tonight.

She walks a little route that travels around a large cream sofa, two armchairs, and a liquor cart where Trey is standing, and then back again. Malcolm seems to enjoy it. Ellie Grace's husband is in the dining room, where a technician has set up a little station for fingerprinting and collecting DNA. As Danit walks by the door to the dining room, she can tell Zak is flirting with the tech, which strikes her as odd. But, she reminds herself, people deal with grief in their own way.

"To think there was a murderer, right here, in this house." Danit shudders at the thought. This is the first time she's been alone with Nate's older brother. She's heard the stories of his drinking and bad behavior, but she wants to give him a chance. She knows better than most that some people need second chances.

Trey throws back the last of his scotch, ice cubes clinking against the crystal.

"Pappy Van Winkle," he says. "The good stuff. Bastard can't stop me now."

Danit winces. "You don't mean that."

Trey pours himself a refill. "Just a joke. Want one?"

"Oh, no, thanks." The truth is she would like a drink, but it feels wrong somehow. Besides, she's in charge of Malcolm right now, so sober it is.

Trey holds the cut crystal tumbler in the air. "To Daddy." He takes a swig and then looks directly at Danit. "So, you and my brother, huh? Is it true you were working as the nanny when you guys started dating?"

Danit feels her cheeks grow warm. "No. I mean, yes, it was a nanny share. But it wasn't in Nate's house. It was at the other family's house."

"That's kind of hot."

Danit pretends not to hear him, whisking Malcolm over to the couch where Mr. Panders is lying on his side. "Do you want your Mr. Panders?" She scoops up the stuffed panda and brings it close enough for Malcolm to grab.

"Panders!" Malcolm takes Mr. Panders's one good ear and stuffs it in his mouth.

Back in Mendocino, it didn't bother her how she and Nate met. But here in D.C., people seem to react to the news that she was Malcolm's nanny as if it were something scandalous or embarrassing. She can only imagine how they'd react if they knew the rest of her story.

"Glad that's over with." Zak walks into the room and puts his hand on Trey's shoulder. "Your turn, buddy."

"I am not your buddy." Trey shakes Zak's hand off and teeters a bit. "This is preposterous. Treating us like common criminals."

"Calm down, Trey. They just want to be able to eliminate us as suspects," Zak says.

Danit stops pacing. "Suspects?"

Trey nods his head in an exaggerated way. His eyes are red-rimmed. "You worried? Where were you and Nate when my parents were shot?"

Danit recoils. She instinctively squeezes Malcolm closer. "We were both outside, playing croquet." Danit feels ashamed of how easily this lie slips out. Nate doesn't need her protection. He would never hurt anyone, least of all his parents. So why did she say he was outside with her when he wasn't?

"So what are you so worried about, then?" Trey asks.

"She's not worried, dude, she's upset," Zak says. "A man is dead. Your mom is clinging to her life. It's a normal response to feel upset after a brutal attack like this." He winks at Danit.

"Thanks for telling me how I should feel, *buddy*." Trey slams down the tumbler and stumbles into the dining room.

Danit sinks into the couch, letting Malcolm wiggle out of her grasp. Trey is a lot. She looks at Malcolm, so clearly a Calhoun with his black hair and dark eyes and two bright pink apples for cheeks. *This poor little baby*, she thinks, *will never know his grandfather.*

"Don't let them bother you," Zak says, sinking into an armchair.

"Them?" She looks up from Malcolm at Zak, who is wearing a slightly amused expression on his face. "Do you mean Trey?"

"I mean the Calhouns," he says. "They're just not used to letting outsiders in."

18

Outsiders. The word hangs in the air. Is that what she is? An outsider? Danit wants to press Zak more about what it's like to be married to a Calhoun but doesn't dare. She doesn't want to be conversational fodder for him and Ellie Grace.

Instead she turns her attention to Malcolm, flat on his back on the couch, his head resting on Mr. Panders. His eyes are wide open, but he's not fussing, just staring up at the ceiling while occasionally rocking back and forth, blowing kisses in the air. Danit sits beside him, ready to catch him if he should begin to roll off.

"Little guy doing okay?" Zak takes a seat on the other side of Malcolm. But before Danit can answer, Zak takes out his phone. She can see he is scrolling through Instagram. He looks up, catching her eye. "Ellie Grace and I were supposed to post today. Sponsored posts. We're really screwed if we don't. But at the same time, I mean, do you think that would be tacky? To post when all this is going on?"

"I think maybe waiting is the smart move." Danit tries not to show her surprise that he is even considering posting at a time like this, but she's not a huge social media person. She's technically on several platforms, but she's more of a lurker than a poster. Sometimes she goes weeks without checking her accounts.

"Yeah, you're probably right. It could look bad. Taint the brand. But at the same time, we can't afford to screw up these relationships. You heard of Troop bags?"

She shakes her head, a flutter of nerves in her belly. Was she supposed to have?

"Luxury leather goods, wallets, bags. They're sustainable and fair trade. Ellie Grace has been chasing them for months. But maybe none of it matters anymore. Things are going to change around here."

"What do you mean?"

"Yeah, right." He shoots her a smile like they are in on a joke. Danit chews her lip. *Is he talking about money?*

"This whole thing is so crazy," he continues. "I mean, I didn't see or hear anything. Did you see or hear anything?"

Danit frowns. His rapid-fire questions and comments have her confused, trying to play catch-up. "I don't think so. I was outside; we were outside playing croquet."

"Yeah, me, too."

"You were there?" She jerks back her head. "I don't remember seeing you play."

"Well, I wasn't *playing croquet*. I just meant that I was outside with everyone else at the party."

"Oh." But that wasn't what he'd just said, was it?

"You probably didn't see me because I was on the other side of the big cherry tree, talking to some of the neighbors."

"Makes sense." Danit gets the feeling he is working very hard to convince her of something that isn't true, but she does not press him. He reminds her of a mediocre magician who can't quite pull off a card trick, but everyone pretends to be fooled out of politeness.

He shows her his phone. "Here I am." It's a picture of him and Ellie Grace at the party, but there's nothing about it that indicates what time it was taken. It proves nothing. But she can't help but notice it has more than three hundred comments.

"Wow, that's a lot of comments."

Zak yanks the phone back and stares at it silently for a few moments. "People are going nuts." He looks up at her. "You know, because of the murders."

"Murder. I mean, Ginny is alive." She grips Malcolm's foot as she says this, sending up a silent prayer to heaven on Ginny's behalf.

"Holy she-ite. We have five hundred new followers in the last hour alone! Oh, I see, we were tagged. TrueCrimeAddix posted about us. Dang."

"Is that good?" Danit forces a smile.

"Yeah, it's good. I mean, it's not good what happened to Ginny and Thom, of course. I mean, that's a tragedy. But this might be a silver lining, a real opportunity for Gingham Life. I gotta find Ellie Grace."

"Hell, no!" Trey shouts from the dining room, and they both look up.

"Just part of the process, sir," a woman's voice says.

A few moments later, Nate comes down the stairs with an overnight bag slung over his shoulder. "Hey, Zak. Ellie Grace said we could spend the night with you."

Zak tells Nate the code to the front door. "Take any of the spare bedrooms." He stands. "I'm heading to the hospital to meet Ellie Grace."

Nate drops the bag and sits next to Danit, pulling Malcolm onto his lap. "I couldn't pack everything, but it's enough for tonight. It's crazy that such little creatures need so much stuff. I tried to grab a few of your things. I guess we can come back tomorrow for the rest."

"Oh, Nate. I'm so sorry this has happened to you." She searches his face for the signs of devastation she would feel if she were in his shoes, but finds none. How he and Trey maintain their sangfroid baffles her. Is it because they are men? Or is it just that the Calhouns don't readily show emotion? She wishes Ellie Grace were here. Not because she is particularly fond of her, but she's curious to see how Ellie Grace is reacting.

Trey reappears in the living room, eyes wild, drunk. "And

what am I supposed to do now?" He holds up his inky fingers. In a wild flourish, he swipes them on one of the cream-colored armchairs, leaving ten streaks across the back.

Danit gasps.

"Trey!" Nate barks. "Cut it out!"

"What? Now that Dad's gone, you're going to start in on me?" He storms out.

Danit buries her face in her hands. She can't stand Trey's combative tone, or Zak's bloodless reactions, or even Nate's composure.

"Shh, it's okay," Nate says, rubbing her back. "It's just how he is. He hides all his feelings behind a lot of bluster. You're not seeing the best side of him tonight. Obviously."

Someone taps her on the shoulder. Danit turns to see the fingerprint technician.

"Ma'am? You're next."

* * *

Trey stumbles out of the house and immediately into a pool of light. News crews must have arrived while he was inside being fingerprinted. He feels a pang of shame for the way he behaved in the living room, especially in front of Nate's fiancée. But the shock of everything that happened today has left him disoriented.

The shootings. The police. And, of course, seeing Shawna.

He hasn't had time to process it all. Suddenly, an eager young woman with long blond hair and too much makeup grabs Trey.

"Hey, hi—are you Trey Calhoun?" Her pink minidress and youthful appearance make her look harmless, like a teenager off to prom, but the microphone dangling by her side belies that. Still, he stops.

"Uh, yeah, I guess I am." Trey brings his hand to his eyes to shield them from the bright lights.

"Kylie Rose. Turn this way out of the light." She adjusts Trey so the house is in the background and stands beside him. "Do you mind if we ask you a few questions?"

Trey considers this. "I don't know, Kylie. It's been a rough night."

"It'll be short. I promise."

"I probably shouldn't."

"Terrif." She turns to the cameraman. "Mac, in three."

As soon as Mac is done counting down, Kylie takes a step closer to Trey, raises her microphone to her face, and starts talking directly into the camera. "I'm here with Thomas Brooks Calhoun III—"

"Call me Trey." Looking for something to do with his hands, he adjusts his bow tie. He shouldn't be here, he doesn't want to be here, so why *is* he here? He's halfway to being drunk, having abstained for so long that the Pappy Van Winkle he drank inside has done a number on him. *This is a bad idea*, the voice inside his head says. It said the same thing that night two years ago when he climbed into the driver's seat of his car, Shawna by his side, both of them high as kites.

And look how that ended up.

"Trey? Would you agree?"

Trey blinks twice. He's spaced out, missed the question. "Uh, yes. Definitely."

"Somerwood is such a lovely place to live, but on this night it turned into a scene from a horror movie." She gives a little half nod to the house behind her. "We are standing outside the Calhoun residence right here in Chevy Chase, and as you can see, there are still guests left over from a garden party gone terribly wrong." She turns a quarter of the way toward Trey. "Trey, you've suffered a terrible loss this evening, just terrible. Can you tell us how you are holding up?" She thrusts the microphone at Trey.

"Uh," Trey stalls, trying to think of what his sister would say.

"It isn't easy. I guess I am lucky to have the love and support of not just my brother and sister but of everyone in the neighborhood."

Kylie nods vigorously, turning back to the camera, visibly tense. "And there you have it, an unspeakable act of violence on this normally quiet street—"

"It's just really strange, to tell you the truth," Trey says. "I mean, it's surreal."

The reporter turns back to him, a smile frozen on her face.

"I mean, one minute, we're all together taking pictures for our family's Christmas card." He shrugs and holds up his hands as if to say *I give up*. When he sees the alarmed look on the reporter's face, he remembers his fingertips are stained with ink. "Oh this! This is from the fingerprinting."

"Is that right?" Kylie's voice perks up. "Are you a suspect?"

"Oh, no, nothing like that. It's routine; they have to do it. They're doing the whole family."

"Is that so?" She is looking at him with that fake smile, a gleam of triumph in her eyes. He's lost the game, he realizes, and he didn't even know he was playing. He swivels his head. People are looking at him, at his dirty hands, standing in the spotlight.

"And there you have it," Kylie Rose says into the camera. "Straight from Trey Calhoun himself—he and his entire family are currently being fingerprinted as part of the investigation into the brutal murder that happened right here in Somerwood. Apparently, no one is above suspicion. Back to you, Alex."

19

When the ER doctor comes into the waiting room, Ellie Grace steps forward to greet her. From the corner of her eye, she can see movement. She turns to see the tall detective who was at the house earlier walking toward the doctor, as well.

Annoyance swells within Ellie Grace as she rushes toward the doctor, determined to get there first. *She's* Ginny's daughter. She should get precedence in talking to the doctor. To her chagrin, they both arrive at the same time.

The doctor offers the kind of tight, perfunctory smile that suggests she has been instructed to do so. She's young, not much older than Ellie Grace, which puts Ellie Grace off. The presence of professional women has always made her feel insecure, as if their very existence is a kind of accusation—*What are you doing with your life?* In some deep crevice of her brain, Ellie Grace suspects she could have been a doctor or a lawyer if only her parents had encouraged her. Before she can open her mouth to speak, the detective has produced ID.

"Detective Washington," she says. "I'm here about Virginia Calhoun."

"And I'm here about my *mother.*" Ellie Grace leans hard into that last word. Mother. It's a loaded word implying a deep bond, a history of love and sacrifice, and it should carry some weight with the doctor. The doctor turns away from the detective to Ellie Grace. *Score one for me*, Ellie Grace thinks.

"The good news is that we were able to staunch the bleeding, and your mother is an excellent candidate for surgery."

"Surgery? Is she going to be okay?" Ellie Grace asks, looking into the doctor's large eyes, ringed by purplish half-moons. It occurs to Ellie Grace that a good tube of concealer would do wonders.

"She lost a lot of blood," the doctor says. "We are getting ready to operate on the tibial nerve right now. She's actually really lucky."

"Why do you say *lucky*?" Detective Washington draws out the last word in a skeptical way that rubs Ellie Grace the wrong way. She doesn't see how this line of questioning is going to help her mother at all. The doctor should be with her mom, not answering these pointless questions.

The doctor turns to the detective. "Well, a few inches higher and the bullet could have hit the femoral artery. She could have bled out."

"How quickly would someone bleed out from an injury like that?" the detective asks.

"Wouldn't take much time at all." The doctor shrugs. "Twenty minutes?"

Washington nods before scribbling something on her pad. Ellie Grace cranes her neck as subtly as she can to see what the detective has written, but can only make out the numbers *911*. Washington looks up, and their eyes lock for a moment. Ellie Grace is the first to break eye contact. She clears her throat. "When can I see my mother?"

"Yes, I'd like to speak to Mrs. Calhoun, as well." Washington nods.

The doctor scowls at the much taller woman. "Absolutely not. Like I said, we are prepping her for emergency surgery." She gives Ellie Grace a little nod. "Now if you'll excuse me, I have to get back to work."

The doctor turns on her heels and disappears into the bowels of the hospital. After a curt smile at the detective, Ellie Grace walks back to her spot in the corner of the room. She's commandeered several seats—one for her bag, one for her water bottle, and another for her. In one deft move, she slides into her seat, slips off her shoes, and tucks her legs beneath her. Pulling her phone from her bag, she settles in to scroll through Instagram.

To her shock, her direct messages, likes, and follows have exploded. It's normal to pick up several dozen or even a hundred or so new followers a day, especially if she cross-promotes with a bigger influencer. But the numbers she is looking at go way beyond that. She has two thousand new followers. When she looks at her DMs, they are filled with random people offering condolences, true-crime internet sleuths wanting to interview her, and even a few local reporters hoping to speak with her. The outpouring warms her from the inside. But she finds more than a few sharp jabs among the kind comments under the pictures from the party.

> **Guess she's not as perfect as she pretends hahahaha**
> **Karma is a beyotch**
> **Gingham Life? More like Gingham Lies.**

Ellie Grace deletes those. There are always going to be haters, she tells herself, people who can't stand to see others succeed. She'll focus on the positive messages. The *You got this* and the *Thoughts and prayers*. And on the fact that there is a silver lining to this tragedy. She would never say that aloud, except maybe to Zak, but it feels like with all these new followers, the universe is telling her it's all going to be okay.

But one message makes her suck in her breath.

> **Knew this bitch in prep school. Totally capable of murder.**

"You all right, Ellie Grace? Bad news?"

She looks up at the detective standing over her, aware that her distress is showing on her face. Quickly, she deletes the offending comment, but not before taking note of the name. Sitting up straight, she smooths the front of her blue-and-white-checked dress and slips her feet back into her high heels. She offers her most gracious smile.

"Hello, Detective Washington. How can I help you?"

"You all right?" The detective sits next to her. "You looked like you had seen something upsetting."

"Not at all. Just looking at some of the news coverage and—"

"I get it," Washington says. "I always tell my victims and their families to stay away from the news, at least for a while. The media invariably get details wrong, or put things in a less-than-sensitive light. No need to add more stress than you're already under."

"You're probably right."

"Trust me, I've been doing this awhile." Washington takes out her little spiral notebook, and Ellie Grace's heart sinks—more questions. Washington nods knowingly. "Just a few more questions for tonight, I promise. Let's start with the basics. I know this is difficult, but do you recall where you were when Renée came out of the house?"

Ellie Grace tugs at the hem of her skirt. "I was outside. I was watching the croquet game."

"Were you standing alone?"

"Oh, no, I was with Danit, and Cookie and Bob—they're our neighbors." She picks up her phone. "A waiter took a photo of us. Do you want to see?"

"That won't be necessary." Washington shakes her head. "Did you hear or see anything unusual before that?"

Ellie Grace shakes her head. "Nothing. Not until Renée came out. I had no idea what was going on inside." This part is true, and it feels good to deliver a line with the kind of conviction only truth will allow. "It was a total shock."

"Did either of your parents seem upset or concerned at all at the party?" she asks.

"What do you mean?" Ellie Grace can feel her throat tighten.

"It was a lovely party. Everyone was in a good mood." She knows her voice is strained and that she didn't really answer the question the detective asked.

"Has anything been bothering them lately?"

"Bothering them how?" *Play dumb*, she tells herself. *She knows nothing. She can't possibly.*

"I don't know. Suspicious mail. Upsetting phone calls. Any arguments or disagreements, maybe between family members?"

Ellie Grace purses her lips together. "No. We're a very happy family. We all get along. I mean, look at us!" She lets out a weak sob, remembering her mother is in surgery at this very moment.

"What about with tradespeople? Employees?"

"No." She pauses a moment, remembering the fiasco with the flowers earlier. "I mean, Mommy was upset when the hydrangeas didn't show up this morning, but we worked it out."

"Hydrangeas?" Washington asks.

"It's nothing. She always gets white mopheads for the party, and the florist sent them to a different address by accident. We couldn't get them back in time, so we made do with calla lilies."

"That must have been stressful!" Washington says in a neutral tone that Ellie Grace can't decipher. Is the detective mocking her?

"It was. My mother was very stressed," Ellie Grace says. "She was worried the calla lilies were a little too modern, too minimalist, but I told her no one would notice."

"Anything besides the hydrangeas?" Washington asks. "What about your dad's business? Anything unusual there?"

"I don't know." She is surprised by the sharpness of her own tone. "Daddy doesn't talk to me about his business." Ellie Grace exhales. "I mean, he *didn't* talk to me about his business."

"Your father must have hired and fired many people over the years."

She shakes her head stiffly. "I told you, I don't know anything about that. You can ask Trey or Fabiola."

"Fabiola?"

"The office manager."

"And your brother Trey works there?"

Before she can control her reaction, she feels her eye twitch. "Yes. Trey is employed there."

"I see. Family business. Was there anyone who had done work on the house recently?"

"Maybe?" She shrugs. "My mother is always renovating something. She did the powder room last year. I don't know. Why? You think someone working on the house did this?"

"We're not ruling anything out at this point. Including everyone who was at the party today."

"I don't believe that anyone who knew my parents would want to hurt them. They were beloved. You understand? Beloved."

Washington clears her throat. "One last thing, Ellie Grace. According to a witness, you had a heated disagreement with your father earlier this afternoon."

"What? Who said that?" Her cheeks redden. "It was just a chat. Not a disagreement."

Washington leans in. "This witness heard raised voices," she says in a stern but affectionate tone, the kind you might use with a kid caught red-handed sneaking candy. "Saw you leave the study crying."

Ellie Grace opens her mouth as if to speak, then closes it again, like a guppy. *How the hell does the detective know about that?*

"There you are, baby." The two women turn to see Zak standing there. He opens his arms wide, and Ellie Grace jumps up to embrace him, burying her head in his chest. His familiar scent unhooks the latch where she has been storing all her emotions, and she lets out a giant sob. Zak hugs her tighter and over her shoulder says to Washington, "I think we're done here."

20

An hour later, the guests have all gone home, the media has packed up, and most of the onlookers have dispersed. The front lawn is a ghost town of empty folding chairs and tables. The breeze blows cocktail napkins across the grass like tumbleweeds. Inside the house, crime scene technicians are finishing up while the Calhouns' housekeeper, Anya, rubs her hands together nervously.

"Do you have to leave, Miss Renée?"

"I do have to, Anya, but I'll be right across the street." Renée leashes up Ginny's two French bulldogs, juggling a navy-blue tote in the other hand. It's filled with a few things that Ginny will want to have when she wakes up at the hospital. "And anyway, the police will be finished soon. I promise. As soon as they are, you can lock up and go home."

"Yes, Miss Renée."

Asti and Spumante leap up in the air. "You excited to come stay with Mumbo?"

Renée peers out the front window. The neighborhood looks quiet again. A few stragglers walk down the street, but whether they are true-crime lovers or simply lovers is a mystery.

"Do you think he is out there?" Anya asks. "The murderer?"

Renée lays her hand on the smaller woman's shoulder. "Anya, I promise that you are safe. And like I said, I am right across the street."

As Renée leads the dogs through the living room, where a technician is packing up equipment, she calls to Anya over her shoulder, "I'll be back tomorrow." At the doorway, she half expects someone to stop her. Funny thing, how just being close to police officers makes a person feel guilty.

It is only after Renée crosses the threshold of her own house that she starts shaking and can't stop. Once off the leash, the three small dogs take off in a pack, their little claws scratching on the hardwood floors as they scurry around the house at top speed.

It wasn't a lie, she tells herself. None of what she'd said was technically a lie. She walks over to where she keeps the liquor and takes out a bottle of bourbon. She'd won this Blanton's Single Barrel bourbon two years ago in the countywide liquor lottery. The contest, held each year, allows residents of Montgomery County a chance to win coveted and limited bottles of liquor that would otherwise sell out to collectors as soon as they are released. She's been saving it for an important occasion.

She pours herself two fingers in a glass. After gulping it down, she pours another glass and drinks that one as well. The hot liquid coats her throat and goes straight to her stomach. The trembling stops.

Renée calls the hospital and asks about Ginny, but they won't tell her anything. Not even whether she is alive. She checks her phone. Surely one of the kids would tell her if Ginny was in serious trouble.

She is debating contacting Nate or Ellie Grace to ask about Ginny when the doorbell rings, startling her. Renée lets out a little shriek, dropping her phone. The three dogs run to the front hall, yapping and scratching at the door. Renée follows them and peers through the peephole.

"Renée, sweetie," her next-door neighbor calls loudly. "I hope you don't mind my calling so late."

Renée rolls her eyes. She adores Cookie and Bob. They have been wonderful neighbors to her over the years, and when Drew up and left her five years ago, they swooped in with cold sauvignon blanc, shoulders to cry on, and invites to events on the weekend so she wouldn't be alone. They helped her realize there was life after marriage. But she has to be in the mood for Cookie. He can be—as her daughter says—*extra*.

Renée opens the door but keeps it only slightly ajar so the dogs can't get out. She tries to shoo them away with her foot. "Cookie, hello. What's going on?"

"May I?" Without waiting for an answer, Cookie barges inside. "I was walking by your house, and I saw that your lights were on. I just thought, poor Renée, I should check on her. She's had quite the night."

"That's true, but you needn't have bothered. Just having a cocktail and then heading right to bed."

Cookie slips past her and into the living room.

"I love how classic this room is. That you don't feel the need to constantly renovate and follow trends. Timeless. That's the word." He points to a floral chaise longue in the corner. "But we need to discuss that chaise." He spins around. "I know. Not the time. How are you, dear? You must have been terrified walking in on that. Tell me everything." He sits on the sofa and pats the seat next to him. "You shouldn't have to bear this alone."

Renée is tempted to take him up on the invitation. She would love to unburden herself, to hear someone else's perspective. But telling anything to Cookie would be like posting it on Facebook.

"Oh, I don't think I possibly could. I'm exhausted from this evening. And I just took an Ambien." The lie slips out easily.

"Ambien and a cocktail?" Cookie wiggles his eyebrows. "Living dangerously, I see."

Renée makes a show of looking at her watch. "I have about ten minutes until I'm unconscious." After she fakes a yawn for effect, she walks back to the foyer. "I'd better let you go, or you're going to have to carry me up to bed!" She lets out a hearty laugh that lasts a beat too long. "But thank you so much for checking on me."

Cookie stands up, a pinched look on his round face. "I'm here for you, you know. Bob and I are right next door." Cookie walks into the hall and peers up the stairs. "Let's touch base tomorrow and see if there's anything we can do for the Calhouns. Those poor children."

"Indeed."

Cookie is almost out the door when, changing his mind, he turns back. "You don't think, I mean, it's not possible that one of them had anything to do with this?"

"Now, now," Renée says in a motherly tone.

"You're perfectly right to kick me out. Bob says I gossip too much. But with all that money at stake, you do wonder." He takes a tentative few steps onto the stoop.

"Good night, Cookie." Renée shuts the door and locks it.

Once she is sure Cookie is gone, Renée walks around the house shutting off lights. Doing so calms her down. It's a night-time ritual she has performed for fifteen years. As she passes by framed photos of her kids marking their milestones, she pauses to wish them good night. She likes to think that the message she sends through the universe somehow reaches them wherever they are and whatever they are doing.

Mumbo, Asti, and Spumante chase after her as she walks up the stairs, passing her easily. They have already jumped onto the foot of the bed by the time she enters the room.

"Silly rabbits," she says. "Are you all going to sleep with me tonight?"

At the window, before she pulls the curtains shut, she pauses to look at the street. Fifteen years on this block, and nothing more scandalous than a resident putting a dog poop bag in another's recycling bin has ever taken place. Until tonight.

A gust of wind tears the blossoms from their branches and lifts them swirling into the sky, pale pink and white against the black night. Despite the violence of the wind, it's one of the most beautiful things Renée can recall witnessing.

This afternoon, she was in this room readying for a party, worried as always about money. Now her prospects have changed.

And if she can navigate the dangerous waters of the next few days, that change might be for the better.

A wave of guilt washes over her when she thinks of the statement she gave to that detective. What did her grandmother always say to her about lies? *Don't tell me half a story*, she'd say. *That's a sin of omission.*

So maybe she did tell half a story.

Maybe she did commit a sin of omission.

It wasn't the worst thing she did tonight.

Not even close.

21

A clanging from outside startles Ellie Grace. She freezes in front of her open closet, one arm reaching for her bathrobe. "What was that?"

"Just the wind banging. Don't worry," Zak grunts out between pushups. "How long do you think they're going to stay here? Not that I mind or anything."

Ellie Grace pulls on her robe and ties the belt tightly. They are in the master bedroom on the third floor of the house they live in but don't own. The Chalfonte—one of Calhoun Development Group's latest endeavors. Instead of designing a house from scratch, busy buyers can choose one of a dozen luxury designs to build on the site of the smaller house they have bought and torn down. At three stories, the Chalfonte is taller than it is wide, fitting nicely into the narrow lots that are typical of the older neighborhoods of D.C. and some of its suburbs.

"Who? Nate?" Ellie Grace feels hurt. She knows how important Zak's evening workout is to him—he's practically OCD about it—but she wishes he would abandon it in favor of comforting her. "I don't know. Probably for the rest of their trip."

"Hmm." Zak stands up and frowns. Sweat glistens on his chest.

"Is that a problem?" Ellie Grace asks, looking at his naked torso. Sometimes her husband can be very distracting. "I mean, this is a five-bedroom house. He's my brother, Zak. And our father was just killed."

"I know that. It's cool. I was just curious. I like your brother. And Danit seems nice. But you know, houseguests? Don't love it." Zak moves to the area rug, where he lies down and begins doing sit-ups. "Maybe we should turn the room they're in into a workout room, you know? Now that the house is ours. Mirror up one wall. Put a squat rack in."

She perches on the edge of the bed and watches him. She's always liked watching him exercise. "*If* the house is ours. My father may have already alerted someone at the company that he was kicking us out. What did he say to you when you spoke to him?"

"Uh, he said it was fine. We could stay."

"Really?" She cocks her head to one side. He is obviously lying. She chalks this up to Zak trying to protect her feelings. One of the things she loves about him is how chivalrous he can be—he opens doors for her, always whips out his credit card at restaurants. Yes, it's her money. But the point is he likes being the white knight. "So you went into the study to talk to him?"

"Yup." Zak pauses in a sitting position, his arms on his bent knees. "Remember? You told me to go talk to him. So I did."

Gently, she pushes. She doesn't want to nag—she'd never want to be a nagging wife—but she does want to know if the two really talked. "Really? Because I went to look for you, and I couldn't find you."

"Well, it was a pretty short conversation."

"Oh yeah? What did he say?"

"He said the same thing to me as he said to you, that he wanted us to move out, and I asked if he could see his way to letting us stay for three more months. To give us time to save up some money and get a place of our own."

"And?"

"And he was very receptive. He said he appreciated me coming to him man to man, that he respected me for it. And that he would give us three more months."

Ellie Grace nods, but it doesn't sound like her dad. She's pretty sure this conversation never happened. He grins up at her from the floor. "Eleven, twelve, thirteen." A wave of empathy engulfs her. Poor Zak. It must have been so emasculating to have Thom Calhoun for a father-in-law. She has never really appreciated, up until this very moment, just how hard it's been on Zak. Of course he's lying about the conversation; he probably never made it past the foyer of the house. He is one of the least confrontational people she has ever met. She had naively hoped that people would see Zak the way she did—as kind and loyal and loving—but as her father made clear tonight, he saw Zak as a loser. The memory of that humiliating conversation sends a ripple of rage through her. Suppressing it, she smiles. She won't call out Zak on his lie. She won't continue her father's campaign of humiliation.

"Well, what can I say? That's what he said," Zak says. "And he told me he hadn't mentioned us moving out to anyone. So basically . . ."

"Basically what?"

"Well, I don't want to be insensitive, but basically, the house is ours. I mean, no one else knows about your talk earlier, right? I mean, you didn't tell anyone."

"That's true."

"Then we're in the clear."

She instinctively recoils at the phrase *in the clear*. It makes it sound as if they did something wrong. She puts her head in her hands. "I don't like this, Zak. I don't like any of this. That detective at the hospital? She wasn't nice."

"Well, she's not trying to make friends. She's trying to find a killer."

"What? What does that mean?" she says. "You think the police think I had something to do with this? Is that what you're saying?"

He pulls his head back sharply. "That's not what I meant at all. Just that it's normal for her to question you. She has to question everyone. I mean, you were in the study."

"Right, of course. But you were, too, right? You just said so yourself." She exhales sharply. "Are you going to tell them you were in his study? They're going to ask tomorrow. They want to talk to each of us. Alone. You're going to tell them the truth, right?"

"The truth?" He grins up at her from the floor. "Which truth? My truth?"

"There's only one truth, Zak. Are you going to tell them or not?"

"Depends on the circumstances."

A shiver runs through her. That sums up her husband's morality in one sentence: depends on the circumstances. And what exactly is her moral code? She used to think there was an absolute right and wrong, but now she doesn't know. Not after tonight.

She walks to the bathroom to take off her makeup, but as soon as she flips on the lights, she turns and marches back into the bedroom. "We need to be on the same page, Zak. I don't like surprises, you know that. And sometimes it feels like you play according to your own rules."

"Isn't that what first attracted you to me?" He smiles. He knows she cannot resist that devilish half grin.

"It's just . . . were you in my dad's study or not? Why won't you tell me?"

"You asked me to go, so what do you think?"

"Who cares what I think!" She throws up her arms in exasperation. "We need to be honest with each other." The irony of this statement makes her cringe. She has no intention of being honest with him. "I just think we both need to play by the same rules."

As quickly as it appeared, his smile vanishes.

"Yeah? That's pretty funny coming from a rich girl whose mommy and daddy have given her everything she ever wanted since she was a baby."

Ellie Grace recoils at his sharp tone. "That's not fair, Zak."

"Life isn't fair." He jumps up. "You think your dad played by the rules? I've got news for you. Your dad had the scruples of a bookie, and I should know. My dad was in debt to one of those guys almost my entire childhood. He died with the broken bones to prove it."

"Wait, what? You think my dad was a criminal? Since when?"

"Just because you slap a Brooks Brothers suit on it and park it in Chevy Chase doesn't make it legit."

Tears spring to Ellie Grace's eyes. "Why are you being so mean to me? I just lost my father. My mother is in the hospital."

Zak walks to the door. "I'm gonna go grab some water."

After Zak leaves, Ellie Grace goes into the bathroom and allows herself a good, hard cry. Tears fall for her dead father and her injured mother, but most of all for herself. When she looks up at her face in the mirror, she revels in how ugly it is—swollen eyes, red nose, blotchy skin. Without mascara, her eyes seem to disappear. She's hideous. Zak would never love her if he saw her this way.

"You look like a naked mole rat," she tells herself. The self-castigation feels good.

She looks closely in the mirror at her pores. They are getting larger by the day.

She lets out a little yelp.

One of her sapphire-and-pearl studs is missing. They were a gift from her mother two Christmases ago. She must have lost one somewhere at the party. Her heart sinks as she mentally retraces her steps throughout the party, trying to remember where she might have lost it.

What has she done?

* * *

Danit stares out the picture window of Ellie Grace and Zak's kitchen. Everyone else is upstairs—Nate taking a shower, Malcolm sleeping, Ellie Grace in her bedroom, and Zak leaving the kitchen to join her with a glass of water, grunting good night. Nate mentioned the house was a model home, and it feels that way. Everything gleams and shines—from the white marble backsplash to the gold-toned hardware. There's not a single indication that human beings with personalities or, God forbid, flaws live here.

Danit finds a mug and a box of chamomile tea. Next to the faucet is a spout for instant hot water. She fills her mug. She's seen Ellie Grace's Instagram. She's pored over it, looking for clues as to who the Calhouns are. Back in California, she thought Ellie Grace might laugh about all the work it took to look so perfect, that in reality her sister-in-law would be as agreeable and down-to-earth as Nate. But after meeting Ellie Grace, Danit knows Gingham Life is no act.

Her phone rings, and she answers with a hushed "Hello?" just as she reads the caller ID.

"Hey, gorgeous girl." Charmaine's familiar voice hits her hard, causing a wave of homesickness to wash over her.

"Hey! How are you?" She takes the mug and heads to the den area, which features a sectional couch in front of an immense TV. If anyone can help her process the day's events, it's Charmaine.

"How am I? Who cares! How are you? I was just sitting down to watch *Rebecca*, it's on AMC, and it made me think of you and Nate's mysterious ex. You remember, the husband shot his first wife in *Rebecca*?"

"I remember he had a good reason."

"You sound weird. What's wrong?"

"That obvious?" Danit pulls her legs under her and sinks into the deep couch. "I don't even know where to begin." Danit steels herself for Charmaine's response. *Cool* and *measured* are not words she would use to describe her honorary aunt. "You know the big annual party I told you about? Well, there was a murder right in the middle of it. Nate's father was shot. And his mother was shot, too, although she's still alive, thank God."

"A murder!" Charmaine yells so loudly, Danit has to pull the phone from her ear. She spends the next few minutes filling Charmaine in on what has transpired.

"Honey, I am so sorry. That sounds incredibly scary."

"I'm just numb, honestly."

"A murder, and you were right there." Danit can hear ice cubes clink in a glass as Charmaine takes a sip of something. Probably rum and Coke, her favorite. "I don't like this. Maybe you should come home."

"Charmaine, wherever Nate is, that's my home. And he needs me, now more than ever."

"You asked him about Helena yet?" A note of disapproval has crept into her voice.

"There really hasn't been a good time. And now, with all this—"

"Danit, sweetie, there's *never* gonna be a good time. Just do it."

Danit sips her tea and considers this. "I know you're right. I promise I'll do it." She decides to change the subject. "You should see the way these people live. You'd die."

"Yeah, like what?"

"Like the oldest son, Trey? He's in his early thirties, barely works, lives in a gorgeous house owned by his parents, and they gave him a Range Rover. When I wasn't working, I was considered a loser."

"No one ever thought you were a loser, Danit. That's your inner critic talking," Charmaine says. "Rich people are funny— they can do things that if poor people did 'em, we'd be called degenerates."

Danit laughs. "So true. And don't get me started on the drinking. These people drink—a lot! You should have seen all the empty bottles of alcohol at the party. And then as soon as Nate's father dies, they all bust out the heavy liquor."

"Don't you know that it's okay to be a drunk if you're rich, but it's practically a crime if you drink when you're poor?"

They talk for a few more minutes while Danit sips her tea. "All right, dear," Charmaine says. "I'd better let you go. Manderley is calling. I know it's getting late there, and you have a tough conversation ahead of you."

Danit groans at the *Rebecca* reference and promises to keep Charmaine updated.

"Be careful out there," Charmaine says. "All joking aside, this is no movie. Someone was murdered, Danit. And you don't want to get mixed up in the middle of that. The sooner you leave D.C., the happier I'll be."

"It's Washington, not the Wild West. But I will be careful," Danit says, feeling less flippant than her comment suggests. "And I'm kind of looking forward to leaving, if you want to know the truth. It's pretty intense here." She says goodbye before rinsing her mug in the sink and heading upstairs.

The lights are off in the bedroom in which they are staying, and Danit slips under the covers next to Nate. "You still awake?" she whispers.

"Sort of." He turns over and presses himself into her back, his face nuzzling her hair. "You smell good."

She squeezes his forearm where it crosses her body. This is a good time. She once read that tough conversations can go more smoothly if you're not eye to eye with the person you're talking to. Like if you're walking together, or driving. Or spooning in bed.

"It wasn't always like this," he says quietly. "Believe it or not, there were some happy times."

"I know, sweetie."

"I do love my brother and sister, it's just that we're so different."

She doesn't say anything, waiting for him to continue. It's so rare that he opens up, she doesn't want to say or do anything to make him shut down.

"We had a sort of clubhouse when we were kids, not a real one, but we'd meet on the roof right outside our bathroom window. Trey and I would pretend that Ellie Grace couldn't be a member because she was a girl." He lets out a quiet laugh. "It was kind of mean. We would make her do all these challenges to try to join."

"Like what?"

"Oh, I don't know. Like run down to Ledo Pizza, get a napkin with their logo on it, and put it in the hidey-hole."

"The hidey-hole?"

"Yeah, we had an old lockbox we shoved in a hole in the side of the chimney. That's where we'd hide treasure or secret messages."

"That sounds sweet."

"It was. There's this huge oak tree, and in the fall, the roof would be covered in acorns." He laughs. "Once Trey slipped on one and went flying. He almost fell off the roof. We used to be really close for a while. I don't know what happened."

"You guys all grew up, I guess." They are quiet for a moment. Charmaine's advice weighs heavily on Danit's mind. It's as good a time as any to ask him about Helena. "Nate, I know it's late, but I have to ask. Meeting your family, everything that happened today."

"Yeah?"

"What really happened with Helena?"

"Danit, it's midnight."

"I know. But can you tell me anything?"

"This is hard for me to talk about, Danit. And it's really late, and it's been a horrible day."

"The one-sentence version. That's all I need tonight."

He sighs heavily, and she can feel his warm breath on her neck. She wonders if she has pushed too far. "The one-sentence version," he says, "is we should never have gotten married, but neither of us wanted to admit it. Malcolm changed everything. I wanted kids, she didn't. There, that's three sentences. Satisfied?"

"Yes, thank you."

But she's not satisfied. If anything, his answers raise more questions than she'd had before.

22

Sunday morning, Ginny opens her eyes to see a nurse standing in the doorway, checking a clipboard. Her head throbs, her body feels like a sack of wet sand, and it takes several moments before the images in front of her make any sense. The room is a blur of shadows and light.

She's in the hospital, she remembers, the events from last night flooding back.

The nurse raps twice on the doorjamb before dragging in a cart laden with a computer and medical equipment.

"Good morning, good morning!" She smiles broadly as she approaches the foot of the bed and lifts the flimsy white blanket. "How are we feeling this morning? Better?"

"A bit." Ginny scooches up as best she can, considering the scratchy hospital gown she is wearing has gotten tangled up, and her wounded foot is suspended in a sling from a contraption that hangs over the bed. "Whatever is in this drip, it's divine. I can barely feel a thing." She gestures toward the IV beside her.

"Glad to hear that." The nurse pulls her portable computer closer to the bed. Ginny extends her arms so the nurse can read her wristband to make sure she is, indeed, Virginia Calhoun.

"Don't want to mix you up, that's for sure," the nurse says as she readies the blood pressure cuff.

If this was supposed to be reassuring, it has the opposite effect on Ginny. Mix her up? She stares straight ahead, waiting for the whole thing to be over. Sleep is wearing off, and the reality of her circumstances is becoming all too clear. She is alive, but her lower leg is badly injured. And Thom?

Thom is dead.

The thought catches her off guard, and she inhales sharply.

"You all right, hon?" the nurse asks.

Ginny nods. "I just . . ." She stops, unsure of how to finish that sentence. *I just what? Remembered my husband was murdered?* Even in the hospital, in an unflattering seafoam-green gown that exposes her backside, Ginny cannot bring herself to break with etiquette. *Never complain. Don't whine.* She has to be even stronger now; her children will need her to get through this. They don't have the grit she has. "I was just wondering if my children have been by yet."

"Now, *that* I don't know, but there was a woman who dropped off a bag early this morning." She gestures at a navy-blue canvas tote in a chair.

"That would be Renée. God bless her."

After she has completed her examination, the nurse types the information into the computer. "Looking good. The doctor will be by later this morning." She packs up the cart and starts toward the door.

"Excuse me." Ginny nods toward a bag on the chair in the far corner of the room. "Would you be a dear and peek in that bag and see if there's any moisturizer? This hospital air is brutal."

The nurse smiles. Ginny knows the look—the nurse is wondering if she can come up with some excuse why she has to leave, but then she reconsiders. "Sure." The nurse goes to the chair and rummages through the bag until finally she pulls out a small glass jar. "This it?" She holds it up, squinting at the label. "Crème de la Mer?"

"That's the one. To be honest, I cannot tell the difference between it and Ponds. That's what my mother used all her life, and she had the most beautiful skin." Ginny extends a hand. "Now, be a dear and open it for me. I'm a little shaky."

Visibly irritated, the nurse twists off the lid. As she is placing it on the mobile tray table, Ginny reaches out and wraps her fingers around the nurse's wrist.

"Tell me, will I be discharged today?"

"I don't know, ma'am. That will be up to the doctor." The nurse yanks her arm free.

"Hmm." Ginny doesn't like this noncommittal answer, but what can she do? She'll have to wait. She's no good at that. She's a woman of action with not one but two planners—her calendar on her phone and a kelly-green Filofax she's had for years that stays on the desk in her bedroom. Each December, right after Christmas, she ritually replaces the paper calendar in the leather-bound Filofax with next year's calendar, taking a full afternoon to write down not just standing appointments but goals—for herself, her house, her family.

One of this year's goals was *recommit to Thom*, and she had three action points—*join him on the golf course 2x a month, dinner just the two of us 2x a week, a romantic getaway (maybe Charleston?)*. Unfortunately, achieving goals is not as easy as setting them. Golf season is just starting now, and Thom usually professed to be too tired or too busy to have dinner with her. As for the getaway, she never found the right time to bring it up.

As the nurse turns to go, Ginny dips her fingers in the jar. With her eyes closed, she massages the cream into her face. Now she will be using her planning acumen to arrange a funeral.

Once through the doorway, the nurse doesn't get very far before someone stops her to chat. Ginny can't see who it is—the person is quite short and is partially hidden by the computer cart—but she guesses it's another nurse by the scrubs and the cheery voice.

"Crème de la Mer? That's like three hundred and fifty dollars for a small jar!" the other nurse says. "That's about what I make in a day."

The first nurse shushes her and looks back into the room. Ginny shuts her eyes and stays very still.

A fit of whispering ensues, but even though she is straining to hear, Ginny cannot make out what they are saying. Suddenly, the younger nurse's voice breaks through.

"It's been all over the news. Somebody broke in and shot her husband last night. She's lucky to be alive."

A loud beeping comes from somewhere down the hall, and the women part, heading in different directions. Ginny opens her eyes, unsettled. But why should she be surprised that the shooting is all over the news? It was bound to happen, so no, that's not the disturbing part. The hard part is being stuck here, unable to control the situation. Without her there to manage them, she imagines Ellie Grace melting into a puddle of hysterics, Trey crawling back into the bottle after all that hard work getting him sober, and Nate—would Nate even bother to stick around?

Not if he found out the truth. He'd be furious, and she can't blame him.

Fury is too weak a word to describe what she felt when she learned the truth. Just the thought of what that son-of-a-bitch husband did sends the blood rushing to her head.

And once Nate finds out, she is sure he will be gone. Maybe forever.

Ginny reaches her hand out and slaps around on the mobile tray table next to her bed until she locates her phone. The to-do list is forming in her head, but she'll need help.

It's time to text Renée.

23

Trey wakes up to a pounding at the door. He stumbles downstairs, muttering curses under his breath. The clock in the hallway reads nine o'clock. Who the hell is coming by this early?

Then he remembers the police telling him they'd be by, and Ellie Grace offering to show up for moral support. He groans, his head throbbing from having had too much to drink after such a long abstinence. And then it all hits him. Everything has changed. His father is dead.

His father has infused almost every aspect of his entire life. Even during those few years in California, he internalized the man's voice so well that he could carry out entire conversations without his presence. And with the right substances, he often did.

And these past two years, since returning home, he has felt his father's judgment heavy on his shoulders as if he is wearing a thick, woolen cloak.

Who was he if his father wasn't watching and judging? Trey shivers with fear. No, he is not ready to face what happened last night, not prepared to deal with the fact that his last words to his father were *I hate you, you son of a bitch.*

He unlocks the door and swings it open. His sister and her husband are standing on the porch, looking like they stepped out of a catalog. Behind them stand Nate, holding Malcolm, and Danit.

"Welcome to my nightmare." He steps aside to allow them to enter.

Danit waves two brown paper bags at Trey. "Well, we brought bagels. Georgetown Bagelry."

Trey watches as Ellie Grace swipes the bags from Danit and peers inside. "These are everything. And cinnamon raisin. Blueberry are Trey's favorite."

"I don't mind," Trey says, and his sister shoves the bags into his chest and marches past everyone into the kitchen. Trey shuts the door. "I'm not even that hungry."

Nate frowns at him. "Are you hungover?"

Trey heads to the living room, his brother on his heels. The last thing he needs right now is a lecture on his drinking. "If you can't get drunk when your dad dies . . ."

"Yeah, I just thought you were sober, that's all. It seems a shame." Nate stops and surveys the mess—piles of clothes on the couch, fast-food wrappers and pizza boxes on the floor. "What happened here?" Nate kicks at an empty energy drink can. "Actually, don't answer that. You know the police are coming, right? Here. They're coming here."

"Can I help?" Danit asks.

"Well, I think I should clean up." Nate passes Malcolm to her. "Do you mind taking him while I deal with all this?"

"Sure." Danit and Malcolm head off to the kitchen.

"She seems nice," Trey says, and he means it. Danit is the one person in the house who isn't shooting gamma rays of disappointment in his direction. And maybe Malcolm.

"She is," Nate says. "Now, I need a garbage bag and some paper towels. Hall closet? Kitchen?"

"Kitchen." Trey feels his shoulders sink. Once upon a time, Nate looked up to him. When he was a senior in high school, and Nate a freshman, he'd let Nate hang around with his friends sometimes. He has a fond memory of taking Nate to his first show at the 9:30 Club in D.C.—an Incubus concert—how cool Nate thought he was. But Nate hasn't thought he was cool in a long time. He knows what Nate thinks of him, and it is even worse than how his parents feel, because coming from Nate, it isn't tinged with anger or disappointment. Nate would never use the word, because he isn't unkind, but Trey knows his little brother thinks he is a loser.

In the kitchen, Trey pours himself a large glass of orange juice and then splashes it with some vodka from a bottle that is sitting on the counter.

"Really, Trey?" Ellie Grace asks.

"Hair of the dog. It's scientifically proven to work."

"Uh-huh."

Ignoring her, Trey turns his attention to Danit, who has just given Malcolm a cinnamon-raisin bagel to gnaw on. "Bagel," she says.

"Bay-bull!" the kid shrieks. Trey feels a momentary pang of jealousy for Malcolm. He's got a great dad and is about to have a loving stepmom. Trey wished he could start over with parents like that.

Trey grabs the cleaning supplies and heads to the living room to clean up his mess. He leans against the kitchen island for support, aware that he is the one who should be doing the cleaning and half hating himself for not being up to it. His sister whirls around the place, tidying, prepping, and organizing as if her book club friends were on their way over and not a homicide detective. When Ellie Grace finds a saucer with delicately painted flowers that Trey has been using as an ashtray, she gasps.

"This is Mommy's china, Trey!" She searches his face for a glimmer of remorse. "Never mind. Since when did you start smoking again?"

"Only sometimes."

"Do you think maybe you should get dressed? I mean, look at your shirt."

He looks down at his stained Fugazi T-shirt and boxers. "Dude, this shirt is vintage. The Ritz, 1999. The Ex opened."

"You were nine in 1999, Trey. You were obsessed with Power Rangers, not listening to hard-core."

"Are you calling me a poseur?"

"I'm sorry, aren't you the one who called us? Because the police are coming?" Ellie Grace's voice rises in pitch with each question. "They'll be here at ten, and I kind of think we need to get our stories straight before they get here."

"Stories?" Danit asks.

"Just an expression." Ellie Grace squeezes out a smile. "I hope you don't feel like you *have* to be here. This is probably so boring for you."

"I want her here," Nate calls from the living room.

"I can go," Danit says.

"No, don't leave." Nate appears in the doorway with a full trash bag.

"No, that's perfect, of course. Super," Ellie Grace says. "We need coffee. Can you make coffee, Danit? That would be such a big help."

Danit goes in search of a coffee maker.

Ellie Grace turns to her brothers. "We need to figure out what we're going to tell them about Mommy and Daddy."

"What's that supposed to mean?" Nate asks.

"I just think we should be on the same page. We don't want to air our dirty laundry in front of these people."

"You just tell us what to do, Captain Smelly!" Trey clicks his heels together and salutes his sister.

"Just follow my lead, okay, Trey?" She is trying not to smile.

"Aye, aye, Captain." He hoists his hand up to his forehead and salutes his sister again. Ellie Grace grabs his hand and yanks it down.

"What the hell happened to your knuckles?" she asks.

Trey looks down at them, raw and red, and pulls his arms free. They still ache, although not quite as badly as they did last night when they made contact with his father's chin.

"It's nothing," he says. "Scraped them on some shrubs."

Ellie Grace considers this for a moment and, to his relief, seems to buy it. "Nate, tell Trey it's time to shower and get dressed."

Nate turns to Trey. "Your sister says it's time to shower and get dressed."

"Orders received," Trey says.

Ellie Grace can't help but laugh. "It's probably not a good idea to look like the basement dweller that you are."

For a moment, Trey basks in genuine fondness for his siblings. There was a time before all the competition and judgment, before their parents pitted them against each other to fight for Thom and Ginny's limited affection, when it was the three of them against the world. But that was a long time ago, and he's not sure they can ever go back.

24

A sullen orderly has just cleared away her breakfast dishes when Ginny senses someone at the door to her hospital room. She sits up, pinching both her cheeks, eager to welcome her children in, to show them that despite these dismal surroundings, this hideous garb, this humiliating foot sling, their mother is in fighting shape.

To her dismay, a tall woman in jeans and a button-down white oxford enters followed by a uniformed officer. Ginny sinks back into her pillow.

"Good morning. I'm Detective Washington, and this is Officer Amatangelo. We're here to ask you a few questions about last night, if that's okay."

Ginny offers a wan smile. "What choice do I have?"

"Let's start with the basics, Mrs. Calhoun. Yesterday afternoon—"

"Ginny. Don't you dare call me *Mrs. Calhoun*. That was Thom's mother." The old bat had never approved of Ginny. Thought she was uppity, too ambitious, didn't know her place. Of course, she didn't refuse the Cadillac, or the house in Florida that Thom's money bought her in her later years. Money Thom only made because of Ginny and her *ambition*.

"All right. Ginny." Washington pulls up a chair and sits near the bed while Amatangelo stands back. "What can you tell me about the party? When did it begin?"

"Well, the royal family holds three garden parties a year at Buckingham Palace—from three in the afternoon until six. If that's good enough for them, it's good enough for me." It's a line she has repeated many times over the years and is usually good for a chuckle. But it falls flat with these two.

"So you're saying the party started at three o'clock?" Amatangelo asks.

"Generally speaking."

"I know you throw this party every year," the detective says. "Was there anything unusual about the party this year?"

Ginny frowns, trying to recall.

"Your daughter told us there was some problem with the flowers," Washington says. "You ordered hydrangeas, but they didn't arrive. Any other issues?"

"Other than that, things went swimmingly. Until, of course—" Her throat catches. An image of Thom flashes before her. His unseeing eyes, his mouth agape. "There was a small trickle of blood," she says quietly. "Coming out of his mouth."

Washington takes a step forward. "Are you talking about when you found your husband? Mr. Calhoun? Because that's not unusual, ma'am, when people are shot in the lungs," the detective says in a soft tone. "Sometimes they cough up a little blood."

Ginny takes a deep breath, trying to steady herself as memories threaten to overwhelm her. "Please excuse me. The pain medication has me rather disoriented."

"Of course. Let's start with what brought you into your husband's study."

Ginny nods. She can't tell them the truth, of course. But she can tell them something *akin* to the truth. Or rather, *a* truth.

"I hadn't seen him in a while, so I went looking for him. Thom sometimes takes refuge in his study during parties."

"Was he upset or angry?"

Ginny thinks about this. "I don't think so," she says with honesty. Now, *she*, on the other hand, was a different story. *Upset* and *angry* don't begin to cover it. But they weren't asking about her state of mind. "He was in his typical mood."

"Which is?"

"Oh, well. Calm, in control, very much the man of the house."

"So you go looking for him in his study, and when did you realize something was wrong?"

When the hydrangeas didn't arrive.

When that redhead dared to show her face at my party.

When he whispered in my ear, "I'm filing for divorce. I've already had the papers drawn up."

Ginny reaches for the large cup of water with trembling hands and takes a long sip. "When did I realize something was wrong? I suppose when I saw his body there, lying on the floor."

"And then what did you do?"

"It's really all a blur." Ginny is silent for a moment. "I can only remember bits and pieces. When I saw him on the floor, I thought, *He's had a heart attack*, but when I went to him—" She chokes up remembering Thom's large body on the ground looking so helpless. Instinctively, she had rushed to him; after all, she'd been tending to him for the past thirty-five years. That devotion trumped whatever anger she was feeling. "When I knelt, I saw the blood. My phone wasn't with me, so I started to stand, to go for help. That's when I must have been shot. I remember a searing pain. And then I collapsed."

"Did you get a look at who shot you?" Washington asks.

"No, I did not."

"Height, race, sex, clothes—anything at all?"

"I'm sorry I can't be of more help. I must have had my back to the shooter."

"And there was no one else in the study when you entered?"

"Not to my knowledge. That doesn't mean they weren't there. They could have been behind the door. It's tremendously large. Thom had it custom-made based on a wonderful old castle in Ireland. Kinkillan? Kinkaid? It'll come to me." She brings her hand to her mouth. They had been at a friend's wedding near the Galway Bay, the reception held in the castle. They had danced late into the night. "Thom had the entire study re-created. He loves it so. Loved." She inhales sharply. "I still can't believe he's gone." Tears spring to the corners of her eyes. It's true. No matter what a bastard he was, he was her bastard for thirty-five years. She'd lived more of her life with Thom than without him.

"Did you notice anything odd when you went in? Anything at all?"

"Let me see." She closes her eyes for a moment. "I can't think of anything."

"How about his safe? Was it open?"

"I can't say that I noticed one way or the other. It's behind his desk, anyway." For a moment, Ginny feels sorry for herself. She wishes one of her children were here with her so she wouldn't have to endure this interrogation all alone. Where are they? And what must these police officers think, her all by herself, in a hospital gown?

"Who else, besides Thom, had access to the safe?"

"No one. It's biometric. Only Thom could open it."

"Not even you had access?"

"Not even me."

"And what did he keep there?"

"I haven't the foggiest." A slight iciness creeps into that last answer, but she is getting tired. And she doesn't like what this woman is insinuating. She looks at the detective's hands, large for a woman's, Ginny thinks, to go with her height. Despite their size, she has long, slender fingers—a pianist's hands. Ginny wonders if she plays. But no ring. "Are you married, Detective?"

The question catches Washington off guard. "Uh, no, ma'am. Divorced."

"I am," Officer Amatangelo offers from the corner of the room, where he has been standing silently. "Going on three years this June."

Ginny offers him a conciliatory smile. "Three years. That's sweet. But after thirty-five years, you learn a little about privacy. And I gave Thom his."

"Fair enough. Let's talk about staff. You have a housekeeper?"

"You mean Anya?" Ginny can't keep the annoyance from her voice. They can't be serious. Anya who is scared of her own shadow. "Oh, after all these years, I think of her as more like family."

"How often does she come in?"

"Every day. There's always something to do. Thom's very fussy about having things ironed. I was never one for ironing."

"Did she know about the safe?"

"I imagine she did. She dusted in there every other day." She lies back and closes her eyes. That's about as much time as she's willing to waste on discussing Anya, who would rather catch a cricket and let it outside than kill it. It was simply preposterous they were even asking about her. "Excuse me, Detective. But this little conversation has worn me out. If you don't mind."

"Just one more question. In the event of your and your husband's deaths, who are the beneficiaries?"

Ginny's eyes open to slits. "I know what you're driving at, but it's ridiculous. We have been more than generous with our children. No one has any need of money."

"But if both of you died"—she pauses a millisecond to let the word sink in—"the children would each stand to inherit quite a large sum, correct?"

Ginny struggles to sit up. "Are you suggesting that one of my own children killed their father and then tried to kill me as well?"

"I'm not suggesting anything, ma'am. But how much is the estate worth—in totality?"

Ginny glances around the room as if searching for someone, some *thing*, that can bring this interview to an end. If only one of those nurses would barge in, demanding to take her vitals right now. Finally, she shakes her head. "I apologize, Detective, but I simply cannot . . . You'll have to talk to the lawyers."

"We only need a general ballpark," Officer Amatangelo says,

approaching the bed. "Promise we won't hold you to it." He winks. A slight shudder runs down her back. She supposes the officer thinks that little move is charming, but Ginny finds it quietly threatening.

"I can't possibly."

"Here." Detective Washington hands Ginny a notepad and pen.

Ginny stares at the woman's outstretched hand. It's a game of chicken. How long can she hold that pad and pen? How long can Ginny refuse to take it from her? Finally, she breaks. "If you insist." With a shaky hand, Ginny grabs the pad and scribbles something down. "Somewhere around that number. But I could be off. I just don't keep track of these things. Thom did all that."

She thrusts the pad and pen back at the detective and watches as the woman's eyes widen.

Ginny knows that number has just elevated her children to prime suspects in their father's murder.

25

Cookie pumps his arms in rhythm with his power walking, while Renée hustles to keep up. This is their Sunday-morning ritual, and while Renée thought they might skip it in light of yesterday's events, the knock came at 8:00 a.m. sharp.

"Slow down, Cookie."

"It's not too fast if you can keep up a conversation. C'mon, Renée, put some gas on it."

"I'd like to put some gas on you," Renée says.

Cookie laughs. Renée rolls her eyes, but with every step she's more grateful that he dragged her outside. After she delivered Ginny's bag to the hospital this morning, she could have easily crawled right back into bed. But the sky is a lovely bright blue, and daffodils seem to have sprung up overnight in the neighborhood to complement the cherry blossoms. Like most Sundays, they wind their way through the streets of Somerwood, then onto the Capital Crescent Trail, an old railway line that was turned into a hiking and biking trail. From there, it's a straight shot into downtown Bethesda. She's been around long enough to remember the fierce opposition to the trail back when it first opened—including Cookie and Bob's. There were lots of SNOB meetings with raised voices, where residents complained that it would become an artery for criminals, camouflaged by the joggers and cyclists, who would hop on and off the trail robbing people from dusk to dawn. Tears were shed then, but now having a house on the trail can add a half a million dollars to its value, as well as coveted bragging rights.

"Remember when you wrote that op-ed for the Gazette opposing the trail?"

Cookie shakes his head, his gaze focused on the path in front of them. "You must have me confused with someone else. Someone closed-minded." He turns and winks at her.

Once they're in downtown Bethesda, Cookie and Renée stop at Quartermaine and order coffee. They grab a recently vacated table against the wall of the small shop where someone has left a *Washington Post*.

Chevy Chase Couple Attacked During Garden Party
Husband Dead, Wife Injured

Renée is reading the first paragraph when Davida, the manager, places two small paper cups on the table. "Here you go. Two doppios—one Splenda, one stevia." She twists her head to read over Renée's shoulder. "Grisly crime."

"We were there, you know," Cookie says while Renée pulls her espresso to her face and inhales deeply.

"Were you?" Davida asks. "How terrifying."

Renée listens as Cookie recounts the previous day's events to Davida in the same breathless manner he uses whenever he has a captive audience. "I mean, looking back, we were all just inches from death, right, Renée?"

Renée nods. She's tempted to point out that Cookie was nowhere near Thom's study when either Calhoun was shot—she should know—but that would be a terrible idea.

"But at the time, we had no idea," Cookie says. "That's the most horrifying thing; I was just telling Bob last night. Your life can change in an instant." He snaps his fingers.

"I'd better get back to work." Davida sighs. "It'll be strange not seeing Thom in here."

"Oh, was he a regular?" Renée asks. Somehow Thom didn't seem the type to frequent their quirky local coffee shop.

"For the past six months or so. Started coming in every day, right after the morning rush."

"Alone?" Cookie asks in a low voice.

Davida looks up at the ceiling, her brow furrowed. "Now that you mention it, he was usually with a young woman."

"What young woman?" Cookie's voice is pitched.

A tingle runs down Renée's arms. She has an idea, but she keeps it to herself.

"Lovely girl. Red hair. Always dressed to the nines. I think he said she worked for him? Not sure."

"Oh yes, *that* woman." Cookie laughs. "Of course. Such a sweetie."

Davida steps back behind the counter to deal with the line snaking out the door. The small coffee shop has filled with customers, including a young man clutching a laptop who is hovering over the table.

Renée gets up. "I can't enjoy this coffee with this fellow breathing down my neck." She takes the cup outside and swallows the last of the thick, black liquid as she wonders about this redheaded woman and whether she's going to be any trouble.

The caffeine seems to hit her almost immediately. Cookie joins her a few minutes later. "Well, that was interesting, don't you think?"

"Uh-huh." If the walk into Bethesda was brisk, on the way back she is speed-walking. *Swish, swish, swish, swish.* Renée wants to get home as soon as she can. But Cookie seems to have lost his mojo.

"Slow down!" He touches her arm, and Renée eases her pace. "Did you know Thom was having an affair?"

Renée presses her lips together, and Cookie gasps. "You did! How long has it been going on?"

"No idea. At least a few months. I saw the two of them at a restaurant in Georgetown."

"You didn't! Which one?"

"Filomena."

"Poor Ginny. Filomena is not a place you take a gal when you want to hide."

"I know."

"Did Ginny know?"

"Hello, Renée! Hello, Cookie!" Marty calls as he cycles by.

Renée gives a little nod to Marty, but as soon as the man passes, Cookie groans.

"You have a problem with Marty?" she asks.

"He just rubs me the wrong way. Pompous. Take that hideous addition on the back of his house. Monstrosity. Ruins my view from the second floor. And who needs their own pool when the club has such a lovely one? It's downright antisocial. I mean, it would be different if Marty had asked for my expertise on interior design—I've only owned my own firm for fifteen years—but no, it's clear Marty made his choices of finishes one afternoon at Home Depot."

Renée relaxes a little, relieved Cookie has found a new topic of conversation. No one, besides she and Ginny, knows that Thom was leaving her. Divorcing her. And she swore to Ginny she would tell no one. After all, that would make her a prime suspect in her husband's death, wouldn't it?

"Lovely girl. Red hair," Cookie mumbles. "I think I know exactly who Davida was talking about. The girl was at the party yesterday in that extremely short pink dress. Don't get me wrong, she had fantastic legs, but it was completely inappropriate for the occasion."

"Yes, I saw her, too."

"You don't think she might have . . . I mean, you hear of jilted lovers."

Cookie and Renée take a sharp right off the trail, past a small playground, and into the neighborhood.

"I don't know. We should leave the detective work to the police, don't you think?"

"Maybe. But maybe the right thing to do is just mention the redhead to the police. Just to err on the side of caution, of course. It may have been just a professional relationship," Cookie says. "But I pride myself on being helpful."

26

Ellie Grace assigns everyone seats in the newly straightened living room. Nate, Danit, and the baby on the chesterfield create the image of a perfect family. She and Zak will be on the love seat, and Trey—freshly showered, thank God—sits in one of the overstuffed armchairs that flank the fireplace. As long as everyone stays on script, this meeting with the police will go well.

"I can't wait to move out of here," Trey says to no one in particular.

Ellie Grace winces. Can't her brother at least try to stay on point? Control his emotions? It's not like she wanted to get up the day after her dad was murdered and do her face and hair, put on shape wear, slip into a pair of navy-blue—not black but still somber—pants that fit in all the right places but don't let her exhale. She'd love to stay in her PJs, pull the covers up, and bawl. Maybe dig into a pint of Graeter's black raspberry chocolate chip, her absolute favorite indulgence, which she allows herself one day a year—on her birthday.

But no, she rallied because *that's what you do*.

"Really?" Danit asks. "This is such a cute house! I love it. Especially those chairs. They look super comfy."

Ellie Grace stares at her future sister-in-law, trying to figure out if her kindness is real or just a big act. No one can be that nice. What's her angle? "Can we maybe focus on the fact that the police are going to be here any minute? I mean, I don't want to be a *b*, but maybe it's not time to talk decorating."

"Aww, be nice, Smelly," Trey says. Turning to Danit, he adds,

"I think her Spanx are cutting off her circulation. Makes her cranky."

"Shut up, Trey. Maybe I'm sad. Did that ever occur to you? And maybe I'm a little freaked out." Ellie Grace adjusts the platter of bagel slices she has laid out on the coffee table. Her hand hovers over one, but she does not take it. Zak nods in approval. Thanks to his encouragement, she hasn't eaten a bagel in almost a year. "I can't believe Daddy's gone. I woke up this morning, and for the tiniest moment, I didn't remember. And then it all came back." She lets out a hiccup of a sob. "And I started crying and crying."

"And then you stopped when you realized how much money you were going to inherit," Trey says.

Everyone in the room gasps. Ellie Grace glares at her brother. She knows he doesn't mean it. He has no filter. And he's under the impression that he's witty. But the stakes are too high for his nonsense.

"Not cool, Trey," Zak says. "The police will be here any minute. Can we take it down a notch?"

"Oh, he speaks! He doesn't just smile at the camera and show off his forearms and jawline," Trey says. "He actually talks!"

"Now you're being nasty." Ellie Grace wipes at her eyes. "And I won't stand for it."

"Why? Because your makeup might run? Tell me, Smelly—how many photo shoots do you have booked for today? Tomorrow?"

"That's not fair," she hisses. "That's how I make my living." Ellie Grace stands up and runs to the bathroom. She can hear them whispering behind her. In the bathroom, she dabs at her eyes with a piece of toilet paper. The worst part is Trey is partially right—she doesn't want her makeup to run. She does have a photo shoot later. But this is the way she's handling all this—putting one foot in front of the other and continuing with her life. It's like that science experiment in middle school, where she spun a bucket filled with orange juice on a string so fast that none of the OJ spilled. If she stops spinning now, her whole life will splash all over the floor.

Besides, her follow count was up another thousand today. People are watching.

A hard knock comes at the front door, and Ellie Grace rushes out of the bathroom to answer it. With a pleasant smile fixed on her face, Ellie Grace opens the door to the same detective who was at the hospital last night.

"Oh, hello, again. Please come in."

Washington nods and steps forward, followed by a uniformed officer with a shiny shaved head that reminds Ellie Grace of a hard-boiled egg. "This is Officer Amatangelo. He's going to be helping me out."

"Ma'am." He nods at Ellie Grace.

"Is Trey here?" the detective asks.

"Please, follow me."

The two follow Ellie Grace into the living room, and she can sense the detective stiffen when she sees everyone sitting, staring at her. "Trey didn't mention you all would be here," Washington says.

"We're here to support our brother," Ellie Grace says. "He told us you were stopping by. Anything you ask of him you can ask in front of us."

"That's not really how this works," Washington says. "We can chat with you as a group now, but we'll need to talk individually later."

Washington sits in the only empty seat in the room, a floral armchair across from Trey. She perches on the edge of the chair, her long legs folded in front of her, creating a little lap table. Officer Amatangelo finds a spot against the wall, declining the chair that Nate offers to bring in. Ellie Grace's eyes are drawn to the large black gun sitting on his hip, and she has to consciously look away.

Malcolm lets out a little yowl. "I guess that's my cue," Danit says. "I'd better take this little guy."

Everyone waits patiently for Danit and Malcolm to exit the room. Washington makes a little show of taking out her notebook, putting it on her lap, and uncapping her pen. "Shall we? I'm trying to get a sense of what was going on in your parents' lives before this happened." Washington looks at Trey. "How would you describe their marriage?"

The question lands with a thud. Trey stays silent, and no one else says a word. Finally, Ellie Grace clears her throat.

"Wonderful. They were role models for Zak and me. Right, honey?" She grips his hand.

"That's right, babe."

"Nate?" Washington asks. "How did you feel about your parents' marriage?"

"Fine, as far as I can tell."

"And, Trey? Do you agree with your brother and sister?"

"Eh, fairly typical D.C. power couple. He has affairs, and she spends his money."

"Trey, don't," Ellie Grace says.

"Is that right?" Washington cocks her head. "Your father had affairs?"

"He's exaggerating," Ellie Grace says. "Daddy could be a flirt. But my parents were married for thirty-five years, thirty-six come this August. Yes, they had their ups and downs, but they loved each other very much. You can see for yourself." She pulls out her phone and taps at it furiously like a chicken on cocaine. "Here, look at this." She gets up and brings her phone to Washington.

Washington takes the phone and looks at each picture as Ellie Grace leans over her, swiping every few seconds. "This is us skiing at Vail. And here we all are at St. Barts. And this one is a family vacay in Carmel—the boys golfed, and Mom and I went to a spa. Oh, and this is Christmas, up at Stowe. We all wore matching tartan plaid that year."

"I get the idea." Washington hands the phone back.

"Does that look like an unhappy family? I don't think so. Pictures don't lie."

"They say a picture is worth a thousand words," Zak offers.

"That's right, Zak." Ellie Grace nods. "Exactly."

"Let's move on," Washington says. "Nathaniel, I understand you are a marine biologist in California."

"Correct. Although technically, I am on a sabbatical for two years."

Washington shifts a little. "That sounds interesting. Where are you going?"

"Saipan. It's an island in the South Pacific, off the coast of Australia, but it's actually a US territory. I'm working on a project where we record whale communication."

"I didn't know that," Ellie Grace says. "Since when?"

Nate shrugs. "I applied about a year ago—"

"You didn't tell us!" Ellie Grace looks at Zak for confirmation. "I know for a fact that Mom and Dad didn't know, because she was talking about a trip this summer to California."

"I didn't tell anyone when I applied because it's very competitive. But I told Mom and Dad yesterday."

"How did they take it?" Washington asks.

"Fine. Great." Nate picks at some imaginary lint on his pants. "They were happy for me. For us."

Ellie Grace pinches the back of her thigh through her pants to stop from scoffing loudly. It's so obvious her brother is lying. He can't even look up. Besides, does he really expect Trey and her to believe their parents were happy he was moving to Saipan? Number one on her mother's list of chronic complaints is that her son and grandson live three thousand miles away in California.

"Trey, Ellie Grace, what do you do?"

"I work—correction—*worked* for my father's company." Trey leans back and crosses his legs, a wide, easy smile on his face.

"And why is that a correction? Did you leave recently?"

"I quit." Trey brings his large glass of spiked orange juice to his mouth and takes a gulp.

"When was that?" Washington scribbles something.

"What was my father's time of death?" He taps his chin. "Tack about ninety seconds onto that time."

"You're not funny, Trey," Ellie Grace says, fidgeting in her seat. Zak squeezes her arm.

"And you, Ellie Grace?"

"I am an influencer."

"And you can make a living doing that?"

"It can be very lucrative."

"And, Zak? How about you?"

"I help Ellie Grace out with the business. And I do a little fitness training at Equinox."

"That's where we met." Ellie Grace beams at him. Finally, a topic that makes her happy. More than ever, she thanks the universe for sending Zak her way.

"I see. And have any of you spoken with your father's lawyer yet? About the estate?"

Ellie Grace gasps. "We have not. That's rather a crude question. I mean, he died yesterday."

"I have." Trey holds up his hand. "They said we can have a meeting whenever Mom is ready."

"When did this happen?" Ellie Grace swivels in her seat to glare at her brother.

"I called him last night."

"You called the lawyer last night?" Despite her effort to remain cool, Ellie Grace can sense the blue vein that snakes up the left side of her temple beginning to throb. No amount of cover-up can hide that vein once it gets going.

"Well, if you could give me that lawyer's name," Washington

says. "I'm going to need a copy of your father's last will and testament."

"Of course, Detective."

"One last thing. Officer Amatangelo?"

After pulling a small plastic bag out of his pocket, Amatangelo strolls around the room, displaying its contents in his open hand. "It looks like a pearl, surrounded by little sapphires. We found it at the scene. Does anybody recognize it?"

The question is met with silence.

"Anyone?" Washington asks.

"Where did you say you found it?" Ellie Grace asks in a pinched voice, feeling woozy. "Is it some kind of clue?"

"We found it in your father's study," Washington says. "Was your mother wearing these earrings last night? She had no jewelry on her when she left for the hospital. We just assumed everything she was wearing had been stolen when she was attacked. But perhaps this was dropped."

"Maybe she was." Ellie Grace shakes her head. "I don't recall."

"I don't think so," Trey says, looking at his phone. "In this photo, you can see she's wearing—what are these, diamonds?"

"Oh, that's right." Ellie Grace snaps her fingers. "She was wearing diamond studs."

Washington stands up. "That's about it. Is there someone at your father's company who could walk us through its daily operations?"

"Fabiola Balindong," Trey says. "She's his secretary."

"Not *secretary*," Ellie Grace says. "Office manager."

"Whatever," Trey says. "She knows every little thing about that company. Been there how long? Fifteen, twenty years?"

"We'll start with her. And as for individual interviews, Trey, Ellie Grace, Zak—we'd like you each to arrange to come down to the station. You too, Nate. We can have a more private chat. Trey, if you're free, we can do it right now."

"I'd love to, but I can't." He shakes his head, feigning disappointment. "The rest of my morning's jammed."

"I see."

"But I'll try to stop in later."

"By the end of the day," Washington says. "Find the time, or I'll find it for you."

27

From where she is kneeling on the kitchen floor alongside Malcolm, Danit cannot see the police leave, but she hears the door shut. And then a little screech.

"Sounds like Ellie Grace," she whispers to Malcolm.

"Wagaagaga." Malcolm looks up at her from the plastic sippy cup he's been banging against an overturned pot.

"That was a complete disaster." Ellie Grace's voice comes through loud and clear. A moment later, she comes into the kitchen and begins a frenzy of activity—checking inside the refrigerator, opening and slamming drawers.

"Everything all right?"

Ellie Grace freezes as if just realizing Danit is in the room. She pulls out one of the counter stools and takes a seat. "This is all too much."

Danit leaves Malcolm on the floor and brings Ellie Grace a glass of water. "Tell me how I can help. Errands? Phone calls?" She is eager to show she can be of use to Ellie Grace. She remembers when her mom died, how Charmaine showed up in a hundred tiny ways. Long after her mom's coworkers and friends had sent flowers and cards, and a few neighbors had dropped off casseroles, Charmaine continued to provide a steady trickle of support. A bag of groceries. Taking Danit's car in for its smog check. Going to the crematorium to pick up her mother's ashes.

Turned out even Charmaine's persistent presence wasn't enough to stop her life from unraveling, but Danit knows it would have been much worse without her.

"Thanks for the offer, but I don't know. There's so much to

do—people we should call. Relatives of my dad's who don't live nearby. I don't want them to find out from the news."

"I'm happy to make some phone calls." Danit peers over at Malcolm to make sure he isn't getting into trouble, and finds him busy pulling his shoes and socks off.

"Oh, no," Ellie Grace says quickly. "Someone in the family should do that, no offense. We'll also need to contact St. Giles's to find out when we can have the funeral. And the funeral home. Have to call them. And someone has to write the obituary. Oh, God." Ellie Grace lets out a small sob. "There's so much."

"Let me help. You shouldn't have to do all this alone."

Ellie Grace smiles and wipes at the tears in her eyes. "You're sweet. I'm sure you didn't think you'd be dealing with all this when you planned your trip."

"Life happens. My mom died six years ago. And it was really hard."

"I didn't know that. I'm sorry. Nate never told us. He doesn't tell us much. He's lucky to have you."

"Thank you for saying that." Danit feels dizzy from the compliment. This was what she had hoped for, to break through Ellie Grace's hard candy coating to the gooey inside and make a real human connection. Danit loved when people turned out to be kind; it reaffirmed her belief that people were fundamentally good.

"Much better for him than Helena."

Danit's tummy does a little flip. "Oh yeah?"

Ellie Grace rolls her eyes. "Helena cared about one person—Helena. When they met at Stanford, I think she thought my brother looked good on paper, but Nate is just a regular guy. I mean, you know, he's just not that interested in"—she flicks her hand to take in the kitchen's fancy appliances and the marble countertops—"all this."

"I know. It's one of the reasons I love him."

Ellie Grace laughs. "Well, there you go."

"But to leave Malcolm . . ." The words are out before she realizes what she is saying. But Ellie Grace seems unfazed.

"She never wanted kids. I'm surprised that she agreed to have him in the first place. I mean, maybe she thought she would change her mind and then didn't? It was all kind of weird. Like, hey, we have a newborn and, oh yeah, Helena left me and moved to Tokyo."

"Tokyo?"

"Yeah, her dad was Japanese, you know; she always wanted to live there at some point. She made partner in the Tokyo office of her law firm, and boom, she was gone."

"What are you two talking about?" Nate appears in the doorway.

"Oh, just girl stuff," Ellie Grace says, and Danit feels a wave of gratitude. They didn't get off to a great start yesterday, but maybe some good will come out of this horrible tragedy—she and Ellie Grace becoming friends.

"Where's Malcolm?" Nate asks. "There you are, bud. Don't chew on your socks."

He sits down on the floor, pulling Malcolm onto his lap, and begins putting his socks and shoes back on.

"I guess we should head to the hospital," Ellie Grace says. "You ready?"

"Malcolm looks pretty tired. He didn't sleep last night, and I think he needs an early nap." He looks up at Danit. "Unless, can you take him while I go to the hospital with Ellie Grace?"

"Sure," Danit says, slinging her tote bag over her shoulder.

"Actually," Ellie Grace says. "I was going to ask Danit if she could do me a favor. The party rental company is coming for all the chairs and tables and everything, and someone needs to be there. Literally all you have to do is sit there and then sign the paper."

"You don't have to do that," Nate says. "Sit there and wait?"

"I'll be fine." Danit pulls out a well-worn copy of *Jane Eyre*. "I've got a book. When are they coming?"

Ellie Grace looks at her phone. "Between like right now and noon."

"It's no problem, and it'll give me a chance to pack up the rest of our things," Danit says.

"Tell you what," Nate says as he stands up with Malcolm. "I'll drop this guy off at Cookie's so you don't have to worry about finding a place for him to nap at my parents'."

"You sure?"

"Cookie said they had a playpen, and he's dying to babysit. I'll tell him you'll come grab him when you're done at the house," Nate says. "Come on, we can walk outside together." He turns to Ellie Grace. "I'll be back soon. Tell Trey to get ready to go visit Mom."

Outside on the stoop, Danit holds the door open for Nate and the stroller. She takes a deep breath of the cool spring air. It's so humid here, her curls have exploded into frizzy corkscrews. She surveys the street—twigs and branches lay strewn on the ground, evidence of last night's windstorm. A cluster of people are huddled next door in front of the Calhouns' house, some standing, some sitting on the curb.

"Thanks for helping. I really appreciate it," Nate says once he has the stroller on the walkway. Malcolm writhes in his seat, a last expulsion of energy before he collapses into sleep.

"It's not a problem at all. What's going on over there?" She points to the small crowd.

Nate turns and scowls. "Oh, great." A young woman with hot pink hair who had been sitting on the curb looks their way and gets up. She taps a scrawny guy in a bucket hat, and the two start jogging over toward Danit and Nate.

"Stop right there!" Nate steps in front of the stroller and holds up his hand. "This is private property."

The girl smirks. She's in her midtwenties with the sort of pale, puffy face that Danit associates with people who are too online. The guy next to her takes one step off the street and onto the grass, holding up his phone as he does. "The town of Chevy Chase has a right-of-way setback of between eight and ten feet," he says.

"He looked it up," the girl says. "So it's not private property." She takes another step forward and turns her back to Nate and Danit, facing her friend.

Danit turns to Nate. "Is that true?" she whispers.

"Behind me is Nathaniel Calhoun," the girl says in a clear voice, holding a cell phone a few inches from her mouth. "He's the second oldest of the Calhoun children, and he lives in California. He came back to D.C. the day before his parents were brutally attacked. I know some of you have been wondering—"

Nate leans into Danit and whispers, "I'm heading to Cookie's. You go to my mom's. Look! Renée is heading there now, she'll let you in. Don't stop and talk to any of these people." He kisses her before turning Malcolm's stroller sharply to the left. She watches him cross the street to Cookie's and knock on the door. Once the duo realizes Nate is gone, they rush to the other side of the street, but they get there too late. Cookie has opened the door and swept Nate and Malcolm inside.

Danit imagines what it was like for Nate to grow up on this block, how safe he must have felt. It looks like something out of a Norman Rockwell painting, if Norman Rockwell were a partner in a high-end law firm. He's told her stories about his brother and sister running wild in the neighborhood, staying out until the streetlamps went on, getting into all kinds of scraps.

When he told her those stories, she had imagined he had a perfect childhood, like a sitcom about a boisterous but loving family. She had been wrong; the Calhouns weren't perfect, after all.

But then again, neither was she.

*   *   *

Cookie opens the door and clasps his hands together, and Nate pushes past him into the foyer, wrangling the stroller over the door's raised bottom sill.

"Oh, Nate! Malcolm! What a wonderful surprise! Do come in." He turns his back for a moment and calls, "Bob! Bob! Nate Calhoun is here. And he's brought the baby."

Once Nate is safely inside the foyer, he tries to catch his breath. "Sorry. Being chased by a bunch of wannabe crime podcasters."

Cookie peers out the window. "Can they do that? Just sit on the lawn like that?"

"Technically, it's the right-of-way." He hates that the smarmy guy was right.

"Well, forget them." Cookie peers into the stroller. "Look at this little one! What a wee thing, and how old are you, little fellow?"

Nate transfers a sleepy Malcolm from the stroller to Cookie's arms. "He's almost eighteen months. But he's very tired."

"Almost eighteen months! No wonder you're exhausted."

Malcolm rests his head on Cookie's broad shoulder as the man carries the baby into the living room. Nate follows him in, taking in the scene. One half of the large room has been set up as a play area, with a playpen, a mat, soft toys, and an enormous stuffed rabbit. Above the fireplace is an oversized framed black-and-white photo of Cookie, Bob, and a grown-up Olivia with a baby in her lap.

"That must be Willow," Nate says.

"Oh yes, our little angel. Shall I put him down to nap here? We also have a crib upstairs."

"I think down here is fine. It's quite the setup."

Cookie deposits Malcolm in a playpen, where he lies on his back, clutching Mr. Panders. "We watch Willow on Tuesdays and Thursdays when her preschool gets out. And of course whenever Olivia and Bryce need a weekend away."

"You're good grandparents," Nate says. "Willow's lucky to have you."

"It's just so sad that your dad won't get to see Malcolm grow up. Losing one's parent is devastating," Cookie says, taking a seat on a cream-colored sofa. "I can remember when my father died. It was the day before Olivia's ninth birthday party. Had to cancel the whole thing. Flew back to Michigan. I was in a dreamlike state for months. Now, can I get you a cup of coffee? Tea? Something stronger?"

"That won't be necessary—"

"Bob!" Cookie calls in the direction of the kitchen in a stage whisper. "Put the coffee on, will you?"

"On it," comes the reply from the kitchen.

"I really can't stay," Nate protests. "I was just hoping I might take you up on your offer of babysitting today. Ellie Grace and I are headed over to the hospital to visit my mom, and my sister assigned Danit some chores."

"Say no more. Mi casa es su casa." Cookie turns to brush a piece of lint off his blue button-down shirt. He has the wide shoulders and softness of a former linebacker. "We have everything you could possibly need right here. Bob and I call it Daddy Day Care—you know, like the movie?"

"Sure. I get it."

"By the way, your fiancée is delightful. What a sweetie. I'm sure she's a real comfort to you at this time." Cookie turns to the kitchen. "Bob! How's that coffee coming?"

"Almost ready!"

"Olivia gave us a Keurig for Christmas. I personally don't touch the thing, but Bob says it's very efficient. Getting coffee at Quartermaine is my reward for my morning walk. I said, if I drink coffee at home, I'll never leave the house! Olivia put together a spreadsheet, if you can believe it, showing I spent something like two thousand a year on coffee. I told her I can't think of a better use of my hard-earned money. Olivia's the CFO of AltraTech, you know. She just loves her spreadsheets."

Bob comes in with a tray containing three steaming mugs of coffee and a plate piled with macarons.

"They're from Trader Joe's," Cookie says as Bob serves them. "Shh. That's our little secret. You'd never know when you taste them."

A rustling comes from the corner, and the three men turn to see Malcolm sleeping on his tummy, his legs tucked under him, his butt high in the air.

"Is that not the cutest thing?" Cookie whispers.

"The absolute cutest." Nate smiles. "He didn't sleep well last night, so I'm glad he's getting an early nap." Nate takes a pink macaron off the plate, enjoying the moment. In contrast to his parents' house, Cookie and Bob's place feels lived-in and family-friendly. The slipcovered sofas, the tasteful but well-worn antiques that are just battered enough that you wouldn't worry about damaging them. People live here, play here. His parents' house, by contrast, always felt like a set piece, perpetually picture-ready.

"If you don't mind my asking," Bob says, "how is your mother?"

"The doctors said she's going to be fine—physically, that is. But that's about it. I'll know more when I see her today."

"Well, send her our love," Bob says. "Will you? And let her know if she needs anything at all, we're here to help."

"Anything," Cookie repeats.

Nate stands up, and so do Bob and Cookie. "Thank you for the coffee. And for watching Malcolm. I'd really better get going."

"Let me walk you out," Cookie says. In the foyer, he opens the front door but pauses. "Do look after yourself. We're happy to host little Malcolm overnight if you want to get a good night's sleep."

"It's true that I didn't get a lot of sleep last night."

"Neither did your brother, but I don't think it's because he was beside himself with grief."

Nate frowns. "Why do you say that?"

Cookie covers his mouth with his hand. "Me and my trap. I shouldn't have said anything. It was rude, forgive me. People grieve in different ways. Who am I to judge?"

"What are you referring to? Did he do something?"

"Well, it's more the company he keeps. I mean, where does he find these people? I shouldn't judge, but honestly, Nate—the very night of your father's death."

"What are you talking about?"

"I wasn't spying, mind you. I just happened to be at the window looking outside. You know the cherry blossoms look like snow when the wind blows them in the moonlight."

"What did you see, Cookie?" Nate cannot keep the note of annoyance out of his voice.

"Oh, it's nothing. Only . . . it was odd. I saw a car pulling up at the house, and a girl got out and went inside. I took note because the car didn't look like it belonged here. A Ford Fiesta." He lets out a little laugh. "My goodness. How two brothers who grew up in the same house can turn out so wildly different, I'll never know."

"What girl?"

"I really couldn't say. Just some trashy girl. Tattoos up and down her entire arm."

28

With Nate and Danit gone, and Zak in the bathroom, Ellie Grace has a moment alone with her oldest brother.

"Trey, I don't know what kind of games you are playing. But you are putting this whole family at risk," she says, trying to keep her voice calm and steady. "We don't want to give the police reasons to be suspicious of us."

She watches his face, trying to gauge his reaction. As a teenager, Trey had a sort of bad-boy charm, as bad a boy as you can be in Chevy Chase. He had some swagger, more confidence than he deserved, and an acid tongue that, when it wasn't directed right at her, could make Ellie Grace pee her pants from laughing. Girls loved him. You'd think they'd have gone for Nate—who had inherited his father's square jaw and athleticism—but Trey was the one who they went nuts over. Mostly because he gave off an air of indifference, catnip to girls. In middle school, she found it fascinating how a seemingly endless parade of girls would write him poetry, drop off gifts, prank-call the house, stop by "on their way" to see if he might be home. He never seemed to give them a second thought, always preferring to hang out with the guys.

But this morning, he just looks a mess. Red eyes, bloated, the beginnings of a gut.

"Trey, are you listening?"

"What if you knew something, something that would really destroy the family?"

Ellie Grace jerks her head back, surprised. "What do you mean?" A wave of nausea hits her. Could he know about her father kicking her and Zak out of the Chalfonte? "Listen, Trey, I don't know what you think you know—"

"Oh, I know the truth is what I know!" Trey lets out a warped laugh. "For two years, they lied to me, Ellie Grace. Two years of my life I'll never get back."

Ellie Grace sits down with a thunk. Her lungs take in a full breath. He's not referring to her dad's decision to evict her and Zak. This is about something else entirely, that has nothing to do with her.

"Are you talking about Mom and Dad? What did they lie to you about?"

Zak strides into the kitchen, phone a few inches from his face. "Dude, Ellie Grace, we hit two hundred K! This is sick!"

"Let me see." Ellie Grace grabs the phone from him and looks. Sure enough, they have just over two hundred thousand followers. The last picture she posted, a very tasteful shot of white tulips on her windowsill, has fourteen thousand likes. That's what—a 7 percent engagement rate? Below, she had copied and pasted a poem she found about grief. Excitedly, she scrolls through the comments—the *beautiful*s, the *so sorry*s, the emojis.

But her attention always snags on the vicious ones—*you're not fooling anyone you know you did this.*

Ellie Grace gasps. "What the—?" She deletes the comment.

"Ignore the sickos," Zak says. "This is good news."

"Yeah, it's good news, Smelly. Hundreds of thousands of strangers are rubbernecking your dad's murder. Maybe you can monetize this. Sell water bottles?" The vulnerability her brother had shown before Zak entered the room has been replaced with an obnoxious bravado.

"Stop it, Trey."

"Yeah, you need to stop, bro." Zak's tone is low and controlled, but the anger is palpable.

Ignoring his brother-in-law, Trey looks at his sister with wide eyes. "Maybe like, blue and white checked. Printed across the side—*The Calhoun Murders*—who would want to kill such a lovely family?"

Zak lunges at Trey, catching him off guard. Ellie Grace shrieks, jumping back. Soon the two men are on the kitchen floor, rolling around. A millisecond ago, she was angry enough to punch her brother herself, but now seeing him on the floor getting dominated by her stronger, more athletic husband, she again feels pity for him.

"Stop it, you two!"

In the chaos, none of them notices that Nate has returned from dropping Malcolm off. Nate inserts himself into the middle of the fight, easily separating the two brawlers. The physical exchange does not seem to have done any actual damage. Like two cocks on a dusty patch of land, Trey and Zak retreat to opposite sides of the kitchen, both puffing out their chests, thrusting up their chins, bouncing on the balls of their feet.

"Just cut it out, both of you. You look ridiculous." Nate's authoritative tone slices through the bluster in the room. The macho energy leaks out of them like air from two punctured tires. Trey slumps in a seat at the island.

Zak heads out the front door, letting the screen door slam.

"Zak!" Ellie Grace calls after him.

"Let him cool off," Nate says.

"We should get going to the hospital, anyway." Ellie Grace's voice is soft, barely audible.

Nate nods. "I agree. We can drive over together."

"I'm not going." Trey does not lift his head, which he is cradling in his hands.

"Of course you're going," Ellie Grace says, trying to remain calm. "She's our mother. She needs us."

"Ha ha." He raises his head, but he's neither laughing nor smiling. "What she needs is a gin and tonic and some lipstick. She'll be fine."

Ellie Grace looks to Nate to see how he is taking this. Something isn't right with Trey. His usual age-inappropriate affectation of teenage rebellion is infused with a heavy dose of despair. Ellie Grace realizes she is actually concerned for him.

"Nate," she whispers. "Do something." Nate's face, however, is unreadable as usual.

Her brother nods. "Trey, look, I know you're upset. I know we all deal with grief in our own way. But don't do something you'll regret later."

An abrupt laugh. "That's rich! Really rich! You think I'm going to regret not visiting her? I *relish* not visiting her."

"Why would you say something like that?" Ellie Grace says. Trey and his mother had an enmeshed relationship—she doted on him, and he pretended to be annoyed by her smothering, but since he moved back to D.C., he could barely make a move without her. Her mother often ran interference, trying to protect Trey from her dad, so what had she done to make him so angry? "At least think about how that might look to the police if you don't visit."

"I don't give a flying—I don't care how it looks. I'm over the games this family plays. You want to play them, Smelly? By all means. Play stupid games, win stupid prizes. But I'm done. Now can you leave? I have a few things to do before I have to talk to those cops again."

Nate turns to his sister and says in a low voice, "Maybe you could go outside and give us a few minutes. Let me talk to him alone?"

"Fine." She heads out to the front to join Zak, seething at being left out. She always hated to be excluded from what her brothers were doing. Her whole life, the two of them had their own secret way of communicating—with fewer words, but more meaningful ones. She studied their brotherly language, but she never learned to speak it. It was so unfair. Their parents seemed to encourage this gendered alliance. Like when Nate and Trey tacked up a *No Girls Allowed* sign on the bathroom window, forbade her to follow them out onto the roof. Her mother thought it was hilarious. *Boys will be boys!* Her father was confused as to why she would want to climb out on a roof, anyway.

But she did. She wanted to be near them and their energy.

Instead, they sent her to Miss Sherry's etiquette classes where, along with the girls of other well-heeled Washington, D.C., families, she learned how to hold a fork and dab her mouth with a cloth napkin.

Ellie Grace pauses at the front door, hoping she can catch just a snippet of the conversation in the kitchen. She strains, trying hard to isolate individual words from the murmurs.

"—he saw you get into her car last night," Nate says.

Saw Trey get into whose car? she wonders.

Zak bangs hard on the storm door, making her jump.

"Let's go!" he calls, so loudly that she is sure Nate and Trey can hear from the kitchen.

Ellie Grace rushes outside, not wanting to be caught eavesdropping.

An unbidden image flashes through her mind—Trey standing over her mother, pointing a gun, pulling the trigger. She shakes her head as if she can knock the picture right out of her brain.

Her brother might be a screwup, but there's no way he would shoot their mother—is there?

29

Renée marches past the small crowd gathered outside the Calhoun house and up the front walk, inwardly daring them to talk to her. She'd give them a piece of her mind, the same way she addresses the eighth-grade boys who dillydally after lunch is over.

But no one says a word to her. At the front door of the Calhoun house, she's about to punch in the key code when she senses someone coming up behind her. She spins around, ready to lash out, but sees it is only Danit.

"Hi, Renée! How are you?" The young woman manages to sound both cheerful and concerned at the same time. She must have made a terrific nanny, Renée thinks. There's not a sharp edge on her.

"How are you holding up?" Renée asks, one hand still clutching the door handle. *You have to pull it tight,* Ginny said on the phone, *when you type in the code. Otherwise, it won't open.*

"I'm okay. I mean, it's just so sad. Nate and Ellie Grace are at the hospital. I'm just here to pick up the rest of our stuff."

"Of course. You're staying at Ellie Grace's, right?"

Danit nods.

"Well, come on in. I'm here to do a few things for Ginny while she's in the hospital." Renée turns back, types in the code, and gives the door a push with her shoulder. Once they are both inside, Renée shuts the door and locks it. Who knows—one of those crazies might try to get inside. "Hello?" she calls out. "Anyone here?"

She takes a few tentative steps from the foyer into the living

room, Danit at her heels, when a figure appears in the doorway
to the kitchen.

"Oh, Anya!" Renée clutches her chest. "You scared me!"

"Good morning, Miss Renée." Anya wipes her hands on a
dish towel she is holding. "Miss Danit. Would you like some
coffee?"

"I'm just going to run upstairs and grab my things. But thank
you!" Danit walks to the staircase. "Just pretend I'm not here."

"No, I couldn't possibly," Renée says. She watches Danit as-
cend the stairs and disappear, then reconsiders. "I suppose if
you're making some. If it's not too much trouble."

"Yes, Miss Renée." Anya nods. "I will make you some."

Renée follows Anya into the living room, clutching a piece
of paper with a list of things to do for Ginny. She was relieved
when Ginny called her an hour ago, sounding much like her
old self. The surgery had gone well. She would need rehab, but
other than that, Ginny was fine. The sense of relief was so overwhelming for Renée that she slid down onto the floor, only to be
pounced upon by all three dogs.

"Thank God," Renée said, her voice breaking.

"Now don't you shed a single tear for me," Ginny said. "We
have more important things to deal with. How is Asti? Spumante? Do they miss me?"

After Renée recounted how well the dogs were getting along,
Ginny dictated to her a list of chores. Renée didn't ask why she
hadn't assigned these tasks to one of the children. She didn't
need to. When you want something done, you ask a mother.

Now Renée takes a seat at the wide marble island as Anya
gets to work making coffee.

"Mocha, hazelnut, or French roast?" Anya gestures toward
the rack of coffee pods behind her.

"Ooh, let's go with hazelnut."

She's never had a housekeeper herself. Back when she and
Drew were together, and the kids were small, she had a cleaning

crew come in. Those were her two favorite days each month. She would come home from a long day of work, scoop the kids up from day care, and enter a house where everything gleamed and shone. But when Drew left, she was forced to cut expenses.

"I am glad you're here." Anya places a mug and two biscotti on a napkin in front of Renée. A loud thump comes from above—Danit doing Lord knows what—and the women make eye contact for a moment. "I had to get here early to let the police in, but now they're gone and I'm alone. It's very spooky to be in the house all alone."

"I'm sure it is." Renée dunks a biscotto in the hot coffee before taking a bite. "Oooh, delish."

"Pistachio cranberry. It was Mr. Calhoun's favorite." Anya sniffs. "I am so sad about Mr. Calhoun." She shakes her head. "I have to clean his study today, but I don't want to."

"I completely understand." She thinks of little Mumbo and how the police said there was blood on him. Even though she couldn't see any, when she gave him a full bath last night, the water ran pale pink. "You shouldn't have to clean that study. Maybe Ginny'll hire someone to come in and do it. There are people who do that for a living, you know. Clean up after crime scenes. They have special cleaning materials and everything."

"What an awful job." Anya shakes her head.

"Let me talk to Ginny."

"Yes, I would appreciate that, Miss Renée." She clicks her tongue. "The police left so much dust."

"Dust?"

"Yes." Anya walks out of the kitchen. Grabbing her coffee cup, Renée follows her into the study, where Anya flips on the lights.

Renée gasps. Although she has been in and out of this house many times over the years, she has spent little time in Thom's study. A fine layer of dark gray dust coats everything, making it look like a bomb went off in the room.

"The police did this." Anya shakes her head in disgust. "Last night. They made a big mess in a lot of rooms. It's too much for one person. Please tell Miss Ginny."

"I will, Anya."

Anya leaves Renée alone in the study for a few moments. As Renée turns to go, she notices an arc of dark paint dots on the wall.

Drawing closer, she can see it's not paint at all but a fine spray of blood droplets.

She backs out of the room and pulls out the to-do list. The sooner she can accomplish these tasks, the sooner she can leave. First, Renée retrieves a bowl of ice from the kitchen and places three cubes in each of the orchid pots in the sunroom. Anya could very well have done this particular job, she knows, but Ginny is finicky about her orchids. She prides herself on getting them to rebloom year after year.

Next she collects Asti's anxiety medication and Spumante's favorite blankie that he likes to sleep on and puts them in her tote bag. She consults the to-do list again.

"I have one more thing to do on the list," Renée says to Anya, who is cleaning the stove top in the kitchen. "Bulbs and potting soil for the May Flower Mart."

"Did you say something, Miss Renée?" Anya turns around and takes the earbuds out of her ears.

"Just that Ginny wanted me to pot up the rest of her bulbs for her so they'll be ready for the May Flower Mart. She has this down to a science. She says they need a full six weeks, so it has to be done this week."

"Oh yes, Miss Ginny loves the Flower Mart. I hope she is better by then."

"She will be, Anya. She will be. She hasn't missed a May Flower Mart, in what . . . twenty years? She's not about to miss one now. Our girl is tough."

Anya smiles, but she looks like she might cry. "I'd better get back to work, Miss Renée."

"Of course. Don't mind me. I'm just going out to the garden shed to gather up what I need. Is that red wheelbarrow still in the shed?"

Anya nods. "Go ahead and take it. Only Miss Ginny uses it, anyway."

Renée crosses the back lawn toward the garden shed. The yard is Ginny's gardening lab, where she experiments with different perennials and annuals. Every year, she grows the most beautiful zinnias for the Flower Mart.

The backyard is an oasis, protected from the gawkers clogging the street. The only sound is the chatter of sparrows, a cardinal chirping, and the distant hum of a leaf blower. Renée holds her breath as she enters the dark and musty shed. The place stinks. She takes the wheelbarrow out and sets it down outside the shed. She returns to the shed twice more—once for a bag of bulbs and then again for a large, open bag of potting soil. She rolls the top over several times and carries it out, careful not to spill it.

"This is going to take more than one trip," she mutters to herself, gazing at the full wheelbarrow.

"I'll say. Need a hand?"

Startled by the voice, Renée jumps back, knocking a terra-cotta pot behind her onto the ground, where it shatters. "You scared the devil out of me." Renée bends down to scoop up the pieces. "Pass me that pot, would you? If I don't get this mini boxwood replanted, it will die."

Zak hands over an empty pot and bends down. "Didn't mean to startle you." He watches her scoop the dirt with her hands but doesn't offer to help.

Renée focuses on the job in front of her. The sooner she can get away from Zak, the happier she'll be. Doing this errand already has her jittery. The last thing she needs is someone nosing around, watching her every move. When she finishes repotting the boxwood, she stands up to see him poking around the red wheelbarrow.

"Excuse me," she says, trying to insert her body between him and the wheelbarrow.

"Cyclamen, snowdrops." He reads the labels of the bagged bulbs out loud.

"That's right, I'm helping Ginny out. She needs these potted up immediately for them to be ready for the May Flower Mart." She has practiced this line so many times today, it has lost any real meaning to her.

Zak reaches around her and grabs a bag of bulbs. "Fifty snow-drop bulbs. That's a lot of potting up, dude."

Renée snatches the bag from him and puts it back. "Is there something I can help you with, Zak?" She clears her throat and attempts a more conciliatory tone. "I mean, I thought you'd be with Ellie Grace at the hospital."

He narrows his eyes. "How did you know she was at the hospital?"

Renée's fingers flutter to her neck. "Danit told me. And I just assumed you'd be going as well."

"Well, I wasn't invited." He frowns. "Sometimes I wonder if they even think of me as part of the family."

Renée tries not to show her surprise. She never figured Zak for the reflective type. Maybe he was alluding to something specific. Fishing for information. *Thom certainly didn't consider you part of the family.* She doesn't say that, and she's not sure if it's because it's rude and might hurt his feelings, or if she's a little afraid of him. Ginny would laughingly refer to her son-in-law as the *gigolo* when they gossiped over cocktails, but Renée always sensed a darker side to Zak. He isn't just a pretty face. She's known enough juvenile delinquents in her years teaching middle school to recognize that.

Renée hoists the handles of the wheelbarrow up to her waist. The wheelbarrow wobbles under the weight of its load.

"Can I give you a hand?" Zak asks.

"No, thank you."

"Sure? That looks heavy." The twinkle in his eyes unnerves her. He's toying with her, but why? He can't possibly know what she's done, can he?

"I'm stronger than I look."

"At least leave the potting soil. That's got to weigh twenty pounds."

"This isn't just *potting soil*, Zak. It's Elm Dirt." She nods her chin to the big letters on the side of the bag.

"And what's the difference?"

"Oh, about a hundred and seventy-five dollars a bag."

His eyebrows shoot up. "Wow. A hundred and seventy-five dollars for a bag of dirt?"

"Clearly, you are not a gardener," Renée sniffs. "This isn't *dirt*. It's a special blend of organic soils that includes worm casings, sea kelp, bat guano—"

"Bat guano? You mean poop?"

Renée shifts the wheelbarrow to one side and maneuvers past him.

"If you'll excuse me," she says as she pushes the wheelbarrow. "The dogs are waiting. Asti needs his anxiety medicine."

30

Ginny lies on her back while the monitor beside her beeps, punctuating the silence every few seconds. She is on the brink of dozing, recalling the list she gave to Renée and picturing her friend entering the house with that determined look she gets on her face. Ginny's mind drifts back through the years to the first time she ever set eyes on the house in Somerwood. It was much too big, Thom said; they needed a starter house. But Ginny fell in love. She knew as soon as she entered the house that Trey would not be an only child. There would be more children to come. There would be dogs. And friends. And parties, wonderful parties. To become the successes they were meant to be, they had to begin living as if they already were.

She was right.

It was a financial stretch at first, but no one can tell her that the dinner party in 1994 with the French-dressed lamb roast, the one where money, politics, and real estate dovetailed with exquisite Italian wine and smiling wives, didn't propel Thom's career forward. They would not impress the right men with a potluck at a split-level ranch deep in the hinterlands of Montgomery County. No, proximity to D.C. was essential. A beautifully set table was a business expense.

Her own parents lacked such imagination. Hard workers, yes, and honest as the day is long. But not risk-takers. They lived in fear that their little slice of the American pie would be snatched from them. Coming of age in the Great Depression haunted their adult lives. Those memories of men out of work and women struggling to feed their families. Foreclosures, instability. Those experiences shackled them. Everything in cash. No debt.

It felt glorious to break free of that stranglehold of doom. She knew Thom wanted to, as well, and it was she who gave him permission.

She and Thom were such a wonderful team once. But now, lying here, Ginny begins to doubt her memories. These past few years, as she tried so hard to reignite the passion they once felt for each other, were all in vain. The damage had already been done in California.

How could she have fallen for his lies?

Because she trusted him, that's why. She believed every word of his ridiculous tale. She never even thought to question it, to double-check the accuracy. And why should she? Thom was her rock—sturdy, unflappable. If anything, she thought he suffered from a lack of imagination. What a fool she had been.

Ginny becomes aware of voices in the room and opens her eyes.

Her vision is blurry for a moment, but when she can focus, she sees Nate and Ellie Grace standing by the bed.

"Oh, hello, dears." The words come out creaky. She reaches for the cup beside her with a trembling hand, and Ellie Grace rushes over to help.

Ginny takes a long sip of the lukewarm water—what she wouldn't do for a prosecco—and pats her daughter's hands. The poor thing. Ginny appraises her—her long, dark hair is pulled into a tasteful ponytail, her makeup is perfect, and she manages to look quite chic, but not too trendy, in the navy pants and silk shirt that convey she is grieving. But there's a lot more to Ellie Grace than meets the eye. Ginny knows that under that perfect façade, her daughter must be in turmoil. How could she not be, after last night?

"How are you doing? You sleep all right?" She notices Ellie Grace won't meet her eye.

"Not really. I'm just really shaken. And I'm worried about you."

Ginny shakes her head. "Uh-uh. Don't you dare. I'm going to be fine." She squeezes her daughter's hand, hard. "We'll all be fine, mark my words. We will get through this."

"People are saying things, on the news, the internet—"

"Now, Ellie Grace, listen to me, you're going to have to tune all that out. Now is the time to focus on the family, not on random strangers." Her tone is stern, perhaps too stern, and she holds her breath waiting to see if Ellie Grace will protest.

"You're right, Mommy."

"I know I am." She turns her head to take in the sight of her son. So handsome. She searches his face, looking for a sign that he knows the truth, but sees nothing that indicates it. A twinge of guilt zaps her for having allowed him to become embroiled in the whole mess. But she didn't know the truth back then, either. That son of a bitch had them all fooled. "How are you holding up? How are Danit and Malcolm? I can only imagine what is going through that girl's head."

Nate laughs. "Malcolm's Malcolm, and Danit's fine. She's been a huge help."

"Well, that's good. Do me a favor, honey, have Fabiola at the office box up your father's personal things today and then pick them up, okay? Make sure she gets his calendar."

Nate nods. "Sure. Does it have to be today?"

Ginny laughs to show that she knows she's being silly. "It probably doesn't, but indulge your old mother, will you?"

"Of course. I'll call her as soon as we leave."

If it is hard to deny his mother under normal circumstances, she knows it is impossible now.

"Thank you." Ginny cranes her neck and looks around the room. Her smile disappears.

"Where's Trey? Isn't he with you?"

Her children exchange the tiniest of glances that only a mother could detect.

"He said he would come by later." Ellie Grace sounds a bit too chipper when she says this.

"Come by later?" Ginny wrinkles her brow in confusion. Ellie Grace was never very good at obfuscation. "What in the world? Why didn't he come with you?" She puts her hand to her heart. "Is he all right? Tell me he's all right."

"He's fine, Mommy."

"He's just tired," Nate says.

"Oh." Ginny sinks back into her pillow. "He's not angry, is he?" Her blue eyes search her son's face for an unguarded reaction.

"Why would he be angry?" Ellie Grace asks.

It's a good question, but she can't tell Ellie Grace the real reason for her oldest son's fury. "He reacts to things more deeply than most people. He's a very sensitive soul. I'm sure his father's death is hitting him hard. I'm worried about him. Will you keep an eye on him, Ellie Grace?"

"Sure, I guess." Her daughter's nostrils flare, a most unbecoming tic. Ginny sighs. Poor Ellie Grace. She was always jealous of her brother. Both her brothers, really.

"And you, Nate? I know I've asked a lot of you. Maybe too much. But please don't let Trey do anything foolish."

"We're here, Mom. Doesn't that count?" Ellie Grace asks in a high-pitched voice.

"Of course, dear. It's everything. Absolutely everything." Ginny nods vigorously. "I couldn't ask for more wonderful children than you two."

Ellie Grace beams. She leans over and kisses her mother on the forehead. "Oh, Mommy."

Ginny smiles back at her daughter. "But all the same, promise me you'll look out for your brother, won't you? He needs us now more than ever."

31

Upstairs in the guest room, or what Ginny called *the pink room*, Danit gathers her things and places them on the bed. Two days ago, they'd set Malcolm's playpen next to a single bed in Nate's old room down the hall, where a Roger Federer poster still hung on the wall, and settled in to the guest room for a weeklong stay. It felt like she was staying in a luxury hotel. Not that she had ever done that. The walls were the palest pink, the color of the inside of a conch shell, and both bedside tables had small bud vases with a single flower, and a carafe of water with matching glass. A wooden four-poster bed with pineapples on each post held a thick white duvet atop a feather bed so high off the ground that when she sat on it, her feet dangled, barely skimming the floor.

Just yesterday, she was worried about how she would fit in, that she might commit some terrible faux pas that would reveal she didn't grow up in a house with monogrammed hand towels but in a small apartment with peeling linoleum.

What a difference twenty-four hours make. Now all she can think of is the murder that took place under this roof. She digs into the back of the closet where she shoved her duffel bag, but when she pulls it out, there is something stuck to the bottom. She wriggles it free to examine it and realizes it's a crumpled-up shirt.

The slam of a drawer in the distance startles her, and she pauses, ready to shove the shirt back inside. But no one comes up the stairs. Her heart races as she uncrumples the shirt. She feels guilty, although she's unsure why. It would be embarrassing and difficult to explain if anyone walked in at that moment.

But as she flattens the white shirt, she knows in her gut that she has found something important. It wasn't there when she'd unpacked her bags and thrown her duffel in the closet two days ago, and it clearly didn't just fall off the hanger. Someone shoved it in there. Recently.

She turns it over and sucks in her breath. The front is marred by splotches of dark brownish red.

Blood.

Danit looks inside the collar, where someone has stamped *Capitol Catering*.

Capitol Catering. That was the name of the company that did the food at the party yesterday, she's sure of it. She reaches for her phone, but once it's in her hand, she freezes. She can't call 9-1-1. This is not an emergency. What would she even say? *I found a shirt. I think it might have blood on it?* No, that was definitely not an emergency. On the other hand, she has to do something. This could very well have something to do with the murder of Nate's father.

She'll bring it to Nate. He'll know what to do. She crumples it back up, shoving it inside a dry-cleaning bag on the floor of the closet, and puts the whole thing in an outside, zippered pocket of her duffel bag.

Call when you get a chance, she texts Nate. And then adds—**not an emergency.** She doesn't want to worry him. He has enough on his plate. The shirt probably belonged to one of the catering staff who cut themselves or something. Or maybe the stain was something else entirely, like wine.

Danit pulls out *Jane Eyre* and settles herself into an armchair by the front window. She's at the point where Jane has just arrived at Thornfield Hall, when the doorbell rings.

Thinking it must be the folks coming for the chairs and tables, Danit heads downstairs, where Anya is opening the door to a man. Danit approaches and signs a form he offers on a clipboard, and Anya agrees to take him around the side where everything is stored.

Mission accomplished, Danit gets her things and lets herself out only to find that the crowd on the street has doubled. All eyes are on her as she hurries down the walkway, her duffel bag over her shoulder.

"Excuse me, excuse me," she says as she pushes through several people who are in her way. As she crosses the street, she can hear them right behind her.

"Are you a Calhoun?"

"Do you work for the Calhouns?"

"Hey, curly, what's in the bag?"

She rushes up the path to Cookie's house, pounding the front door with her fist as soon as she gets there. The door springs open. Cookie takes one look at his yard and yells past her, "Get off my property or I'll call the police!" He ushers Danit inside. "Hurry, hurry."

He shuts the door behind her. "Monsters. Are you okay?"

Danit nods, but she is shaken. "What do they want?"

"They want fame. They want to fill that black hole of emptiness inside them with the validation of strangers on social media. And they're using this horrible tragedy as a way to do it." He holds his fingers up to his lips. "Now Malcolm is fast asleep, so why don't we wait for Nate in the kitchen? Bob baked banana bread, and I swear if someone doesn't stop me, I'm going to eat the whole loaf myself."

Danit follows Cookie into a large, bright kitchen whose french doors overlook a patio outside. She takes a seat at the marble counter while Cookie walks over to a fire engine–red stove to light the burner under a kettle. She settles into her seat, feeling drained. So much has happened in the past twenty-four hours, she is exhausted—emotionally and physically.

"What a stove," Danit says.

"Isn't it? A Chambers from 1950. I grew up with it in Michigan, and when my parents died, I had the thing moved here and designed the whole kitchen around it. That was more than ten years ago, and would you know that every single appliance we installed—the microwave, the dishwasher, the fridge—has broken since? But not this baby. They just don't make them like they used to."

Danit shifts in her seat. "I grew up in an apartment, and I remember in seventh grade, one of the electric burners on our stove went out, then the other. Then a third. We had one working burner for about a year before our landlord replaced the stove."

"That's simply criminal." Cookie puts two red mugs on the counter. "And I should know. I am a recovering lawyer."

"Really?"

"Yes, ma'am. Now black, green, or herbal tea?" He frowns. "Or do you prefer coffee?"

"Green tea, please."

Cookie produces a wooden box and places it in front of her. "I recommend the jasmine pearls. I buy them at the Bethesda farmers' market. They're wonderful."

"Let's try it." Danit takes a silk sachet filled with tiny orbs and puts it in her cup.

"How you doing over at Ellie Grace's? She have everything you need?"

"Oh yeah. It's a huge house. And I just finished packing up—" She stops short, remembering the shirt she stuffed into her duffel. "Hold on a sec," she says. "Can I show you something?"

"Sure. What is it?"

Danit slips off her chair and starts walking back to the foyer, where she'd dropped her bag. "I think it might have something to do with the murder."

"Well, now you have my interest."

Danit unzips the outside pocket of the bag, pulls out the shirt still wrapped in the dry-cleaning bag, and returns to the kitchen. "I found this in a spare closet when I was packing up. It has *Capitol Catering* on it. And look." She spreads it out a little, revealing the dark stains.

Cookie gasps. "Is that what I think it is?"

Danit nods. "Looks like blood, right? Do you think I should call the police?"

"Well, yes. Obviously." Cookie yanks at his left ear a few times and then shakes his head. "Maybe not. What does Nate say?"

"I haven't told him yet. He's with his mom at the hospital, and I thought I'd just wait until he came here to get Malcolm."

"You need to text him, honey. This could be important."

"I did." But she takes out her phone, anyway, and taps out a message before placing it on the counter. "Okay. I told him I was here and he should come as quickly as possible."

"You didn't mention the shirt?"

"No, that didn't seem like a smart thing, to put that in writing."

"Good point," Cookie says, picking up the shirt and gingerly moving it off the counter and over to a nearby side table. "I don't want to look at that while I drink my tea. Let's talk about something more pleasant. Like you. You grew up in San Francisco, and you lived in an apartment, and you graduated from UC Berkeley with a degree in English and became a nanny. Do I have that right?"

Danit opens her mouth to respond, but the kettle begins whistling. While Cookie's back is turned, she makes a decision—she's going to tell the truth. She needs to tell someone. The thing about a lie is that it attracts other lies, growing larger, the same way one tiny piece of dust grows into a dust bunny. She might not be ready to tell Nate the whole truth, but as she watches Cookie pouring hot water into her mug, she decides confiding in this kind man will be her practice run. She will carefully gauge Cookie's reaction before he has a chance to cover it up so she knows what to expect from Nate. If only she can get the words out of her mouth.

"So yes, most of that is right."

Cookie peers up at her, his eyes twinkling with interest. "Most of it?"

32

Outside Ginny's hospital room, Ellie Grace grabs a hold of her brother's shirt. "Can you believe that? All she cares about is Trey. She doesn't even think about all that I've done for her."

"She's drugged to the gills," Nate says. "Don't overthink it."

He walks away from her toward the bank of elevators, prompting Ellie Grace to march after him. "How dare you!" Whenever someone tells her not to worry, or that she is overreacting, or that she should relax, it always has the same effect on her—that of dousing a barbecue with lighter fluid. Whoosh!

"Do not tell me not to overthink it," she snipes once she catches up to Nate. She reminds herself to speak softly. She doesn't want the nurses looking or, worse, recording her. "I will overthink anything I feel like overthinking." She frowns. That didn't come out quite right. "Mommy has always favored Trey, and you and I both know that."

"You'll get no argument there."

Ellie Grace straightens up, surprised by the slight bitterness she detects in her brother's response. "What do you mean?"

"I mean I see the same things you do, Ellie Grace. I just try not to let it get to me."

"I'm worried, that's all. What if the nurses tell the police that Trey didn't come to visit? What if they post about it?"

Her brother shoots her a look that brings her straight back to childhood. The same look he gave her when she refused to drink from a water fountain because someone at school told her the water came from the toilets. "Who cares what they post?"

The sheer absurdity of this question leaves her momentarily

speechless. How is it that her brother, one of the smartest people she knows, has no understanding of how the modern world works? What a privilege, she thinks, to never have to worry about what other people are saying about you. Ellie Grace, on the other hand, was born exquisitely sensitive to even the tiniest slights and rejections. High school at Washington Prep was a war zone, every day a new battle for her to win or lose. And she lost. A lot. She had all the trappings of a popular girl—she was *good on paper*—the right name, the right income bracket, the right address. But her neediness seeped out of her pores and re-pelled people like a putrid scent. She was always the one to laugh last, after finally getting the joke, and after the laughter had died down. The one whose birthday gifts were a bit too extravagant, as if she knew her wealth was the most appealing thing about her. College was no better. She pledged, and was accepted into, her first choice of sorority, but she knew she was filler. She wasn't one of the hot girls, or the outgoing, funny ones. She was just there. A body in a ruffled minidress, wearing her requisite Kendra Scott necklace, who would do what was asked of her.

All that changed when she met Zak and they started Gingham Life. Thanks to Instagram, she could curate what people knew about her and how they saw her. She was the one in control, offering up the best version of herself.

Who cares what they post? Ellie Grace cares, that's who. Because her life is online. That is her reality. She takes a deep breath, wondering how she can explain this to her brother without sounding condescending.

"So, our image matters. Like, a lot. I know that may seem stupid to you, but people are going to decide if we are innocent victims or a terrible family that deserves what we got. And all it takes is one or two viral photos, or videos, and people's minds will be made up forever." She pulls out her phone. "There are already TikTok videos about what happened and who did it. This girl, she claims to be a psychic, and she's been posting about us all morning. She posted a picture of our family, Nate! She has one-point-two million followers, Nate! Do you want to see?"

"No, actually, I don't."

"The worst part is they are hate-following me on Insta."

"Hate-following?"

"Yeah, they're only following me to troll me and leave mean comments. They're not fans. And yes, I am grateful that Gingham Life is up to, hold on—" She squints at her phone. "Holy cow, we're at three hundred and fifty thousand. That's insane!"

"You are addicted to this." He plucks the phone from her hands just as the elevator door opens. "You need a break." He steps inside.

"Give me my phone." Ellie Grace follows him onto the elevator, where she grabs the phone back from him. "You should see the comments on my Insta. I mean, most of them are super supportive, but some—listen to this one. *Guess the Calhouns aren't so perfect, after all. Karma is a beyotch.* Cats4_life wrote that. I mean, do you see what's going on?"

She scrolls down, and the words and emojis begin to swim before her eyes. **Liars. Fake, fake, fake. Bwaaaah!! Hate these people.** The casual cruelty is devastating. Each of these gleeful insults was created by a real person—is she that loathsome? That unlikeable? Suddenly, the tears burst forth. Here, in the closed confines of the elevator, where no one can possibly see, she weeps. "I . . . can't . . . take . . . it—"

Nate pats her awkwardly on her shoulder. "Don't cry, Ellie Grace. These people don't know you." He jams the button marked *L* a few times.

"Yes, they do," she hiccups. "They know a lot about me."

"That's where you're wrong. They know your image, but they don't know the real you."

"The real me?" She stops crying and looks up at her brother. *Is there a* real *me?* she wonders. She knows who she would be without Instagram. The old Ellie Grace. The one no one liked.

"A lot of people are going to be talking about our family for a while," he says. "You need to keep your gunpowder dry."

"My gunpowder? What kind of toxic masculinity is that?"

This makes Nate smile. "It means calm down." The elevator doors open in the lobby, and he steps out.

"Did you just say *calm down*?" Ellie Grace stands still and glares at her brother.

"Stay off of Instagram for a while," he says as the elevator doors begin to close.

Ellie Grace wedges her shoulder between them, shoving them back open. "I can't do that. You know I can't do that. It's my job." She jumps out as the doors close once more.

"Then at least don't read the comments," Nate says. "You need to stop caring so much what other people think."

"Ha. Easy for you to say. You work with fish."

"Sea mammals."

"Same difference."

After a few moments digging through his pockets, he produces a ticket for the hospital's parking garage. "Aha!"

Nate walks briskly out of the front of the hospital and turns left toward the parking garage. Ellie Grace hurries to keep up. "What did Mommy mean when she said she's asked a lot of you? What has she asked you to do?"

"The usual. You know how Trey is."

"What's the usual?" She has to jog to keep up with Nate's long strides.

Nate sighs. "Little things over the years. Check on Trey when he was in LA. Sometimes I would drive down from Mendo."

"What did happen in LA, Nate? No one ever told me."

"He crashed his car. He was pretty high."

"I knew about that. But that's not all, is it?"

Nate shrugs. "I think a car accident while high is enough, don't you?"

Ellie Grace frowns. "No, something else must have happened. I mean, why did he move back? Just because he was in a car wreck?"

At the kiosk, Nate inserts his ticket, then his credit card. "I don't know, Ellie Grace."

"Trey hates D.C. He swore he would never come back. There has to be another reason."

As soon as the machine spits out the ticket, Nate grabs it. "Cool it, Ellie Grace. This feels like an interrogation. You're worse than the cops were this morning."

"Tell me! I have a right to know."

He turns and gives her a hard look. "It's not my place to say. And my advice would be to drop it."

"Maybe I don't want to drop it. Did you ever think of that? I'm sick of all the secrets in this family."

"You mean you're sick of not being in on the secrets, isn't that what you mean? Trust me, it's no better when you know all the dirt."

"All the dirt! So there is dirt?" She knows she sounds hysterical, but she can't rein herself in. She doesn't want to. Nate, of all people, is keeping secrets from her.

An elderly couple approaches them, eyeing the parking kiosk. Nate pulls his sister out of the way so the couple can use the machine. "Ellie Grace, for the love of God, just keep your eyes on your own paper, okay?" He turns on his heels and begins walking up the ramp toward the car.

"Where are you going? Wait up!"

Nate keeps walking until he has turned the corner, out of sight.

Ellie Grace clenches her fists so tightly that her long nails dig into her palms. The pain is the only thing stopping her from screaming.

33

"So, I didn't actually graduate from UC Berkeley." Danit looks down and focuses on her hands. She said it. She can't take it back. Panic envelops her. She jumped the gun. What has she done? Cookie will tell everyone. Nate will know, and it will ruin everything. It's one thing for him to date a nanny. But a college dropout? She knows how important college is to him, to his family. Will he even want to marry her once he knows?

"Oh, no?" Cookie pours the hot water into the two mugs. "Give this two minutes—three, tops."

"Thank you." Danit pulls the mug close to her and inhales the flower-scented steam. "I kind of dropped out."

"Kind of?" Cookie puts two plates and a loaf of banana bread between them and sits down next to her, adjusting his stool so he can look at her. "What happened? Did this have something to do with your mother?" He sounds calm, not surprised at all. She breathes a sigh of relief and nods.

"Yes. She got sick my freshman year, and I didn't go back after summer break. She died that fall, and I just kind of, I don't know, I became lost. Adrift. I never went back." She doesn't want to let herself get swept up in those painful memories. It was a dark time. One she thought might never end.

"But you can quote Charles Dickens!"

Danit laughs nervously. "Books were my escape. I read a lot. I always thought I would go back to school someday, get my degree, but I just couldn't seem to get it together. And then a few years went by, and it was just embarrassing. I was depressed, actually. My mom was my only family, and pretty much my best friend in the world. When I lost her . . ."

Cookie places his hand over hers. "I understand. My mother's death hit me very hard. If it weren't for Bob and Olivia, I would have crawled under the covers and not come out."

He understands. This is what she needed—someone from this world, Nate's world, to make her feel like it was okay.

Danit smiles as she plucks the tea bag from her mug and places it on the edge of her plate. "I cried every day for a year. I still cry. If I smell her perfume—she wore Beautiful by Estée Lauder—or if I hear a Fleetwood Mac song. They were her favorite."

"For me, it's the birds. My mom was the biggest bird lover," Cookie says. "Had feeders all over the backyard—drove my dad crazy. Every time I see a goldfinch, it's like a knife in my heart."

"So I pretty much did nothing until the small amount of life insurance my mom left me ran out," Danit says. "Then I had to get a job, only I had no degree. I had no confidence. But I ran into a friend of mine from high school who was making a killing as a nanny for this tech couple, and I started doing that. I worked for a few families and realized how much I loved working with children. And it paid well. During the pandemic, the Steins, the family I was working for, moved to Mendocino and asked me to come with them."

"And that's where you met Nate."

"Right."

"So why does he think you graduated from Berkeley?"

Danit bites her lip. "I might have told the Steins that I went to Berkeley. Which is technically true. I did go for one year."

Cookie shoots her a look.

"Okay, it was not the *whole* truth. In my defense, I have never said I graduated."

"Now, Danit."

Here comes the judgment, she thinks. Her defenses flare. "I know, I know. It's just that when Nate was looking for a nanny, the Steins told him I had gone to Berkeley. You have to understand, these are very competitive people. They want everyone who comes into contact with their children to be overachievers. I've been turned down from jobs in San Francisco because I only spoke one language and didn't play a musical instrument."

"And when do you plan to tell Nate the truth? Before or after you get married?" He pauses for effect. "Or maybe on your tenth anniversary. *Oh, sweetie, there's something I've been meaning to tell you.*"

Danit groans. "Ugh. I know. I was planning to while we were here, I swear, but then all this happened."

"Take it from someone who was in the closet for the first twenty years of his life. Keeping secrets is exhausting. Just tell the damn truth." He comes closer to her and opens his arms wide. "C'mere. You need a big ole hug."

Danit sees no option but to stand. She gives Cookie a quick embrace, but her resistance melts once she feels his strong arms around her. "You don't need to pretend to be anybody else," he says softly into her ear. "You're perfect just the way you are."

He pushes her back, holding her at arm's length, and Danit is surprised to feel tears spring to her eyes.

"I'll tell you what I've told my own daughter countless times, and I mean it every time I say it: you don't have to *do* anything to be loved. Just existing is enough."

Danit nods, wiping at her eyes. "Thank you for saying that."

"Well, it's true. In this crazy striving world, we can forget that sometimes. And I'm sure Nate feels the same way. He doesn't love you for some darn degree, he loves you for you." He lets his hands drop from her shoulder. "But you need to tell him the truth, honey."

"I know it's no way to start a marriage. It's just, this is going to sound bad, but Nate and me, we just have fun together. We don't talk about serious stuff. I don't know if he will still accept me once he knows."

Cookie scowls. "You can't avoid the tough conversations. I mean, you can. But the issues don't go away just because you aren't discussing them. And if Nate loves you half as much as he appears to, he will understand."

Danit swallows a mouthful of banana bread despite the lump in her throat. She wants so badly to believe Cookie. "It's true. I never should have let it get this far. Like his first marriage—I keep wanting to ask him about it, but when I do, he doesn't like to talk about it."

Cookie leans back. "Oh, well. Helena. She was a piece of work."

"You met her?" Danit feels a quiver of anticipation in her belly, tinged with a sense of dread.

"Sure, she came back here with Nate a few times. They met at Stanford, and she was type A-plus-plus. I mean, don't get me wrong. Gorgeous. Smart. Ambitious."

"Great," Danit says, instinctively patting down her unruly curls.

Cookie pats her leg. "Now don't you worry. She was as cold-blooded as they come. A real reptile. She had a list—law school, make partner, marry perfect guy—all before thirty. Nate had the bad misfortune of wandering into her crosshairs. But the one thing that was never on her list? Children. And that turned out to be a deal-breaker." Cookie reaches into his back pocket and pulls out his phone. "Let's see if I can find her. We're still friends on Facebook. I know she's a big marathon runner. She ran the Tokyo marathon last year—oh, here she is."

"So she had Malcolm and then just left?"

Cookie turns the phone toward Danit, who braces herself for the wave of emotion upon seeing image after image of Nate's ex. But when she looks at the photos, none of the insecurity or jealousy she anticipated materializes. Cookie was right—Helena is a big runner. The majority of her pictures are either of her running in races, or dressed in all black, her sleek hair pulled back in a tight ponytail, seated in front of complicated-looking minimalist dishes.

"Huh," Danit says, taking the phone. "She likes food and running, that's for sure." She scrolls down, the years whizzing backward before her eyes. All of a sudden, Danit stops scrolling at a picture of Helena at the finish line of a race. She reads the caption—*Personal best at the Redwood Summer Trail Run!*

"Hold on a sec," Danit says, a chill running through her body. Are her eyes deceiving her? This can't possibly be true. She double-checks the dates. "If Malcolm was born October 3, 2022, and this was taken on September 22 of 2022, how can this be?"

Cookie stands up and leans over her shoulder. "What am I looking at, exactly?" he says. "I mean, besides Helena running another race?"

Danit taps at the image of the sweaty, muscled woman in racing shorts and a sports bra, with the number 522 pinned to her chest. "You're looking at her washboard abs, when she was supposed to be eight months pregnant with Malcolm." She looks up and meets Cookie's eye. "Malcolm was born less than a month later."

34

Zak pulls up in front of the police station and puts the car in park.

"I'm nervous." Ellie Grace examines her face in the visor mirror. "I'm sweating already. Are you sure we have to do this?"

"I'll be there the whole time, babe."

After visiting the hospital, Ellie Grace went home and changed into a navy-blue blazer over a white shirt, and a pair of tan cigarette pants. She thought she looked cute in the full-length mirror in her bedroom, but now she's worried she looks like she's going to a job interview.

"Don't be scared," Zak continues. "Just remember—be cool. You don't have to answer anything you don't want to answer." Zak puts his hand on her knee. He's being especially sweet after their little tiff last night. "They just need to talk to everyone in the family so that they can cross us off their list of suspects."

"They're not going to make me take a polygraph, are they?"

Zak laughs. "You watch too much TV. It's routine. Just keep your answers short and don't volunteer any extra information, 'kay?" He takes her hand and kisses it. "You sure you don't want me to call a lawyer?"

Ellie Grace flinches. "What? A lawyer? Won't that just make us look guilty? I mean, when I think about what people would say if they knew we hired a lawyer—" She shudders. "No. We can handle this. As long as you're by my side, I'll be fine." And it's true. All she needs is Zak, holding her hand, giving her strength. She only wishes he had changed out of the joggers and T-shirt that are practically his uniform. Some people can be very judgy about appearances. "I'm so lucky to have you. Let's not fight ever again."

He takes her face in his hands and stares into her eyes. "Let's never fight." He gives her a deep kiss that she feels all the way down to the molecular level. He hasn't kissed her like that in months. Maybe this tragedy will have a silver lining—bringing them closer together.

After announcing themselves to the desk sergeant in the police station's front room, Ellie Grace and Zak sit side by side holding hands. It's a little awkward, since the plastic molded chairs are bolted to the floor about a foot apart, which means they both have to stretch their arms out to grasp the other's hand, but it's worth the strain. They are sending a message—Zak Miller and Ellie Grace Calhoun Miller are a team. You want to interview one of them? Well, you're getting both.

Finally, the officer who was at Trey's house earlier that morning pops his head in and motions for them to follow. Ellie Grace stands, shaking out her stiff arm before looping it through Zak's.

The officer deposits them in a windowless room that smells of sweat and stale coffee.

"Yuck," Ellie Grace says, dragging two of the chairs together for her and Zak to sit on. Zak sits down, pulls out his phone, and immediately begins playing *Candy Crush*. She's slightly miffed that he can lose himself in such mindless entertainment as they are about to be questioned by the police, but then decides to join him. She scrolls through social media on her phone to check the latest coverage of her family. It's not good. They are being portrayed as rich monsters. One viral video refers to them as "*Succession* in the D.C. suburbs."

She shoves the phone back in her bag, feeling worse than before. But with nothing to distract her from the fact that she is waiting to be interviewed by the police about her father's murder, her entire body quivers from her trembling hands to her tapping feet. She tries tucking her hands beneath her thighs, but nothing helps until she grabs the phone and resumes her scrolling.

When Detective Washington and Officer Amatangelo finally enter, she puts it away for good and nudges Zak to do the same.

"Thank you both for coming in," the detective says, taking a seat across from her. "We're still waiting for your brother to show up. He seemed a little out of sorts this morning."

"Trey's a very sensitive soul. He reacts to things more deeply than most people realize. Our father's death is hitting him hard." It's only after she's finished speaking that Ellie Grace realizes she just paraphrased the insipid speech her mother gave at the hospital this morning.

Detective Washington offers a placid smile. "Sounds like Trey isn't expected to play by the same rules as everyone else. That can't be easy for you, Ellie Grace."

Ellie Grace feels her eyelid twitch. "I'm not sure what you mean."

"Oh, believe me, I get it. I have four brothers. There are always favorites in a family."

Ellie Grace digs her nails into the palm of her hands. "I'm sorry your parents played favorites," she says in a conciliatory tone she picked up from her sorority days. She had been in charge of mollifying girls who had been cut during rush but wanted to argue their way into the house. "That can be really hard. Thankfully, my parents never did that."

She can't help but notice the look Washington and Amatangelo exchange.

"Anyway, there are a few things we need to ask you both that we didn't get a chance to this morning," Washington says. "Besides, we thought you'd appreciate the privacy."

Ellie Grace nods. "I appreciate that. I have a professional image to consider."

"Gingham Life?" Officer Amatangelo asks, standing off to her side.

Her face brightens, and she swivels to face Amatangelo. "Yes. Are you familiar?"

"We are now," he says. "But we'll get back to that."

"Do you remember what time you left your father's study?" Washington asks.

Ellie Grace snaps her head back. "No. I mean, why would I?" she splutters. "I don't keep track of every second of my day. But he was very much alive when I left his study, I can tell you that."

"What were you and your father discussing that was so distressing to you?"

Ellie Grace looks to Zak. He gives her a little nod. "Just life. Stuff."

"C'mon, Ellie Grace, you can do better than that." Washington perches on the edge of the table. "Something must have upset you enough to make you cry. What was it? Was it about money, by any chance? We all know Gingham Life isn't exactly bringing in the big bucks."

"Although you have a lot more followers today than you did before your dad was killed," Amatangelo says. "That's a lucky little development for you."

"What are you implying?" Ellie Grace stares, horrified, at the officer. "That I killed my father for Instagram followers?"

35

After the hospital, Nate heads out to Calhoun Development. His phone pings and a quick glance tells him that Danit has texted him, wondering when he is coming back to get her at Cookie's.

"Siri, text Danit," Nate says loudly into his phone when he is stopped at a red light in front of the NIMH buildings on Rockville Pike. "Headed to my dad's office, and then I'll come to Cookie's after that."

When the light changes, Nate tosses the phone on the passenger seat and continues to drive past the immense campus. He is suddenly struck by a memory of when he was in fourth grade and had just finished *Mrs. Frisby and the Rats of NIMH*, the children's novel about a widowed mouse who helps free some highly intelligent rats being experimented on at NIMH. He talked Trey into biking over to the campus to explore the area where he thought Mrs. Frisby must have lived.

His big brother indulged him, even though by that time, in middle school, Trey must have thought the whole thing a bit ridiculous. The two of them searched the grounds for at least an hour until a security guard found them and strongly recommended they go home.

Nate slows down as the high-end office park where Calhoun Development is located comes into view. Remembering the old Trey, a sensitive guy with a quirky sense of humor, always makes him upset. If Nate thinks about it too much, he can sink into a pretty dark pit. His brother had so much potential that just went nowhere. Trey might have thrived in a different family, one that wasn't as competitive and status-oriented.

But you can't pick your family.

A lump has formed in Nate's throat. He loves his brother. That's why he did what he did in California, as crazy as it was. He thinks of Ellie Grace, demanding to know about Trey's reason for coming back. She would never understand.

But what about Danit? He owes her the truth.

Nate parks, gets out, and enters the gleaming lobby of the office building in front of him and jabs the elevator button. He'll tell Danit tonight. He knew the day would come, that he can't keep putting it off.

He rides the elevator to the eighth floor, where the doors open onto a large reception area. Nate approaches the young woman seated behind a wide desk below a sign reading *Calhoun Development Group*.

"Hi. We haven't met, but I'm Nate Calhoun," Nate says.

The young woman looks up at him, her eyes almost hidden by a thick curtain of bangs. "How can I help you?"

Nate shifts uncomfortably. "I'm Thom Calhoun's son." He's not expecting her to jump up, run around the desk, and hug him—but he finds her lack of emotion disorienting. "Can I talk to Fabiola?"

"I'll call her now." The receptionist motions to a cluster of low-slung metal and leather chairs.

Nate wanders over and parks himself by a tall, potted fig tree. "I'll never get out of that chair if I sit in it," he says to no one. This is one of the few spaces in his father's life where Ginny clearly had no input. There was no way she would have approved of the low-slung modern chairs, or the gray-and-black abstract paintings on the wall. A few moments later, a middle-aged woman with dark hair in a severe cut comes out.

"Oh, Nate. I am so sorry for your loss." She wraps her arms around him and gives him a little rocking hug before pulling back. "It's so awful."

"Thank you, Fabiola. I know you worked with my dad a long time."

"Twenty years next month. Longer than my marriage! Now, how can I help?"

"I just wanted to box up a few of my father's personal effects. My mother asked me to."

"Of course. Come with me. I have some boxes you can use." Fabiola pivots, leading Nate down a long hallway and into his father's office. It's been years since he was in here, since he seldom had reason to visit his father at work. "I think the last time I was here was for a take-your-kid-to-work day when I was in middle school."

"Well, not too much has changed."

He takes in the floor-to-ceiling window that offers sweeping views of a slice of the Washington suburbs filled with tree tops, highways, and office parks.

"Your dad was a wonderful boss. He took a chance on me when I came to this country. I worked my way up and made a very good life. Put my three children through college with this job. I owe the life I have to this company. I just don't know what we are going to do now. I only hope one of you children will keep the company going. Not just for me. Hundreds of people depend on CDG."

"Well, there's always my brother. Maybe we can convince him to stay on." Nate realizes how ridiculous this sounds as soon as he utters it. It's the type of filler talk he's terrible at.

"Trey? He's a bum." She claps her hand to her mouth. "I apologize. I shouldn't have said that. Don't tell him I said that, please."

Nate makes a zipping motion over his mouth.

"It's been a long day. The police were already here asking all kinds of questions."

Nate straightens up. "Like what?"

"Oh, *Can you think of anyone who might hold a grudge against Mr. Calhoun?* Things like that—disgruntled employees." Fabiola shakes her head in disgust.

"And what did you tell them?"

"The truth! That your father was a wonderful boss. One of the kindest men I've ever known. You're so lucky to have had him for a father." She sniffs the air, jutting her chin out in a haughty manner. "A few employees took it upon themselves to repeat unsavory rumors about Mr. Calhoun, but the police didn't get very far with that line of questioning with me."

Nate rubs his neck. "What unsavory rumors?"

"You know, there's always talk in a workplace. There have been attractive young ladies working here over the years, and of course, your father went out of his way to make everyone feel welcome. People can be so suspicious. I'll get those boxes now."

Fabiola turns and leaves Nate standing there feeling numb. He struggles to make sense of Fabiola's words. He can't reconcile the memory of his authoritarian father with Fabiola's version. Kind? He could think of many words to describe his dad, but *kind* was not one of them.

A grief tinged with anger hits him unexpectedly in the chest, and he steps back, steadying himself on the desk. Perhaps this is where his father was his true self, at the office. How awful to consider that his employees got the best of him, while he, his mom, and his siblings made do with the emotional scraps that were left.

And what was that about unsavory rumors? Trey had joked about his dad being a philanderer, but Nate had chalked that up to his brother pushing buttons. But could it be true? He walks over to the gray sofa and sits down, head in hands. The thoughts come fast—is there another woman? If there was, it might have bearing on his father's murder. The more he thinks about it, the more he is sure the police ought to look into it. Maybe there was a jilted lover, angry at his father, who took revenge at the party. It would explain why his mother was shot, too.

On the other hand, if there was no other woman, or if there was and she had nothing to do with his dad's death, does he really want to drag all this out into the light? He thinks of Ellie Grace and her thousands of Instagram followers and what she said about the true-crime junkies trawling through their lives for juicy bits of gossip. He couldn't put his mother through that for nothing. He decides to look into it for himself.

He gets up and sits behind his father's desk. The first drawer he opens is filled with promotional flyers. He pulls out one glossy brochure that features a smiling couple in front of a new house. He flips it over and reads: *Calhoun Development Group is a privately owned real estate development firm with almost thirty years of experience. CDG develops, leases, and markets a variety of properties, with an emphasis on residential, retail, and flex buildings.* Nate shoves the brochure back into the drawer. He can't think about what will become of this company now. He has too much else to worry about.

He searches in all the drawers for anything that might be a clue as to what was going on with his father—a diary, personal correspondence, anything—but finds nothing. Only office supplies. He feels silly—what was he expecting? A handwritten letter? *Dear Nate, I've been having an affair, and this is exactly why . . .*

Where the hell is his diary? He must have kept his appointments somewhere.

Just then, Fabiola returns with several boxes. "Can I get you anything else?" she asks, putting them on the sofa. "Water? Coffee?"

"I'm looking for an appointment book or diary. Any idea where that might be?"

Fabiola nods. "Ashleigh, his personal assistant, kept his appointments. I believe she uses an iPad. But she's not in today. I can give you her address if you want. I'm sure she would want to help. She was very fond of your father, and I think his death has hit her hard."

36

Ellie Grace guffaws. "No, I did not murder my father for Instagram followers. You people are sick."

Zak inches his chair closer to her, and Ellie Grace remembers his admonition not to take the bait, no matter what the police say.

"But you were fighting over money?" Washington asks.

Ellie Grace wills herself to smile. "No, nothing like that." In the car, she and Zak went over how to respond to this exact question. What was a reasonable and believable answer? They discussed saying that she was upset Nate was moving so far away, but that sounded ridiculous even to her own ears. They considered telling the cops the truth, about her father booting them out of the Chalfonte model house, but that seemed like a bad idea. She wasn't going to mention the manila envelope. Even Zak didn't know about that. Instead, she delivers the little speech she practiced, punctuated with slight sniffling at opportune moments.

"We were talking about me having a baby. And I was telling him how hard it was for me. And how we weren't having any luck." Here she hitches a bit, not quite a sob, but just enough to convey her deep sadness. "It's so hard when you want to get pregnant and you can't. And every single month you're reminded. You have no idea!" She takes a tissue out of her bag and brings it to her nose. There's just enough truth to what she's saying that tears spring to her eyes.

"And what did your father say about all this?" Washington asks.

Ellie Grace brightens. "Daddy was wonderful. He told me

to keep trying. That it would happen. But I did get upset, it's true. I may have accused him of being insensitive." She sniffles. "That was the last conversation I had with him. I didn't get to say goodbye." She dabs at her eyes.

"How about you, Zak?" Washington says. "How's the personal training going? I keep meaning to take my gym up on their offer of two free sessions, but I never get around to it."

"Good, good." Zak bobs up and down. "Business is steady, growing. You should do it. You won't regret it."

"But it doesn't pay a lot, does it?" Washington wrinkles up her nose. "I mean, not real money."

"Dude." Zak spreads his hands wide. "All money is real money. Besides, I'm a simple guy."

"Simple guy, huh?" Amatangelo folds his arms across his chest.

"Tell me about your in-laws," Washington says. "You close with them?"

Zak looks to Ellie Grace before answering. "Sure."

"He was like another son to my dad," Ellie Grace says. "I think Daddy saw a lot of himself in Zak—hardworking, entrepreneurial." She searches Washington's face to see if the detective is buying any of this, but it's impossible to tell.

"Your father didn't mind that he was supporting you and Zak?" Washington's manner is warm and welcoming. Ellie Grace sees how some people might be lulled into saying things they ought not to, but she won't be.

"I wouldn't say he was supporting us. He's been helping us get on our feet."

"And I bet that help came with a few strings attached, huh?" Washington winks.

"You're not exactly in the same league as Ellie Grace and the rest of the Calhouns, are you, Zak?" Amatangelo asks. "Money-wise, class-wise, and I'm guessing education-wise. You go to college?"

"That's rude!" Ellie Grace says.

"A couple of years at Arizona State," he says. "Ellie Grace doesn't care about any of that stuff."

"No, I don't." She picks up Zak's hand and squeezes it, leaving their entwined hands on the table in full view. If they think they can drive a wedge between her and her husband, they don't know what they're up against.

"But Thom did, didn't he?" Washington asks. "He didn't think you were good enough for his little girl, did he?"

The two lock eyes, not speaking. About five seconds of silence pass before Zak leans back and grins. "Is there a question there?"

"Yeah," Amatangelo says. "Did you kill your father-in-law?"

Erupting in laughter, Zak's entire body begins to shake. "Did I what?"

"That is not okay!" Ellie Grace says. "We're done here. C'mon, honey."

But neither she nor Zak makes a move.

"Do you know where your father kept his handgun, Ellie Grace?" Washington asks.

"What?" Ellie Grace laughs, several staccato barks in succession, thrown off guard by the sudden shift in topic. "What on earth? I didn't know anything about a gun. I suppose I knew he had one. We all knew. He kept it in the study."

"What about you, Zak?" Washington asks. "Were you aware that your father-in-law kept a gun in the house?"

"What? I mean, I guess."

Washington leans in a little. "We know your father-in-law and Ellie Grace had a serious disagreement, serious enough for her to leave the room crying. I'm gonna guess it was about you."

"You went in there, didn't you, Zak?" Amatangelo asks, adjusting the walkie-talkie on his belt. "You got into it with the old man. Maybe you were just sticking up for Ellie Grace. You were angry because he made your wife cry. Was he trying to come between you and Ellie Grace?"

"Dude, that's crazy," Zak says.

"We dusted the place, found Ellie Grace's prints, Ginny's, Trey's—but not yours, but you said you spoke to Thom. How do you explain the absence of prints? Did you wear gloves, Zak?" Washington asks.

Zak pulls his hand from Ellie Grace's and crosses his arms. "I'm sorry, Ellie Grace," he mumbles, his chin pressed into his chest. Ellie Grace leans in closer to hear him. "I lied to you. I never went in and talked to your dad."

"You never went into the study?" she asks.

"I'm sorry." He looks up at her. "I know you wanted me to, and I planned to, I was just avoiding it."

"It's okay." Ellie Grace rubs his upper arm, and pulls his hand free, back onto her lap. "I'm not angry." *I knew you never went in.* She looks up at the detective. "See? That's why his prints weren't there. Because he never went inside."

"So now you are saying that you weren't in his study?" Amatangelo asks. "So you lied to the officer on the scene."

Washington raps her knuckles on the table, catching Zak's attention. "Ginny must have caught you off guard. That wasn't part of the plan, was it? Where'd you hide the gun, Zak?"

"Did you hear anything I said? I never went into his study." Zak drops Ellie Grace's hand before pushing his chair back from the table. "I think we're done talking to you. We were trying to be helpful, coming in here and everything, but just forget it."

Amatangelo looks at Washington, who nods.

"All right," Washington says. "But, Ellie Grace? Zak? Don't leave town. I'm sure we'll be speaking again. Quite soon."

37

From Cookie's front window, Danit watches Nate park his car and hurry up the walk before any of the gawkers on the street notice him. She flings the door open. "Quick, come inside."

"Dadadadaada." Malcolm comes running into the foyer and wraps his arms around Nate's legs.

Cookie appears and ushers them all into the living room. "Malcolm just woke up. He was down for a good hour."

"At least someone can sleep around here," Nate says, sitting on the sofa.

Danit is clutching the bloody shirt wrapped in the dry-cleaning bag.

"What's that?" Nate asks, frowning.

"So I was getting my stuff from your parents' house, and I found this." She sits next to him, torn between wanting to tell him what she found and not wanting to add to his worries. "It's a Capitol Catering shirt, and there's blood on it." Her voice quivers as she passes him the shirt.

"Whose blood?" he asks.

"We don't know," Cookie says. "We think we should call the police."

Nate looks down at the crumpled shirt. "I agree."

Cookie pops up. "I'll do it. I have that detective's card right here."

Danit sits next to Nate as they listen to Cookie talk on the phone. "Uh-huh . . . uh-huh . . . that's right. Blood. The Calhoun house . . . Calhoun. *C-A-L-H-O-U-N.*" After a moment, he gets off the phone, disappointment on his face. "Detective

Washington wasn't available, so I left a message. They said a uniformed officer would be by in about an hour to pick it up and not to handle it any further." And with that, Cookie plucks the package from Nate and deposits it on the mantel. "Out of Malcolm's reach."

While they wait, Nate fills them in on how his mother is doing at the hospital and that they plan to discharge her tomorrow. He then goes on to describe his visit to his father's office. "I'm going tomorrow to visit his assistant, Ashleigh, to get his appointment book. I'm hoping if my dad was having an affair, there might be a clue in there. I know it's a long shot."

Danit curls her legs under and scooches closer to Nate. "Do you really think your dad was cheating on your mom?"

Nate shrugs. "I don't know. Up until this happened, I would have said no way. But it turns out that I didn't really know him that well."

"I know the feeling," she says. "I never even met my dad."

Cookie clucks his tongue. "You poor kids." He takes the seat next to her. "I have an offer to make. How about you consider me an honorary uncle? I don't have any nephews or nieces, and Bob and I have more love than one child and grandchild can handle. Just ask Olivia. She'd be thrilled if I had someone else to text all the time. What do you say?"

For the second time today, Cookie's kindness has brought tears to Danit's eyes. "Deal," she says, holding out her hand.

"Oh, screw that!" Cookie says and gives her a big hug instead.

The doorbell rings, and Cookie gets up, wiping at his own eyes. "I should get that." In a moment he is back with a uniformed police officer. "This is Officer Lee, and he's here for the . . . evidence."

"Which one of you found it?"

"I did," Danit says, raising her hand. She describes how she discovered the shirt in the back of the closet, on top of her bag. "So it couldn't have been there for long."

Officer Lee's lip quivers. *Disgust* might be too strong a word, but it's clear to Danit that he thinks she screwed up.

"I wasn't sure what to do."

"You shouldn't have handled it at all, but at least you called," he says. "Where is it now?"

Cookie points to the mantel, and the officer pulls out a large plastic bag, unfolds it, and slips the shirt into it. "Next time you find something that could be related to a murder investigation, call us before you touch it."

Danit feels her face grow warm under the admonition. "Sorry about that."

After the officer leaves, it takes another twenty minutes for Danit and Nate to pack up Malcolm's things and disentangle themselves from Cookie's hospitality. They politely decline his offer of dinner and get everything into the car as quickly as possible so as not to draw attention from the people hanging out across the street.

"I'm exhausted," Nate says, turning onto Wisconsin Avenue. "Maybe we should just pick up some takeout."

In the back seat, Malcolm arches his back and howls. "I think he's hungry," Danit says. "Why don't you drop us at the house and then grab food?"

Nate nods. "Don Pollo okay?"

"What's that? I never heard of it."

"Peruvian chicken. You're in for a treat." Nate turns down a narrow street to go to Ellie Grace and Zak's house, a leafy neighborhood with a mix of older homes and recent builds that tower above them. Their large modern farmhouse comes into view. Nate pulls up in front. It's the tallest house on the block, straining at the property's edges. It's objectively a nice house, but it leaves Danit cold. It's too perfect, with none of the charm of the painted brick colonials on either side. Nate had told her that was one of Calhoun Development's specialties. Not just planned communities but tearing down older homes in established communities and building these newer, bigger houses so that the neighborhood quickly took on the look of a planned one. Nate made it sound like a virus his father was injecting into these older neighborhoods.

"You like spicy?" he asks, putting the car in park.

"You mean the chicken? You know I do." Danit unclicks her seat belt. "Listen, before I go in, I want to tell you something."

"Can it wait until I get back? I'm starving."

"No, I need to tell you now, while I have the nerve. Who knows what's going to happen later, with your sister and Zak around. We never really have time to talk."

Malcolm shrieks, and Danit reaches back to undo his buckle. Nate sighs, annoyed. "Okay, what is it?"

This doesn't feel like the right time. Malcolm is in a bad mood, Nate is hungry and tired, and yet she has an overwhelming urge to confess. She feels as if she doesn't tell him *right now*, she never will. She's kept this secret from him for six months, but the act of telling Cookie put it front and center in her mind. She won't be able to think of anything else until she tells Nate. "I never graduated college," she blurts out. "I dropped out of Berkeley after my freshman year."

"Wait, what?" He scrunches up his face in confusion. "That's out of left field."

"When my mom died, I never went back."

Malcolm clambers over the console between them and into Nate's lap. "But I thought . . . the Steins, they said—"

"I let them think I graduated from Berkeley," she says quickly. "They just assumed, and I didn't correct them."

"Danit, how could you let me keep thinking that? You let me tell other people that you graduated from Berkeley. I told my whole family, and you never corrected me. Why would you let me do that?"

"Oh, please! Why? You went to Stanford. Then you got a master's and became a marine biologist. Your ex-wife went to Stanford. Your dad went to Penn. Don't pretend you don't care about that kind of stuff. It made you happy to think I graduated from a prestigious school. That's why you told everyone."

"That's not fair."

Malcolm leans toward Danit and reaches for her shoulders. "He's hungry," she says, feeling sick to her stomach. She hates quarrels. "I should go in."

"I feel like you're trying to blame me when you're the one who lied," Nate says. "Or at least didn't tell the truth."

"No, that's not it. I take full responsibility!" Danit says. "I was just trying to explain why I would do it. I'm not perfect, Nate. I made a mistake. I was worried you wouldn't think I was good enough if I told you." She pauses and takes a deep breath. "I was worried that you wouldn't want to date me if you knew I never went to college."

He is silent for an excruciating moment. She longs for him to laugh at this suggestion and say that it wouldn't have mattered. Even if that was a lie, she needs to hear it. It would mean he loved her. And sometimes a lie can tell a bigger truth.

"I don't know what to say, Danit. I'm sorry you felt that way, I really am. But this is messed up. I need to be with someone who is honest. We're engaged. We're building a life together."

"I agree. That's fair. And that's why I am telling you now." She takes a pause. "But it works both ways."

"Meaning?"

"Meaning you haven't told me everything about Helena. Have you?" She waits for him to respond, to open up freely about what she has seen today on Helena's Facebook page. There has to be a reasonable explanation for her not looking pregnant, but she can't imagine what it is.

Nate frowns, shaking his head. "I'm sorry, Danit. I can't get into this right now. It's all too much. My dad murdered, my mom shot. There will be plenty of time to talk about Helena later."

"Of course," she says, her heart sinking.

"The flight to Saipan is what—twenty-four hours?" He offers

a weak smile, an effort she recognizes as an olive branch. "Trust me, huh?"

Danit pauses, a part of her burning to push harder, to force him to crack and tell her the truth. But the peacemaker in her prevails. He's right that she has to trust him. The alternative is too terrifying. She gets out of the car with Malcolm, grabbing the diaper bag and tossing it over her shoulder.

"I'll be back with the food soon," he says before driving away.

"Let's go, buddy," she says, reaching out her hand. She tries to give the little boy a genuine smile, but she feels like crying. Her insides feel like mush. That's the closest thing to a fight she's had with Nate so far, and she doesn't like it.

For the first time ever, she wonders how well she knows the man she is about to marry.

38

By the time Trey arrives at the police station, he feels like an entirely different guy from the Trey of this morning.

As soon as he left the house, he swung by an old friend's place to pick up some Desoxyn, which he ground up and immediately snorted. He didn't like the way his friend—his dealer, if he was being honest—kept calling it *meth*. It was a legit prescription. Not his, of course, but somebody's. And Trey doesn't consider it meth if a doctor can prescribe it.

With newfound energy coursing through his bloodstream, he hit Georgetown, picking up a pair of three-hundred-dollar kicks, rigid Japanese jeans, and a new watch. All of which he is wearing now.

It felt good to tap the Calhoun company credit card on the card reader, knowing there would not be an accountability meeting with his dad at the end of the month.

The reign of terror was over. And anyway, his parents owed him. They owed him two years of his life. They owed him his sense of self-respect, which they had smashed to pieces with their lies. The new clothes hardly made a dent in their debt to him.

"Here for an interview with Detective Washington." He raps his fingers on the bulletproof glass separating the officer behind the counter from the small waiting room, admiring his watch as he does so. She tells him to take a seat in one of the plastic molded chairs, but he's too wired, so he just paces back and forth until finally the detective appears.

"Trey, glad you're here. It's almost five and we were worried you might not show up at all." Washington holds open a door that leads to the back rooms. "Follow me, please."

"Sorry about this morning." Trey follows her down a brightly lit corridor. "Was a wee bit hungover. Plus, family. That's always tense. You know what I mean?"

Once inside the interview room, Detective Washington takes a seat at the table, which is the only furniture in the place, other than two chairs. A moment later, Officer Amatangelo steps into the room and pauses.

"Can we get you something?" he asks. "Maybe a cup of coffee or a soda?"

"Maybe herbal tea?" Washington asks.

Trey points a finger at her. "I get it. I'm a little wired, so you suggest herbal tea. You're funny."

Washington shakes her head at Amatangelo, who shuts the door and leans against it, his arms crossed over his chest.

"I'm glad you came in, Trey," Washington says. "We were curious about a few things, things we didn't really want to discuss in front of your family."

"Happy to help." Trey spreads his arms wide on the table. "I'm an open book."

"All right. Were you close with your father?"

"Close? I mean, we lived next door to each other. Can't get any closer than that." He grins.

"Uh-huh. Other people say there was tension between you two."

"Yeah, just normal stuff. He wanted me to be a certain kind of guy, you know, follow him into the family business or go into banking or something. I get it. He's old-school."

"But you wanted what?"

"I wanted to do something big, you know? Huge! And when you want to do something big, there's risk." He rubs his nose for a bit too long. "So yeah, I had some failures, but who didn't? Bill Gates, Steve Jobs, Elon Musk. They all failed."

"So you were a tech entrepreneur?"

"What? No. I was trying to get into entertainment. Adult entertainment." He waits a beat, but there is no change of expression on Washington's face. "Nothing gross. Just light kink. A subscription model. You know, you pay what, ten bucks a month, and you get personalized live streaming kink."

"Doesn't that already exist?" Amatangelo asks. "I think it's called OnlyFans."

Trey bobs his head up and down in agreement. "That's what you might think, and you would be mistaken. This would be a classy, primo service. We would vet our providers."

"Classy kink?" Washington raises an eyebrow.

"Exactly." Trey crosses his arms, satisfied.

"I imagine your parents didn't approve," Washington says.

"My mom never knew, thank God. And my dad, well, it's complicated. He came out a few times, met with my backers, saw the business plan. I mean, he didn't *love* it. But he didn't interfere."

"So what happened?" she asks. "Why did you come back to D.C.?"

"Lost an important backer. Things went south from there." Trey can sense a dark cloud threatening to descend upon him. "I was in a car accident. My parents brought me back here to recuperate."

Washington leans forward. "Must have been serious."

"Broke a couple of ribs. Nothing too bad. But I decided to, like, regroup, you know. I was partying pretty hard in LA, and I had run out of capital. So I came back to D.C. for a temporary reset."

Washington opens the folder in front of her. "Looks like you have quite the record, going back to when you were a student at Washington Prep."

"And when you were a student at Bethesda–Chevy Chase High School," Amatangelo says from behind him. "And when you were at Blackridge Military Academy in Pennsylvania."

"What's your point? That I knew how to have fun as a teen-ager? Check." He holds up one hand. "Guilty, Your Honor."

"I'm actually more interested in the series of arrests when you lived in California." Washington runs her finger down the paper as she reads. "Possession. Possession. Operating a vehicle under the influence. Possession. Public intoxication. Disorderly conduct."

"That last one wasn't my fault. This other guy started with me. That was dropped."

Washington looks up. "How did you manage to avoid any jail time?"

"What can I say? I was born lucky." He looks at his watch.

"New watch?"

"You like? Just got it this morning. Patek Philippe."

Washington takes Trey's wrist in her hand. "Mind if I have a look?"

"You know what they say, don't you? *You never actually own a Patek Philippe. You merely look after it for the next generation.*"

"Lefty?"

"Yeah." Trey tries to pull his arm free, but Washington holds tight, turning his arm so that the knuckles are facing her.

"What happened to your hand?"

Trey jerks back his hand. "Scraped it at the car dealer. Opening the hood of a Tesla can be a little tricky."

"Buying a Tesla, huh?"

"We all have to do our part for the environment, right?" Trey grins, but his heart is thwomping so loudly in his chest, it feels like it might crawl up his throat and pop out of his mouth. He has to get out of here. "We done?"

"One more thing. We checked and your father had a .22 Ruger registered to his name. That's the same caliber of bullet that killed him. We searched the house but couldn't find it. Any idea where it might be?"

"Yeah, no. I haven't seen that gun in a while."

"But you knew he owned it?"

"Sure, sure. He bought it a couple of years ago. For when he was out of town, so my mom would feel safe. You should ask her."

"We will, Trey. Thanks."

"Anything else?"

"That's all for now."

Back outside in the sunlight, Trey slips on his new sunglasses. All those goddamn questions. It's like they knew things, things they weren't telling him, but also weren't asking him. It was a total mind fuck. He flexes his fist. His red, raw knuckles glisten against his white skin like a neon sign in Vegas. What message did his knuckles telegraph to those cops?

Fear spreads through his guts, liquifying them, and for a moment, he worries he might soil himself right there in the parking lot of the Montgomery County Police Department.

Or maybe it's not fear at all. Maybe it's just all that meth.

39

Ginny can tell it is evening by the darkened windows, but the exact time eludes her. One more night in this godforsaken place. Every time she thinks about what's going on back at her house, she panics. Questions ping-pong around her head—will Renée complete all the tasks on the to-do list? Is Trey going off the deep end?

Thom was always so good at reining him in. Maybe he was too tough on the boys sometimes. That's why she was such a pushover. If Thom had been a little more sensitive, a little more understanding, then she wouldn't have had to overcompensate. Like when Trey was caught drinking and driving at the end of his junior year in high school and Thom grounded him for the whole summer. It was a brutal punishment for just one youthful error. All the poor boy could do was ride his bike to the club and come home. So when Thom went away on business, she said yes to a long weekend at Dewey Beach with his friends. She honestly didn't think Thom would ever find out. She shudders at the memory of his angry reaction.

The TV is on. She looks up, then blinks twice. No, she is not imagining it. It's her house with a reporter in front of it. And so many people in the background.

Murder in Somerwood, the crawl reads.

She turns up the volume. "—rocked this wealthy enclave. Police have no suspects at this time, but our sources say they are interviewing witnesses and family members and that it is too early in the investigation to speculate. However, that hasn't stopped dozens of citizen journalists from showing up at the scene and posting their theories about the crime online."

As she presses madly at the Off button, Ginny drops the remote. She yanks at the cord that is attached to the remote, but doing so causes the whole thing to get stuck in the hospital bed.

She presses the Call button. "Help!" she yells. "Help!"

A headshot of Thom appears on the screen.

"Don't look at me like that." Her dead husband's steely eyes glare at her from the TV, as if he is reaching out to her from beyond. She hears his voice, measured and cruel, whispering those words in her ear yesterday. "Help!" She presses the Call button again.

A nurse comes running in. "What in the world? Are you okay?"

Unable to speak, Ginny points to the TV. The nurse looks up to see a commercial for antacid.

"Now, now, Ms. Calhoun. You know the remote is right here." The nurse untangles the long, cabled remote that is dangling by the side of the bed and places it on the table. "The Call button is for emergencies." She lifts Ginny's arm and places two fingers on the inside of her wrist. "Goodness, your pulse is racing!"

"Off." Ginny lifts her free hand toward the TV as if she has magic powers in her fingers. "Off!"

"You want it off? Okay, okay." The nurse shuts it off. "Here, have a sip of water."

Ginny gulps it down. Her breathing steadies.

"Good girl. Now, let's get you ready for bed. Shall we use the bathroom one more time?" The nurse helps Ginny, whose injured leg prevents her from walking on her own, into the bathroom. How she detests being helped onto and off the toilet. How humiliating to be called "good girl" every time she accomplishes the most basic task. The nurse takes her back to the bed and tucks her in. A low-level fury toward the nurse threatens to erupt, but

Ginny tamps it down. She knows it's not wise to anger a caretaker.

"Have you heard the good news?" the nurse asks. "The doctor says if everything stays the same overnight, it looks like you'll be going home tomorrow."

Ginny smiles and lays her head back. "Good. Fine." She's found her voice.

"I'll let you rest now," the nurse says and leaves the darkened room.

Ginny closes her eyes. She'll need the rest. Tomorrow the hard work will begin.

*   *   *

Shawna pulls into the parking lot of her apartment complex. All she wants is to change out of the clothes that she's been wearing since yesterday, take a warm shower, and crawl into her own bed.

But as she drives through the lot, she spies a dark sedan parked in the handicap spot in front of her building. Shawna slows—no stickers or decals are visible on the sedan, and the front of the car sports an extra protective bumper. A chill runs through her. It's an unmarked police car, she is sure.

They found the shirt with the blood.

Trey kicked her out of the house around four in the morning, and she spent the rest of the night sleeping in her car at the far edge of a Home Depot parking lot, if you could call it sleeping. She should have been knocked out cold—she and Trey finished a bottle of bourbon between them, just like the old days—but instead, her mind was racing, trying to reconcile what she had witnessed at the Calhouns' party with what Trey told her.

The Calhouns were one twisted family.

Trey swore up and down he had nothing to do with his dad's death, but Shawna knows what she saw. The blind rage that overtook him when he followed her into the study to talk to Thom, and the violence that ensued. Not that she blamed him.

What kind of parents tell their son he killed someone? Her own mom and dad might not win any parenting awards, but what Ginny and Thom did was sadistic.

But she knows exactly what kind. Thom and Ginny Calhoun. They used her and the car accident as an excuse to take control of Trey's life. It was all he could talk about last night, ranting and raving at the injustice.

He seemed less relieved that she was actually alive, that she had survived the crash with only superficial injuries, than angry at his parents. Which sort of miffed her. But she wasn't a real person to Trey. Or to Thom or Ginny. She was a chess piece to be moved about.

She didn't tell Trey the whole truth—he might have really lost it if he knew everything. And she was pretty sure there would be no payout if she did spill. She told him that his parents had paid her off to disappear, and now she was back for more money.

And he bought it.

She spent the day bouncing between Dunkin' and the public library in downtown Rockville, where she used the computer to read and watch everything she could about the murder investigation. So far, it didn't look like they had much. But she knew that meant nothing.

Shawna continues through the parking lot as it loops around behind her building, dead-ending where the garbage dumpsters are. The spots here are her least favorite, thanks to the rats and raccoons, but her car will be hidden from view. She parks and gets out.

Pulling her hood over her head, she jams her hands in the front pocket and walks back to where she saw the police car. A row of trees serves as a buffer between the lot and a medical office park next door. It's no forest, but there is enough cover that she can find a spot among the overgrown brush and trees to duck behind. Shawna crouches on her haunches and takes out her vape pen. She's been hitting the pen so much lately, she can barely taste the apple flavor anymore. From here, she has a good view of both the car and the external stairs that lead up to her apartment.

She does not have to wait long. Soon, the door to her apartment opens, and a woman and a man leave. As they descend the stairs, she recognizes the woman as the police officer who interviewed her last night at the Calhouns.

Her chest tightens.

This is no routine visit. Her roommate, Kaycee, appears at the door in a bathrobe. *Lazy bitch*, Shawna thinks. Never gets up before 2:00 p.m. No wonder she can't hold a job.

After the police drive away, Shawna shoves her vape pen into her pocket, hunches her shoulders, and walks across the parking lot to the stairs, taking them two at a time. As soon as she lets herself in the apartment, Kaycee is in her face.

"What the hell is going on, Shawna? The police were just here. They say you're involved in a murder. What the actual?"

Shawna turns her head away from the blast of bad breath that accompanies her roommate's diatribe.

"I can explain. I was working a party—"

"I know all about it. The Calhoun family in Chevy Chase. It's all over social media, Shawna. I told them everything I knew." She says this in a triumphant tone, then crosses her arms.

"What's that supposed to mean?"

"About the photos I saw on your phone? Of their house? Of that woman who was shot and her husband?"

"Why did you do that?"

"Why? Because I don't want to be on the wrong side of the police. You're selfish and dumb. You know Alejandro is undocumented. He could lose his job, his scholarship. He could be deported because of you, Shawna."

"This has nothing to do with Alejandro. He doesn't even live here."

"And neither do you." She turns and walks into Shawna's bedroom. Shawna rushes after her. Her bedroom is in chaos. On the floor lies a large black garbage bag stuffed with her things.

"When did you do this?"

"As soon as I saw the murder house on TV. I did a little googling about you. I should have done it before I let you move in, *Naughty Schoolgirl*."

"That was a job." Shawna squares her shoulders. "It was legal. I'm not embarrassed."

"Well, you should be. And if it was so great stripping online, why did you move out here and start catering? Pretty suspicious, if you ask me. Were you involved with that murder?" Kaycee holds up a hand. "No, wait. Don't answer that. I don't want to know. Just leave."

"You can't kick me out."

"Yup. I can. As of right now. Get your shit and go. I already told Alejandro he could move in. He's going to use your room as a recording studio."

"So that's what this is about. Your boyfriend is moving in. Just let me stay one more night. Then I promise I'll leave."

"I'm gonna take a shower. And if you're still here when I get out, I'm calling the cops. Keys, please?" She holds out an open hand.

Shawna pulls her keys out, slips the apartment key off the ring, and places it in Kaycee's palm. She has no other choice.

Shawna finds her one suitcase in the closet and pulls it out, then packs it full. As she drags the garbage bag and the suitcase out onto the landing, she can hear the shower running. She pauses to catch her breath before reentering the apartment to turn the sink on full blast.

She hears Kaycee shriek from the bathroom. The shower pressure drops dramatically whenever someone is using the kitchen sink. Shawna leaves it running and shuts the apartment door behind her. Immature? Maybe. Satisfying? Definitely.

She peers over the railing to make sure no other police car has shown up while she was inside. When she is confident that it's all clear, she lugs her things to her car before tossing them in the trunk.

She is officially homeless.

Where is she supposed to go now?

All the way back home, empty-handed? Hell, no.

Not after what she's been through.

She's not going home without something to show for all this.

Inside her car, she takes out her phone. Yes, the police are looking for her. But maybe she can use that as leverage. She thinks of her metaphorical poker hand. Maybe last night gave her one more card to play. Thinking of it like that lifts her spirits a little.

The police are looking for me, she could say.

And the things she could tell them. She could even get a lawyer, go on one of those cable shows, tell her story.

She dials a number.

"Yeah, this is Shawna. The police were at my apartment, and I need a place to stay. Tonight."

She sucks in her breath at the response.

"Yeah, well, actually, it is your problem," Shawna replies. "And if you don't help me, I'm gonna make it an even bigger one."

40

"Does the TV have to be so loud?" Trey is sprawled on an enormous sectional, head pounding, as a human Ken doll pontificates about his father's murder on the television. Everyone is gathered this morning at Ellie Grace and Zak's, at Ellie Grace's insistence. Trey estimates the screen is at least five feet wide, which makes each tooth on this so-called journalist the size of a slat on a white picket fence. "If I am going to be forced to watch this, I'll need more coffee." He holds out his mug, but no one comes to take it. "This reminds me of how at Guantanamo they would lock prisoners into wooden boxes and blast 'Night Fever' by the Bee Gees night after night."

"Oh, please." Ellie Grace picks up the remote control and lowers the volume a few notches, although not as far as Trey would like. "Any other complaints?"

"Coffee." His sister grabs the cup from his hand and passes it to Danit, who then hands it to Nate, who is standing in the adjacent kitchen. "Don't pretend you don't like waiting on me." He can still hear that smarmy, perma-tan anchor intoning about *what could have gone wrong in Chevy Chase* and the *murder that rocked this upscale community*.

"Here's your coffee. Two sugars, right?" Nate asks, walking over and handing it to him. "Please, don't get up."

"With ambassadors, journalists, and White House administration higher-ups for neighbors"—the talking head, Hunter Blake, punches each word for emphasis—"the Somerwood neighborhood is an unlikely target for this kind of brutal violence—"

"Turn it off, Smelly!"

"Fine." His sister mutes the TV just as Blake's robotically handsome face is replaced by a picture of their house from the night of the murder, police wrapping yellow crime-scene tape across one side of the lawn. Is this why she came to get him at the crack of dawn this morning? So he could lie on her sofa and watch cable TV? If it weren't for Ellie Grace, he would still be asleep in his warm bed. But she let herself into his house at 7:00 a.m. and dribbled ice water on his face until he got up.

Zak walks to the window and looks out at the front yard. "You're not going to believe this, but there are two girls outside, and one of them is filming the other in front of the house."

Ellie Grace rushes to the window. "What? They must have followed us here when I picked up Trey."

"You think they followed you from Somerwood?" Nate asks.

"I'm sure of it. When I went to get Trey, there were a bunch of losers just camped out in front of Mom's house. They must have seen us leave and followed us." She turns back to the room. "As we were driving away, I saw a neighbor arguing with one of them who had blocked his driveway. He was yelling, *It's Monday morning! I have to get to work!*"

"Thank God none of us work," Trey says.

"For your information, I work," Ellie Grace says.

"Why are we here?" Trey asks.

"Because we need to be more proactive. Zak and I had a very unpleasant experience at the police station yesterday. I think as a family we ought to hire a lawyer and maybe a PR person," Ellie Grace says. "I mean, look—Hunter Blake has been talking about us on his show all morning. And don't get me started on social media. People want to know why I haven't put out a statement. They think it looks suspicious."

"Meaning?" Nate asks as he settles into the end seat of the L-shaped sectional.

"Meaning I don't know! Meaning that they think I'm involved, or covering for someone, I guess."

"Are we seriously making this decision based on what your followers on Instagram are posting?" Nate asks. "That's not real life."

"Actually, it is real life, Nate. Maybe you don't realize it, but this is how I make my living."

"Am I going to have to separate you two?" Trey asks. He's not *not* enjoying this. It's rare to see a family conflict that isn't centered on him and his bad behavior. "So if it's not Smelly, or you, or me, who do we think did this? I think it was Professor Plum with the candlestick."

"Not everything is a joke, Trey," Nate says, exhaustion in his voice.

But Nate's obvious weariness just spurs his brother on. Trey peers up at everyone in the room and then fixes his gaze on Danit. "In the movies, the nanny is always a psychopath." Danit pauses in the middle of biting her blueberry muffin, crumbs tumbling down her chin to her lap. She looks so forlorn that Trey quickly adds, "I'm kidding."

"That's not funny," Nate says.

Nothing is funny to his brother anymore, Trey thinks. "Sorry I'm not as mature as you. I'm just trying to lighten the mood."

"Well, don't."

"Actually, there was an interesting development, right, Nate?" Danit asks. "Can we tell them about the shirt?"

"Shirt?" Ellie Grace squawks. "What shirt?"

"Danit found a shirt upstairs, with blood on it," Nate says, and Danit proceeds to fill them in on all the details.

"I know I shouldn't have moved it," she says. "That was dumb. I just panicked."

"I would, too." Ellie Grace smiles at her.

"What does it mean?" Zak asks.

"It means whoever did this was on the catering staff. That's what it means." Ellie Grace crosses her arms over her chest as if she's settled it for once and for all. "I knew it was going to be someone like that. Someone jealous of what we have."

Trey has a pretty good guess of who that shirt belongs to, but he has no desire to place himself in his father's study moments before he was shot. Not even with his siblings. Just then, Malcolm runs babbling toward where he is lying on the sofa and scrambles onto his chest, erupting in giggles.

"Hey, buddy," Trey says, helping the boy up.

"I can take him if he's bothering you," Nate says, starting to rise.

Trey bristles. Is he such a degenerate that he can't be allowed to touch his nephew? "I can handle a kid for two minutes. I'm not going to break him."

"So they finally have a lead." Ellie Grace taps her lips with one manicured finger, the pale blue nail as perfect as a Jordan almond. "Maybe we can get this info out somehow. Like not directly, but if we hire someone who's really good at PR, they can use this to help direct attention away from us."

"I'm pretty sure that would fall under the heading of impeding an investigation," Trey says. But his sister makes a good point. A little misdirection might be a good thing. "I think I heard somewhere that the chances of solving a murder are cut in half if a suspect isn't found within the first forty-eight hours."

The room is silent for a moment except for Malcolm, who holds his hands in the air and calls out, "Dada, dooce. Dooce."

Nate stands up. "You want some juice, Malcolm?" Malcolm nods, sliding off Trey and onto the floor, where he toddles after Nate.

"I think I might have a lead," Nate says when he returns from the kitchen.

"A lead?" Trey pulls himself up on one elbow. "Okay, Columbo."

"So, it looks like Dad might have been having an affair."

"Not this again!" Ellie Grace looks up from her phone. "How is this relevant? Do you have any idea how this would make Mommy feel if she knew about this? I mean, the man is dead. Let sleeping dogs lie."

"Ellie Grace, you have to face facts," Nate says. "We can't be in denial. This woman may have been involved."

"Why do you say that?"

"When I was at the office yesterday, Fabiola mentioned it. She said the office gossip was that he had a history of carrying on with some of the female employees."

"So what's your theory?" Ellie Grace says.

"I don't know," Nate responds. "This woman wanted more? Maybe she wanted Dad to leave Mom—"

"He would never do that," Ellie Grace interjects.

"Fine. But maybe that's what she wanted. Maybe whoever she was, she came to the party to push the issue, and when he rebuffed her, she shot him in a jealous rage. And Mom came in, and she shot her, too."

"It doesn't add up." Ellie Grace cocks her head to one side. "And I don't see what this has to do with the bloody shirt that Danit found. I think you're barking up the wrong tree."

"Maybe you're right. But there could be a perfectly logical explanation for that shirt. It doesn't prove anything. We have to keep our minds open," Nate says. "I'm going to Dad's assistant's house and getting his agenda. There may be some answers there."

"What? When are you going?" Ellie Grace sits up straight.

"Why do you always sound so irritated?" Trey asks.

"Because we're supposed to pick Mom up from the hospital, Trey. We have a schedule."

"I'll be back in time," Nate says. "This won't take more than an hour, two tops. She lives out in Potomac." He starts to gather his things.

"I'll go with you," Danit says.

It takes about ten minutes for Danit, Malcolm, and Nate to pack up everything and get out the door, and once they are gone, Ellie Grace lets out a low groan.

"He'd better make it back in time to go to the hospital," she says, scrolling through her phone. "I just know there's going to be press. It's going to look weird if one of her sons isn't there."

"Both her sons," Trey says.

Ellie Grace whips her head up. "What? You're not going?"

"I'm not going."

"You have to go."

"No. I don't." Trey swings his legs around so he is sitting up. That second cup of coffee is kicking in. "Now that Dad is dead, I don't have to do anything anymore."

"How can you be so cold? He was your father. He loved you."

"Because I hated him," he says in a quiet voice.

"Don't say that, Trey." Ellie Grace comes and sits beside him. "I know he could be tough on you. He was tough on all of us. But you loved him."

"I used to. Even when he told me what a screwup I was. I wanted to please him and make him proud. I thought, *Achieve this one thing and Dad will love me.* But it turns out I'm not great at achieving things."

"Dad was complicated. He was from a different generation. But that doesn't mean he didn't love us," Ellie Grace says, nudging Trey a little with her shoulder. "And that you didn't love him."

"Don't tell me what I feel." Something inside Trey starts to unfold, something dark and urgent. "You don't know what he did."

He sees the look of fear on Ellie Grace's face. She doesn't want to know, he thinks. She'd rather go on believing their family is as perfect as those Christmas cards they send out, as flawless as her Instagram photos. He almost feels sorry for her. For what he is about to tell her.

"So what did he do that was so terrible?" she asks in a quaking voice.

"What did he do? You wouldn't even believe me if I told you."

"Try me," she says.

"Remember that car accident I was in two years ago—in California?" He stares at his hands, unable to look up. He's never told this story out loud to anyone.

"Of course," Ellie Grace says in a soft voice. "That's when you came back to D.C."

"I didn't have a choice. They transported me back while I was still heavily medicated. I didn't want to come back. There was a girl in the car with me; her name was Shawna." He catches himself, remembering that Shawna is alive. "*Is* Shawna. We worked together." He pauses here. He doesn't go into what they were working on. He doubts his sister would approve of his adult-entertainment subscription idea. "We were together that night. Dad was in LA, actually, and Shawna and I were heading down to Malibu to meet him for a late dinner. I was fried out of my mind when I crashed the car. Broke three ribs, had a concussion. And Shawna? She didn't make it. She died."

Ellie Grace's sharp intake of breath is the only reaction.

"That's what Mom and Dad told me, at least. They said if I stayed in California, I could be arrested and charged in her death."

"Oh my God, Trey. You killed a girl?"

"That's what I was told. And it's what I thought for a long time. Two years. Until yesterday. When I saw Shawna at the party."

"You saw her here?" Ellie Grace asks, her face ashen. "At our house? I'm so confused."

"She wasn't dead, after all. Dad had paid her off to go away two years ago, and she came back for more money." He doesn't try to keep the bitterness out of his voice. He almost adds, *In fact, I'm pretty sure that's her shirt that Danit found*, but he keeps his mouth shut. He wants to keep his sister's focus on him. He's the victim here.

"That's all she said?" Ellie Grace asks. "That she was here for more money?"

"Forget the money," Trey says, getting angry. "Do you hear what I'm saying? They lied to me and told me I killed someone! I lived with that guilt for two years, and it was all lies! What kind of people do that to their kids?" He searches his sister's face, but there are no answers there. Just shock. "So, no, I'm not going to play the role of the perfect son for your photo op, Ellie Grace. And yeah, I do mean it when I say I hated Dad." He waits, but for once she doesn't try to argue him out of his feelings. "I hated him, and I'm glad he's dead!"

Ellie Grace wraps her arm over his shoulder. "I'm sorry that happened to you," she says quietly. "You didn't deserve that."

Trey puts his head in his hands as he is convulsed by sadness. He loved his dad. He hated his dad. He was a total screwup. He was a victim of other people's manipulations. He had everything he could materially want. He was miserable, a nobody. The tears come fast and hot, the waves of shame crashing against the grief and anger. Ellie Grace pulls him closer.

"Poor Trey, it's okay. Let it out." He allows himself to be taken into his sister's embrace, and he weeps.

41

Shawna wakes to a vibrating phone. She lets the call go to voice mail and tries to fall back asleep, but she can't. She's in limbo, waiting for a payout that might not happen.

Every day she stays in the D.C. area she risks getting dragged into the Calhoun murder investigation. While she prides herself on bending the truth to get what she wants, she's never had to lie to the police. And she doesn't want to have to start now—even if she has one million reasons to do so.

Shawna stretches in the immense bed, taking in the vaulted ceiling, the large windows, and the pale gray walls with not a single scuff mark or nail hole, so unlike the mobile homes, rentals, and crappy apartments she's lived in her whole life. As she drove out here last night on winding roads, first passing a horse farm and then a nature preserve, it occurred to her that she might be entering a trap. That suspicion was only reinforced when she turned into Fox Grove Homes, a Calhoun development that seemed deserted. She almost turned back.

Her heart was racing as she drove deeper into the private neighborhood, passing large houses in various states of construction, but the model house was just as promised, at the end of a cul-de-sac and fully furnished.

It wasn't a trap, after all. The Calhouns clearly wanted to keep her happy.

She grabs her phone to check her voice mail. The message is from Sunniva at Capitol Catering. "I have your check. Come by and pick it up today, or I can pop it in the mail."

Mailing it won't work, Shawna thinks. Not while she's on her former roommate Kaycee's shit list. She'll have to pick it up.

After a quick shower, she rummages through the black garbage bag filled with her clothes and grabs a T-shirt and jeans. Feeling like Scarlett O'Hara, she waltzes down the wide spiral staircase, basking in the reflective glow of the crystal chandelier that hangs above. In the large kitchen, Shawna runs her hand across the sleek glass induction cooktop, opening the Sub-Zero fridge, pleased to find it packed with some basics like yogurt and juice. A bowl of fresh fruit sits on the marble counter, and she takes a bite of an apple before returning it to the bowl.

It looked perfect enough, but the flesh is mealy.

Instead, she decides to make coffee and wanders over to the dedicated coffee and tea station, complete with a Nespresso machine, an instant hot-water spigot, and ten ceramic mugs dangling from little hooks.

This is what it's like to be rich, she thinks. And any doubts about her plan vanish. She deserves this. She's had some terrible experiences in life, some too horrible even to think about, and the universe owes her. As she pops a pod into the coffee maker, scattered memories swirl around her like debris picked up by the wind.

Her parents' divorce when she was six.

Her dad's descent into drug addiction.

Failing out of school and no one caring. Her guidance counselor advising her to get a job at the Walmart twenty miles away because she was *not college material*.

Her mother's carousel of boyfriends. The best ones just mooched off her mom. The worst one put her mom in the hospital with a broken jaw.

The impulsive decision to move to LA to try to break into the entertainment industry, which instead left her stuck in a moldy apartment, broke. The only job she could get, the only decent-paying job, was as a topless waitress at a sports bar called Girls & Grills. No one looked twice when she gave them her sister's ID, even though she obviously wasn't twenty-one. No one ever said, *Hey, shouldn't you be in school, getting your diploma?* It was there she learned she could make hundreds a day streaming herself on OnlyFans. She had a niche—Naughty Schoolgirl. She can't blame the world. It was her choice.

When Trey reached out to her with his business idea—OnlyFans but more elite, classier, *more money*, she could have said no. She had enough income by then to enroll in community college, get a nursing degree like her sister. She thought about it once or twice—but Trey's enthusiasm was contagious. And when she met Trey's dad, she knew there was real money there.

Shawna takes her coffee, sits down at the kitchen table, and looks out the large window at the empty street. No one lives here now, but in a year, it will be filled with rich people. Why shouldn't she be one of the people who gets to live in a house like this? The Calhouns aren't better than she is. In fact, despite their outward appearances, they are awful.

Her mother, her sister, her friends back in Oregon. They struggled so hard and got nothing for it. Last year, her sister was diagnosed with lupus. She is probably going to have to go on disability.

Shawna looks down at her arm. In a T-shirt, most of her sleeve tattoo is visible—the twining roses representing the sweetness of life, the thorns signifying the pain she has endured. It took four sessions, eight hundred dollars, and hours of her life, but the artist achieved what she asked—a beautiful transformation of the ugly red scars from the car accident.

The physical wounds, at least, are hidden.

Shawna still doesn't recall the details of the accident. She only remembers partying with Trey and then waking up in a private hospital with Trey's dad by her side. But her memory of what happened in the following months is clear. And if she ever forgets, she has the document that Thomas Calhoun made her sign. Not that it's legally binding anymore.

She goes out to the attached garage, where her Ford Fiesta sat overnight, tucked out of sight. That was one of the requirements of staying here.

Don't let anyone see you.

Ridiculous, she thinks as she backs out onto the street—there's not another car or person in sight. But she understands the caution. And she's happy to hole up in that beautiful house until the money comes through. Then she'll put D.C. in the rearview mirror. Maybe try for Austin. She has a friend there.

Twenty minutes later, on the eastern side of the county, after navigating a sloping, pothole-riddled driveway leading to an industrial office park, Shawna pulls up in front of a squat brick building with a small sign reading *Capitol Catering*.

When she yanks open the business's glass door, nothing in the small front room seems to indicate the headquarters of a catering company except the overpowering scent of sautéing garlic. She peers past the dingy white counter and a fridge filled with bottled water, glimpsing a large kitchen through a porthole in the swinging door.

Shawna rings an old-fashioned silver bell on the counter. In a moment, a burly man with a red beard barges through the door, wiping his hands on a pristine white apron. He has a tattoo of a snake wrapping itself around his neck, like a boa constrictor ready to squeeze.

"Nice tat," she says, wondering how Sunniva feels about it.

He looks at her arm. "You, too. What can I do you for?"

"I'm here to pick up my check. Sunniva called."

The man grunts. "She's in the back. Follow me."

He turns and pushes through the door, which swings shut after him. Shawna hustles to catch up, following him as he weaves through the large industrial kitchen, where men and women in white aprons rush between ovens and metal tables. Music blares from speakers, punctuated by the sounds of chopping, whirring, and blending. When they arrive at the rear of the building, her guide stops before a small office with an open door.

"Hey, boss, somebody's here for a check."

Shawna peers inside at Sunniva, who is tending to a pile of papers, muttering to herself.

Sunniva curses loudly and straightens up, recognition crossing her face. "Tiny, watch the croissants. Don't let them burn."

"Sure thing, boss," Tiny says, backing away, leaving the two women alone.

"Hi. Shawna, right? Hold on, lemme send this text." Sunniva taps at her phone before sticking it in her back pocket. "We have one hundred and twenty mini ham-and-cheese croissant sandwiches to make by five o'clock."

"That's a lot."

"It's a crazy week. Now let me see where I put your check."

Someone turns up the music in the kitchen, and the thumping bass makes the entire office vibrate.

Shawna suppresses a sigh of annoyance. The room is chaotic, papers everywhere. She hopes this won't take too long.

"This Calhoun thing has been terrible for my business. I've been catering the cherry blossom party for years. It rarely changes. This year, she wanted figs wrapped in prosciutto instead of oysters. People are very concerned about oysters. You hear about that man who had oysters at a Bethesda restaurant and landed in the hospital with a flesh-eating disease?" She looks up at Shawna and shudders. "The Chesapeake Bay is warming, and now oysters are off the menu for half my clients. Ahh, here it is." She holds up a white envelope.

Shawna extends her hand. "I'll take that."

She slips the envelope into her pocket and turns to go. But when she opens the door, a short uniformed police officer is standing there.

"Shawna Douglas? I'm gonna need you to come down to the station for questioning in the murder of Thomas Calhoun and the attempted murder of Virginia Calhoun."

42

After about fifteen minutes of driving, Danit and Nate find themselves in a part of the county known for large estates that look like mash-ups of French châteaus and Disney castles. From the back seat, Malcolm lets out a steady stream of nonsense mixed with nursery rhymes. "Twinka, twinka, lil lamb . . ."

Danit lets out a low whistle as they pass an immense mansion. "That looks like the castle in *Beauty and the Beast*."

Nate stares straight ahead, silent, working his jaw. He's been like this on the whole drive. She figures he is anxious about getting his hands on his father's agenda and learning the truth about whether his father was cheating on his mother. But all Danit can think about is that photo of Helena and her washboard abs. Oh, how she wishes she could just compartmentalize it like Nate wants her to. Pack it up in a shoebox and stick it in the back closet of her mind, to be opened at some later date.

But her brain doesn't work that way. She was up half the night, tossing and turning, imagining increasingly elaborate and fantastical reasons that Helena might not have been showing a pregnancy. The front-runner was that they had the baby by surrogacy, that Helena never really wanted a kid, and when Malcolm was born and the reality of it hit home, she left. It made enough sense to Danit at four in the morning that she was able to fall asleep, but now on this drive in the bright light of day, it seems farfetched.

"Nate?" she asks. The silence between them feels oppressive. "Honey, do you want to talk?"

"Huh?" He glances at her. "What was that?"

"I asked if you wanted to talk." She glances in the rearview mirror at Malcolm. "Actually, I want to talk." She swallows down what feels like a giant lump in her throat. Trusting Nate doesn't just mean following his lead blindly, it also means that he will allow her to voice her concerns and to ask questions. "I want to talk about Helena."

The statement hangs in the air for a moment, and she wonders if she has made a terrible mistake. Men are not her area of expertise. She never had a father, and while her mother had boyfriends over the years, there was never anyone serious. No brothers, no uncles. The way a man's mind worked was a mystery to her. She and her mother had communicated constantly, sharing every little thought no matter how mundane. Same with Charmaine. But her relationship with Nate is so different. There was so much unsaid. Has she violated some unspoken arrangement by bringing up Helena after he asked her not to?

"You're right," he says.

Danit tries to hide her surprise. This was not the answer she was expecting.

"I need to tell you something, and you're not going to like it." Danit's stomach clenches. "Oh God, what?"

He gives her a tight smile. "I love you. I want to marry you, but I screwed up. I didn't tell you the whole truth about Helena."

"All right. Tell me now," she says, suddenly afraid to hear what he has to say. What if it changes everything? Her whole body is on edge. For a while, she's been hungry for the whole truth, but now that it is about to be revealed, she wants to run and hide. Go back to when the specter of Helena didn't exist, those first blissful months with Nate and Malcolm. That first Friday he asked her out, at the end of a long week. "What are you up to this weekend?" They picnicked at Glass Beach, spending an overcast afternoon trying to keep Malcolm from swallowing the tiny blue and green glass stones. She still kept a small jar of them to remind her of that day. She knew then that she had found the thing that would fill the void her mother's death had left. An instant family. "I'm sorry I've been pushing you about Helena. There's so much going on with you. I trust you. I know you'll tell me when you're ready."

"I'm not sure I'll ever be ready, but . . ." He shakes his head. "I really owe you an explanation. Plus, I need to tell someone."

Danit laughs nervously. "Gee, I don't know if I want to hear this."

Nate pulls the car over into a small dirt lot that has a trailhead leading into the woods.

"What are we doing?" Danit asks. "I know we're not going hiking."

Nate smiles, and Danit's heart flutters. "No. Just wanted to give you my full attention."

Danit peeks back at Malcolm, whose head is lolled to one side, mouth wide open. "Well, you've got it."

"Here goes." Nate puts his hands on the steering wheel and exhales. "Two years ago, I was in an unhappy marriage. Looking back, it was obvious we weren't a good match, but at the time, I still thought—I don't know what I thought. I didn't want to have been wrong. I didn't want to look like an idiot, if you want to know the truth. Divorcing after two years? I had never failed at anything. I knew how my parents would take it."

"I'm sure that was tough," Danit says, feeling a mix of guilt and relief that Nate's marriage to Helena never really worked. While that's what she always wanted to hear, that he wasn't happy with Helena, she knows it's her insecurity speaking. It should be okay that he loved other people before her. He's with her now, and that's what counts. "So what happened?"

"I wanted kids, she didn't. She wanted to make partner at the law firm she was working at in San Francisco and did not want to take the time off. And honestly, she was really worried about what it would do to her body. She's an athlete. A runner."

Danit nods as if this is news to her.

"I suggested adopting, but she had loads of reasons why we couldn't do that, which I now know were all bullshit. But then, everything changed."

"I don't follow."

"A few months after Trey had his car accident, my mother came to see me about a *very delicate matter*." He makes quotation marks with his fingers when he says those last words. "At the time, I had started working at the Noyo Center for Marine Science and was renting a house nearby during the week, returning to San Francisco on the weekends."

"That can't have been easy on the marriage," Danit says, trying to sound neutral. But she hates the mental image of them reuniting in the city after a week apart. If it were her and Nate, they'd tumble into bed and only come up for air to feed Malcolm.

"No, it wasn't. I remember exactly when my mom visited. It was early October. We were getting ready for the whale migration from Baja that starts in November, doing all kinds of prep. I didn't really have time, but she said it was urgent."

"What did your mom want?"

"She had a newborn baby with her." He looks over his shoulder at Malcolm and smiles. "She said that Trey had gotten some girl pregnant in LA. That the girl was—how did my mom put it? In the adult entertainment field."

"Aha. She must have loved that."

"Exactly. And that the girl had threatened to put the baby up for adoption, so my mother had to step in."

"Oh my God. Did Trey know?"

He shakes his head. "No. The way my mom described it, the girl had reached out to my parents and told them she was planning to essentially sell the baby to the highest bidder. She told my parents that there was a couple in Los Angeles who were willing to pay a lot of money. At that point, they had moved Trey back here and he was recovering from his injuries. They made it sound like his drug use had been pretty bad. I remember my mom saying, 'He is not a father, can never be a father.'"

Danit feels as if someone has struck her with a spell and turned her to stone. Her chest is tight, and her breaths are shallow. She can see where this is going, but at the same time, she can't believe it. "Nate, are you saying that Malcolm's—"

"My dad flew out there," he says. "Got a paternity test done. You can do that before the baby is born, did you know that?"

She shakes her head silently. She doesn't want to interrupt and break his momentum. He has to tell this story his way, in his time, so she keeps her mouth closed even though she wants to interrupt with questions.

"Well, you can, and the test showed it was Trey's. My mother asked me if Helena and I wanted to adopt the baby. I mean, she basically put Malcolm in my lap. She said she and my dad were too old. And that Dad was dead set against it. He didn't care what happened to the baby, but my mother couldn't stand the thought of her grandchild being raised by strangers. I immediately said yes."

"Did she ask Ellie Grace?"

Nate sighs. "No. Ellie Grace wasn't with Zak yet. But I think the real reason they didn't want to ask her was it would look bad. Single mother, not married? Not the Calhoun style. My being in California worked perfectly."

"So Malcolm is Trey's." This comes out as a statement, not a question.

His dark eyes flash. "No. Malcolm is mine. But yes, Trey is the biological father, if that's what you meant."

"It is what I meant. Was he all right with this?"

"He doesn't know. He never knew. The messed-up part? The condition of taking Malcolm was that I could never tell Trey the truth."

Danit presses her lips together so tightly they hurt. *There is no one messed-up part*, she wants to scream. *The whole thing is insane.*

How could her Nate, the sweet man she fell in love with, who rinsed out Ziploc baggies to reuse them, how could that conscientious guy have been a part of this?

"I know how it sounds. But they wanted him to focus on getting sober and getting his life in order. So I agreed. I mean, look at him, Danit. He can't raise a kid!" He massages his forehead. "It sounds like an excuse, doesn't it? It was. I was selfish. I wanted Malcolm."

"He deserves to know that Malcolm is his son." She glances at the back seat, where Malcolm is still asleep. She understands why Nate would have wanted him so badly that he lied. After all, she wanted Nate and Malcolm so much that she lied to them. "Being a parent can change you. It might have changed Trey."

"It might not have."

"True, but he should at least know the truth."

He nods. "I know. You're right. I am going to tell him. I swear, before we leave."

"So what happened when you told Helena that you wanted to adopt Malcolm?"

"She was furious. She gave me an ultimatum. Malcolm or her. It was a pretty easy choice."

He smiles that amazing smile, and she feels an overwhelming love for this man who loved that little baby so much he was willing to end his marriage. Her earlier doubts recede. She can't help but feel it was all fated—Nate adopting Malcolm, divorcing Helena, and Danit meeting him. But can something beautiful be born out of so many lies?

Nate's phone buzzes in the console between them. "It's Ellie Grace," he says, glancing at the screen. "She wants me at the hospital at noon." She can see his face rearrange itself as he starts the car. Back to reality. His father was murdered, and his mother is in the hospital.

"Do we still have time to get the calendar from your dad's assistant?"

"Yeah," Nate says, pulling back onto the road. "I have to do it. I need to see that calendar."

They drive along in silence for a few minutes as Danit thinks about what he's told her. She is stunned by the depth of lies and manipulations in the Calhoun family. She had naively thought that because they were so rich and good-looking and successful that they had life figured out. But they had problems like everyone else, and they had an outsize sense of entitlement that they shouldn't have. And they had the kind of money that can make those problems go away. At least for a while.

Danit glances at Nate's profile. Nate was different, she thinks. He got sucked into their vortex, but for a good reason. And he knows what he did was wrong. "I'm glad you told me," she says, squeezing his hand.

He gives her a quick smile. "I wouldn't blame you if this was a deal-breaker for you. I mean, this is a pretty big crack in our family's perfect façade."

"Everything has a crack; that's where the light gets in," she says.

"I like that."

"Can't take credit for it. I'm paraphrasing Leonard Cohen," Danit says. "But we have to tell Trey. It's the only way we can start our life together. With no more secrets."

"I agree," Nate says. "Just promise me you'll let me tell him?"

"Of course."

"This is it," he says as they slow down, turning onto a driveway bordered by an eight-foot hedge. As the house comes into view, Danit spots a pool, a two-story pool house, and tennis courts.

"Wow. Pretty fancy for an executive assistant."

"Well, this is weird," Nate says, parking the car next to a wooden stake sticking out of the ground with a sign that reads *Calhoun Development Group*.

Nate gets out and unbuckles Malcolm from the car. Together,

the three of them take the wide steps that lead from the gravel driveway up to the portico.

"Here goes nothing." Nate presses a bell whose chime echoes through the house. Soon one of the double doors swings open, revealing a young woman in leggings and a tank top. Her red hair is piled on top of her head in a messy bun, her face is free of makeup, and her eyes are swollen as if from crying. But it's her belly that takes Danit by surprise. The round little bump is all the more obvious on her slender frame.

"Oh my God, you're pregnant!" Danit blurts out.

The woman's hands go to her belly as if protecting it from an attack. She looks directly at Nate and says in a steely voice, "I was wondering when one of you would show up."

43

In an interrogation room at the station, Shawna sits cross-legged in her chair like a little girl, hands cocooning a Styrofoam cup as if it were as delicate as a robin's egg.

"Let's begin here." Detective Washington pushes the evidence bag containing the oxford with the blood on it across the table. "This is yours, right? You were wearing this at the party?"

Shawna nods. "How did you find it?"

"Forget how we found it, Shawna. Help us understand. How did Thomas Calhoun's blood end up on it?" Washington says.

"It's complicated."

"Try us," Amatangelo says. "You'll find we are extremely patient."

"All right." Shawna takes a sip of the water. "I saw Thom—Mr. Calhoun—was bleeding, and I went to him, and that's how I got blood on my shirt. So I went upstairs to change." As soon as the words come out, she knows by the look on the detective's face she has said something wrong.

"*Thom?*" Detective Washington asks. "Did you say *Thom?*"

Shawna feels her cheeks grow hot.

"Don't bother denying knowing Mr. Calhoun," Washington says. "Two years ago, he transferred a hundred thousand dollars into your bank account. Want to explain that, Ms. Douglas?"

"I thought you wanted to know about the shirt."

The detective lets out a little laugh. "However you want to start. It's all going to come out."

Shawna takes in the bare room, the bulldog of a uniformed cop by the door, the buzzing fluorescent light in the popcorn ceiling tiles. *One million dollars*, she reminds herself. "It started a few years ago in LA when I met Trey Calhoun. He wanted to start a high-end adult subscription service, and I was going to be one of the marquee performers."

"Go on."

"There was a car accident. Trey was driving. I don't remember it, only that we were pretty fucked up that day. My arm got burned up pretty bad." She lays her left arm on the table and traces the tattooed vine that runs along a section of pink rippled skin. "If you look really closely, you can see some of the burn scars."

"Is that when you found out you were pregnant?"

Shawna tries to hide her surprise. "I . . . How did you know that?"

The detective taps the folder on the table. "We got your hospital records from that night. There was a criminal investigation, as I'm sure you know."

"So you know that I was pregnant. So what?"

"What happened next, Shawna?"

Shawna debates how much she should tell them. Just enough to flesh out what they already know, she decides, but no more than that. "I woke up in a hospital, but it wasn't like any normal hospital. It was like a cross between a hotel and a rehab. I got clean there. They took good care of me while I detoxed." Shawna lowers her gaze, staring at her fingers interlaced around her coffee cup. "They told me I was four months along, which was news to me. I stayed there until the baby was born, and I signed the adoption papers over to her. To Ginny. She came and got the baby. Said her other son was going to raise him." Shawna looks up searchingly.

"You just turned your child over to this woman? Why would you do that?"

"They told me I could go to jail for doing drugs while I was pregnant, endangering the welfare of an unborn child and shit like that. They said the state would find me an unfit mother and put my baby in foster care, and that if I signed the adoption papers, the other brother would raise him. Make sure he never wanted for anything in the world. It was an easy decision."

"Was it?" Washington asks. "I can't imagine that it was."

Shawna can't meet her eye. The patronizing bitch. Smug. As if this woman had any idea what it was like to be broke, twenty, and pregnant. Who was she to judge?

"What were the terms?"

"I don't know what you mean."

"C'mon, Shawna. People like the Calhouns don't turn over one hundred thousand dollars with no strings attached. What did you agree to? Besides giving up your child?"

Shawna pulls her hands from the table and tucks them under her legs. "Not to contact anyone. Ever. Disappear, basically. They told Trey I had died so he would never look for me."

Washington lets out a low whistle. "They told their son he had killed a girl? That's a new low. And I've been a detective for ten years."

"I'm still stuck on the fact that you gave these people your baby for a hundred thousand dollars," the officer behind her says. "As a father, I have to tell you, that sounds pretty cold."

"It's not like that," Shawna says sharply. "You don't get to judge me. I wasn't ready to have a kid. Here was this rich family that was going to take care of him. I mean, if the state was going to take him, anyway, I might as well get a hundred grand, right?"

"Sure, there's a certain logic to it," Washington says. "A girl's gotta do what a girl's gotta do to survive. So what went wrong with the plan? Why'd you come to D.C.?"

Shawna straightens up. "I ran out of money. I'm not embarrassed to say it. Why should I give up my baby for only a hundred grand? That barely lasted one year."

"All right. I get it. You came back for another bite at the apple," Amatangelo says. "But why the whole charade with the caterer?"

"I tried calling the Calhouns, back in California, but they

wouldn't take my calls. So I came out here. I knew the only way to get them to talk to me was to surprise them."

"You mean ambush them?"

Shawna squirms in her seat. The detective is twisting her words. "No, not *ambush*. Just surprise. I was outside their house the week before, trying to figure out how I was going to do it when a catering van showed up. I watched Sunniva, my future boss, walk around the lawn with Ginny. They were obviously talking about some party or event. That's when I got the idea. If I got a job with the caterer, Thom and Ginny wouldn't make a scene in front of all their guests. They'd have to hear me out. I needed to talk to them somehow, show them how serious I was. I realized that if I had kept the baby, I would have been getting child support, wouldn't I? So I came back. To renegotiate."

"And did you *renegotiate* on the afternoon of the party in Thom's study?" Washington asks.

"I wanted to, but I didn't get a chance. Literally seconds after I got to his study, Trey busted in. He had recognized me at the party and followed me inside. He completely flipped out when he realized I was alive."

"I'm sure he did," Washington says. "Must've been furious."

"He was. Ranting about being lied to. Then they got in a fight. Trey punched his dad in the nose, and he started bleeding."

"What did Trey do then?" Amatangelo asks.

"Nothing. He just stormed out. He was really upset."

"How about you? Were you concerned?"

"Yes, I went to Thom. He had fallen down, and I helped him get into his chair. That's when I got the blood on my shirt."

"So who shot him? Was it Trey? Was it you?" Washington shakes the bag with the shirt at her. "This isn't from a bloody nose, Shawna. This is blood from a gunshot wound."

"No, that's not what happened. It's from his nose, I swear."

"Maybe. Or maybe you witnessed a murder. Maybe you and Trey cut a little deal." Washington leans in close. "You promise to tell the police that he left the room, and in return, you get a nice little payout down the line. When he gets his inheritance."

"That didn't happen. I wouldn't lie about murder."

"That's where you draw the line?" Amatangelo demands. "You'll sell your baby for money, but you won't lie for money?"

"That's bullshit! I did the right thing for that kid, and you know it. What do I have to offer a kid? Besides, you know what childbirth does to your body? Huh? Didn't think so." She crosses her arms over her chest and leans back, a satisfied look on her face. "They fucked up my arm. They fucked up my body. I deserve compensation."

"Sounds like you're pretty angry," Washington says. "Angry enough to shoot the people you hold responsible?"

"Why would I kill the person who I was going to ask for money?"

"Maybe he said *no*. Maybe you lost it," Washington says. "Tell us about the shirt."

"I went upstairs and grabbed the first white shirt that looked like it would fit me," she says. "I couldn't go back outside with blood all over the front of my shirt."

"And then?" Amatangelo asks, coming into her field of vision.

"I stuffed the stained shirt in the closet, and I went back to working the party. I thought it would be weird if I just left."

"You didn't check on Thom again?" Washington asks.

She laughs. "Uh, no."

"You came all this way to ask him for money. You see Trey punch him, and you give up? It doesn't add up, Shawna." Washington looks at her watch. "This isn't looking good for you. You've put yourself in Thom Calhoun's study moments before he was killed. You have his blood on your shirt."

"Yeah? But I was outside when that lady came out. There are about fifty witnesses. I wasn't anywhere near the study." She crosses her arms over her chest, looking from the detective to the officer. Has she pulled it off? It's time to call their bluff. If they have enough to charge her, they'll arrest her right now. But if they don't, she's going to get the hell out of here, get her money, and get out of town. Only this time, not deposited in some bank account where there's a record that will connect her to the Calhouns. This time, she wants cash. "Unless you're gonna arrest me, I want to go. Now."

44

"I'm Ashleigh Dixon." The woman steps back to allow them into an immense two-story foyer, but she does not invite them in farther. "And you're Nate. I've seen your picture."

"Right. This is my fiancée, Danit, and this is Malcolm." Malcolm squirms in his arms, wriggling to be let free. Nate lowers him to the floor, where he wraps his arms around Nate's calf. "Is there someplace we can talk?"

"I'm good here," Ashleigh says. "I was about to jump in the shower, so can we make this quick?"

Coming here seemed so urgent, but now he doesn't know what to say. "I came here to see if you had my father's calendar. Fabiola said you might."

"Hold on." She holds up a hand and walks to the back of the house. A moment later, she returns with an iPad. "It's technically yours, I guess. I unlocked it. All his email is on here and so is his calendar." She passes it to Nate. "Anything else?"

"My father, how long did you work for him?"

"Almost a year. And this house is in my name, in case you were wondering," Ashleigh says.

He wasn't. But now that she mentions it, he wonders how she could afford a house like this on an executive assistant's salary. He knows a Calhoun house this size in Potomac has to be at least two million. He hates himself for being unable to ask the burning questions inside: Whose baby is that? And was she sleeping with his father? Malcolm grunts in frustration before taking off in a run around the circular foyer, tracing the wall with his hand, no doubt leaving greasy prints on the wall. This is not a kid-friendly house. The marble floor. The wide, slippery staircase. Suddenly, Malcolm stops short, pivots, and runs full speed into another room.

"Sorry about that," Nate says. "Danit, do you mind?"

"I'm on it," she says, already following Malcolm into the other room. He feels a shard of guilt about how easily he still slips into the role of employer and nanny with her and makes a mental note not to delegate so much childcare to her. Not that it seems to bother her, but he wants them to be equals now.

"Look, I already talked to the police yesterday. I'm really sorry for your loss, but I don't think I can help you or your family in any way," Ashleigh says. "I'm not feeling well, and I'd like to get back to bed." She coughs for emphasis, and Nate takes a step back.

"I thought you were about to jump in the shower," he replies. The skin on her pale neck turns pink. "Either way, I need to go. So you need to go." She walks to the front door and opens it. "I'd hate for you to catch my cold."

From somewhere in the house, Danit calls out, "Nate? You'd better come see this."

Nate turns away from Ashleigh. "Where are you?"

"Over here," Danit calls from the other room.

"Now hold on just a minute—" Ashleigh says, but Nate ignores her, following Danit's voice through a large doorway. He finds her standing in a living area the size of an airplane hangar with a freestanding fireplace in the center. Done up in pale neutrals with pops of hot pink, the room extends all the way to the back of the house, where a massive picture window overlooks a terraced back garden.

"Check it out." Danit gestures toward various areas of the room. Every single surface overflows with voluptuous bouquets of white flowers.

"What am I looking at?" Nate asks, confused. "The flowers?"

"I think I know what happened to your mom's hydrangeas."

Nate rushes to grab Malcolm as the boy begins pulling the throw pillows off the couch and tossing them on the floor. "I'm confused. Is this supposed to mean something?"

Danit lets out a short laugh. "How did you not know about the flower drama? I think I heard your sister mention it about ten times. They ordered white hydrangeas for the party, but they got delivered to the wrong address."

Nate sits on one of the long couches, allowing Malcolm to bounce next to him. "I still don't get it."

"I think these flowers were supposed to be for the party," Danit says, sitting next to him. Malcolm turns his attention to Danit's curls, plucking one at a time, pulling it straight and then letting it snap back, giggling each time. "Somehow they ended up here."

Ashleigh appears in the doorway, her shoulders slumped, tears in her eyes. "I know I shouldn't have kept them, but . . ." She stumbles into the room, crumples onto a cream divan, and sobs face-first into a pillow.

"What the—?" Nate whispers.

"Go find some tissues," Danit says, getting up.

After searching the living room unsuccessfully, Nate returns with a roll of paper towels from the kitchen to find Danit seated next to Ashleigh, rubbing her back.

"Go on, you just let it all out." Danit grabs a paper towel from the roll, giving Nate a look. "No tissues?"

Nate shrugs.

After she takes the paper towel, Ashleigh sits and blows her nose loudly.

"You really loved him, didn't you?" Danit asks. Nate sits at the edge of the sofa, confused. He must have missed something key when he went to get the paper towels. Malcolm scrambles onto his lap.

"Yes." Ashleigh drops the used towel on the floor and grabs another from the roll Danit is holding. "I really did."

"It wasn't just an affair, was it?" Danit crinkles her nose.

"No, it was true love. I know you don't want to hear that." She looks up at Nate bashfully. "But it's true. Your father and me, we were in love."

The words feel like a glass of ice water thrown on his face, shocking him. *True love?* He was willing to concede that his father was a cheater, but now he was supposed to accept that he was a romantic who had found true love with a woman the age of his own children? It was too much. "Are you suggesting that you and my father were in some kind of serious relationship?"

"I'm not delusional," Ashleigh insists. "He was going to leave your mom. I'm sorry to be the one to tell you that."

Nate laughs awkwardly. "Come on, you can't expect me to believe that."

Ashleigh sits up straight and pats her belly. "We were having a child together. He bought me this place."

Nate's eyes drop to her belly, the impact of her words sinking in. His father was having another child. This woman is carrying his *half brother.* "You're lying."

"He had contacted a divorce lawyer."

"I don't believe you," Nate says, surprised by the anger in his voice. Ashleigh takes the iPad he's holding and, after a few swipes, turns it around so he can see the screen. "See? Raibman and Raibman. Best divorce lawyers in town. He had a meeting last week, and he had the papers drawn up. It was only a matter of timing when he was going to tell her. He said he would do it at the party."

"Is that right?" Nate says in a steely tone, snatching the iPad back and looking for himself. Sure enough, it's right there. He looks up, all the rage he feels toward his father directed at her. "You expect me to believe my dad was going to drop this bombshell on my mom in front of her closest friends and family?"

"He thought she wouldn't be able to make a scene in front of every single person they knew. He finally had everything in order. He's been reworking his finances. You know he built this company from the ground up." Ashleigh looks up at Danit. "If you're not careful in Maryland, the wife can get half."

Nate opens his mouth to speak, but finds he is unable to articulate the mix of disgust and anger he is feeling. He stands up. "I've heard enough."

"I mean, Thom wasn't a bad person. He wasn't going to leave Ginny totally unprovided for."

"Oh, that's sweet. Come on, Danit. Let's go." He lifts up Malcolm, not bothering to put the pillow he was playing with back on the sofa. But when he gets to the edge of the room, he sees Danit is still seated on the chaise.

"Tell me about the flowers," she says.

"That was a mistake." Ashleigh bites her bottom lip. "Thom sends me peach roses here every week. That's his nickname for me, Peaches. The florist must have seen the name Calhoun and mixed up the two addresses or something. Early Saturday morning, all these hydrangeas arrived. I realized right away what had happened. I knew these were for the party."

"Did you call Thom?" Danit asks.

She looks down at her feet. "No. I should have," she murmurs. She picks her head up and straightens her shoulders. "I'm not going to lie. I loved the idea of Ginny losing her mind over not getting the flowers she ordered. I thought maybe she would even put two and two together and force the issue with Thom. But no, when I got to the party, there were calla lilies everywhere, and they were acting like the perfectly happy married couple."

"Thom invited you to the party?" Danit asks, surprised.

"Not exactly." She sighs. "I know I shouldn't have gone. He didn't want me there, but I couldn't help myself. I'm only human. I was afraid he might chicken out and not tell her."

"And did he?"

She shrugs. "I have no idea. But I can take a wild guess."

"Which is?" Nate can't keep the bitterness from his voice.

Ashleigh looks over at him before returning her gaze to Danit. "Either he told Ginny, or she figured out what was going on. Either way, once she realized that she might actually have to work for a living, she killed him. I am sure of it." Her eyes flash with anger.

"Maybe my dad didn't want you at the party because he wanted to cool things with you," Nate suggests, hoping the words will make her feel as wounded as he does. "The way he has with all the other women he's had affairs with."

Ashleigh's face scrunches in disgust. "That's not true. He already told me about the other girls. I know what you're trying to do, but it won't work. I had no reason to hurt Thom."

"He was breaking up with you, and you were pissed," Nate says. "You were about to lose your sugar daddy. You came to the party to confront him. Maybe you threatened to tell my mom, and things got out of hand."

Ashleigh stands. "I don't have to sit here and listen to you insinuate I had something to do with your dad's murder." She walks past Nate and Malcolm into the foyer and opens the door. "Please leave my house. And don't contact me, or my child, again."

45

Ginny Calhoun's protective gear is in place.

Covering her head is an Hermès scarf adorned with images of blue-and-white ginger jars against an orange background. Large glasses hide the dark circles under her eyes. Her favorite pink lipstick lends her an air of health. She's not crazy about having to sit in a wheelchair, but it's hospital policy, and practically speaking, she still cannot put any pressure on her foot.

"Now there may be some press outside, Mommy, but Nate texted. He's going to pull the car around." Ellie Grace walks briskly beside her mother as Zak wheels Ginny through the lobby. "So be prepared."

Ginny waves her daughter's concerns away as if they are as insignificant as gnats in a spring garden. But as soon as the sliding glass doors of the hospital open, Ginny realizes she ought not to have been so dismissive. The cameras begin clicking even before Zak has pushed her outside. Reporters rush up to her. At least she thinks they are reporters.

"Mrs. Calhoun!"

"Ginny! Over here!"

"Who shot you, Ginny? Did you see?"

"Who killed Thom?"

Nate pulls up in the car and jumps out. Ginny experiences the strange sensation of hands all over her body, lifting her, moving her. She is being whisked inside the car. Her seat belt is barely buckled before Nate hits the gas and they roar away. Beside her, little Malcolm lets out a whoop. On the other side of her, Ellie Grace's body is twisted so she can stare out the back window.

"Animals!" Ellie Grace turns to her phone and begins typing. "This should be illegal! They shouldn't be allowed to say this stuff. They're saying you and Daddy were swingers, in some kind of sex club."

"Maybe not now, Ellie Grace?" Nate says from the driver's seat.

"I'm not saying that. *They're* saying that."

"How about no one says it?"

Ginny closes her eyes. She is transported back to the many car rides with her three children. Those long drives to the Outer Banks when they were very young. The fighting. The bickering. More than once, Nate rode in the front with Thom while she rode in the back between Ellie Grace and Trey, serving as a barrier, a human DMZ. The family would arrive at its destination already soured on each other, having exhausted their fill of togetherness before the vacation even began.

She doesn't bother asking where Trey is. He's clearly pulling away from the family. It's a physical sensation in her chest, as real as the throbbing in her foot. Everything she has done for him is forgotten. The only thing he will ever remember is the one lie.

A lie told to protect him, no less. But he obviously doesn't see it that way.

Maybe she's done it all wrong, but hindsight is twenty-twenty.

There is no manual that comes with a newborn baby, only love. And maternal instinct, if you're lucky.

Has she made mistakes?

Of course. You don't raise three children into adulthood without making a few. But whatever mistakes she made, she made for them, out of love.

So many sacrifices.

And for what?

She opens her eyes and looks to her left. Ellie Grace hunched over her phone, scrolling endlessly. Nate getting ready to take her grandchild to the opposite side of the world.

Did I create this?

They gave the kids every opportunity that neither Thom nor she had when they were young. Did it backfire?

Zak, in the front passenger seat, turns around to face the back seat. "Everything okay back there, Mom?" She cringes inwardly at his use of *Mom*. Zak looks her directly in the eyes, that weaselly grin on his face. She'd like to wipe that grin right off it, but she smiles tightly.

She's going to need Zak's cooperation.

"Just so thrilled to be going home."

46

After Nate drops everyone off at the house, he drives directly to his father's estate lawyers—Brumfield, Brumfield, and Gritz. The iPad he'd retrieved from Ashleigh Dixon's house turned out to hold a lot of tantalizing information and not just the appointment with the divorce lawyers; his dad had recently seen his estate lawyers as well. There was also a mysterious meeting with a "JB" scheduled for tomorrow at the Tastee Diner in Bethesda that caught his eye. The same "JB" his dad had met with the day he'd died.

Nate follows the receptionist down a long hallway, his footsteps silenced by the thick carpeting. The entire office suite has an unnaturally hushed feeling—it's easy for him to imagine clients whispering their dirtiest secrets behind sealed doors.

The receptionist leads him to an office where a short man in his early fifties, with visible hair plugs and the orange-tinged skin of a tanning salon addict, stands at the doorway.

"Hello." The man sticks out his hand. "Frank Brumfield. Please come in, sit."

Nate sits in the low-to-the-ground leather sofa, sinking into it. Across from him, Brumfield sits in one of two matching wingback chairs, towering over him.

"First let me say, I am very sorry for your loss. I counted your father as not just a client but a friend. His loss will be felt in the Washington community."

"Thank you for saying that." Nate wipes his sweaty hands on his pants, dreading the awkward conversation to come.

"And your mother? How is she faring?"

"She's doing well under the circumstances. She came home from the hospital today."

"Good. Very good."

They sit in an uncomfortable silence. Nate searches for the right words, but there is no gentle way to ask if his father was about to leave his mother. He's spent a lifetime avoiding conversations that probed too deeply into people's personal lives. Emotions are treacherous terrain; he likes to stick to facts, numbers, quantifiable elements.

Finally, the lawyer clears his throat. "How can I be of help today?"

"I know that my dad had an appointment with you here about a month ago," Nate says. "I was wondering if you might share the nature of that appointment."

"I think under the circumstances, we can. Your father was here to change his will."

Nate is shocked. "His will? Why did my father want to change his will?"

"This is a bit awkward," Brumfield says. "But your father came to us on the advice of a different law firm that he had engaged. A firm that specializes in divorce." Brumfield chuckles. "We don't handle divorce. We're an estate-planning firm."

"I don't understand." But he has a sinking suspicion in his stomach that Ashleigh Dixon wasn't lying, after all.

"Well, any decent divorce lawyer would advise him to change his will before delivering divorce papers. Too many people make the mistake of waiting until after the divorce to revise their will, but that can be very risky. Problems can arise if one party dies during the divorce. I've seen that happen a few times. One gentleman I know went on to get remarried, but he hadn't updated his will. He had a heart attack and died about a year later, and his new spouse was none too happy to learn that the man's ex-wife was an inheritor, since he hadn't changed his will."

"So my dad came in to update his will," Nate says slowly, unable to deny the reality any longer, "because he was planning to leave my mother." His chest feels like it might cave in. His father was about to launch an entirely new life with a woman half his age, and was jettisoning his old family in the process.

"I'm afraid so. I know this is tough to hear. As you said, he came in about a month ago. We worked on the new will and testament together, in this very room." He raises one eyebrow and pauses for effect.

"So there's a new will?"

Brumfield sighs. "Technically, no. Your dad never executed it, at least not to my knowledge. Our office FedExed it to his house a few days ago," he says. "He called me with a few minor concerns. We scheduled an appointment for him to come in this week, actually. But then . . ."

"Then he was murdered," Nate says.

"Precisely." Brumfield crosses his legs. "You should know I've already shared this with the police. They had a court order."

Nate's head throbs. All of a sudden, the room feels too hot, too small. Ashleigh Dixon wasn't some delusional jilted lover. She was telling the truth. His dad was about to divorce his mom. The bastard. After thirty-five years of marriage, he was leaving the wife who helped him create his perfect life for a woman half his age. It is such a pathetic cliché that Nate almost laughs out loud. But did his mom know? If she did, she must have been terrified. She belonged to a generation that viewed marriage as the cornerstone of a successful life. There was no hyphenated last name for her; she was proud to be Mrs. Thomas Calhoun. She couldn't have taken the news well. In that case, could she have had something to do with his father's death? He blinks twice, pushing the question back into the dark corners of his mind. He must be losing it.

"So, what was the difference in the wills?" Nate asks.

"The original will is very straightforward. The bulk of the

estate goes to your mother, with sizable inheritances for you and your two siblings. And by sizable, I mean somewhere in the mid-seven-figure range."

Nate coughs into his hand. "That means like, what, five, six million each?" He has trouble getting the words out. He knew his dad and the company were worth millions, but it had never been spelled out like this before. Money was never discussed in the Calhoun house except in the vaguest sense.

"Again, I cannot recall off the top of my head, but something like that. Mrs. Calhoun would retain control of the company, inherit all properties and other assets."

"And the new will?"

"That one's a bit more complicated. Essentially, your mother is cut out entirely. The house, as you may or may not know, is in your father's name."

"I didn't know that." Nate wrinkles his brow. "Was he going to leave her anything?"

"He was planning to leave her the condo down in West Palm Beach."

"Bastard." Nate has to give it to his father. He never wanted that condo, and he rarely went. He supposed his dad justified his cruelty with this one act of kindness, but it was one that meant nothing to him. "And us? My siblings and me?"

Brumfield shakes his head. "I'm sorry, Nate. This will be hard to hear. But he left you and your siblings an inheritance of one hundred thousand dollars each, with the remainder of his estate to be split among any other children he sired outside of the marriage. If he signed the new will, that is."

"Jesus." Nate sits back and stares at the ceiling. His father was starting over. Not just a new wife but a new kid. He was done with family 1.0 and was moving on to the Calhouns 2.0. Maybe he figured he had done all he could for Nate and his siblings and wanted a second chance. Nate is angry, but he isn't panicked. He never counted on his parents' money to make it in life. When they were teenagers, his dad made them all get summer jobs, trying to teach them the value of a dollar. Trey worked as a lifeguard at the country club until he got fired; Ellie Grace put in a few weeks at a boutique in downtown Bethesda until she quit. He was the only one who seemed to enjoy working. He got a job stocking shelves at Rodman's in D.C. He liked the camaraderie with his coworkers, the sense of purpose each day he went to work, and the financial freedom he felt when he deposited that first paycheck. No, Nate knows he would be all right, but what about Trey and Ellie Grace? He got the impression they were counting on that money.

"Is there any chance I could get a copy of the new will?"

Brumfield runs his hand through the sparse hairs on his head. "Just remember that this will carries no legal weight or authority." Brumfield pauses. "Unless you can produce a signed and witnessed copy. If someone showed up with that, it could get pretty messy. But it's possible. It might be in a safe-deposit box. Or under the mattress."

"Or in a safe?" Nate asks, thinking of the open and empty safe in his father's study the evening he was murdered.

Brumfield frowns. "Of course, that's an obvious place. The point I was making is that some people keep wills in the oddest places. We had one client who kept his in the glove compartment of his car. Against our advice, of course. But to be frank, it's not unusual for a will to go missing, never to be found," he says. "People do execute new wills and then have a change of heart. It's not unheard of."

Or perhaps the heirs who find the new will inconvenient make it disappear. The thought pops into Nate's head before he can stop it. And if the thought occurred to him, he is sure it's occurred to the police.

47

The afternoon sun, filtered through the sheer white curtains, bathes the master bedroom in a lovely pale light. On each night-stand flanking the king-size bed, matching crystal bowls overflow with pink peonies.

Trey stands in the corner of the room, unsure of what to do with himself. He didn't go to the hospital, but when he saw the car pull up with his mother, something kicked in and he went outside to help.

He didn't do it because there were people watching, even filming. He did it because he wants to confront his mother face-to-face and get some answers.

Anya and Ellie Grace hover over Ginny, playing ladies-in-waiting to their queen. Fluffing her pillows, adjusting her blankets, they coo and cluck like roosting birds. Trey's practically drowning in all this estrogen. He should have stayed downstairs with Zak, who is probably helping himself to a cold beer right about now. Trey examines the room, growing more uncomfortable by the minute at such a raw display of feminine intimacy. How could his dad stand sleeping in here every night? With all these pale pinks and lace, the ruffles, the throw pillows.

Of course, the answer is that his dad couldn't stand it. He knew his dad was sleeping in one of the guest rooms. It almost makes him pity his mother, but he reminds himself that she was in on all the lies, too.

"Where is Trey, darling?" Ginny asks.

Ellie Grace freezes, mid-fluff. Trey can sense his sister's discomfort from across the room.

"He's right there, Mommy." Ellie Grace steps back, and Trey offers a little wave.

"Darling, there you are. Why didn't you come to the hospital?" Ginny turns to her right and says sharply, "Watch it, Anya, dear. One more pillow for my leg, I think."

"Yes, Miss Ginny." Anya rushes to the closet and digs around for a while before returning with a fresh pillow.

"Come closer so I can get a good look at you. Scoot out of the way, Ellie Grace." Trey watches his sister's face harden. He feels bad for her. Always so desperate for attention, like a golden retriever puppy but sadly not as cute.

Trey takes a few steps forward. "I'm right here."

Ginny winces as Anya tucks the pillow beneath her injured leg, elevating it like the doctor ordered. "Can you pull up a chair? We need to talk."

Ellie Grace pulls the vanity chair over, tapping it to indicate that Trey should sit.

Trey pulls the chair back a few inches so he's not so close to his mom, then sits down. It feels weird to see her in such a private and vulnerable position, in her bed. He's used to her striding through a room, grabbing her tennis racket, dictating orders. She was the one who tended to them, not the other way around. For the first time, his mother looks old to him, and fragile. He's annoyed with himself that her being injured is causing some of his anger to seep away.

"I just don't understand why you didn't visit me once in the hospital," Ginny says. "I was very concerned."

"But Nate and I did," Ellie Grace says brightly. "And Zak and I picked up these flowers for you. Peonies, your favorite."

But Ginny doesn't crack a smile. In fact, she wears the expression of a woman who has just smelled a particularly noxious fart. "Ellie Grace, dear, might your brother and I speak for a moment? Alone."

Ellie Grace sits ramrod still, and for a second, Trey wonders if maybe she didn't hear. Then she stands, smoothing the front of her dress. "Sure. Of course. Zak and I have some things we need to take care of, anyway." She starts to walk to the door but stops. "I just think we should have a family meeting. We have to make some decisions—about the funeral, I mean. We need to start contacting people. I didn't want to do anything until you got home, but I really think—"

"Ellie Grace, you are the most organized, efficient daughter a mother could ask for. I have no doubt we'll figure all this out in due time. But right now"—Ginny cocks her head toward Trey—"I need to speak to your brother."

"Of course." Ellie Grace pulls the door behind her. Once it clicks, Ginny turns her attention to Trey. "Do you want to tell me what's going on?"

An endless stream of clever retorts runs through his head. *I think I saw a ghost, Mom.* Or *Tell me about your friend Shawna.* Or, *I was curious what cemetery Shawna was buried in.* But for once, he can't locate the energy for sarcasm. He shrugs. "I know, Mom. I know all about Shawna."

Ginny's face is expressionless. "Meaning?"

Trey throws his hands up in exasperation. "I know she's alive, Mom. I spoke to her. She told me everything."

Ginny gives a little nod. "Everything? What did she tell you?"

"Well, she told me you paid her off to go away. To never contact me again. To help you keep this lie going that I had killed her."

"Is that all?"

"Is that all?" Trey jumps up. "Is there more?"

"No." Ginny sighs deeply and sinks into the pillow. "All right, let me have it."

"Let you have what?"

"The anger. I can take it. It's a mother's job."

Trey is pacing the room. "I am angry. You lied to me for two years. You let me think I killed someone," he says. "Do you have any idea the toll that has taken on me?"

Ginny puts her hand to her chest. "I told your father this was a terrible idea. I told him you would find out and would hate us. But he was determined."

"So you're saying it was all Dad's idea?"

"But it was!" Ginny pats the bed. "Come back and sit. I know I am to blame, as well. I went along with it. But you know your father."

Trey walks slowly back to the chair and sits. What his mother is saying is true, but it also reeks to high heaven of bullshit. His dad's not here to offer a different side of the story. It's true that his father was controlling. He remembers so many family dinners when they were teens that ended in hostile silence or, worse, tears. They dubbed them "*Jeopardy*" dinners. In lieu of conversation, their father would quiz them on what he considered relevant knowledge. It could be anything. He vividly remembers the humiliation of not knowing the currency of China and his father not letting anyone speak until Trey came up with the answer. Finally, his dad tossed the question to Nate, who answered easily, "Yuan."

"You're not going to make it very far in life if you're not paying attention," his dad said.

Could his mother have stopped this awful ritual? Perhaps she was just as much of a victim. At least she would come and check on him later, try to make him laugh, cheer him up.

"You should have told me," he said, sounding like a sulky boy. "You're my mother."

"I should have. And I failed you," Ginny says. "I'm so sorry."

There was almost nothing he could say to that. The person he really wanted the apology from was his father. But he would never get that.

"Your father is dead, and nothing can bring him back. Nothing. We must focus on the future now." She leans forward and tousles his hair. "I need you, darling. More than ever." Trey

chews on his bottom lip, a nervous habit from when he was a little boy and would chew until his lips were bloody. Ginny gently
tugs at his chin so he stops.

"You and me, kiddo, we've always had a special bond, and you
know it."

Trey bristles, but at the same time, he is flattered. He always
knew his mother preferred him over Nate and Ellie Grace.
They knew it, too. "You're probably going to deliver the same
little speech to Ellie Grace and Nate."

Ginny smiles at him. "I assure you I am not. I love your siblings very much, but neither of them can ever know of the things
we are about to discuss. You and I are the same," she continues
in a gentle voice. "We want to enjoy life. Nate is hobbled by a
rigid sense of morality. Your sister is blinded by a desperate need
for love and validation. But not us. We're survivors. And we are
willing to do what it takes to get what we want. Now listen
closely, because the next thing we do is going to determine the
rest of your life. And mine."

He sinks into his chair, eyeing the prescription pill bottle on
the nightstand. "Go on."

"I know you've always wanted to return to California, but I do
wish you'd reconsider. You know how terrible I am with money,
and your father left everything to me. What am I going to do
with a multimillion-dollar company? And all his investments?"
Her eyes search his face. "I need you, Trey."

Millions of dollars. That's what she is offering him. Without
his father around, the urge to flee is subsiding. He has friends
here in D.C., a mother. She is offering him a deal, although the
terms aren't clear yet. Trey picks up the pill bottle. "Hydroco-
done," he reads aloud. "Can I have one?"

Ginny looks at the clock on her bed stand, which reads 4:05.
"Just one," Ginny says. "You have to get to the bank before it
closes. And you're going to need your wits about you."

Trey opens the bottle, pops one in his mouth, and follows it with a swig of water. He feels different from how he did just an hour ago. The anger that felt like a hard rock in his chest is gone, replaced by a sense of purpose. The idea of hitting the road and going back to California seems silly now. This is his home. He sits back and waits for the pill to kick in.

48

Ellie Grace angles the laptop toward Zak so he can see the photo she's zoomed in on.

"What about this one? You look superhot." It's a shot of Zak, his hair glowing in the sun and creating a halo effect. He's smiling and looking slightly beyond the camera, with the cherry blossoms in the background in soft focus, creating a pale pink backdrop. It would be perfect for Gingham Life. "Zak, are you listening?"

"Huh?" He turns away from the large TV and looks at her. "What was that, babe?"

"I need your help. I can't go through all these photos myself."

"I can help," Danit says, entering the room with a mug of something steaming while Malcolm trails behind, clutching an armful of plastic lids and bottoms. "He found the Tupperware drawer."

Malcolm carries the items over to the corner of the TV room and begins stacking them. Ellie Grace takes in Danit's bleached-out, baggy jeans and cream-colored T-shirt. The girl has a look, all right, but not exactly the one Ellie Grace is going for. "Aww, that's sweet."

"Hey, Zak, can you come here a minute?" Trey calls from the hallway. A second later, he is in the TV room. "Did you hear me? I said, I need your help."

"What's going on?" Ellie Grace looks up at her brother. He has a strange half smile on his face, and she wonders if he's baked. But that's impossible. He's been upstairs with their mom for the past half hour. "What do you need help with? Is Mom okay?"

"She's fine. She wants us to move some furniture or something. Gimme a hand, huh, Zak?"

"Guy stuff." Zak grins and kisses Ellie Grace on the cheek before getting up and following Trey out.

Ellie Grace mutes the news and returns to the photos. "There are too many," she says, mostly to herself. "This photographer was definitely snap happy. I mean, look at this—" She looks up at Danit and motions with her head for her to come closer. Danit sits down beside her, and Ellie Grace turns the laptop so Danit can see. "Why was he taking a picture of this catering girl? Because she's cute? I mean, are we paying him to do that? He literally took more than five hundred photos."

"What are these for, exactly?"

"Some are for our Christmas card, some I'm going to use on Gingham Life, and some are for a story in *Chevy Chase Style* magazine. I went to Washington Prep with the editor. She said she'd love to do a feature on our cherry blossom party and we should send over a dozen pictures to pick from."

"Don't they usually send their own photographer?" Danit asks.

Ellie Grace laughs. "Everybody's cutting corners. When I pitched her the idea, she was lukewarm, but when I told her we were hiring a professional photographer, all of a sudden, she loved the idea." She clicks her nails against the keyboard of her laptop. "Of course, now she's saying the story will have to be on hold until my father's murder is resolved. So I told her, 'Oh, maybe I should pitch the whole thing to the *Washingtonian*?' And she panicked. 'No, no, no. We just want to make sure we get the tone right.' But I'm just going to move forward like the story is happening. And if they don't want it, I am sure someone else will."

Ellie Grace looks up at the sound of the front door opening. Moments later, Nate enters the room, and Malcolm squeals, running to greet him. "Hey, buddy!" he says. "What have you been up to?"

"He found the Tupperware and has been stacking them over there," Danit says, adding quickly, "Don't worry, I'll put it all back."

Ellie Grace waves the comment away. "Anya can do it. That's why we pay her."

"I don't mind."

"Maybe I should take him down to the park and let him run around a little," Nate says. "I can unload all the stuff I brought over later on."

"What stuff?" Danit asks.

"Everything. I thought we'd stay here now that my mom's back from the hospital," Nate says. "I just think it would be better, you know, if she needs something in the night. I don't want her to be alone. You don't mind, do you, Danit?"

"No," Danit says. "Makes sense."

"Maybe I should stay, too," Ellie Grace says, feeling a little left out. She's the obvious choice. Why didn't Mom ask her?

"You don't have to do that. You'll probably have to be here a lot once Danit and I leave after the funeral."

"Oh." She tries to hide her dismay. "So you're still planning to go? I thought you might postpone."

"I have a job starting, Ellie Grace," he says. "It's not a vacation."

"Right, I know. I just thought that your dad being murdered was a pretty good excuse to postpone it."

"I'm not looking for an excuse to postpone it."

Ellie Grace feels her lower lip tremble. She hates when he uses this tone. Like she's some dumb employee who got his order wrong at a chain store. She wants him to stay, and she wants him *to want* to stay. It bothers her how little he seems to need her, to even like her. When she was younger, her brothers played such a central role in her life, even after they went off to college. When they came home for vacations or summer break, she'd learn all about their girlfriends, their guy friends, their roommate drama, their habits, and then *poof.* They were gone. And it seemed like all communication ceased. She sometimes wondered: If she didn't make an effort, would she ever hear from Nate again? She was jealous of her friends who had sisters, especially the ones who texted all the time with little inside jokes. How could she come from a family of three and still feel so lonely?

She looks over at Danit, who's scrolling through the photos. Maybe they could become friends. At the very least, Danit seems like she would encourage Nate to stay in touch, unlike Helena. Helena never had time for her—in Helena's eyes, she was a basic sorority girl. But Danit seemed impressed with what she had done with Gingham Life. "Hey," she says to Danit. "How would you like to help me cull these photos? It's really too big a job for one person."

Danit's eyes light up. "Happy to."

"Great. Give me your email, and I'll send you the link to the website and the password. Just go ahead and heart what you think is good."

"Ellie Grace, quick," Nate says. "Turn up the volume."

She looks up at the TV. A large yellow graphic reading *BREAKING NEWS* is splashed across the top of the screen as a wide-eyed young woman walks out of the Montgomery County Police Department, trying to rush past the reporters.

"Wait, isn't that the catering girl from the photos?" she asks as she turns up the volume.

The camera pans to a reporter on the steps of the station. "Police have issued a statement that Shawna Douglas, twenty-one years old, is not a suspect but merely a person of interest in the murder of prominent developer Thomas Calhoun and in the brazen attack on his wife, Virginia Calhoun."

"Shawna Douglas? That's the girl who was in the accident with Trey," Ellie Grace says.

"Do you think—I mean, could she be the one who left the

shirt upstairs?" Danit asks. "It had *Capitol Catering* printed on the inside. And Trey said she came back for more money."

"That's right," Trey says. "She told me herself."

Everyone turns to see Trey and Zak standing there.

"Did she get arrested?" Zak asks, striding over to the couch where Ellie Grace is sitting. He lays his hands on her shoulders.

"I don't think so." Ellie Grace leans back and looks up at him. "They said she was just brought in for questioning. It must be because of the shirt." She grabs her phone.

"You're not going to post that on Instagram, are you?" Nate asks.

Ellie Grace scowls. "I'm not an idiot. I'm not posting—*Hey, they found my daddy's killer!*" She pauses a moment as she types into her phone. "I'm just DMing someone who will do it for me. A friend who has a true-crime podcast. She's mostly on Twitter. Don't worry, it won't come back to us." She finishes typing the message and hits Send. Finally, a suspect and some evidence that doesn't point to the Calhouns. It's red meat for those following the case. If she's lucky, this one little nugget of info will snowball out there in the ether, take on a life of its own, and by tomorrow be considered gospel on social media.

"I don't think that's a good idea," Nate says. "We should let the police do their job."

"I know what I'm doing. Trust me." She drops the phone next to her.

Nate exhales loudly, then bends down to grab Malcolm. "I was going to head to the park before it gets dark. Want to join me, Trey?"

"Can't," Trey says to Nate. "Sorry. Promised Mom that Zak and I would help with something."

Nate nods. "Maybe we can grab a beer later? Just you and me? I feel like we haven't had time to talk—just us two."

"You don't ask *me* to hang out—just us two." Ellie Grace crosses

her arms over her chest. It feels like when they were kids all over
again and Trey and Nate would go off on their own. It made sense,
when they were in high school and she was in middle school, that
they wouldn't take her to Nate's games or to concerts on a week-
night. But there's no excuse to exclude her now.

"Maybe," Trey says. "I got some shit to do."

"What are you guys doing that's so important?" Ellie Grace
asks.

"Mom wants us to deliver this sideboard to this guy who
does restoration," Trey says, nodding at the sideboard in the
hallway.

Ellie Grace twists her body so she can look at the sideboard.
It's an antique mahogany piece with inlaid panels, slender legs,
and a lovely curved front. It's been in that spot for as long as she
can remember, and it looks perfectly fine to her. "What's wrong
with it?"

"How do I know?" Trey bristles. "You know how Mom is."

Ellie Grace sighs. Her mom is probably going nuts bed-
ridden up there and is coming up with all sorts of chores and
errands for other people to run. If she can't schedule every moment of her own life, she'll settle for scheduling the lives of
those around her. She shuts her laptop. "I'll tag along. We can
grab dinner after."

"That's okay, sweetie." Zak leans over her so his mouth is close
to her ear. "It'll give me a chance to bond with your brother."

Ellie Grace leans back and opens the laptop again with a
flourish. "Fine." She draws the word out. But she doesn't protest.
She knows how much Zak wants to be accepted by her broth-
ers, by her family. He'd do almost anything to belong. And if
Trey's actually willing to hang out with Zak, that's a good thing.
"Danit and I will watch stupid TV and order takeout. Right,
Danit?"

"Sounds fun!" Danit says.

"Great!" Ellie Grace says, trying to match Danit's enthusiasm. But inside, her stomach churns with anxiety. Something is going on. She knows when people are lying and covering up. She should. She's had enough practice.

49

After changing into a comfy velour sweatsuit, Renée heats a Trader Joe's dinner, pours herself a glass of wine, and sits down to watch an episode of *My Lottery Dream Home*. She finds it very soothing. She especially enjoys the more outlandish houses, like the one tucked into the cliffs of Maine that had to accommodate a couple and their fourteen cats. When she was younger, she would fantasize about all the different places she might live—Tokyo, Paris, London—but now the thought of downsizing into a smaller house overwhelms her.

No, she's leaving this house feetfirst.

It's been a long day. Someone called in a bomb threat to the school. It turned out to be a prank, but these days, even if it is a hoax, they must follow protocol. Twenty-one years teaching with the county. Nine more years until she is eligible for a pension of 60 percent of her salary. She'll be in her late sixties by then. It had once seemed like a workable plan, although she tried not to think about the future too much. But now, for the first time since Drew left her, she dares let herself dream that there might be another option.

In the kitchen, she rinses off her dishes in the sink, puts them in the rack, and grabs the dogs' leashes.

"Mumbo! Asti! Spumante! Ready to go see your mommy?" The three dogs run into the kitchen, yapping. She needs to return the frenchies to Ginny, but she is hesitant to go over. She knows her friend is back from the hospital—as soon as she came home and got out of her car, Cookie informed her. But the thought of dealing with all those onlookers exhausts her. The last thing she wants is to end up a side character in some online conspiracy theory. She read about how an innocent man's life was ruined by some cyber-sleuth just because he was at the same food truck as a girl who was later murdered. A true-crime YouTuber managed to ID the poor guy and blasted his name and address all over the internet, claiming he was a suspect. The man lost his job, had death threats, and developed severe anxiety.

But she knows how much Ginny must be missing her fur babies. Sometimes knowing she will be coming home to Mumbo is the only thing that gets her through the day. After leashing them up, Renée nudges the dogs out of the way so she can slip on her garden clogs, which she keeps by the back door. Pulling the door shut behind her, she steps into her yard, enjoying the sweet scent of springtime. A house nearby boasts an enormous viburnum that blooms this time of year, releasing a spicy scent that wafts across the entire block. It will be wonderful when things get back to normal and she can put this whole awful experience in the rearview mirror. Besides that initial interview with the police the night of Thom's murder, no one has contacted her since.

So far, Ginny has been right. The police don't seem to suspect a thing.

Mumbo yaps, straining at his leash toward the side yard between her house and the Cooke-Andersons.

"What is it, little buddy?" She takes a tentative step forward.

Suddenly, Mumbo breaks free, causing all three leashes to slip from her hand. The dogs race around the corner.

"Mumbo!" she calls as she runs after them. "Asti, Spumante!" The last thing she needs is for the dogs to get out into the street. That side of the house is dark, lit only by the moon and the lights coming from inside the house next door, but she sees the dogs have stopped short.

"Silly dogs," she says.

"Hi, Renée."

Renée lets out a shriek. She jumps and almost falls before

grabbing a hold of the coiled green hose on the side of the house to steady herself. The owner of the voice comes into focus. "Zak. What are you doing here?"

"I, uh, I thought I saw a fox." He flashes that grin. It might work on Ellie Grace, but it doesn't work on her. A thought intrudes: Did Ginny send him here? With a message? But she dismisses it right away. Zak can't possibly know.

"You saw a fox?" She knows a lie when she sees one. She sighs, exasperated, reaching down to pick up the leashes.

"I was just following it." He adjusts the backpack he is wearing.

"In my yard?" Renée wraps the leashes around her hand twice.

"Everything all right?" Cookie appears at the garden gate before letting himself in. "I thought I heard a scream."

"That was me, Cookie. Zak surprised me." Normally, she's annoyed by Cookie's nosiness, but tonight, she's grateful.

"I see." He takes a few steps toward them. "Coming to bring the dogs back to Ginny, Zak?"

Zak laughs. "Oh, no, I don't do dogs."

"He claims he saw a fox in my yard," Renée says in a weary tone.

"That's funny, because when I heard the scream, I said to Bob, 'I wonder if it's the bear?'"

Renée stares at him blankly.

"Haven't you heard? There's been a black bear sighting in Chevy Chase, over near Woodlawn. It's all over the LISTSERV."

"No bear." Zak holds his hands up. "Just me." A car horn honks from the street. "Must be Trey. Better go." He turns and walks away. After he's gone, Renée realizes he was standing in front of the bag of cyclamen bulbs she lugged over from Ginny's place. The bag is wide open. Her stomach drops.

"Zak hanging out with Trey?" Cookie asks. "Since when are those two buddies? I thought Trey couldn't stand him."

Renée stares at the bag, speechless. She's sure she had the top rolled down. She would not have left it open like that.

"You all right, Renée? You look like you've had a shock," Cookie says, his gaze following hers. "Now what are you doing with those cyclamen bulbs?"

"I'm potting them up for Ginny," Renée says robotically.

"Sweetie, I hate to be the bearer of bad news." Cookie walks over to the bag. "But these are fall bulbs. You can't plant these until much later."

When he bends down to take a closer look at the bag, Renée shouts, "No! Don't touch it, Cookie!"

Cookie jumps up, his hand on his heart. "Renée, what on earth?"

She walks over and peers inside the bag, frowning. Sticking her hand in deep, she feels around, praying that her hand will hit something solid, but she knows in her gut she won't find it.

"Oh my God," she says, pulling her hand out and looking up at Cookie in dismay. "The gun is gone."

50

Trey stands on the front stoop of the house, shivering in his T-shirt and jeans. It was sixty-five degrees today, but now that the sun has set and a strong night breeze is blowing, he's freezing.

He rings the bell, glancing back behind him toward his car, the only one on the street. Although the car's windows are tinted, he gives a little nod, knowing that Zak is watching. Never in a million years did he think that he and his brother-in-law would pair up like this. But his mom was right when she told him earlier: *We're survivors. And we are willing to do what it takes to get what we want.*

He rings again and looks around. This place is depressing. He never understood the appeal of moving out to the middle of nowhere and then jamming a bunch of houses together like this. If he had to live out in the country, he'd want fifty acres. Not neighbors within spitting distance.

Finally, the door opens, and Shawna stands there barefoot in sweatpants and a T-shirt.

"Trey! It's about time. I was wondering if you were going to show up. Did you bring it?"

Trey hoists the duffel bag to shoulder level. "Are you going to let me in or what? I'm freezing my tits off."

Shawna looks past him at the empty street before allowing him in. "Those reporters ambushed me at the police station. I was worried they were going to follow me here."

"It's nobody but me. Just relax." He steps inside the foyer, and she shuts the door. Trey is confident she cannot see Zak through the tinted windows.

"Relax? I spent the afternoon getting grilled by the police. I don't like lying to the police." She looks at the duffel bag. "Is it all there?"

"No, not all of it—"

"Your mom promised me!" Some spittle from her mouth hits his chin.

Trey steps back, surprised by her vitriol. He was fighting off pangs of guilt the whole way over. Vacillating between thinking of Shawna as a victim who got caught up in his family's lies, and a conniving bitch who ruined his life. In a flash, he makes his decision. Any residual reluctance disappears, the tiny flame of tenderness extinguished.

In its place—a blinding anger. She ruined his life, he can see that now. She could have reached out to him at any point in the past two years and told him the truth—that she was alive and well. But no, she stayed quiet for money. And why did she come back? To rescue him from the personal hell those lies had created? No, she wanted more. She would have come and gone from Washington if things had worked out as she'd wanted, and he would still be in the dark, still thinking that he had killed her.

Well, if she wants to be dead so badly, he can help make those dreams come true.

"I need a drink," he says. "It's been a long day." Trey walks into the kitchen, where he pulls a bottle of tequila out of his backpack. "Let's celebrate."

"I don't see what we're celebrating. How much money did you bring?" But she gets two glasses down from the cupboard, anyway. That's the Shawna he remembers, always up for a drink, a line, a bump.

"This is one hundred thousand." He places the bag on a stool and unzips it. It's closer to thirty, but he's counting on Shawna not figuring that out at this moment. Thirty thousand in bills looks like a lot of cash. And it's the amount that his mother had in her safe-deposit box at the bank. She called it her *mad money*. "My mother always said to have a little mad money," she told Trey when she gave him the key. "She used to give me a ten-dollar bill to tuck in my bra whenever I went out on a date in high school. I was never sure if it was for when the guy you're with gets mad at you, or when you finally go mad."

Trey agreed with Ginny that withdrawing a large sum of cash from their accounts wouldn't be a great idea right now.

Shawna pulls a block of twenties out of the bag, brings it up to her nose, and fans it. "Yum. I love the smell of money."

"Yeah, okay. Whatever." Trey takes the tequila bottle and the two glasses, walks into the living room, and plops himself down on a large gray sectional. "Grab a lime, will ya?" he calls.

Moments later, she comes in with a small bowl containing lime wedges and sits on the floor cross-legged, a giddy smile on her face. "First thing I'm gonna do is buy a new car. I always wanted a jeep. You know, the kind with no top?"

"Sounds good." He fills the glasses and hands her one. Shawna squeezes a lime wedge into hers and then his. "Cheers."

They both down the tequila.

"Damn!" She wipes her mouth with the back of her hand, grinning.

"So you like the place? I thought it was a nice ironic touch. You getting to stay in one of my dad's fanciest builds."

"I like it fine. When are you getting me the rest of my money?"

"It'll take a week or so."

"A week? What the hell, Trey? I can't stay here a week."

"Don't sweat it." He refills the glasses, sloshing some onto his hand. "This is enough to get you out of town, and then I'll bring you the rest."

She laughs bitterly. "The hell you will."

He lowers his chin and looks directly at her. "You have us over a barrel, Shawna. We're good for the money. Now one, two, three, drink!"

They both down their shots. "Hey, you got any snacks back there?" Trey asks.

"I think so," Shawna says, standing, clearly woozy from the tequila, and walks into the kitchen. "Cheddar popcorn, teriyaki seaweed, bison jerky, peanut butter cups," she calls from the kitchen.

"Bring it all!" Trey yells back. He reaches inside the back pocket of his jeans and takes out a tiny glass vial. After squeezing a few drops from the vial into Shawna's empty shot glass, he fills it with tequila and stirs it with his pinkie. He almost licks the excess off his little finger, then, remembering, wipes it on the sofa.

Funny thing—Shawna and he used to take GHB together back in LA. The dose was much smaller, of course, and they wouldn't take it with tequila. There would be no point, since with alcohol you would almost be guaranteed to pass out.

Shawna returns, loaded with snacks, and dumps them on the coffee table.

"You know, Trey, you have one fucked-up family, and I don't say that lightly. I mean, my dad walked out on me and my mom when I was five and then dropped dead of a drug overdose, and I still think your dad was worse."

"To dads everywhere." Trey raises his shot glass.

Shawna lifts hers, as well. Both throw back their shots, then slam the empty glasses on the coffee table.

They lock eyes for a moment, and Trey searches for a glimpse of recognition that Shawna realizes what is happening. Her eyes widen and her mouth makes a wide O as she struggles to stand up, falling instead to the floor.

Trey stands above her, watching her eyes flutter.

"Damn, that was fast."

Once he is sure she has passed out, Trey picks up his shot glass and takes it to the kitchen, washes it, and pops it into his backpack. He double-checks that there are no signs he has been here, using a rag he brought with him to wipe down the bottle and any other surface he touched. He looks around and spots Shawna's car keys. Grabbing them, he moves to the front door, where he flashes the porch light once. In a few seconds, Zak is on the stoop, and Trey lets him in.

"Where is she?"

Trey leads him to her.

"Here, hold this." Zak shoves a brown paper bag at Trey's chest. It's heavier than Trey had thought it would be. But then again, he's never held a gun before.

"You got the keys?" Zak asks.

Trey pulls them out of his pocket and jangles them.

Zak takes something crumpled and blue out of his pocket. "Put these on," he says, tossing two blue latex gloves to Trey while putting on a pair himself. "And wipe those keys down."

Trey snaps on the gloves, feeling dumb. He should have thought of that. He wishes Zak weren't here, that they didn't need him, but they do. Trey knows himself. He can spike someone's drink, but he's no killer. His mom was right about looping Zak in. *Once he does this, he'll be loyal to us for life*, she said. *We'll have leverage over him.* It had revolted him when she'd said it, but now the realization washes over him like one of those waves that knocks your breath out of you. His mother was right. She was always right. She could read people, and she knew exactly what buttons to push—greed for Shawna, acceptance into the Calhouns for Zak. And what about himself? A need for her approval. As much as he hates himself for it, he can't live without the warmth of her praise, the seal of her blessing. It's why he had come back to Washington, to earn back her favor. It's why he is here tonight. Yes, the money, of course the money. But it is a mother's love he craves, the oxygen he can't live without.

Zak picks Shawna up and carries her toward the kitchen. He's bigger and stronger than Trey is. Shawna has to weigh at least 130. No way he could carry her across the house like that.

"Get the door," Zak barks.

Trey rushes over and opens the door in the kitchen that connects to the garage. He flicks on the light. The double car garage is empty except for Shawna's crappy red Ford.

"Open the door," Zak says, clearly straining. "Hurry."

Trey rushes around to the driver's side. He unlocks and opens the door before stepping back. He watches as Trey wedges her into the front seat. "Put the gun in the car."

Trey walks around to the other side and opens the passenger-side door. "Where?"

Zak looks up from trying to get Shawna's left leg into the car. "It doesn't matter. Tuck it under the seat. Dude, take it out of the bag first."

"Right." Trey pulls the gun out of the bag. It's still wrapped in the wastebasket liner from his father's study. It's a brilliant touch, he thinks, keeping the liner. Was there no detail too small for his mother? Leaning over, he shoves the wrapped gun under the passenger seat among the fast-food wrappers and napkins.

"You can go," Zak says without looking up. "I'll meet you back at the car."

Trey goes back inside the house and looks around one last time. In the kitchen, he grabs his backpack and the duffel bag filled with cash, then lets himself out. He gets into the car and slips in an Arctic Monkeys CD—*Whatever People Say I Am, That's What I'm Not*. Zak made him leave his phone back at the house. "It's better this way. The GPS on our cell phones will say we never left."

In a few minutes, Zak comes out of the house and punches the door code to lock it. Trey glances at the garage. From the outside, there is no hint at the destruction that is taking place behind the pristine white electric doors.

"Let's go," Zak says as soon as he gets in the car. "We still have to stop by my house and drop this thing in our basement." He nods his head at the mahogany sideboard in the back seat.

Trey cranks up the music as he heads to Zak's house, driving carefully, not just because he has had several shots of tequila but also because he can't afford to trigger any red light cameras or the speed traps along Connecticut Avenue. It pains him to drive thirty miles an hour when there is no traffic, but he knows the Town of Chevy Chase is always watching.

As he drives, questions pop in his head. How long will it take for Shawna to die? Will it hurt? But he can tell that Zak is not interested in talking. He feels a little giddy, a strange sense of elation. Shawna's death will be his rebirth. She's done him a favor in a twisted way. All her lies and schemes have stripped away his pretensions—he's not a producer or an entrepreneur. He's not the loser rich kid who couldn't cut it on his own. He doesn't belong in LA; he belongs right here.

He's a Calhoun.

It's just taken him a while to come to that realization.

51

"Do you know who Shawna Douglas is?" Detective Washington asks.

"Yes. I do." Nate feels that Detective Washington is closely watching his face as she delivers this line. It is early Tuesday morning, and they are standing in his mom's kitchen as Malcolm, sitting at the table, tosses Cheerios onto the floor. "She was brought in for questioning yesterday. I saw it on the news."

"That's right. She was a suspect in your father's murder."

"A suspect? I thought she was a person of interest?" Nate asks, trying to keep his voice steady. He was in the middle of making coffee when the doorbell rang this morning. Anya wasn't there yet, so he was the one who had answered it.

"She was until she died last night. Carbon monoxide poisoning. She was in her car," the detective says. "She had been drinking. She must have passed out."

"I'm very sorry to hear that. But what makes her a suspect?"

"We found the gun that was used to shoot your parents in her car. It was registered to your father."

"So, she did it." Nate crosses his arms over his chest. "Is it settled? That she shot my dad? And my mom? Is it over?"

He watches Detective Washington look around the kitchen, pausing to take in the wall adorned with shiny copper pots that cost his mother a small fortune. She couldn't use them with the glass stove top on the new induction stove, they were just for show now—each week, Anya polished them to gleaming perfection. Every room in this house was like that—decorated with an eye to signaling their wealth. What must this detective think of his family? "Well, we still have to cross some t's and dot some i's," Washington says, "but as far as our department is concerned, the case is closed." Her tone is wry, as if she's repeating lines she's practiced but doesn't believe in.

"But you don't think it is," Nate says just as Malcolm throws his plastic bowl onto the floor and laughs maniacally. The bowl lands at Detective Washington's feet. "Sorry about that."

"Not a problem." She bends down, picks up the bowl, and puts it on the counter. "To answer your question, there are a few things that don't add up. The sales rep for the Fox Grove development stopped by the house and found her. She was quite upset, obviously. She said she had no idea how Shawna got in or why she was there. She said the house was locked with a code. Do you have any idea how she got a hold of that code? Who might have given it to her?"

Nate shrugs. "I don't know."

"Who would know? Your siblings? Your mother?"

"A half dozen people at Calhoun Development would probably know."

"But we don't think anyone at Calhoun Development would give Shawna Douglas the code. Why would they?"

"Why would anyone in my family give it to her?" he asks.

"You tell me, Nate."

He jerks his head back, startled by the sharpness of her response. "I told you, I have no idea."

"Danny!" Malcolm howls, arms extended as Danit enters the room, hair still wet from the shower.

"Morning, everyone," Danit says as she goes to give Malcolm a hug. "What's going on?"

Nate gives her a quick recap of what he has just learned, before turning to the detective. "Is there anything else?" he asks. "I'm not trying to be rude, but we have a lot to do. Like plan for my father's funeral on Friday."

"There is one more thing," she says. "I knocked on Trey's

door, but no one answered. Any idea where your brother is this morning?"

"Honestly, he's probably still asleep."

"I see. He must be a sound sleeper. I was knocking pretty hard. Tell him we came by. We'll need to talk to him later today."

"Why? Do you think my brother is involved?" He shakes his head in disbelief. "Why would he give this girl the code?"

Detective Washington squints at him as if his face is one of those posters you need to look at from a certain angle before you can spot the image. Nate squirms under her scrutiny. "What is it?" he asks.

"Do you not know who Shawna Douglas is?"

Nate feels an icy grip around his throat. Something about her tone scares him. He tries to swallow but can't. "I'm not sure what you mean."

"Nate, maybe you'd better sit down."

Slowly, he pulls out a stool and sits, a feeling of dread descending on him.

"Shawna was in the car with your brother when he crashed it."

Nate nods. "Yeah, I know."

"Your parents paid her off to go away. She came back to D.C. because she wanted more money." Washington inhales deeply. "Nate, I'm sorry to be the one to inform you of this—but Shawna is Malcolm's mother."

Her words are like a spell, immobilizing him. His face feels frozen, his lips unable to move. He stares at her unblinking, with a thousand tiny thoughts flitting through his brain at once. Each time he tries to grab one, and hold it long enough to try to make sense of it, another flies by demanding attention. The car accident. The porn star his mother told him about. The girl from the news coming out of the police station. The bloody T-shirt. It's all connected. It's as if someone has taken a story and flung the pages in the air. He has all the pages, but they are out of order. He just has to piece it back together for it to make any sense.

"Are you all right, Nate?" Washington asks.

Danit puts a glass of water in front of him, and he lifts it to his lips, grateful for something to soothe his dry throat.

Malcolm's birth mother is dead. His son will never have a chance to meet her. A tiny part of him had always worried that she would come back and try to take Malcolm. But knowing now that she will never come back does not offer any relief. All he feels is grief mixed with confusion.

"So this Shawna Douglas came back here for more money?" Danit asks. "And then when she didn't get it, she killed Nate's father and shot his mother? Is that what you're saying?"

Nate feels a wave of gratitude toward Danit for asking this. He doesn't feel like he could string a coherent sentence together right now.

"That's what the evidence points to," Washington says. "By the way, before I leave, where were you two last night?"

"We were here the whole night," Danit says, stiffening, and Nate loves her for her protectiveness of him. "We ordered takeout and watched TV."

"And you two slept here?"

"That's right," she says.

"Was anyone else here?"

"My sister," Nate says as if in a trance. "And her husband until around midnight."

"But not Trey?"

Nate pauses. "No, Trey was here." *After he and Zak came back from their errand.* "Everyone was here in the evening."

"Watching TV together, how cozy." She flashes a tight smile. "I guess that's all for now. I can let myself out."

A few moments later, after the detective has left and the front door has clicked, Danit goes to the window. "She's gone."

Nate puts his head in his hands, the base of his skull throbbing. "I never knew her name. My parents never told me."

Danit comes over and rubs his shoulders. "This is a lot to deal with."

"She was here, Danit. In this house. What if she came back for Malcolm?" Nate asks. "That detective obviously thinks my brother had something to do with Shawna's death. But why?"

"Look, if they found the gun on her, doesn't that mean she did it?" Danit asks. "I mean, she had a motive. She had opportunity."

Nate gives her a weak smile. "What are you, a detective now?"

"Are you still going to tell Trey?" she asks. "That he's Malcolm's biological father?"

Nate nods. "I have to," he says glumly. "I'm sick of all the lies. I don't want to be a party to them anymore."

He stands up, taking her in his arms, and pressing his face into her damp hair, which smells like fresh flowers. He closes his eyes, wishing they were far away, starting their new life in Saipan. The house is already rented—a three-bedroom bungalow in the Capitol Hill section, overlooking a popular beach called Old Man by the Sea because of some rocks that jut into the ocean. It's not hard for him to picture the three of them walking on the shore, laughing, carefree. He opens his eyes. "So you still want to marry me? Even though my family is nuts?"

She laughs. "I do. More than ever."

As he hugs her closer, anxiety ripples through him. In the craziness of the past few days, he has almost forgotten to get what he came to town for.

It's time to confront his mother.

*   *   *

Renée turns away from the window and back to Cookie, who is sitting at her dining room table, cradling a cup of coffee.

"The detective is gone," Renée says. "She just drove off."

"Stop worrying, then. She's not coming over here. Now come sit down." He looks at his watch. "What time did you say the lawyer was coming?"

"Ten o'clock. He said we would talk and then go down to the police station together." Renée takes a seat at the table and drums her fingers on the wood. A smudge catches her eye, and she jumps up, returning moments later with a wet chamois.

"Renée, what are you doing?" Cookie asks with affectionate exasperation.

She rubs at the spot with tears in her eyes. This cherry table, with its four leaves, has been the setting for two dozen Thanksgiving dinners over the years. She had anticipated hosting many more, once Eva and Seth have their own children. "I might have to sell this. I want to keep it in good shape."

Cookie places his hand over hers to stop her cleaning. "Don't be dramatic. You're not going to have to sell your belongings." He waits a beat. "But if you decide to sell this gorgeous table, I want first dibs."

Renée lets out a small laugh and sits down again. Her chest is tight, but Cookie's silly jokes always make her feel better. "I won't be able to stay here once word gets out. Just imagine what the neighbors will say. I'll be a pariah."

"You're a survivor. You can sell this place, and with that money, you can get an adorable house farther out, near where you work. Or take early retirement and move someplace less expensive. You wouldn't be the first."

Renée smiles through tears at her neighbor. He really is a good friend. Last night, after she realized that Zak had taken the gun from the bag of cyclamen bulbs, the whole story came out. Cookie listened eagerly as they shared a bottle of sauvignon blanc in her kitchen, talking late into the night. By the end, they were both in tears, and he had given her the name of a good criminal defense lawyer.

"I don't want to go to prison." She can barely say the words without choking.

"Now you stop that, young lady. You are not going to prison." Cookie holds his hands out and picks at a cuticle. "You know, I always thought there was something off about the Calhouns."

Renée stops sniffling. "You did?"

Cookie nods vigorously. "Oh yes. I mean, they appear to be this amazing family, but you could just tell it was a façade." He wrinkles his nose. "Nobody's that perfect."

Renée frowns. Her friendship with Ginny is genuine. At least, it feels genuine. "I don't know. Ginny's been kind to me over the years."

Cookie scoffs. "Please. She groomed you! She manipulated you! And look what ended up happening."

Renée cocks her head to one side. She doesn't like to think of herself as a victim, and yet there's something appealing about the tale that Cookie is weaving. Perhaps Ginny did take advantage of her. "Maybe."

"Not *maybe*, Renée. *Definitely*. That's your story, and those are your key words—manipulated, cornered, pressured. You're just as much a victim here as anyone else."

A knock at the front door startles them both. "That must be the lawyer," Renée says, standing. She smooths out her navy pantsuit, the one she wears when she has her annual performance review with the school administration. She looks professional in it, trustworthy. She walks to the front door to let the lawyer in, pausing to see if Cookie is getting ready to leave. But he's still seated.

"I'd better stay." Cookie winks at her. "I think I can be helpful."

52

Nate leaves Danit and Malcolm in the kitchen and heads upstairs to talk to his mother. After knocking, he lets himself in and finds his mother awake, having opened the blinds with the remote control.

"Who was that downstairs?" she asks.

"That was the police." He sits in the chair near his mom's bed. "Shawna Douglas is dead." He watches her face for reaction to this news, but she looks back at him impassively. He's not accustomed to seeing her like this, but up close she looks so vulnerable without her makeup and pink lipstick. Even when he'd visited her in the hospital, she was fully made-up.

Ginny sits up, adjusting a pillow behind her. "Is that right? How?"

"She got drunk and fell asleep in her car in the garage. She died of carbon monoxide poisoning." He takes a deep breath. "That's not all. They found the gun in her car, the one that was used to kill Dad and to shoot you."

"Good God. So she is the one who shot me." She fusses with the lapels of her pink silk pajamas. "I guess I shouldn't be surprised. She'd been trying to wring more money from us for several months now. I was worried she might show up here sooner or later." His mother shudders. "The whole thing is just too awful."

"Yes, it is." He presses his lips shut, hoping his mother will take the opportunity to tell him about Shawna. He doesn't want to be the one to bring it up, but after a few moments of uncomfortable silence, he realizes how delusional it is to expect his mother to confess to anything. "I know," he says. "The detective told me. That she's Malcolm's mother."

"That's no mother." Ginny spits out the words. Despite everything she has done, Nate can't help but be shocked that she doesn't even blink when confronted with her duplicity. She doesn't have the decency to be ashamed.

"You knew, all this time," he says. "And you said nothing to me? Malcolm's mother was here, and you said nothing."

"She may have given birth to him, but believe me, she was more than happy to trade him for a nice fat check."

"I don't know anything about that. I wasn't there."

"No. You weren't," she snaps. "But your father and I were."

"She was in the car with Trey. In the accident. The police said you paid her off and she came back for more. I'm confused. Did you pay her off because of the crash? Or did you give her money for Malcolm?"

"Both. What's the difference, Nate? The girl was trash. She was trying to extort this family any way she knew how. We had to get her out of Trey's life. We used the tools we had at our disposal." She nods vigorously. "And yes, I mean money. I'm not ashamed of that."

"And Trey? He didn't wonder what had happened to her after the crash?" Nate adjusts the chair near her bed so that it's a few feet farther away, as if his mother were a wild creature and he doesn't want to be within striking distance.

"We let your brother think she had passed in the accident," Ginny says. "It was for the best."

Nate lets out a strangled laugh. "You did what?"

"Don't give me that. Your brother was slowly killing himself while you were off gallivanting with the whales," she says. "We did it for his own good. And we were right! She's a murderer. I assume the case is closed?"

Nate ignores the question. "Do you have any memory of her being in the study when you found Dad on the floor?"

She shakes her head. "None. Like I told the police, she might have been hiding when I went in, but I didn't see anyone."

"You know where they found her? In the model Fox Grove house. Any idea how she got in?"

His mom sighs and shuts her eyes for a moment. "Who's asking?"

"I am." He sits back in his chair. *This should be good.*

"I gave her the code. She called me the day after the party."

"Is that right?" Anger seeps into his voice. His mother is a shape-shifter, presenting a façade that serves her purpose at any given moment.

"I was still in the hospital. She basically blackmailed me, said that if I didn't find her a place to stay, she would go public—go to the media. Tell them everything she knew about our family." She lowers her chin and glares at Nate. "Tell them about Malcolm."

They are silent for a moment. *What does she want*, he thinks, *a thank-you?* Nate knows what his mother is doing. Using his love for Malcolm to blind him to her behavior. "Did you know when you helped her that she was the one who shot Dad?" he asks.

His mother opens her mouth as if she's appalled by such a thought. "Absolutely not! I was only thinking of you and Malcolm. I had to help her, Nate, you can see that. She was willing to drag that little boy's name through the mud. If you think the attention is bad now, imagine what it would have been like if she had come forward and started blabbing."

"I guess it works out well for you that she's dead."

"For *us*. And don't say it like that. I'm not an evil person. I'm a mother. And a grandmother. I would do anything to protect you all, and twice as much for little Malcolm. You're the same way, and you know it," she says. "What's one or two nights in a model home if it made her happy? If it kept her quiet?"

"The police think Trey gave her the code. When they find out he didn't, they'll come question you."

She waves her hand at him. "Let them. I'm not guilty of anything but loving my family to bits. Now how is my little fellow?" she asks gaily. "I'm about ready for a visit from my favorite grandson." And just like that she slips into the role of doting grandmother. She leans forward and tries to adjust the pillow under her foot. When she can't quite reach it, she smiles at Nate. "Be a love."

Nate gets up and is momentarily tempted to wrench the pillow from her and toss it on the floor, but he fixes it for her. "Malcolm's downstairs with Danit. And that's the second thing I wanted to ask you about." He stands over her. "Mom, I want you to sign the papers. And I need Malcolm's birth certificate."

His mother brings her pointer fingers to the sides of her forehead and massages gently. "You have got to be kidding me, Nathaniel. After all this, you're still planning on leaving?"

"This isn't up for discussion. I have a job that's starting."

"I need you."

"Trey is here. Ellie Grace and Zak are here. You'll be fine."

"Hasn't this horrible experience taught you anything? You need family. Let me buy you a house here. Budget is not a consideration—"

"Mom, no."

"A pool? I think Danit would like a pool. Or maybe not. She's very social. Perhaps she'd prefer the club. I will pay your initiation fee at the club. Think how wonderful it would be to bring Malcolm up near his only remaining grandparent, his doting aunt and uncles."

"Mom, stop. I'm going to Saipan with Danit this Sunday. That means I will need you to sign the papers and give me an original copy of Malcolm's birth certificate."

"Well, I can't help you." She sticks out her chin, defiant. "Your father had those things. He kept them in his safe. And as you know, that little bitch emptied it out."

"Don't call her that." He winces at the term. Whatever crimes

Shawna has committed, it is because of her that he has Malcolm in his life, and he will always be grateful to her for that. He gets up and walks over to the window to look out at the street. Even this early on a Tuesday morning, there are stragglers hanging about. *Wait until they hear about Shawna's death*, he thinks. *The street will be overrun.* "That was Malcolm's mother, and she deserves a modicum of respect."

"Oh, excuse me, Nathaniel." Her voice drips with sarcasm.

Something occurs to him, and he spins around. "If Shawna killed Dad and took all the stuff—then where is it? The police didn't mention it."

"How am I to know? She probably threw it in the garbage. It meant nothing to her. But my jewelry, that's what I'd like to find out about. Did the police say they found my jewelry? My Cartier panther ring?"

Nate opens and closes his fist. How can she think of her stupid jewelry, which insurance will replace? He tells himself to remain calm. "So the papers are just gone?" He faces her. "You don't have another copy of the birth certificate?"

"Like I said, your father handled all the paperwork regarding Malcolm's adoption. Look, we can write to the State of California, ask for a new birth certificate. It shouldn't take too long. Maybe a few weeks, a month or two."

"A few weeks! We are leaving on Sunday, Mom."

"Well, there's nothing I can do about that. That awful girl took everything that was in the safe. Cleared it straight out."

Nate looks over at Trey's house. His poor brother, caught up for years in his parents' subterfuge. Is there anything his mother wouldn't do to keep her kids where she wants them? If she weren't laid up in bed with a wounded foot, he might entertain the idea that she killed Shawna herself. It is very convenient. *Stop it.* That detective has planted doubt in his head.

"If I had known you'd be so tedious about these tiny details, I would have given Malcolm to Ellie Grace instead."

Nate pivots, marching to her bedside. "But you didn't, did you? As I recall, you and Dad never even considered it. You said her being a single mother would raise too many questions, look bad for the family." He means this as a stinging rebuke, a reminder of how bloodless and calculating she has been, but Ginny nods, taking it at face value.

"True. Besides, your father was worried about what kind of leverage Ellie Grace might have over us if she knew the truth."

Leverage. That was the currency in this family. Not love or compassion. Not duty or loyalty but leverage. Nate turns, ready to do something he hasn't done since he was a teenager and said he had never tried pot: lie to his mother. "You're going to get me those papers by the end of the week. I don't care how you do it. There must be another birth certificate somewhere."

"Well, there isn't—"

"Find one. Because if you don't, I'll tell Trey about Malcolm and Shawna. I'll tell him he had a child that you kept secret. I'll tell him Shawna was the mother of that child."

She gasps. "You wouldn't dare."

"But let us leave"—he prepares himself for the lie—"and I will keep your secret forever."

53

Ellie Grace is unpacking the Rocklands Barbeque takeout on the counter at her mother's while Zak puts a couple of six-packs of DC Brau in the fridge. She spent the afternoon calling and emailing some of her father's distant relatives and colleagues, explaining to them what happened, and now she is thoroughly drained. She had no idea just how *logistical* death was. And her to-do list seems to grow every day. She is meeting with the pastor at St. Giles's tomorrow to go over the funeral arrangements. *Did your father have a favorite hymn?* he asked her, and Ellie Grace almost hung up on him. Instead, she quickly blurted out, "Amazing Grace," but then felt kind of basic afterward.

"Can I get a drink?" Ellie Grace asks Zak. "One of those can thingies."

"Vodka tonic or mojito?"

"Vodka tonic, and lemon and ice, please." She places serving spoons and forks next to the pulled pork, collard greens, macaroni and cheese, and coleslaw.

"Rocklands. Nice," Trey says when he walks in.

"Want a beer, bro?" Zak asks, reaching into the fridge. "We got the Corruption IPA and Joint Resolution Hazy IPA."

"I'll take a Hazy."

"What are you two, like, BFFs now?" Ellie Grace teases, but it makes her happy to see them get along. It's hard to believe that delivering that mahogany side table to the restorer was some kind of male-bonding experience, but whatever brought these two together, she's grateful for it.

Zak hands her a glass, and she takes a long sip of the vodka tonic. She's in the mood to drink, stuff herself with fatty food, and watch garbage TV. Danit walks over with a plastic divided plate, Malcolm right behind her, and puts a little bit of food in each section. "I don't think Malcolm has had barbecue yet," Danit says. Ellie Grace makes a face of mock horror. "Well, Rocklands is a D.C. institution. And it's soooo good." She plops a big heap of mac and cheese on a porcelain plate decorated with delicate blue flowers. She made an executive decision to use the good china, and why not? How often do they have the whole family here like this? Plus, fine china can elevate the most ordinary meal.

"Is that all for you?" Danit asks, nodding at the plate piled high with food.

"It's for a photo, but Zak and I will eat off it after."

"How's the whole Gingham Life thing going right now?"

Ellie Grace nods enthusiastically. "Great," she says, sounding a little squeaky. The truth is she hasn't really found her footing since her dad was killed. "I hoped that avoiding talking about what happened would make people stop posting about it, but it seems to have made things worse. People are saying I'm insensitive and cold."

"But you're not!"

"I know, right? And last night, I posted a very well-thought-out, well-crafted—" She stops and pulls out her phone. "Let me just read it to you." She clears her throat. "'As many of you know, my family suffered an incredible tragedy this past weekend.'" She looks up at Danit, who nods in encouragement. "'I chose not to say literally that my dad was murdered, because that's kind of ghoulish. Anyway, as I was saying, our hearts are shattered by this loss. We are overwhelmed with grief right now, but we are so incredibly grateful and blessed to have this amazing Gingham Life community to support us at this time. Thank you to everyone for your kind words and messages of love. We appreciate you more than you can ever know. We'll be taking a short break to deal with everything, but we hope to be back soon.'" She examines Danit's face, trying to gauge her reaction. "So, what do you think?"

"I think it's great. Pitch-perfect."

"Thank you." Danit is so nice, it makes Ellie Grace a little squeamish. When she was in middle school, she rode horses with a plump, sweet girl from school named Hope. At the stables, they developed a friendship, but at school, they were in different circles. A few times, Hope tried to expand their friendship into their school lives, and Ellie Grace cut that short, like the time Hope tried to sit with her at lunch. She was doing it for Hope's own good—her friends could be merciless. She still remembers the hurt look on Hope's face when she told her that she wouldn't be coming to her horse-themed thirteenth birthday party. But Hope never held it against her and continued to be kind at the stables. Danit reminds her of Hope. Maybe Ellie Grace has made a huge mistake in spurning all the nice girls—like Hope and Danit—who have tried to befriend her over the years. All that social climbing and trying desperately to be in the right group—where has it gotten her now? She is practically friendless. She has always chalked it up to women being catty, but maybe she has been hanging out with the wrong women. Danit is a second chance at female friendship. "I thought it was good, too, but now people are calling it fake and phony. I swear, you cannot win."

Danit frowns in sympathy. "That's honestly why I'm not on social media. I don't think it would be good for my mental health. People can be so mean."

Ellie Grace dips a serving spoon into the collard greens as she responds to Danit. "I know. If I didn't have to be on it—"

"Excuse me!" Nate bellows.

Ellie Grace stops, spoon midair, and turns to face her brother, who has entered the kitchen and is holding his hand in the air like an overeager student. "Can I have everyone's attention?" he asks loudly.

"Nate, you want a beer?" Zak asks.

"Please," Nate says, "everyone stop for a minute."

The room falls silent except for Malcolm, who is banging together two metal spoons he managed to get a hold of.

"What is it?" Ellie Grace asks.

Nate turns to Trey. "Did the police talk to you today?"

Trey shakes his head. "No. Why would they?"

"Well, they came by here," he says. "And they said they were trying to reach you."

"Oh yeah. That must've been them calling." Trey snorts. "I have about four missed calls."

"Well, I need to tell you all something."

"What?" Ellie Grace takes a look at her brother's face, and her stomach drops. He's never been one for dramatics. Whatever he's planning to tell them, it's big.

"There are two things," Nate says, "and I don't know which order to tell them in."

"Oh my God, Nate—just say what you have to say." Ellie Grace drums her fingers on the counter in impatience. The only way to handle bad news is to get it out there as quickly as possible. Then you can come up with a plan and move forward.

"Fine. Here goes. The police know who shot Mom and Dad."

It takes a moment for the words to sink in. Ellie Grace leans back against the counter in shock. "Oh my God! Who was it?"

"Shawna Douglas."

"My Shawna?" Trey asks. "Holy shit. How do they know?"

"They found the murder weapon in her car," Nate says. "Plus, she admitted she was at the party to blackmail them. She wanted more money."

"Did she confess to Dad's murder?" Zak asks.

"No. And she never will." He pauses a moment. "That's my second piece of news. She's dead."

Dead. The word rings in Ellie Grace's ears. Feeling nauseated, she turns her back on everyone, gripping the counter for support.

Danit comes closer. "You all right? Need water?"

Ellie Grace nods. She hears the whir of the water filter on the fridge, and in a moment, Danit hands her a glass. She gulps it down, and it makes her feel a little better. Questions swirl in her mind. She turns back to Nate. "What happened to her?"

"She got drunk and passed out in her car," he says. "She died of carbon monoxide poisoning because the car was still running, and the garage door was closed. The police aren't sure if it was suicide or an accident."

Ellie Grace brings her hand to her mouth as she pictures the young woman she saw on TV slumped over in her car. She was so young.

"So, it's over?" Trey asks.

"I think so." Nate walks to the fridge and takes out a beer. "There are a few loose ends. But basically, yeah, it's over." He cracks the beer open before taking a long pull.

"You okay, babe?" Zak comes up next to Ellie Grace, putting an arm around her and pulling her into him in one smooth gesture. She allows herself to be folded into his embrace, tears stinging her eyes. Her shoulders shake as her vision becomes blurry. All the stress of the past few days leaves her body in one violent push as a sob wrenches free from deep within her. "Shh," Zak murmurs in her ear. "It's okay, babe. It's all over."

"I know," she sobs. "I'm just so relieved." She pulls back from him and grabs a takeout napkin to wipe her eyes. It smells like corn bread. "I'm just so glad it's over. And honestly, I know this is a terrible thing to say, but since she's dead, there won't be any trial."

"That's not terrible," Danit says. "It's totally understandable. You all have been through so much."

Ellie Grace smiles at her through tears. "Now we can focus on Daddy's funeral. And just, like, start to get on with our lives."

Zak picks up the plate, laden with food, that Ellie Grace made. "C'mon, let's all go eat in the dining room."

Ellie Grace nods. "That sounds good. We just need to take a few photos of the plate first."

54

Later on Tuesday evening, Danit returns to the kitchen and pours herself a glass of wine. Malcolm was just fussing a bit, but he's fine now. She wonders if it's confusing for him to change houses like this. Personally, she wishes they had stayed at Ellie Grace's. She doesn't like sleeping in a house where a murder just took place, but she understands why Nate prefers to be here, in his childhood home. She glances at the TV room, where Zak's and Ellie Grace's faces glow in the light of the TV. She's too restless to watch a movie. She pulls her phone out and checks the time, wondering when Nate will be back from the Tastee Diner, where he went to keep his dad's appointment with someone called JB.

Nate's laptop is on the counter. Danit sits down with her wine and brings the screen to life. She gets lost for a while browsing websites that rate the best beaches for a wedding in Saipan. One in particular catches her eye with its white, powdery sand and bright blue water.

Commenters describe it as an undeveloped gem of a beach perfect for snorkeling and gorgeous sunsets. She loves the idea of getting married on a beach, barefoot. She can't believe she's going to be calling this beautiful island home by next week. She just has to get through the rest of this week, including Nate's father's funeral on Friday at St. Giles's. She's already promised Ellie Grace she will help with the flowers. She wanders over to Instagram and signs in. Her own account is meager, thirty followers and one post. She's really there to lurk. She finds Gingham Life and scrolls. In the past few days, Ellie Grace's posts have become more frantic and unhinged. The apology post did not land well. The comments are merciless, and what's worse is it looks like Ellie Grace has actually responded to some of the cruelest ones. Danit might not know much about social media, but she knows you're not supposed to feed the trolls.

Danit finds the last post that was from the party—the photo dump. It's about a dozen photos of different stages of the party—with Ellie Grace at the center of them all. It was only a few days ago, but it feels like it's been ages since so many people gathered on the front lawn. She scans the party guests' faces. No one, herself included, had a hint of what was to come.

She stops when she comes to a photo of Renée and Ellie Grace clinking glasses of Cherry Smash. She thinks she sees Shawna in the background. Danit enlarges the photo—it's definitely the girl who was on TV. Something gnaws at her. She opens up the photographer's website that Ellie Grace sent her and types in the password. Immediately, the page is filled with hundreds of small photos from the party. Ellie Grace was right—the photographer was snap happy. It takes her a moment, but near the end, she finds the photo with Shawna in the background and pulls up the info—it was taken at 5:21 p.m. Did Shawna already know that she was going to shoot Thom and Ginny? Probably not. The detective said this morning that Shawna had come to "renegotiate," that she wanted more money. The gun was Thom's. It must have been a spur-of-the-moment decision.

She sips her wine, trying to imagine the scene. Shawna, an outsider, confronting Thom in his study. How would she know about his gun? Maybe Thom pulled it out, and she somehow got it away from him? Then she shoots Thom and Ginny and goes upstairs to change her shirt . . . Danit scrolls down a few photos on the website and finds another one of Shawna, taken at 5:49. Cookie said Renée had come out of the house at 5:50. He was sure of it. And Renée said she went to Thom's study after hearing two loud noises, presumably gunshots. Assuming that

Renée came outside more or less immediately after discovering the bodies, that would only give Shawna a few minutes to shoot Thom and Ginny, go upstairs and change her shirt, and come back outside.

Danit shifts in her seat, antsy with a growing sense of unease. Something isn't right.

She toggles back to Instagram and resumes looking at Ellie Grace's photos, not sure what she is searching for, but certain she will know it when she sees it.

The last photo is the one the waiter took of her, Cookie, Bob, and Ellie Grace at the croquet game. Everyone looks happy, but Ellie Grace's smile is forced, her eyes laser sharp. Danit frowns, noticing something. She zooms in on the photo, a hot flush rising within her.

In one ear, Ellie Grace wears a sapphire-and-pearl stud. The other ear is naked. She recognizes the earring as the one the detective showed them in Trey's living room, which the detective said was found in the study. Danit quickly scrolls back at the other pictures of Ellie Grace—in all of them, she's wearing both earrings.

So if that was her earring, why did Ellie Grace lie to the police?

Because she didn't want them to know she was in her dad's study right before that last photo—just a minute before Renée came out of the house at 5:50. Ellie Grace laughs loudly at something on the TV. Danit tries to imagine Ellie Grace shooting her parents and then rushing outside in time to have her photo taken. *It's absurd.*

And yet.

She did seem off right before the waiter snapped that photo. Danit just assumed it was something to do with Zak. But maybe that wasn't it at all. Maybe she was so insistent on taking it to establish that she was outside when her father was discovered.

It doesn't add up, Danit thinks. The safe was emptied and all of Ginny's jewelry taken off of her. That pointed to Shawna. Why would Ellie Grace take her own mother's jewelry? Unless she wanted to make it look like a robbery. But then, where was the stuff she took? Danit looks closely at the second picture. A tiny pink leather handbag attached to a gold chain hangs from Ellie Grace's shoulder. Barely big enough for a phone and a lipstick, much less documents and stolen jewelry.

So if Ellie Grace did take those things, she would have had to hide them. But where? The police were all over the house.

The hidey-hole.

The word pops into her head.

Danit straightens up, remembering Cookie plucking that brown leafy thing out of Ellie Grace's hair. What did he call it? She searches her brain until the word comes to her—catkin. The flower of an oak, he'd said.

Danit looks at the french doors that open onto the backyard. Without hesitating, she walks to the back and opens one of the doors. The night is dark and cool, but she can clearly see the giant oak. She remembers what Nate had said about acorns on the roof when they were kids. It stood to reason that the roof would also be littered with catkins. *If Ellie Grace had climbed onto the roof to hide the contents of the safe and Ginny's jewelry in the hidey-hole*, she thinks, *that could be why she had an oak catkin in her hair.*

"Crazy," Danit says aloud, but she's already on her way upstairs, to the bathroom.

55

As soon as Nate enters the Tastee Diner in downtown Bethesda, a man sitting by himself in a wooden booth in the back waves him over.

"JB?" Nate asks as he slides in across from the man.

"Jon Block," the other man says, wiping his hand on a napkin before offering it to Nate. In his midforties, Block is fit and wiry, vibrating with the energy of the highly caffeinated. "Don't have too much time. But I feel guilty as fuck about what happened to Thom. To your dad, I mean. That's why I came. I thought there was a solid chance one of you kids might show up. I didn't want to come bother you, in your time of grief and all, but I wanted to be here in case you had questions." He leans back to make room for a waitress who has appeared with a pot of coffee.

"Coffee, hon?" she asks.

"Sure," Nate says, leaning back while she flips the mug over and fills it. "My first question is, who are you? And how did you know my dad?"

"Menu?" The waitress holds one out.

Nate glances at his dining companion, who is shoveling eggs and bacon into his mouth as if someone might grab the plate at any minute. "No, thanks."

"I'm a private investigator. Your dad hired me. You know, my first job was here, busing tables in 1987," Block says between bites. "This place first opened in 1939. Can you believe that?" He scoops up a glop of yellow egg yolk with his toast. "Location was originally on Wisconsin Avenue, but they moved the diner to this spot in the '50s. Breakfast served all day. One of the last authentic diners."

Nate reaches for a little silver creamer. He hates weak diner coffee, but decides against sharing this thought. "Can we get back to how you feel guilty as . . ."

"Right." Block takes a big gulp of coffee. "Your dad should have waited like I told him to. I told him not to confront that little turd without me. I said, 'Thom, wait until I get back. Just let me be in the room.' Not that I thought that pretty boy was going to react violently, but at least if I were there, I could get a read on the guy's reaction. It's just smart. But your dad insisted on going ahead. Said it had to be done that day, at the party."

"I'm sorry. You're talking really fast, and I'm not following. Do you mind if we start at the beginning? Why did my dad hire you?"

After wiping all the egg bits off his face, Block places a folder on the table between them. "This is what your dad hired me to do. Look into his son-in-law. Zak Miller." He taps the folder with two fingers. "And it's a doozy."

"May I?" Nate asks.

"It's all yours." Block pushes the folder across the pale yellow Formica table.

Nate opens it and glances at the first page—a criminal complaint for fraud in Florida. "Holy cow. But who's Drake Bailey? Is that Zak?"

"Sort of. Your brother-in-law has a few aliases—Drake Bailey, Zak Miller. His real name is Darnell Hoover, and he's wanted in connection with fraud in several states. But fraud's not the big one."

"Meaning?"

"Meaning Darnell Hoover is wanted for questioning in the death of a woman he was involved with in Arizona five years ago. A widow in her forties. The two had a relationship, and by all accounts, he was blowing through her money. Then she died under suspicious circumstances, and he left town."

"You think he had something to do with her death?"

Block shrugs. "Let's just say the police in Arizona were eager to speak to him. It's all in the report I prepared for Thom. I was supposed to meet your dad on Saturday. Here at the diner, actually. But then I had to leave town, so I swung by his place instead."

"Wait, you came to the house the day he died?" He looks up quickly.

"That's right. I hand-delivered a copy of my report that morning. And I told him, 'Don't do anything. Just sit tight. This is incendiary stuff.'"

"If Zak saw what was in this file, if he thought my dad . . ." He can't bring himself to finish the sentence. He looks back at the folder in front of him. He'd never liked Zak, always found him slippery and vain. His dad thought he was lazy. But a criminal? "Do you think he shot my dad?"

Block pushes his empty plate to the end of the table. "I don't know. But I'll tell you this. Your dad was in a mood when he saw this. I mean, he already knew the basics of what I was compiling—we had been talking for several weeks—but seeing it all in writing like this?" Block shakes his head. "Man, his face turned so red, I thought his head was going to explode. He told me he had a new will drawn up, but it needed a few tweaks, that he planned to sign it this week. But when he saw what was in here"—he motions toward the file—"he pulled that will out and signed it right in front of me. Even asked me to witness it."

"Let me get this straight. My dad signed an updated will, and you witnessed it?"

"Yup."

"Then what did he do with it?"

"Popped it in his safe. Saw it with my own eyes." Block turns away and gestures for the check. "Sorry, I got to get going. Have to get to Maggiano's in Friendship Heights."

"Working another case?"

"Nah." He pulls a business card from his pocket and tosses it on the table. "Bar mitzvah. DJing is my side hustle. I do it all, but my specialty is '80s music. Keep the card. You never know when you'll need a DJ."

"One more question before you go. Did anyone else see the will or the file on Zak? I mean, did my mom come into the study? Or anyone else?"

"Don't think so." He leans back so the waitress can drop the check. "There were a lot of people around—the catering staff were there setting up, the housekeeper was there. I know I saw your mom at one point, but no one came into the study." He raps his knuckles on the table. "Sorry about your dad, man. And thanks for grabbing the check."

After he is gone, Nate motions to the waitress for some more coffee and opens up the folder. One, two, three indictments in different states under different aliases—all for fraud. But it's the suspicious death that he homes in on. WEALTHY WIDOW DEAD, YOUNG LOVER AWOL reads one headline in a newspaper story that Block has included in the file. Friends describe the older woman, Alice Meeks, as besotted, buying the younger man a car, clothes, whatever he wanted. Her sister said that Meeks discovered Hoover had been selling off stock without her knowledge, and she was planning to go to the police when she died.

But when he reads the last paragraph of the story, his blood goes cold.

Meeks was found dead in her garage, her blood alcohol level at 0.28. *She died from carbon monoxide poisoning.*

56

Danit's whole body shivers as she climbs the stairs and enters Nate's old bedroom. She crosses it to the bathroom, which joins his room and Trey's old room, and goes straight to the window.

It occurs to her that she ought to wait until Nate comes back, but then what would she say to him? *I think your sister might be involved in your dad's death. There was an oak catkin in her . . .* It sounds ridiculous. Nate would be dismayed. She'd have to convince him. Besides, it might draw Ellie Grace's and Zak's attention, whereas right now they are absorbed in their show.

She can get out onto the roof, check the chimney, and be back in mere minutes. She tries to remember what Nate said. *Yeah, we had an old lockbox we shoved in a hole in the side of the chimney.* It is a crazy thought, that Ellie Grace had anything to do with the shootings, but it is jammed in her brain, and the only way to get it out is to check the hidey-hole for herself.

Once she is through the bathroom window and onto the roof, her adrenaline kicks in. She's never considered herself afraid of heights, but being out here in the dark feels dangerous. There is no railing, nothing that would stop her from falling off if she were to slip. Swallowing her fear, she takes a step toward the brick chimney. The night air is chilly, and she catches the whiff of a wood fire burning somewhere. Beneath her feet, a carpeting of brown catkins from the oak tree above cushions each step, and Danit is surer than ever that Ellie Grace was here. A full-moon guides her steps as she moves tentatively. Just a few more feet and she can grab the chimney for support. Something scurries in a far corner, and Danit shrieks.

Just a mouse, she tells herself. Finally, her hand hits the cold brick, flooding her with relief. She reaches around the back of the chimney, patting tentatively, afraid of spiders or other creatures that might be making the defunct chimney their home. For a second, the whole theory seems ridiculous, and she wonders if it's all been a dumb mistake, but then she touches the edge of a metal box and a zap of adrenaline runs through her. Once she's wiggled the box free, she stares at it for a moment, not quite believing that it really exists outside of Nate's memories. She slides down to a crouching position, heart thumping, and lifts the lid. This is the moment of truth.

As soon as she opens it, she knows she was right—inside are three manila envelopes and a plastic bag filled with jewelry. Light-headed with a mix of fear and elation, she pulls the biggest piece of jewelry out of the bag. Holding the object up to the moonlight, she can make out that it's a ring shaped like a panther, covered in dozens of tiny diamonds with two sapphire eyes.

Ginny's ring.

Danit places it back in the bag and scans the manila envelopes. They each have large, white labels with block print on them—UPDATED WILL & DIVORCE PAPERS, DARNELL HOOVER, and the last one is marked MALCOLM. Just seeing the word sends a shiver through her. What could it contain?

She reaches inside the one marked MALCOLM and pulls out one of the papers. It looks like a birth certificate, but it's too dark to read. She'll have to examine everything once she's back in the house. She shoves everything back in the metal box. She has to get this stuff to Nate, to the police. Whoever put that stuff in the box had to have been involved with the shooting. She backtracks to the window, clutching the box in both hands, careful with her footing. The last thing she needs is to twist an ankle up here. From below, Danit hears the sound of a twig breaking.

She freezes. Only silence.

The neighborhood is filled with so many animals. Rabbits, raccoons, foxes—one neighbor at the party was telling her there were even coyote sightings in Chevy Chase. It could be any of those creatures. She scans the dark yard but sees nothing out of the ordinary.

Still, her heart pounds wildly in her chest.

Psyching herself up, Danit continues to the window. She has one hand on the sill, about to step through, when Zak appears on the other side of the window in the bathroom, blocking her way. She steps back, startled.

"What's going on out here?" He climbs through the window onto the roof.

"Nothing," she says, moving back slightly.

"What have you got there? A box?"

Instinctively, she jerks the box back behind her. "It's nothing."

"Danit, Danit. What have you done?" he says in a teasing tone. "Let me see the box." He reaches his hand out.

"I want to go inside now, Zak. Please. Let me by."

"When I came into the kitchen and saw the laptop open with that picture of Ellie Grace pulled up, I knew that you figured it out."

Zak takes a step forward.

"Wait!"

To her surprise, Zak stops. Danit tightens her grip on the box. She should have closed out that window on the laptop and shut it. "I found Ginny's jewelry." Danit silently prays that someone, anyone, will intervene. Nate should be home any second. "Do you have any idea who could have put it here? Was it Ellie Grace?"

Zak's mouth spreads into a slow smile. "How'd you even know to come up here?"

"The catkins."

He narrows his eyes. "The what?"

"The oak tree," she says, hoping she can keep him talking long enough until she can think of a way to get past him to the window, or until Nate arrives. "I just guessed it was in the hidey-hole."

"The what?" His face is blank—no recognition.

"Are you saying that you didn't know this stuff was in the chimney?" She can sense Zak stiffen. "Ellie Grace didn't tell you?"

"We've never discussed the details of that night." His voice has hardened; gone is the teasing tone.

Danit can't stop a strangled laugh from escaping her throat. "What? I thought you guys were so close."

"We are. But it's better that way. She gets to keep acting like the grief-stricken daughter, and my conscience is clean."

"But you knew, didn't you?"

"I didn't *know* anything, Danit, and neither do you. Why don't you give me that stuff, and we'll walk inside, have a drink, and pretend this never happened?" As he takes a step forward, she retreats farther, glancing behind her. She's getting too close to the edge of the roof for comfort. It's about a fifteen-foot drop to the hard stone patio below.

"I can't do that, Zak."

"Why not? What's done is done." He moves closer to her, and this time when she steps back, she uses one hand to grab onto a hanging limb of the oak tree.

"It's the Calhoun way," he says. "And you're about to become a Calhoun. Think about what you're doing. You know what's in those envelopes?"

She shakes her head. "Not really."

"Well, I'm pretty sure there's a will," he says. "And if that will ever surfaces, your precious Nate will not inherit a cent. Understand? Not a penny. None of us will."

"That's not my problem."

He laughs. "Well, it's my problem. And it's Ellie Grace's problem. And it's Trey's problem and Ginny's, too. So since you want to be part of the family, that kind of makes it your problem."

"What are you going to do?" she asks, her voice quivering. "You can't just—I mean, Nate's going to be home any minute."

"But you won't be here. You'll have left. It was all too much for you."

She laughs. "That's crazy. He won't believe that."

"Won't he?" Zak cocks his head. "No one would notice if you disappeared, Danit. You said it yourself—all you had was your mom, and she's dead. You're like me. You barely exist on this planet."

"That's not true," she protests. She knows he is messing with her head, but the words still sting.

"If you're gone, no one's going to ask too many questions. Because you don't matter to anyone."

"That's not true!" Cookie's voice rings out from below. "She matters to me."

Zak spins around toward Cookie's voice, giving Danit the chance to swing the metal box and bring it down hard on the back of Zak's head. He stumbles, falling to his knees as she sprints to the window.

"Run, Danit!" Cookie yells as Danit climbs through the window into the bathroom, breathless, blood pumping, her throat too dry to answer. But inside she is screaming, *I am! I am!*

57

Danit sits at one end of the living room sofa, hugging her knees to her chest, waiting for her heart rate to return to normal. If a stranger walked in right now, it would look like a very tense get-together with Trey slouching on the other end of the sofa, a slightly bemused look on his face, Ellie Grace sitting in one of a pair of matching armchairs holding hands with Zak, who's clutching a bag of peas to his forehead where Danit struck him.

Behind him, Cookie paces, agitated, like a panther in a cage, as if ready to pounce should Zak make a move.

There's little chance of that, Danit tells herself, thanks to the fresh-faced police officer standing in the middle of the Calhoun living room looking overwhelmed.

"This is all a big misunderstanding," Ellie Grace says, her lipstick slightly smeared, lending her a deranged look. "You didn't have to come. It's just a family matter."

"Misunderstanding!" Cookie stops directly behind Zak, putting his hands on his hips. "He was threatening Danit. I heard it with my own ears."

"What are you doing here, anyway?" Ellie Grace spins in her chair to face Cookie.

Cookie gasps. "The audacity!"

"One at a time, please." The officer's head swivels back and forth.

The front door opens, and Danit turns to see Nate come in, followed by Detective Washington and two more uniformed police officers. Danit jumps up and runs into his arms. He hugs her tightly. "You all right?" he whispers in her ear. "What happened?"

"I found something, Nate. On your sister's Instagram page."
She tells him what happened—going out on the roof, finding
the metal box, Zak confronting her.

"Did he hurt you?"

Danit looks up at Nate's face, recognizing a barely controlled
rage that she has never seen in him before. "No. In fact, I kind
of hurt him . . ." Her voice trails off when she spots a manila
envelope in his hand. "What is that?"

Nate takes her by the hand and walks into the living room.
Detective Washington nods toward the stairs. "Your mother is
up there?"

"Yes," Nate says.

The detective motions with her chin at the stairs, and the two
officers immediately head for them.

"Excuse me." Ellie Grace shoots up out her seat. "Just what do
you think you're doing? You can't just come in here. My mother
is injured."

"My officers will be very gentle," Washington says. "And this
says we *can* come in here." She hands a folded piece of paper to
Ellie Grace, who opens it up and scans it.

"Arrest warrant?" She looks up. "This is crazy." But she sits
back down without further protest.

Nate clears his throat. "Maybe I can shed some light on what's
going on. I just had a conversation with a private investigator
Dad hired. This guy gave me a copy of a report he had given
to Dad the day he was murdered." Nate sits on the arm of the
couch, and Danit takes a seat near him. She would love to crawl
in his lap right now, but she'll settle for sitting close enough to
touch him.

"May I?" Detective Washington approaches Nate, takes the
folder from him, and positions herself in the middle of the room,
displacing the younger officer, who retreats to a spot next to the
fireplace. Washington turns to face Zak. "Look at this. It turns
out Zak Miller isn't your real name. It's Darnell Hoover. And

you are wanted in several states for fraud, and for questioning in the suspicious death of a woman in Arizona."

Cookie lets out a huff.

Danit watches Ellie Grace's face, but to her surprise, Ellie Grace remains composed. She takes her husband's hand in both of hers. "This is all a stupid mistake."

"The woman in Arizona died from carbon monoxide poisoning," Nate says. "Passed out drunk in her car. Sound familiar?" He turns to Zak. "I guess you figured if it worked once . . ."

The reality of what Nate is implying sinks in, and Danit's chest tightens. He's a killer. And he was coming after her less than an hour ago. No wonder Nate was so worried when he came in. Zak's threats weren't empty. "Did Zak kill that girl—Shawna Douglas?" she asks him.

"No, he did not!" Ellie Grace shouts. "People die of carbon monoxide poisoning every day! It's called a coincidence."

"Some coincidence," Cookie says.

"Mr. Hoover is wanted in four states for wire fraud, identity theft, and insurance fraud," Washington reads from the paper she's holding. "Looks like his MO is to ingratiate himself into a woman's life, someone lonely, a little desperate, not too many friends or relatives—"

"Excuse me!" Ellie Grace shrieks.

"Look, I've made some mistakes," Zak says. "But that's in the past."

"Only this time, you hit the jackpot. Didn't you?" Washington looks directly at Zak. "Ellie Grace is worth millions. Many millions. And by marrying her, and staying married to her, you stood to inherit that money. But only if no one found out about your past."

"And my father figured it out, didn't he?" Nate asks. "And that's why you killed him. And you framed Shawna Douglas."

Zak laughs. "I never even went inside the house during the party. I was outside the whole time."

A scuffle on the stairs catches everyone's attention. Danit turns to see Ginny being half carried by the two police officers. She's wearing a flowing silk robe decorated with flowers, and Danit can see the bright pink lipstick on her mouth even from her spot on the couch. She reminds Danit of the scene in one of her favorite noir movies, *Sunset Boulevard*, when the aging film star descends the grand staircase in her house before she is arrested for murder. Ginny Calhoun, bejeweled in diamonds and pearls, looks ready for her close-up.

"Come sit here, Mommy." Ellie Grace jumps up and helps escort her mother to the chair she was just sitting in.

"What in tarnation is this all about?" her mother asks. "I thought all this was settled."

"Not exactly," Detective Washington says. "The gun that we found in Shawna Douglas's car? We know you put it there, Zak."

"C'mon," Zak says in a breezy tone that doesn't fit with the circumstances. "You can't know that."

"Renée Price, your mother's neighbor, came in for a little chat today," Washington says. "She told us how you took it from her yard last night."

"That's right," Cookie says, nodding. "He was in the yard. I saw him myself."

Ginny clutches at her throat. "Renée was involved in all this? I think I need a drink."

Trey, who has been silently slumped in one corner of the sofa, jumps up. "G and T, Mom?"

Ginny shakes her head. "I'll take a whiskey. The Macallan, if you don't mind."

"Please, spare us the dramatics, Mrs. Calhoun," Washington continues. "Ms. Price told us everything. How she was in the bathroom and received a text to meet you in Thom's study. How she found you standing over Thom's dead body and asked her to help. Well, maybe *ask* isn't the right word. You bribed her, didn't you? You offered her one million dollars to shoot you in your leg—"

Ginny laughs sharply. "What a tale! What utter nonsense!" She gazes at Trey standing by the liquor cart and in a strained voice says, "My scotch, dear. I'm waiting."

"You knew she was desperate for money to keep her house," the detective says as if she had not been interrupted. "And you were desperate to make Thom's shooting look like a robbery, with both of you the victims. Did you already have Shawna lined up as your patsy?"

Ginny accepts the tumbler of scotch from Trey with a trembling hand. "I refuse to answer such a ridiculous question."

"We know you gave Ms. Price strict instructions—after shooting you in the leg, she called 9-1-1 immediately, and then did her little act. Rushing out front, screaming on the steps. In the ensuing chaos, while everyone was distracted, she told us that she took the gun, which she had stashed in her purse, and hid it in a bag of bulbs out back. She was worried the police might look through her purse. She played her part well. But it never really added up." Washington cocks her head toward the back of the house. "The study is wood paneled with thick oak. It's practically soundproofed. So how did Ms. Price hear the gunshots while she was in the bathroom? With the door closed and the exhaust fan on? If they were that loud, surely someone on the catering staff would have heard, too."

Ginny clasps her hands together. "Marvelous piece of fiction. Wonderful. But you have no proof. Show me the text."

"You were smart to delete it from your phone and have Renée delete her text. But cell records still show that you sent her a text at 5:42."

"I'm sure I did. We text regularly. It could have been about anything. Why in the world would I want to cover up my husband's murder?" She leans forward a little, eyeing her bandaged leg. "And why would I let someone shoot me?"

No one says anything. Smiling triumphantly, Ginny leans back. "Besides, we know who did this. That Shawna Douglas girl. You found her shirt with my husband's blood on it. She's the one with a motive. She wanted money."

"It's true," Trey pipes in. "She told me that herself. She came back here to squeeze my parents for more money. And the bloody shirt and the gun. It all points to her. Renée is lying. I don't know why, but she is."

"There is simply no logical reason for me to have been involved."

Danit shifts in her seat, pulling the metal box from the hidey-hole closer to her. Quietly, she opens the box and peers inside. The folder marked UPDATED WILL & DIVORCE PAPERS is on top. She nudges Nate, who looks over her shoulder at the folder, eyes widening. She peels it out of the box and hands it to him.

"I think I know why you might have done it, Mom." He pulls the papers out. "Dad was having an affair, wasn't he? Only this time, he was planning to divorce you."

"What?" Ellie Grace asks. "That can't be true. Is it, Mommy?"

Ignoring his sister, Nate keeps going. "How did you know about it, Mom? Did you figure it out when the flowers didn't come? Or did he straight-out tell you?"

"Nate, what are you talking about?" Ellie Grace asks. "Where'd you get this idea?"

He turns toward his sister. "Dad saw a lawyer. I spoke to him myself. He said there was an updated will, one that cut Mom out, that cut us all out. But that Dad hadn't had the chance to return it signed." He flips through the papers he has pulled out of the envelope. "But the private investigator Dad hired said he did sign it. In fact, the guy—Jon Block—was the one who witnessed it. And whaddya know?" He holds up a piece of paper. "Here's the signature and witness."

Trey is up on his feet and over by Nate in a matter of seconds. "That's not official, is it? Let me see that!" He grabs at the will, but Nate jerks his hand back, causing Trey to stumble. A police officer helps Trey to his feet and deposits him roughly in a cane-back chair, standing over him.

"Don't move, sir," the officer says.

"I did not shoot Thom!" Ginny exclaims. "Yes, I knew he was thinking about divorce, but I would have fought him in court like so many other women are forced to do. You have zero evidence that I killed my husband, and that's because I did not."

"Maybe you didn't," Washington says. "But you covered it up. You opened the safe to make it look like a robbery, didn't you? You took off your jewelry and hid it somewhere, didn't you?"

Danit grabs the plastic bag filled with Ginny's jewelry, eager to show everyone. She has to tell them what she knows, what she discovered going through the photos from the party. But Washington keeps talking.

"It was you, Zak, wasn't it? You saw the file Thom had on you," Washington says. "He was threatening you with prison, wasn't he? Unless you divorced Ellie Grace and her millions. You shot him, and then you and Ginny cooked up this plan. Get rid of the documents in the safe, the will, the private investigator's report. Both of you could keep what you had. No one would have to know. Shawna showing up was a lucky coincidence. She would make the perfect fall guy."

The weight of what Danit knows presses against her chest so hard, she thinks her ribs might burst. Before she can stop herself, she's standing up. "It wasn't Zak. He's not lying when he says he wasn't inside at the time of the shooting." She lifts her hand and points. "It was Ellie Grace who did it. She shot Thom."

The whole room erupts in squawking as Ellie Grace and Zak protest, Nate starts peppering her with questions, and Ginny howls with sarcastic laughter.

"WILL EVERYONE SHUT UP." Detective Washington's command cuts through the noise. Everyone in the room is silenced. Danit looks at Ellie Grace, whose face is beet red, matching the poppies in her silk blouse. Her mouth is set in a straight, angry line.

"Go ahead," Nate says gently.

"It's all in the photos," Danit says. "The earring, the catkin, the hidey-hole." Danit holds up the bag of jewelry. "Here's the jewelry." She pulls out the panther ring and holds it aloft. "I found it in the chimney."

"Catkin?" Washington asks. "Hidey-hole? Chimney? You're going to have to start at the beginning."

58

Ellie Grace glares at Danit, willing her to shut up. How dare she! This nobody, this sloppily dressed nanny who insinuated herself into the family is *ruining everything*.

"Why would anybody listen to her?" Ellie Grace says. "This makes zero sense." She stands up. "I don't have to sit here listening to this."

Immediately, she feels strong hands on her shoulders pushing her back down in her chair. "Yes, you do," Cookie says from behind her.

Ellie Grace faces Zak, terrified of seeing a hint of suspicion in his face, but he's looking at her with the same affection as always.

"I love you, babe," he says. "We're a team, no matter what."

In that moment, she realizes that he knows. That he knew all along and still stayed with her. And still loved her. Her eyes well with tears. This beautiful man, despite his flaws, is so loyal and loving. What has she done to deserve him? She sniffs. "I love you so, so much."

"Tell us about this hidey-hole," Washington says.

Ellie Grace watches Danit take Nate's hand, and it hits her— they are the golden couple now. And to think she once considered making Danit a confidante. It's clear to her that Danit is relishing the attention as she tells everyone about the timing of the photos, the missing earring, and the oak catkin in Ellie Grace's hair.

"So I went out to the hidey-hole—it was just a gut thing— and that's where I found the papers and the jewelry." She picks up the other two folders and passes them to the detective. "And that's when Zak came after me, threatening to make me disappear."

Nate turns toward his sister and Zak, hatred in his eyes, while Ellie Grace's gaze drops. She can't bear the way her brother is looking at her. She stares at her black flats with large gold logos on the toes. At once, she realizes they are hopelessly dowdy. Her look is beyond staid, it's geriatric. No wonder Gingham Life never took off. And now she might go to prison.

"It can't have been easy," Washington says to Ellie Grace. "Your dad, he thought Zak was a loser, right? Couldn't hold a real job, couldn't support you. Then he finds out that Zak's not just a grifter, not just a common criminal, but might be involved in murder."

"Stop it." Ellie Grace bites down on her lower lip to keep from responding. She's not dumb. She won't take the bait. She takes Zak's hand in hers and squeezes hard. What he was doing on the roof wasn't menacing Danit, he was trying to protect *her*, Ellie Grace.

"I don't know," Detective Washington says. "Something doesn't feel right." She takes a few steps toward Ginny. "The whole point of having Ms. Price shoot you in the leg was to give someone an alibi, wasn't it, Mrs. Calhoun? It would have to be someone worth protecting. Someone you loved more than your own freedom. After all, you were willing to risk that freedom to save this person." The detective looks squarely at Ellie Grace. Ellie Grace feels her heart sink.

"We all know that the only person that Ginny has ever truly loved, unconditionally, the person she would literally do anything for"—she pauses and gives Ellie Grace a sly grin—"is her oldest son, Trey. I mean, c'mon, does anybody here really believe she would make this kind of sacrifice for Ellie Grace?" She snorts a little laugh. "Please."

Ellie Grace stands up and lets out a guttural scream, the

eruption of years of pent-up jealousy and rage. "How can you say that when I'm right here? I'm the one! Not Trey! Me! I'm the one she put everything on the line for." She turns to face her mother. "Tell them, Mommy. Tell them how much you love me!"

"Ellie Grace!" Ginny snaps. "Sit down!"

Ellie Grace stomps her feet, the tears coming fast. "Why couldn't Daddy just let me be happy? It's like he couldn't *stand* to see me happy!"

"What happened that day in the study, Ellie Grace?" Washington pulls a packet of tissues out of her bag and offers them to Ellie Grace. "Did your father become angry when you refused his ultimatum? Was it self-defense?"

"Zak and I were building a life together. But no, he wasn't good enough for my dad." She looks up at Washington. "He tried to break us up. Like in *Romeo and Juliet*."

"That is so messed up." Washington tsk-tsks. "I mean, what kind of parent does that?"

Ellie Grace gulps loudly. "As soon as I asked Zak to go talk to my dad, I knew it was a mistake. If my dad was putting pressure on me to leave Zak, I realized he was going to put the same pressure on Zak to leave me. And he would use the only leverage he's ever had. Money."

"You were afraid your father would offer Zak money to leave you, and he'd go for it?"

Ellie Grace nods, and then quickly glances at Zak. "I'm not blaming you, babe. But there's only so much a person can take when you don't feel welcome in a family. I was afraid that you would crack under the pressure, not because you don't love me—I know you do—but because it's so hard to stand up to my dad." She turns her attention back to Washington. "But when I got to the study, Zak wasn't even there. And that's when my father told me that Zak was wanted by the authorities in another state. I told him I didn't care. That I loved Zak no matter what his past was. And he said if we didn't agree to divorce, then he would call the cops, and Zak was going to prison for a long time. I didn't mean to shoot him, I swear! I took the gun from his drawer and pointed at him, but only to get him to give me the file. But he . . . came at me. It was self-defense. The gun just went off."

She looks up to meet Washington's eyes, realizing she may have just made a terrible mistake. At the same time, it felt so good to get it all out. Keeping this secret is the hardest thing she's ever done. She looks at her mother, who is aghast, arms crossed over her chest. Don't they see? It wasn't her fault. She is entitled to happiness, and her father was trying to destroy it. She looks at Zak, fearfully at first, but when she sees his easy smile and remembers what he has done, she feels gooey all over. Their love is so strong, they would literally kill for each other. She sits back down and wraps her arms around his muscular bicep and sighs. As long as they are together . . .

"Don't sit down, Ellie Grace." Washington motions to the officers, who come closer.

"What's going on?" Ellie Grace asks, looking up at a tall officer hovering over her. "I told you what happened. It was self-defense. It was an accident."

"Ellie Grace Calhoun-Miller," Washington says. "You are under arrest for the murder of Thomas Calhoun—"

Ellie Grace's mind goes blank as the officer reads her rights. A moment later, she watches as Zak is yanked to his feet and cuffed, too. And to her horror, her mother is also handcuffed and read her rights.

Bile rises within her. "What is happening? Where are you taking us?"

"To jail," Cookie says, arms crossed.

The officers march her, her mother, and Zak toward the door. As they pass Trey, Nate, and Danit, she examines their faces and sees only shock and disbelief, not a trace of affection or concern. An officer flings the front door open, and she can see the police cruisers lined up outside along with at least a dozen spectators.

Parked a few doors down is a white TV van with a satellite dish on top. As Ellie Grace is pushed outside, she tucks her chin to her chest, already imagining this image of her, blotchy-skinned and cuffed, zinging around the internet. There is no way Gingham Life can survive this.

As she steps onto the stoop, she turns back for one more look at her childhood home. Malcolm pops up from where he was half-hidden under a table, waving his arm furiously. "Byebyebyebyebyebyebye!"

59

Trey slumps in the seat that his mother has just vacated, holding the bottle of scotch by the neck. "That was unreal," he says and takes a swig. Washington still stands in the room, even though the officers have all left with Ginny, Zak, and Ellie Grace.

Cookie returns from the kitchen with a bowl of popcorn. "Sorry. Stress makes me hungry."

He puts the bowl on the coffee table and takes a seat next to Danit, patting her leg. "You were very brave," he says.

She leans her head on his shoulder. "I heard what you shouted from the yard. Thank you."

"Look at you two. Adorable," Trey says as he leans forward to grab a handful of popcorn. "What do we do now?" He is a bundle of nerves and mixed emotions. Glee, from having gotten away with something, and fear about what that new will means. There's so much money, he's got to end up with some of it, right? But he knows better than to ask. There will be time for that later.

"Is there something we can help you with?" Trey asks Detective Washington.

"Actually, I still have a couple of questions," Nate says.

"Of course you do." Trey rolls his eyes.

"So my sister, she shot my father and then went and got my mother?"

"That's what we think. Do you mind if I sit down?" Washington takes a seat in an armchair near Cookie. "We think your mother and Ellie Grace went back into the study. When Ginny realized Thom was dead, she decided to make it look like a robbery. They dragged his body over to the safe and used his finger to open it and take out the documents. I don't think your mother even knew about the updated will and the divorce papers before that, to be honest. But once she saw them, she knew she would be the prime suspect. So she made herself a victim as well. She gave all her jewelry to Ellie Grace and told her to hide it and the documents, and then go back to the party and act normally. That was when Ellie Grace must have lost her earring."

Everyone is quiet for a few moments.

"Too bad Shawna had to die," Trey says. And he means it. She was collateral damage in a bigger war. The question now is whether Zak will keep his mouth shut.

"I need to tell you something," Nate says. "I should have told you a long time ago and I didn't."

Trey narrows his eyes at his brother. He's fried from too many surprises, annoyed that Nate has chosen this moment, in front of the police, to play true confession. "Can this wait?"

"No," Nate says. "It can't."

Trey watches his brother put off whatever he needs to say by picking at some imaginary lint on his pants.

"Nate, c'mon—you're killing me here, spit it out."

"Helena isn't Malcolm's mother."

"All right. That's interesting. But what does it have to do with me?"

"Shawna was his mother. Shawna Douglas."

Trey cackles. He looks from Nate's face to Danit's. "You're kidding, right? You slept with Shawna?"

"No, you idiot. I'm not the father. You are."

"What?" Trey straightens up and stares at his brother. "You're joking, right?"

"After the car accident in California, Mom and Dad found out that Shawna was pregnant. Dad went out and got a DNA test. She was going through with the pregnancy but didn't plan on keeping the baby. Mom suggested that I raise Malcolm as my own, and I agreed. The only condition was that we never tell you." Nate hangs his head. "I'm so sorry. I thought I was doing an admirable thing, but now I see how selfish and screwed up it was."

Trey feels the convulsions of laughter build in his belly, and he doubles over silently, completely overcome with giddiness. When he lifts his head, he is laughing so hard that a tear is falling down one cheek.

"What is so damn funny?" Nate asks.

"That you think . . . you believed . . ." He is overcome with laughter again, and it takes a few more seconds before he can compose himself. "You don't know me at all, do you?" He glances at Cookie and makes eye contact until Cookie's eyes widen.

"No!" Cookie says.

Trey winks at him, enjoying his discomfort. "Yup." He faces Nate. "I don't really like girls, Nate. I tried, in high school and college, but it never felt right. Why do you think I wanted to go out to California so badly? I wanted away from all this. I was finally living my life."

"But you were starting an adult website," Nate protests.

"Subscription service," Trey corrects. "And so what? That just makes me a good businessman. Shawna and I were friends. And coworkers. And we liked to party together."

"Did you do GHB together?" Detective Washington asks.

"Of course!" Trey answers before he realizes what he's doing. He quickly tries to backtrack. "I mean, we did a lot of different drugs."

"And you never slept with her?" Nate asks in disbelief.

"I think I would remember." He tries to keep his answer light, but he casts a sidelong glance at Washington. *She knows.* He can feel it. But can she prove it?

"So who's the father?"

Trey shrugs. "Beats me."

"Hold on now." Detective Washington reaches for the other

two manila envelopes that were in the metal box. She holds up one. "This is marked MALCOLM. That's your son, right?"

Nate nods as Washington pulls out a piece of paper. "Here we go—his birth certificate."

Trey leans forward eagerly.

"Mother: Shawna Douglas. We knew that. Father," she says, pausing to look at everyone. "Father: Thomas Calhoun Jr."

"Holy shit," Trey says. Danit gasps loudly.

"Let me see that!" Nate rips the birth certificate from the detective's hand.

Trey watches his brother read and reread it. "Is it true?"

Nate nods slowly, before looking up to make eye contact.

"So Malcolm's what? Our half brother?" Trey lets out a hoot. "That is wild."

"Did you know that Shawna was sleeping with Dad?" Nate asks.

"Sure," Trey says. "Why do you think he liked to visit me in LA? You think he missed me? He wanted to sample the wares in my new business. If I had gone into, I don't know, water bottle manufacturing, I would never have seen the guy. I tried to tell you all that he was sleeping around, but no one wanted to hear it."

"Do you think your mother knows the truth?" Danit asks.

Nate shakes his head. "No way. She thinks Malcolm is her grandson. My dad had her completely fooled. No wonder Shawna thought she had leverage to ask for more money."

"Who's going to tell her?" Danit asks.

The doorbell rings, and Detective Washington stands up. "I'll get that."

Trey brings the Macallan to his mouth and takes a big swig of the smoky scotch. What a completely fucked-up family they are. He has a tiny grudging bit of admiration for his father, who managed to manipulate everyone in the family by playing off their sympathies—his mom's desire for a grandchild, Nate's desire for a baby, his own fear of having to face consequences for his reckless behavior. There were never any pending charges in California, Trey realizes. Sure, he might have done a month or two of community service for drinking and driving, but he came back because he thought he might go to prison. That he had killed someone. If he and his family were closer, if they really communicated and talked to each other, this would never have happened.

"Hey, Nate, if you had ever bothered to talk to me in the past few years"—he points the bottle of scotch accusingly at his brother—"you'd have known I couldn't be Malcolm's dad."

Detective Washington returns with a uniformed officer in tow, who is holding a plastic baggy. "Found what we were looking for. While I was sitting here with you, I had an officer search the house next door—"

Trey jumps to his feet. "You what? You can't do that."

"And found this bottle, which, according to initial tests, looks like GHB."

"I don't understand," Nate says.

"We found trace elements of GHB in Shawna Douglas's blood." Washington turns to Trey. "Thomas Calhoun III, you are under arrest for the murder of Shawna Douglas."

THREE MONTHS LATER

Danit feels the wind sweep off the blue Pacific Ocean and roll over her. The sun is low in the sky, spilling golden light across the beach and bouncing off the ripples in the water. She stands under the cupola covered in plumeria, which grows wild on the island, emitting a velvety vanilla fragrance, and faces Nate as he says those two magic words.

"I do."

Her heart soars as he slips the ring on her finger. It's not the fairy-tale wedding of her childhood, with lots of guests and an elaborate ceremony. It's better. A few of Nate's colleagues, as well as friends they have made on the island in the past few months, are here. Only a handful of American guests came over—Charmaine from San Francisco, and Cookie and Bob from Washington. Nate's siblings are not allowed out of the country under the conditions of their bail, and Ginny is still in prison. Danit only wishes her mother were still alive to see this.

"You may kiss the bride," announces the officiant, an older man with short white hair who was part of the package wedding deal at the resort. Danit turns to Nate, who takes her face in his hands and kisses her.

The audience, sitting in slip-covered folding chairs facing the water, breaks into applause.

"Yay!" Malcolm shouts as he dumps sand on Danit's bare feet.

Nate hugs her, picking her up off the sand and spinning around. "We did it," he whispers in her ear. The past three months have been the best of her life, but they have also been stressful. Moving across the world, settling in, learning a few phrases in Chamorro and Carolinian. And, of course, keeping an eye on what was happening with the Calhouns and their trials. Renée cut a deal—no prison time in exchange for testifying against Ginny, who then pleaded guilty for her part in misleading the investigation into both Thom's shooting and her own. She is currently serving a three-year sentence in Jessup but will probably be out in about eighteen months, depending on her behavior. Danit thinks that she might just thrive in prison, much like Martha Stewart, her leadership skills serving her well. But Trey, Zak, and Ellie Grace are another story. They are all going to trial—Ellie Grace is claiming self-defense in the shooting of her father, and Trey and Zak are fighting the charges in Shawna's death. From what Charmaine told her, the Calhouns are still a regular topic on cable news. It is so much easier to avoid all that here in Saipan, where no one knows their history.

The reception is set up under a white tent just outside the hotel. The sun has set now, and Danit joins everyone in line at the buffet under the glow of the fairy lights. She loads up her plate with kelaguen, a local version of ceviche, and other Chamorro and Filipino delicacies, then finds a seat between Charmaine and Nate at the long family-style table that is perfect for their twenty-five guests.

"Cheers to the beautiful bride!" Cookie says, holding his champagne glass aloft across the table from her. "This is a glorious wedding."

Everyone nearby raises their glasses and clinks. It isn't until she is done eating and a waiter has cleared away the plates that she has a chance to ask Cookie a few burning questions, questions only he would have the answers to.

"What's it like back in Somerwood? Are neighbors freaking out about everything that happened? They have to be."

Cookie taps his chin. "Actually, less than you might think. At first, there was scuttlebutt, but now no one mentions the

Calhouns anymore. It's weird, it's almost as if they never lived there."

"What about the house?" Danit asks. "I know Ginny sold it before she went to prison. Nate says everything in it is in storage for now."

"Well, a new family moved in. The Moens. Three little tykes, blond, rambunctious. I see them stomping through the perennial beds. Ginny would be livid."

"They've certainly livened up the place," Bob says, his face pink from a day in the sun. "I, for one, like seeing all those young people. The neighborhood needed some fresh blood."

"Couldn't agree more," Cookie says. "The Moens are a wonderful addition. And I've been so busy helping them to settle—nursery school recommendations, finding a nanny and housekeeper—there's so much they need help with. They are a shoo-in for the country club, but until then, we all take turns inviting them to the club as our guests so they can use the pool and other amenities."

"Well, that's nice of you," Danit says. "You've always been generous with your time."

"You're too kind. Some people say Somerwood has a reputation of being snooty, but I just don't find that to be the case at all."

"Oh, the Moens will fit right in," Bob says.

"Yes, they will." Cookie smiles. "They're such a lovely family."

ACKNOWLEDGMENTS

"Thank you" barely seems an adequate sentiment when I think of all the work and support that goes into getting a book published. First, a huge thanks to my wonderful agent—Katie Shea Boutillier at the Donald Maass Literary Agency—who is loyal, encouraging, and tough in the best way.

I've never written a book that wasn't improved by working with an editor, and this one is no exception. Thank you to my editor Kristin Sevick Brown, whose vision and insight helped guide this book. Also to everyone at Forge/Macmillan, who helped bring this book out into the world.

I am incredibly appreciative of the hard work of the sharp-eyed copy editors—Sara and Chris with ScriptAcuity Studio—and proofreader Jaime Herbeck.

Writing is a solitary endeavor and I am so grateful that when I emerge from my imaginary world, I have such a supportive network of friends and family. Part of that community is the book lovers on Instagram who use their time and creative talents to read and review books. The readers who, in an age of endless distraction, still reach for a book and give authors your time and attention. And I am continually amazed by the generosity and kindness of my fellow writers. Thank you.

My deepest thanks to my family—to Theo and Roxy, for bringing so much joy to my life and for keeping me on my toes. I am especially indebted to my husband, John Thompson, who is indispensable both as a line editor and as an all-around amazing human being.

And finally—to Pistachio and Fifi, my dog and my cat, my constant companions—thank you for keeping me company at my desk and on my long walks (Pistachio, that is).